Also by Kevin Powers

The Yellow Birds

Letter Composed During a Lull in the Fighting

A Shout in the Ruins

A Line in the Sand

A Line in the Sand

Kevin Powers

sceptre

First published in Great Britain in 2023 by Sceptre
An imprint of Hodder & Stoughton
An Hachette UK company

1

A CIP catalogue record for this title is available from the British Library

Hardback ISBN 9781399711487
Trade Paperback ISBN 9781399711494
eBook ISBN 9781399711500

Printed and bound in Great Britain by Clays Ltd, Elcograf S.p.A.

Hodder & Stoughton policy is to use papers that are natural, renewable
and recyclable products and made from wood grown in sustainable forests.
The logging and manufacturing processes are expected to conform
to the environmental regulations of the country of origin.

Hodder & Stoughton Ltd
Carmelite House
50 Victoria Embankment
London EC4Y 0DZ

www.sceptrebooks.co.uk

For my mother, who never said no to a book

War is a racket. It always has been. It is possibly the oldest, easily the most profitable, surely the most vicious. It is the only one international in scope. It is the only one in which the profits are reckoned in dollars and the losses in lives.

— Major General Smedley D. Butler

ONE

Arman Bajalan woke in darkness, as was his habit. He turned toward the clock on his nightstand: 4:37 in digital red. Another eight minutes to sleep. Outside his window, a songbird warbled in the yellow glow of an alley streetlight. He swung his legs over the side of his single bed and rubbed his eyes awake instead of going back to sleep. A jet passing overhead from the naval air station washed the morning twilight in the noise of its engines. Arman looked up toward his ceiling's popcorn surface as if to track the jet in its low flight over the city.

He stood beneath another streetlight a few minutes later, waiting for the number 3 bus to take him to work at the motel on Ocean View. He wore his custodial uniform, gray work pants and a matching top with a patch on the pocket where his name had been embroidered in white thread, cursive script. After reading his résumé and offering him the job, Mr. Peters, the motel owner, had added *Dr.* to the name patch. His coworkers called him Professor the first few months he worked at the motel, but that had died down once it was clear Arman would not be moved in one direction or the other by the ribbing. A heavy set of keys hung from a carabiner on his belt, and he shouldered a nylon gym bag with a towel and a pair of swimming trunks inside.

His usual bus never came. Arman waited in the emptiness of the city street and the last cool air of night receding from it. He checked his watch two times before another bus arrived at 5:14 and knelt toward the curb with a pneumatic hiss. Arman and the bus driver told each other good morning.

"The last bus never came," said Arman.

"Engine trouble. Sorry about that," the driver said. "Had to switch buses and the schedule got mixed up."

The bus rose and rumbled off, and he put a pair of earbuds in and scrolled through his iPod until he found a Commodores song and pressed Play. The bus driver glanced at him in the mirror often enough that he pretended not to be when Arman caught him. Arman used to smile when he saw suspicious eyes looking back at him in the rearview, but he had given up on that some time ago. Still, he sometimes wondered who they saw when they looked at him. Once, not long after he'd arrived in America, he'd looked into the bathroom mirror in his apartment and tried to imagine that his gray-green eyes belonged to a stranger, but it didn't work. He could not escape himself. And he knew that people mostly saw what they wanted to see anyway. He put "Sail On" on repeat until the driver let him off at Granby and Duffys across from Doug's Hot Dogs just before 5:45 a.m., almost half an hour later than usual.

He walked through Ocean View Beach Park with his hands in his pockets and headed toward the bathroom to change into his swimsuit. Beyond the beach grass, the rising sun carved a red sliver across the horizon. The sky above was not yet light. Black becoming blue. Stars already absorbed by nautical twilight. Arman reached the public restroom and grabbed the door handle, but movement over his shoulder caught his attention. Two men approached from the beach, carrying themselves with a casual menace. Arman looked down and saw his hand tightened into a fist around the door handle, his knuckles whitened by the reflexive effort. They were near enough when they passed that he could hear their voices but could not make out what they said. They hadn't seemed to notice his presence. He looked up and saw that the light above the bathroom door was out. He was in the deeper darkness of the small building's shadow. His hand still gripped the door handle like he might fall off the earth if he let go of it. One of them said something gruffly, but Arman wasn't sure if he'd heard it correctly. The other sidearmed something into the beach grass, but it was too dark to see what it was.

He watched them walk off toward Ocean View Avenue for a few more seconds, then closed his eyes. Something about them reminded Arman of his childhood. When Saddam's men took his father from the camp at Topzawa during the Anfal, they had carried themselves the same way. He let go of the door handle and flexed his hand until the blood returned. He took a deep breath and counted to ten in his head. When he'd first come to America, a counselor from the resettlement agency had tried to explain why he sometimes felt like he was in two places and times at once. And why it was hard to know which place or time was real. The body remembers what the mind wants to forget, she'd said. He looked back through the park toward Ocean View Avenue, but the men were gone. He remembered then what his body had not forgotten. When he got to ten, Arman opened the bathroom door and went inside.

He left the bathroom a few minutes later and walked to the beach. When his bare feet hit the sand, he wiggled his toes in its remaining coolness. He laid his towel out over the sand and placed his gym bag on it. He entered the water as the sun broke free from the horizon line. He let the bracing waves splash against his legs as he waded in, then up to his waist, and finally up against his chest before he dove into a breaker and began to swim. The bus delay forced him to cut his swim short, but he pushed himself hard up and down an imaginary lane a hundred yards from shore for half an hour. He breathed hard as he reversed out of the water, riding a wave into shallower depths, and then walked down the beach to his towel.

It was warm enough now that the sun felt good against his back, and he toweled the salt water off himself and lingered for a minute. There were not many people out that early in the morning. Even those few seemed content to keep to themselves. An old man walked his dog above the boardwalk in the grassy expanse of the park. Here and there, a runner on the sand went by. Those who wanted to engage in pleasantries satisfied themselves with a wave and a "Good morning." Had they known Arman's history, they would have been surprised how easily a smile spread across his face when the moment called for one. Some caught themselves staring as he dried off in the morning sun, then turned away when they recognized the contradictions written across his body.

He was long and athletic. Years spent carving through the morning waves had made him lean and muscular. He had broad shoulders browned by the sun, but when he raised his arms to towel-dry his black hair, Arman revealed the topography of scars stretching from his armpit to his thigh on the right side of his body. Ragged divots pocked the otherwise smooth skin. A line like a river carving out its banks wove its way from his hip to just above his knee. This much was clear even from the glance of a stranger running past: a long time ago, something had meant to carve this man up into pieces, and roughly, but failed. To Arman, the scars themselves were hardly worth remembering. He knew what they were. Marks in a ledger. A record of his loss. Every day the same since then. A morning swim, a day spent collecting all that others so easily discard, and a return at night alone to a small apartment in a city that would never be his own. His life was a ritual with no purpose he could recall.

All this passed in much the same way it had for the past few years. When it was warm, he swam. When it was cold, he walked the stretch of beach between the park and the fishing pier. He found solace in predictability, in the rote mechanics of wave and tide. But all that ended when he saw the man laid out where the dunes met the level sands of the shore.

Arman had put his towel over his neck and picked his bag up to go back to the public restroom to change when he saw him: The heels of a pair of oxfords half buried in the sand. The fabric of the man's suit pants flapping in the come-and-go breeze. His hands folded across his chest as if he were impatiently waiting for someone or shivering against a cold you wouldn't find on a summer morning in Norfolk.

Arman looked at the figure laid out against the bare beginnings of the dunes. He stood there for a few moments, absentmindedly running the towel over his black hair, then glanced back up toward the bathroom in the park. His watch read ten minutes to seven. His shift started at eight. Perhaps his boss would understand his choice if he was late. Maybe he could say, *Mr. Peters, don't you think we owe something to each other?* Probably his boss would not be persuaded by that.

He walked up to the slope of sand beneath the white chain that bounded the limits of the public beach. He knelt beside the man and put his hand on his shoulder, withdrawing it immediately upon seeing the man's face. The mouth was slightly open, in neither a smile nor a grimace. Simply that of a machine seized at a random moment of its operation.

Arman sat back in the sand next to the body. He crossed his arms over his knees and hung his head. He looked up and watched a plover dart from hole to hole in the wet sand, hunting for hermit crabs. Gulls stacked and circled in the air above the nearby pier. He stood up and unfolded his towel and, as delicately as he could, laid it over the dead man's upper body. He hoped to flag down someone with a cell phone, but it seemed the beach had more or less cleared of the sunrise crowd. He knew a pay phone was near the park pavilion, so he reached into his gym bag and fished in his pants pockets for change. He turned the quarters over in his hands like prayer beads and looked out toward the gray waves. Far in the distance, the outline of a carrier backlit by the rising sun cleared Willoughby Spit and silently left the continent behind.

TWO

Detective Catherine Wheel had her eyes closed, listening. Behind her, a dead man's turbo diesel idled. Farther back, the sounds of gantry cranes and boxes moving ship to shore intertwined into a soft white noise. Closer still, a voice recounted another passage to the afterlife. "Seven forty-five a.m., we responded to a ten-forty-seven. Pretty vague. *Fucking Narcan, I don't know. Goddamn it, hit the motherfucker again.* Dispatch said it's a guy passed out in a coal roller. *Compression, compression.* We arrived. Subject was unresponsive. Vehicle doors were locked. *One, two, three, four, five, six, seven, eight, nine, ten.* My partner made the call to enter the vehicle through the window. Subject was cold, had no pulse, no respirations. We pulled the guy out, administered Narcan. Performed CPR. *Breathe, you fat fuck. Breathe, goddamn it.* Okay, I'm putting the AED on him." Pause. "Nothing. Still no vital signs. Subject declared deceased at seven fifty-six a.m."

Only the sound of machinery remained. The human voices faded into the buzz and hum of the port. She opened her eyes. The Lafayette River was a path of glass and light before her. White yachts and the spinnakers of Flying Scots freed from their slips at the country club across the water. They skated toward her on the wind, colorful and effortless, heading to the deeper water of the bay.

"Who was he, Officer? Maersk? CSX? Some rando just decided to park his truck in the middle of one of the largest ports in the world to shoot dope all night?"

"I don't know, ma'am. Customs said they were bringing someone down. Supposed to be a log. In and out."

Detective Wheel pulled on a pair of surgical gloves, reached through the broken window into the truck, and cut the engine. She opened the door and then the storage container between the two front seats and pulled out a lanyard with an ID card on the end of it. She called the headquarters of the facility operator, read the name off the ID badge, and asked if they had an employee by that name. "Yeah," the guy said. "Tell that son of a bitch he's late, and he's fucking fired."

"You want to send somebody down by the substation?"

"What for?"

"I'm the police, and I said so."

"Why, what did he do?"

"He died."

"Goddamn it. Now I have to find someone to cover his shift. South end of the terminal?"

"Yeah. By Tanner Point, that's right."

"All right. Sure, Detective. Whatever you need."

Detective Wheel made another call and turned toward the two patrol officers who had first responded to the scene. "Medical examiner is on the way. Just sit tight. Rest of your day is paperwork. The commonwealth won't believe he's dead until we all write about it."

She admired the disappointment on their faces. *As if any one of us are fit to contend with death.* "You did everything right, Officers."

Her phone rang again. She looked at the number on the screen and flipped it open. "Hey, Lieutenant Billings."

"How's your morning going?"

She looked back at the body laid out on the port's concrete decking. "Could be worse."

"I think it's gonna be one of those days, Cat."

"I thought you might say that."

"Swimmer called in a ten-thirty-nine at Ocean View Beach a little while ago."

"Come on, Lieutenant. I don't do drownings. I'm just coming off a junk call. Tell dispatch to call the Coast Guard."

"I know, I know. We all got shit to do. Just go have a sniff. You never know. Maybe this will be the case that saves the world."

"Ten dollars says it won't."

Detective Wheel turned her cruiser down Terminal Boulevard and pulled out her phone. She shadowed a double-decker freight train moving from the terminal on the CSX line until she joined the highway and waited for her partner to pick up.

"Adams."

Beside the road, an indistinguishable blur of vaguely institutional buildings slipped past, 1970s apartments and ranches housing young sailors and young wives the same as they always had. Decommissioned Quonset huts with paint stripped off by a half century of sea air. The green trees along the highway left to their wildness. A view from no place.

"Lamar, it's Cat. Meet me in the lot at Ocean View Beach Park."

"What is it, ma'am?"

"I don't know yet. Swimmer found a body."

"Roger that. I'm moving out now."

"Lamar?"

"Ma'am?"

"You can speak normal-people English now."

He laughed. "Sorry. Old habits and all."

"If you're really sorry, you'll bring me a cup of coffee."

She pulled into the lot with her badge in her hand and her arm hanging out the open window of her cruiser. A few uniforms and paramedics milled around the lot and lingered at the rear of an ambulance. She saw a man sitting uneasily in the back of a unit with the door open. *That was quick,* she thought. She parked, got out, and checked her watch: 9:00. The medical examiner would want to get the body off the beach soon. She saw Lamar pull in, and she waved him to an open spot next to hers.

He handed her a cup of coffee, and they walked between the wind-bent pines and followed the boardwalk to the sand. A sheet covered the body. A line of police tape staked in the sand ringed the scene. A small blue portable canopy shielded the forensic team and the body from whatever weather might come. What activity there had been in the immediate aftermath of the authorities' arrival had died down. Beyond the tape, a lifeguard on a four-wheeler sat with his arms crossed and talked casually with someone from the ME's office.

She and Lamar walked up and saw the medical examiner. He was sitting in the sand waiting and got up when he saw the suits coming. "Hey, Cat."

"Hey, Doc. This is my partner, Lamar Adams."

"Pat Martin. New?" asked Dr. Martin.

"Yeah. Off the beat a month or so."

"Good to meet you, Detective." They shook hands. "I'm surprised they sent you down here, Cat."

"You think it's natural causes?"

"I don't know. It's a little weird." He pulled the sheet off the man and squatted down in the sand. He held a pen in his hand, presumably so he could point with it if he needed to, but just spun it in his fingers casually while he talked. "I mean, the guy's in incredible shape. I'm guessing around forty years of age. Probably ten percent body fat." The doc put his pen in his shirt pocket and hiked up the dead man's suit pants. "Look at the calves on this guy. He had to be a triathlete or something like it. People in this kind of physical shape rarely die without there being a pretty obvious cause."

"What about hypertrophic cardiomyopathy?" Lamar asked. Detective Wheel looked at her partner and made a mental note: *The kid is sharp.*

"Possible. But death from that occurs almost exclusively during intense physical activity. He's wearing a suit. Sand around the body wasn't overly disturbed when we arrived. No sweat evident even if he had been working out in the middle of the night in a suit."

"What are you thinking?" Catherine asked.

"I'm definitely gonna need a closer look. Can I have him when you're finished?"

"Sure, shouldn't be too long."

Detectives Wheel and Adams took their places on either side of the body. They pulled on surgical gloves and began to examine the dead man, first looking at the outside of his clothes, then going into each pocket carefully and deliberately. A tech took Polaroid photographs as they went, documenting each item of evidence collected no matter how trivial it might appear.

Detective Wheel found a uniformed officer and said, "Give me a zone search from the beach one hundred yards beyond the parking area. Make it inclusive of the parking area itself, all structures within the park out to the street. Any vehicles other than ones owned by the City of Norfolk arrive or leave since the first officer was on scene?"

"No, ma'am," the uniform replied.

"All right. Well, don't miss anything. Anyone besides Mother Nature killed this guy, we're gonna find out who."

They pulled a matchbook from a DC cigar lounge out of his pants pocket. He wore a silver dive watch on his left wrist. Detective Adams looked at the face: Adina Oceaneer. He wasn't familiar with the brand. It was well-made but not showy. He found a Greyhound bus ticket in his left inside jacket pocket. He looked it over front and back. "Detective Wheel."

"No wallet. No ID. No money," she said.

"Got a bus ticket. Round trip, DC to Norfolk and back, under the name Thomas Brown."

"Thomas Brown? Can't be more than, what, ten thousand Tom Browns walking around, can there? Please tell me something good, Detective Adams."

"Return trip is tomorrow at seven forty-five in the a.m."

"Shit. I was hoping to sleep in. When'd he get to Norfolk?"

"Don't know. Doesn't have the inbound arrival info. Just the originating city."

Cat retrieved a key from the smaller pocket on the inside of his jacket. "What do you think this opens?"

"Too small for a house key. Locker, maybe?"

"Locker at a bus station, perhaps?" she said.

"Least we might find out who the guy is. Get his next of kin notified."

"That'd be a positive outcome, Detective. Don't let me forget to get a picture of the label on his suit."

Lamar opened the body's jacket again. He looked up at Detective Wheel and showed her. "No labels."

Catherine opened the other side of the jacket. She leaned in close. There were holes in the silk lining where the labels had once been stitched in, but the tags had been carefully removed. "This ain't junk, Lamar. We've got a real case now."

They stood up and peeled off their gloves and ducked under the tape. They walked back to the parking lot, found a bench, and sat down. "Run it back to me," Cat said. She pulled a pack of Marlboro Reds out of her jacket pocket, lit one, took a drag, then let the ash grow long while Lamar talked.

"Deceased is an unidentified male approximately forty years of age, excellent physical condition other than being dead. No obvious injuries or signs of trauma. Items in possession of the deceased are one matchbook, one round-trip bus ticket, return ticket unused, and one small key. Clothing of the deceased has had all labels and other identifying characteristics removed. That cover it?"

"John Doe," Catherine began, "dies of unknown causes under suspicious circumstances on Ocean View Beach sometime between midnight and...what'd the wit say?"

"Haven't talked to the wit or first on scene."

"Okay, so sometime between midnight and six a.m., our guy dies on the beach, all alone, wearing a gray suit without labels, a white dress shirt without labels."

"Detective Wheel," Lamar said, "could've just been another overdose. No shortage of those these days."

A jet from Naval Station Norfolk flew by. Lamar's eyes shot skyward. Cat took note of that too.

Arman watched the pair of plainclothes officers approach from the beach. He had a read on the younger man right away, recognizing a certain self-consciousness of posture meant to communicate the opposite. The shoulders thrust back, chest out, spine straight as a flagpole. The Oakleys would have been a dead giveaway besides, but it was clear to Arman that the man walking toward him had been in the military. He had been around enough of them back in Mosul to spot them the way countrymen recognize each other when traveling abroad.

The woman was older, maybe forty-five. She didn't wear makeup, and her hair was a wave of curls, red going gray. He watched her take the short walk to the parking lot from the beach. Saw that her eyes swept the terrain before her with the patient arc of a lighthouse beacon. In her left hand, a ciga-rette burned, and she absentmindedly flicked its ashes without taking a drag off it. They paused about ten meters from the car where he sat and spoke to the officer who'd arrived after Arman made the 911 call. He caught only snatches of the con-versation due to the whipping gusts; he heard "A little ner-vous" and "You like him," but the rest blew out to sea with the wind.

The officers introduced themselves as they approached. "Are you comfortable, Mr. Bajalan?" Detective Wheel asked.

"I'm okay. Can I call my boss? I'm late for work. I don't want him to worry."

"We'll get them notified, let them know you're helping us out," Detective Adams said.

"We just want you to tell us what you told Officer Johnson over there," Detective Wheel said, pointing to the first officer on scene.

"Didn't he tell you what I said?"

"He did, but it's best if we get it from you too. Don't want to play telephone with something serious like this, do we?" said Detective Adams.

"No. I guess not."

"Are you nervous, Mr. Bajalan?" asked Detective Wheel.

"I'm not used to finding dead bodies."

Arman noticed Detective Adams had moved to the back of the police car, where he leaned against the rear quarter panel. Detective Wheel put one arm on the vehicle's roof and the other on the top of the open door, blocking him in the car.

"You're out here every morning?" she asked.

"Yes."

"You ever see this guy before?"

"No."

"Did anyone else see him?"

"I don't know. A few people went by. Dog walkers. Runners."

"No one thought anything of it?"

"I don't know what they thought."

"What did you think?"

"When?"

"When you saw him."

"I thought it was strange that a man was lying on the beach in a suit."

"You went swimming before you called it in."

"I hadn't seen him. It was just getting light when I got here. He was behind me. I saw him when I came out of the water."

"And you tried to help him?"

"I called the police."

"Did you try to help him? Did you touch him? Perform CPR?"

"No."

"Why not?"

"He was dead."

"How did you know he was dead?"

"How did I know? It was obvious."

"You said you weren't used to finding dead bodies, but you knew this man was dead and didn't need your help?"

"I'm not used to finding dead bodies. But I've seen enough of them to know."

Detective Wheel looked up at her partner, resting her chin on her arm and raising her eyebrows as if to say, *Anything to add?* She leaned back, stood up, and shifted so that Arman sat unimpeded. Detective Adams took up the questioning. "So you're out here every morning, Mr. Bajalan."

"Yes, almost always."

"Same time?"

"Except today. Number three bus was late."

"What time did you get here?"

"Quarter to six."

"And you're normally here at what time?"

"Five fifteen."

"You didn't see anybody else except for runners and dog walkers?"

"Two men passed me near the bathroom. I was going in to change, and they were leaving the beach."

"These two guys, they part of the regular crowd? Runners, dog walkers, and you?"

"No."

"Because you know the regular crowd."

"I know some faces. To say hello."

"Do they know you?"

"To say hello, maybe."

"But not more."

"Do people know each other like that?"

"Like what?"

"More."

Detective Adams paused. The answer was not one that he'd expected. "So these guys see you? Did you see what they were up to?"

"No."

"They say anything?"

"Yes."

"What did they say?"

"I'm not sure."

"But you think you know."

"Yes."

"What do you think they said?"

"It was only one of them."

"What do you think he said?"

Arman was unsure how to respond. After all, certain suspicions were nearly impossible to shake. These were police. And for the first twenty-five years of his life, Arman would have told the police anything to get away from them. Any lie, any elaboration, was justified if it meant avoiding the Mukhabarat. But the Americans were supposed to be different. When he was a boy, he remembered his father saying the Americans would save them from Chemical Ali. But they didn't come until Arman's father had been dead more than two years. And what did they do when they finally came? They left Saddam in power. The Baathists were not punished. The Americans always came too late or left too soon. Too late for Halabja. Too late for so many others.

As a grown man, he'd spent almost two years working with the Americans in Mosul, once again choosing to believe in them. And some *were* worth believing in. Although they were ignorant of his people, Arman forgave them for it. Their enthusiasm to help often left little room for curiosity or introspection. But they were not all that way. And he had sometimes wondered: What if even the good ones were only responding to circumstances? What if, when it mattered, they abandoned principles as quickly as everyone else? He took a deep breath now, choosing to believe that the truth was worth his trust, whatever this particular man before him might think or do.

" 'Fucking hajji,' " Arman said.

"What?" asked Detective Wheel.

Detective Adams held up his hand discreetly so his partner would let him follow that thread. "Mr. Bajalan, are you sure that's what they said?" he asked.

"No. I'm not sure. But I think that's what one of them said. They weren't very close."

"But you've been called that before."

"Yes."

"By men like that?"

"Yes. And men like you, Detective Adams."

"You mean soldiers."

"Who else knows what that means over here?"

Detective Wheel saw her partner cross his arms over his chest and hang his head. "What is it, Lamar?" she asked. "What the hell are y'all talking about?"

"I'll tell you later." To Arman, he said, "Mr. Bajalan, we're gonna need you to stay in the area. We'll likely have more questions for you."

"Detective," Arman said, "where would I go?"

THREE

S ally Ewell had faith. And with the state her life was in, she needed it. She had faith that her ten-year-old Geo Metro would start. Sally had bought it with four years' worth of 10 percent tips on twenty-dollar tabs while waiting tables in college. And because it had the manufacturing quality of a Little Tikes car with a cheap two-stroke engine stuffed in it, Sally sometimes suspected that faith was as necessary to its continued operation as gas and regular oil changes.

She had faith that if she chewed a half a tin of Altoids on her way to work, they would mask the fact that she could hardly remember the difference between hungover and still drunk and that her breath itself might still be somewhere north of forty proof by the time she got to her desk. Sally had faith that there were still a couple cans of Milwaukee's Best under the passenger seat. Because if she didn't drink at least two in the parking lot before she walked into the building, her hands would start shaking before she could scrounge two more on her lunch break to get her through the afternoon. And she had faith that no one in her life, not her parents, coworkers, or on-and-off boyfriends, knew that things had gotten that bad. But they had gotten that bad, and Sally guessed they did know, and faith is a handy thing to have when you need to believe in something that probably isn't true.

So, while Sally had a certain kind of faith in abundance, she had very little faith in her fellow man, despite Sally's parents teaching her as a child that that was the best place to have it. She didn't believe that anymore because her fellow man had killed her brother in a desert six thousand miles away. Today would have been his birthday, and Sally didn't think faith belonged anywhere near the fact that her little brother would never have another birthday again.

She stopped the Geo at a red light and looked down the block at the building that housed the *Virginian-Pilot,* where she'd been a junior reporter, primarily working the metro desk, since graduating from UVA a few years ago. She flipped the lever of the Geo's AC to max and turned the knob on the fan to match it, but it only blew the hot air harder. She adjusted her bra's underwire to keep the sweat at bay, but even at eight in the morning, the July sun on the pavement of a downtown Norfolk, Virginia, street meant she didn't stand a chance. She popped another Altoid from the tin, reached under the passenger seat, and felt around until she found a can; she pulled it from the depths and cracked it open as the light turned green. There was a time when a hot beer at eight a.m. would have repulsed her, but that time was long past. In fact, as the beer sizzled down her throat in desperate gulps, Sally was sure her faith had been rewarded.

She was drenched in sweat when she entered the building, and the AC only seemed to make it worse. Sally had already acquired the alcoholic's studious avoidance of mirrors, but she caught her reflection in the elevator doors while waiting to take one to her floor. She followed the strands of long brown hair plastered across her forehead and temples. Sally looked into her own eyes but then turned away from them, reminded again of the difference between the woman she was and the woman she had intended to be. She shivered as the bell dinged and the doors slid open, whether at the chill or her reflection, she could not have said. It was an involuntary tremor, as if her body meant to shake off her crawling skin the way one might shake the folds and wrinkles from the sheets of a messy bed.

When she opened the door to the open-plan office, she kept her eyes locked on the institutional carpet to avoid looking in her editor's direction. She made her way through the maze of cubicles and heard him call her name.

"Sally," he said. She caught a glimpse of him reflected in a pane of glass, leaning in the open doorway of his office with his arms folded across his chest. She pretended not to hear him. She dropped her bag at her desk and turned around, still not risking a direct look in his direction. "Sally," he said again.

"Oh. Hey, Matt. I didn't hear you," she answered.

He waved her toward him, turned around, and sat at his desk.

"Fuck," she muttered to herself. She looked over at a colleague a few desks away from hers. He held out a stick of gum. "That bad, huh?" she said. He shrugged and tossed it her way. She took the gum and shoved it in her mouth. *Okay,* she thought as she began to walk to her boss's office. *Story. Get your story together.*

In the ten paces it took her to cover the ground between her desk and the office door, Sally concocted an elaborate story that neatly explained the circumstances of her early drinking and her late arrival and proved she was blameless for both. When she crossed the threshold into his office and opened her mouth to begin, Matt Jacobson, her editor, held his hand up to stop her. "Sit down," he said.

Sally grabbed the chair, sat down in it, and again began an explanation. "Seriously, Matt. I know I fucked up, but—" She looked down and watched as Matt slid a manila envelope across the surface of his desk toward her. "What is it?" she asked.

"I don't know," he said. "It's addressed to you."

"I'm not fired?"

"What? No. I just wanted to give you this. Mail-room guy brought it here by mistake."

"I just thought…" She trailed off. She turned the envelope over in her hands. Her name and the newspaper's name had been written in block letters with a black marker. She glanced up at Matt.

"You don't have to open it here," he said. "If it's personal or whatever."

"No. Right," Sally said. She looked at him as if she'd forgotten why they were there, then slid her finger underneath the flap of the envelope and opened it. She reached inside and took out a small zip-lock bag. The bag held a single thumb drive and a white sheet of expensive stationery. In the same marker used on the outside of the envelope, someone had written *Re: Lacedaemon. Air gap only. Do not connect to a networked computer. Union Station, Saturday, July 12, 1315. Under Themis.*

She slid the paper across Matt's desk and absentmindedly turned the thumb drive over between her fingers. "Any ideas?" she asked.

He looked up at her, and his glasses slid down the bridge of his nose. "Lacedaemon is Sparta, I think. Themis is something Greek too."

"Yeah, I know. But I don't think I'm being invited to a classics convention at the train station. You want to try it?"

"Try what?" he asked.

"The thumb drive."

He scoffed. "Sally, I'm not frying my computer. And I'm damn sure not frying the paper's network."

Sally stared at the institutional weave of the carpet in Matt's office, twirling the thumb drive in her fingers like a gambler rolling a coin across her knuckles.

"Sally," he said.

His voice brought her out of her thoughts. "Yeah."

"You're not going to fry the network either, right?"

She feigned offense. "How could you ask me that? I'll take it to the nerds and let them do it."

"I don't think they like to be called nerds, Sal."

"Are you gonna let me go to the hearing now?"

"The Decision Tree thing?"

"Yeah."

Matt Jacobson drummed his fingers on his desk while making up his mind. He felt sorry for his young reporter. She was smart. But she didn't know she couldn't hide the pain she was in. That was the problem with intelligent people, he thought. They were never smart enough to know when they needed help.

Sally had enough documents going back and forth between Decision Tree International and the various local governments of the Tidewater region to know that something interesting was happening. There were variance applications. Highest-and-best-use appeals. Requests for exemptions from Wildlife Resources and EPA regulations. Sales of large tracts of land surrounding Decision Tree's current facilities. They were expanding. Business was good. And she didn't think there was anything good about that. Convincing Matt that her efforts were worth the trouble was another story.

As far as he was concerned, what she thought of the war and any particular private military contractor's growing influence on it didn't matter a damn bit. She couldn't prove they were doing anything wrong. She couldn't even give him a plausible theory that didn't depend entirely on her having a feeling they were doing something wrong. But he had to admit she'd worked hard. She probably knew as much about the current operations of Decision Tree as most of the company's employees. She definitely knew a hell of a lot more than the idiots in Congress investigating the role of PMCs in Iraq and Afghanistan. In Matt's opinion, *National Geographic* was the publication best suited to cover Congress, as it had the most experience watching peacocks with their feathers out. He wasn't going to say that to her, though. He didn't put much stock in opinions, even his own, but the manila envelope with the cryptic invitation for a meet intrigued him, so he said, "Go there. See what happens. But this paper doesn't print feelings. We don't print hunches, okay?"

Sally couldn't hide her smile. It happened so rarely now that it surprised her when it came. "You're the best, boss," she said. She took the thumb drive and started to head to the IT department.

Before she'd made it out of the room, Matt picked up the envelope and held it out to her. "I'm glad your secret admirer wants to meet at the train station tomorrow, Sal."

She grabbed the envelope from him and tucked it under her arm. "Why's that?" she asked.

He turned to his computer and went back to whatever he'd been working on before he called her in. "I'm hoping it will inspire you to start taking public transportation. Because there's no fucking way you should be behind the wheel of a car any-time soon. Now get your shit together and get to work."

A few hours later, appropriately chastened by both her editor and her hangover, Sally Ewell watched the elected officials and witnesses settle into their appointed places in a hearing room of the Rayburn House Office Building. A few other journalists around her seemed to be there only because the spectacle was cheaper than a movie. She wondered how many believed that the government had any actual function beyond entertainment anymore.

The man next to her leaned over and whispered, "New?"

Sally nodded without otherwise acknowledging him, hoping he was a good enough reporter to pick up on her colossal lack of interest in talking to him.

He wasn't. He handed Sally a card and said, "Call me if you need someone to show you around town." His name was printed above the name of a well-known political blog. Gossip. Hot lists. Who's up and who's down.

"Thanks," she said, tucking the card into the depths of her open notebook and returning her attention to the dais.

The man slid closer to Sally. She instinctively turned away from him ever so slightly.

"So, who are you with?" he asked.

"Virginian-Pilot."

The scoff that followed was a reflex, the physical manifestation of the kind of dismissive attitude that thinks arrogance is itself sufficient grounds for superiority. Sally knew the type. How could she not? Men or women, Black or white. People who came from money always judged those who didn't. They couldn't help themselves. They took credit and placed blame.

They pitied and shamed and wore out their arms patting themselves on the back for both.

It had been true for her father, who'd spent the better part of his life on a dead rise rocking in the wake of rich folks' yachts. When the yacht owners built their stilted houses on the banks of the Rappahannock, they'd hang five-thousand-dollar oil paintings of oystermen in skipjacks above their hearths. Then they'd raise holy hell when they saw a real waterman working tongs outside their windows. Ruins the view. Negative impact on property values. The usual estimation of what work is by the kind of people who'd never done it.

It was true when she went to UVA on a track scholarship. They'd wondered what she was doing there, this skinny girl from Gwynn's Island who said *y'all* without irony and didn't know which fork to use. After a while, Sally developed a kind of pity for *them*. She was faster than them and stronger. There were days on her father's boat so cold and wet that Sally couldn't feel her hands as they pulled eight hundred pounds of oysters from the bay's brown brack. What of the world could they refuse to give her that she could not arrive at under her own power? What could they possibly have that she might want?

"Oh," he said. "Is that like a small-town paper or..."

Sally ignored him. "I think they're about to start," she said.

"What'd they send you up here for?"

Sally nodded toward the man sitting alone at the witness table. "Decision Tree is part of my beat. I'm doing my job. I'm reporting." It was true enough. She reached instinctively into her bag for the thumb drive that had mysteriously arrived for her at the paper's office. The short note that accompanied it. *Re: Lacedaemon. Air gap only. Do not connect to a networked computer. Union Station, Saturday, July 12, 1315. Under Themis.*

The likelihood that it was bullshit was exceedingly high. But when she'd asked the paper's IT department what an air gap was before leaving the office, their response piqued her interest. "An air gap?" one guy said. "What, are you worried about the NSA or something?" She'd been tempted, but Matt was right. Rather than risk infecting the *Pilot*'s computer system with the thumb drive, she figured she ought to go in person to Union Station and see if anyone showed. The hearing was an important enough story to cover anyway, better than most of her assignments since she'd been hired. July 12. Tomorrow afternoon.

But now, she watched as Trevor Graves, the founder and chief executive officer of Decision Tree International, sat at one of a long line of tables arranged before the gathered committee members. He was calm, but a slight expression of contempt was visible on his face, a face that could otherwise be mistaken for that of a youth pastor. He was clean-cut, closely shaven, and modestly but impeccably dressed in a Brooks Brothers suit. The assembled members of Congress sat across the well from him at their raised positions, a hum of activity in stark contrast to Graves's motionless patience. Bottles of water were opened. Aides leaned in and whispered to their representatives. Papers shuffled and changed hands. The chairman's gavel banged the desk.

The chair of the House Oversight Committee began his opening statement. "Throughout the entirety of my career as a member of Congress, special interests have been trying to convince this body that the tasks and duties once ably performed by members of the armed services would be more efficiently performed by the employees of private companies. Their unshakable philosophy is that corporations can and do perform those tasks at a lower cost to taxpayers than our government is able to. Personally, I remain unconvinced that prioritizing cost above all else is a wise position to take when our young men and women are on the battlefield. Nevertheless, one of the many consequences of our military involvement in Iraq and Afghanistan is that we now have data with which we can evaluate this philosophy as implemented downrange. Mr. Graves, no company exemplifies this philosophy more than yours, and given your prior service in our nation's armed forces, you seem to be uniquely qualified to address this committee's concerns. I'd like to start by asking you the total value of Decision Tree International's government contracts."

Sally tried to get it all in her notebook in shorthand but she had a small recording device tucked underneath it just in case. She glanced over and saw the guy next to her working one of those new iPhones, both thumbs hammering away at whatever the screen held.

"We have a contract currently under review for approval, so I wouldn't be able to give you an exact figure," Graves answered.

"Is it more or less than a billion dollars?" the chairman asked.

"Prior to pending approval?"

"Yes."

"More."

"And what was the total value of your contracts before our country's military presence in Iraq?"

"The figure was much smaller," said Graves.

"Does two hundred and sixty-four thousand dollars sound accurate to you?"

Graves paused and covered the mic. He leaned back so a man in the first row of the audience could whisper something in his ear. He sat back upright and took his hand from the mic. "It does."

"And should the currently pending contract be approved, what will be the total value of Decision Tree International's government contracts?"

Graves leaned back again slowly and deliberately. Sally noted the delaying tactic. "The pending contract is under continuing negotiations."

"Would it be accurate to state that the pending contract with the Departments of Defense and State has a value greater than two billion dollars?"

"As I said, sir, negotiations are ongoing."

The chairman made a gesture of his own, folding his arms and looking away from the witness. He wanted the cameras in the well to capture his indignation from his good side. Sally thought the exchange was about as worthy of her suspension of disbelief as a children's puppet show. They knew what characters they were playing and played them well enough. Their whole lives had been spent practicing for the roles. But she found it hard to believe it was anything more than that anymore. "Let's move on to the services we are paying you to perform. Is Decision Tree International authorized to engage in offensive operations?" the chairman asked finally.

"No, sir, offensive operations are outside the scope of our contracts."

"Has Decision Tree or its employees engaged in offensive operations?"

"No."

The chairman looked up from his prewritten questions with curiosity. An aide handed him several papers stapled together and turned to a specific page. The chairman adjusted his reading glasses, read the short passage, then handed the papers back to his aide. He removed his glasses and rubbed at the bridge of his nose. "No?" he asked.

Graves calmly reached for a glass of water and took a sip. He didn't respond.

"But your employees have been involved in numerous engagements?"

"The situation is fluid, and we are authorized to defend ourselves," Graves said.

"Do your employees find themselves in engagements more or less frequently than the average soldier on the line?"

"There is no line."

Sally switched from shorthand and wrote the phrase out in her notebook. *There is no line.* She underlined it three times.

"But you understand the question?" the chairman asked.

Graves leaned back and listened to the man behind him again, then said, "Our duties are often more conspicuous than those of our military counterparts. We are responsible for the protection of high-value and high-visibility individuals within the Coalition reconstruction effort."

"Have any Decision Tree employees shot and killed innocent civilians?" the chairman asked.

"No," Graves answered.

"Have any Decision Tree employees been accused of shooting and killing innocent civilians?"

"It's easy to accuse."

"Nevertheless, Mr. Graves, if you'd answer the question."

Graves began speaking through gritted teeth, but by the third or fourth word of his answer, he'd gotten himself under control again. Sally wasn't sure anyone else noticed, but she had. "Our guys are stuck on defense in a war zone, Congressman," he said. "They act like any other soldiers would."

The chairman smiled condescendingly. "You were formerly a member of the armed forces, Mr. Graves, weren't you?"

"I was."

"As was I."

"I know. I saw one of your campaign ads during the primary. You made it hard to miss."

The chairman took a moment to stare at the witness. He didn't think Trevor Graves would be intimidated by the look, but it was necessary for his performance. "Can you tell me what happens to a soldier accused of shooting and killing an innocent civilian?" he asked.

"They'd be subject to prosecution under the Uniform Code of Military Justice."

"And they have been."

Again, Graves did not respond.

"Are employees of Decision Tree International subject to prosecution under the Uniform Code of Military Justice?"

The man in the first row leaned toward Graves, who leaned back to meet him. A moment later, Graves sat upright and answered, "No."

"No. No, they are not," said the chairman. "Because your employees are not held to the same standards as are members of the armed forces, isn't that true?"

"They are private citizens."

"Has Decision Tree International or its employees been sued in any U.S. court by the relatives of Iraqi civilians killed as a result of their conduct?"

"Those cases have been dismissed."

"On what grounds?" asked the chairman.

"I'm not a lawyer, Congressman."

"Were those cases dismissed because Decision Tree is included under the Department of Defense's Total Force? And the courts found that you, your company, and your employees are therefore not subject to personal or corporate liability?"

"Again, Congressman, I'm not a lawyer. I can only tell you that those cases have been dismissed."

"That's a miraculously well-threaded needle, wouldn't you say, Mr. Graves?"

Silence.

"Just a couple more questions, Mr. Graves, as I can see the ranking member pointing to his watch."

Scattered nervous laughter worked through the committee members and into the audience. *The show's almost over,* Sally thought.

"Mr. Graves, earlier in your testimony, you mentioned that your employees act like any other soldiers."

"I did, and they do."

"What are the terms of their employment?"

"Excuse me, Mr. Chairman," said Graves. "I'm afraid I don't understand the question."

The chairman leaned back in his leather chair. "What I'd like to know, Mr. Graves, is whether or not employees of Decision Tree International swear an oath to the Constitution of the United States, as you and I both did when we were inducted into the armed forces."

Graves was visibly annoyed by the question. Sally wasn't the only one to notice this time. He smirked and checked the clock on the wall above the members of the committee sitting across from him.

The ranking member spoke up from his seat next to the chairman. "The gentleman's time is expiring."

"I'll take that as a no," the chairman said. "I just have one more very brief line of questioning, Mr. Graves. Was Decision Tree International incorporated in the United States of America, and does your company pay U.S. taxes?"

Graves and the chairman stared each other down for a few moments. The dismissive smirk on Graves's face was bolder now.

"I'm sorry, Mr. Chairman, your time has expired," said the ranking member. "Mr. Graves, we thank you for your testimony today. You are free to go."

Graves stood up without saying anything. His demeanor had already shifted into naked contempt. He glared at the committee members. He appeared to be about to speak, but then he visibly collected himself and calmly turned and headed up the aisle to the exit. Sally waited for him to pass her row as he left the committee room and followed him out.

FOUR

Arman looked over his shoulder before he ducked under the police tape and began the short walk down Ocean View to the Sea Breeze Motel. The sunlight slanted over the beach, washed unbroken over the silent police lights, and fell hot on the concrete street and sidewalk. A breeze off the dark gray water gave a little relief, but Arman's collar was ringed in sweat when he crossed the wide beachfront road to the motel grounds.

Arman swung open the glass door, and a bell dinged, and Mr. Peters looked up from his seat behind the check-in desk. He put down the Western he'd been reading, raised his hands, shrugged in frustration, and said, "Arman," as if his name might hold both a question and an answer.

"Did they tell you why I'm late?" he asked.

"Late? Arman, it's almost ten thirty. Late is five after eight. Eight thirty, tops. And did who tell me what?"

"Did you see the police down the street?"

"Yeah, someone drowned or something."

"They were asking me questions. They said they'd tell you."

"Are you in some kind of trouble? Jesus, Arman, I don't want any more ex-cons on staff."

"I found the guy. The dead guy."

Mr. Peters stood up slowly so that as much of his eighty-three-year-old body as possible could straighten out simultaneously. He leaned forward against the check-in desk and took his thick glasses off. "Are you okay, son?" he asked.

Arman found it strange that Mr. Peters called him *son* on occasion. After working for him these past four years, Arman recognized that it was as much an old Virginia man exercising his paternalistic prerogative as it was a term of endearment. Nevertheless, Arman appreciated it, as a long time had passed since someone addressed him with even accidental affection before he'd come to work at the Sea Breeze. He wasn't sure exactly how it had happened. He knew that Mr. Peters was obliquely connected to a few civic organizations, like the Veterans of Foreign Wars and the Lions Club. One of the organizations had a group that assisted in resettling refugees. Arman was sometimes still surprised to be reminded that he qualified as one.

His had been an unusual case. Most of the time, recipients of special immigrant visas would bring immediate family with them to the States. Or, failing that, they'd have some kind of familial connection to an extant community in the U.S., like, for the Kurds, Dearborn, Michigan, or Little Kurdistan in South Nashville. But Arman had left no family behind in Mosul, only graves. And there would not be anyone waiting for him on arrival. Not if the U.S. government could help it. He'd gotten out quickly. Favors were called in and passed up the chain, first by the platoon's lieutenant, whom he'd translated for and fought beside for a year, then up to the company commander, then to the battalion executive officer. The appeal finally reached someone at Multinational Brigade North with enough heart to read and act upon a request written in the cold bureaucratic language of the military that was summarized as follows:

> Arman Bajalan, 26, survived assassination attempt, 9 Nov 2004, Mosul, Nineveh Governorate, Iraq. Subject's dependents deceased. Subject served honorably as an interpreter for brigade infantry elements for 16 months, 24 days. Recommended for special immigrant visa and resettlement in CONUS.

"Sure, Mr. Peters. I'm okay. Just a strange morning. I'm sorry I was late."

Arman looked at the wall behind Mr. Peters. A shadow box with the artifacts of a forty-year military career: Unit patches. Medals. Ribbons stacked on ribbons. Below it were two framed photographs of Mr. Peters's children, long since grown to adulthood and long since gone. Arman had never met them, and he felt he wasn't likely to.

"I know you are, but don't worry about it. Lucy's almost done with the rooms, so why don't you clean up the pool, and I'll take you over to Doug's for lunch. Oh, and change out the letter board outside. I want to get a new saying up."

"That sounds great," Arman said.

He went out through the motel office's doors and into the atrium where the pool was and onto which the two floors of small rooms opened. He looked up to the second floor and saw Lucy's cart through the metal railings, and Lucy came out of one of the rooms and called down to him, "You all right, doll?"

Arman shielded his eyes from the sunlight that fell through the open courtyard and reflected the chlorinated pool water's blue-white movement. "I'm okay. Sorry to stick you with all the rooms, Lucy."

She waved him off. "I need the reps," she joked.

"Yeah?" he said.

She pulled a pack of smokes from her cart, lit one, and leaned back against the wall next to the room's open door. "Thinking of going pro," she said.

Arman watched her put out the smoke, close the door to the room, and go into the next one with her spray bottle and paper towels. He went over to the wall and grabbed the skimmer from its rack. He stood at the pool's edge and set the water moving with the net. There was not much debris, so he put the skimmer back, got the brush, and cleaned the tile above the water's surface. He knelt on the concrete next to the pool to check the pH. The man from the beach floated in the water at the bottom. Arman caught his breath flooding in and sat back from the edge. When he looked again, a woman and a young boy floated where the man had just been. Blood dyed the water pink around them. He shut his eyes, took deep breaths, counted to ten, and opened them again. There was nothing but clear blue water in the pool, the sunlight dancing on its surface. He sat there for a moment with his arms resting on his knees and stared at nothing on the far side of the courtyard: a row of doors, a row of plastic-ribboned sun loungers. He sat there for a while longer, trying not to think of anything at all. Then he set his hand in the water like a cup and splashed it over his face and the back of his neck and let it trickle down coolly between his shoulder blades. He took another minute to collect himself, then went back to his hands and knees poolside with the pH testing kit.

At noon Mr. Peters came out to where Arman was, up on

a stepladder, changing the outdoor letter board. He had the pole extended and had just put up a letter when Mr. Peters waved his cane at him and said, "Come on, son, I'm hungry as all get-out. It'll keep." Arman climbed down and looked back at what he'd done. The letter board read THE REWARD FOR LIVING A GOOD LIFE IS.

"You sure you want to leave it?"

"It's fine."

Arman folded up the ladder, took off his tool belt, brought it and the ladder to the service closet, and locked the door with a key from his carabiner. They went out into the hot sun, and Mr. Peters shuffled along with his cane as Arman walked next to him slowly.

They got to Doug's and went inside and ordered two chili dogs each and two cherry limeades. They sat down at a booth away from the sun-beaten windows and ate quietly for a little while, and then Mr. Peters leaned back, put his hands out flat on the table on either side of his plate, and looked at Arman.

"Can I ask you something, Arman?"

"Sure."

"You been with me how long? It's going on several years now, ain't it?"

"Yes, sir."

"You got any friends? A gal?"

"No. Not really."

"But kind of?"

"It's not easy, Mr. Peters."

"Yeah." He sighed. "I expect it's not. I worry about you is all, son, especially after this morning." Mr. Peters knew that death was hardly ever a welcome guest. He'd faced it more times than he could count. He knew that Arman had as well.

At some point in Mr. Peters's life, he'd started to look back and wonder if it hadn't been there all the time, if he ought not to just let the world go by and wait for it to come and get him.

"I'm okay, Mr. Peters. Really."

"No shame if you ain't. That's something new for a man. Weren't always that way. Anyhow. I'm just trying to tell you if the world gave you a weight to carry around, you can put that sumbitch down any old time you like. It's a thing I wish I'd done sometime well before I got around to it."

Arman looked at the old man across the table. Large-framed glasses over the cloudy gray of his eyes. He had that big Screaming Eagle ball cap set up high the way he'd seen only old men wear them. Mr. Peters leaned back again and looked away from him and started tapping at the ground with the end of his cane, wrapping and unwrapping his fingers around the carved duck handle, his right hand still big and strong despite being liver-spotted and afflicted with tremors.

You can't put down an absence, thought Arman. And he didn't know how to tell anyone, even Mr. Peters, that he felt more like a ghost than a man. Until that day at the university, his world had been his wife and his son, and his world before they'd entered it seemed in retrospect to be little more than the path that had led to them. Now the path was obscured, if it remained at all. He looked out the plate-glass window over the pavement and dry grass and over the gray ocean. Now his world was divorced from the irrelevance of area, of distance. Its chief feature was its emptiness. His life was behind him and would remain there no matter where he went, and it would be this way until he joined them. He felt a mix of envy and shame at moments like this. Shame at his survival. Envy of his wife and son for avoiding the emptiness into which he woke each

43

morning. Then shame again for thinking of their deaths as something to be envied.

He had a sense that Mr. Peters understood something of this. Arman knew that Mr. Peters's children were still alive. And he knew that the photographs Mr. Peters kept on his office wall tracked a family as it grew through time. But he also knew that the chief characteristic of these pictures was how abruptly they stopped and how Mr. Peters had aged alone long past the time the last one had been taken. Arman did not know the circumstances that had created Mr. Peters's estrangement from his family, whether he was blameless for it or tortured himself over being its cause the way Arman did. But the circumstances of the loss were not important to Arman's estimation of the older man, only its fact.

"Can I tell you something, son?" Mr. Peters asked.

"Sure."

"I know you don't owe me nothing to listen, but there are some things a man of my age ought not to wait on. I'd like to have it said even if it's just between you and me and this wall here." Mr. Peters looked out the window into the shady parking lot. "I fought in three wars. You'd think even to get three wars going in the span of one man's life would be tough. Hell, turns out from my history books, it's peace that's the aberration. By the time I turned forty-five, I'd spent damn near half my adult life in combat. And somehow, in the other half, I managed to get married and have kids. But when my wife got sick back in '68, I was off in a jungle somewhere. My kids were teenagers or younger then. Even when I found out she was really going, I didn't make it back till she was already in the ground."

"Mr. Peters, I'm sorry."

"You don't have nothing to be sorry about, son. Point is, I

thought I was supposed to be okay, you understand? I thought that's what everyone needed from me. But you let grief go on too long, and it spreads like a disease." He shook his head. He was tearing up quietly across the table, his chin buried in his chest.

"Mr. Peters, you know what happened to me."

"I know, Arman. I know. And I know hurt like that goes all the way down and don't ever find a bottom. I just wanted to tell you I probably went and used up what portion of love the world had on offer for me. But you ain't, son. You ain't."

FIVE

Detective Wheel rode in Lamar's cruiser from Ocean View back to Violent Crimes. The sun burned up the morning's clouds and sent heat waves rippling down the blacktop ahead of the car as it nooned above them. Cat lit a cigarette, opened the window, and folded down the visor.

"I don't think we're supposed to smoke in the units, ma'am."

"We're not. I am," she said.

Lamar raised his hands off the wheel to signal *Whatever you say*. "You want to bring this guy in later?" he asked.

"Yeah. Probably. When we get to the house, call Homeland Security and see what kind of visa Mr. Bajalan's here on. I want to hear from Dr. Martin before we talk to him again. See if he can nail down a cause of death on the guy Bajalan found."

"Pretty sure he's here on an SIV."

"SIV?"

"Special immigrant visa. I'd bet money he worked as a terp"—Lamar paused, catching his partner's confusion out of the corner of his eye, then went on—"an interpreter for us in Iraq. He clocked me as former military pretty quick. The way he reacted when he said *hajji*. Bajalan's a Kurdish name, I'm pretty sure. Anyway, I'm guessing that's his status."

Cat looked out the window as they rolled toward the city proper on the highway. "How do you get one of those?"

"Usually, they get passed out as favors by higher-ups. Somebody important has a nephew working for us. That kind of thing. Maybe a guy gets made as a collaborator, but to be honest, they're usually left hanging."

"You think someone owed this guy a favor?"

"I don't know. No family. Shitty job taking out the trash at a cheap motel on Ocean View? Maybe that's an improvement. I'm not sure."

"Tell me why the hajji stuff got your wheels turning so hard back there."

"Look, I'm not proud of it, but that's what we called them."

"So it's like a slur or something?"

"Didn't used to be. It's an honorific. One who has gone on the hajj. Someone who made the pilgrimage to Mecca. Or it's what you say to be cool to an important dude in a village. It's a sign of respect. Maybe the biggest."

Catherine figured out the rest pretty quick. It doesn't matter what you call someone if you say it with enough venom. If the word is always preceded by *motherfucking* and spoken by twenty-year-old kids with M4s, it's gonna turn into a slur pretty quick whether you like it or not. "So you're saying these guys weren't just the kind of guys who happened to pick out Bajalan as Muslim — they were also the kind of guys who would have likely been deployed to Iraq or Afghanistan."

"Yeah. Probably wouldn't be just one or the other kind of guys."

"And they were at the very least close to the body, what, thirty minutes before Bajalan found him?"

"It's an unusual place for people to be under any circumstances. What do soldiers do, Detective Wheel?"

"I know."

"So what are the chances these two guys just happened to walk away from that particular beach before sunrise and leave behind a body that they didn't have anything to do with putting there?" Lamar said. "Wait a second, Detective." He kept one hand on the steering wheel and pulled out his notebook with the other. He held it against the wheel and flipped through a few of the small pages.

"What is it?"

"Bajalan said these guys didn't see him. He just heard one of them say the word when they walked by."

"Okay."

"Well, if they weren't saying it to him, why'd it come up?"

"I don't know. Maybe they were reminiscing about the old days."

"You think they were expecting him to be there?" Lamar still had the notebook out in front of him. His eyes darted between it and the road. "Bajalan said he got there late. Problems with the bus and all."

"Could be," said Catherine. "I'll tell you what, Lamar. If this does turn out to be a murder, it'll be a doozy of a first." She looked out the window. They passed over the little highway bridge above Oastes Creek. In the distance, a sliver of white buildings stood at the end of the midday haze through which she looked, a mere fraction of the sprawling naval installation that jutted out into the bay. "Okay. Well. It's a start, I guess."

"Yeah. Nothing to it. All we gotta do," said Detective Adams with a smile, "is find a couple of military guys in Norfolk, Virginia."

"Jesus. Is that all?" They were pulling up to an intersection. "Hey, take Lafayette over to Monticello," she said.

"Isn't that a little out of the way, Detective?"

"Doumar's is never out of the way," said Cat, lighting another smoke. "And I need to think for a minute. We can hit the Greyhound station after. And Lamar?"

"Ma'am?"

"Will you call me Catherine, please?"

They pulled into Doumar's, got out of the cruiser, and sat on the hood. Catherine had her feet up on the front bumper. When the carhop came, she called them both *darling* and scribbled their order across her pad without looking up. The sun tucked in behind the red awning. Catherine worked at an orange sherbet cone with a Marlboro in the same hand. Lamar eyed her curiously, sipped from his drink, and sloshed the ice up and down as he emptied the cup. A seaman in a brand-new plum-colored Dodge at a nearby stoplight laid half the rubber from his tires down onto the pavement. The V-8 growled, and the whole car slowly smoked through the intersection until the tires caught the road again and shot down Monticello.

"You think that's one of our guys?" Lamar asked.

"You think the dead guy sold him the car?"

"Twenty percent interest, we might have to put it down as justifiable."

Cat laughed. It was quiet for a little while, and then a jet roared by above them in the hot clear sky. A pickup full of construction workers went by, blaring out a ranchera that faded in that strange elongated way sound does until the song stretched back into silence, and the truck rolled into the distance. People came and lingered in the parking lot of Doumar's, much like the two detectives and like people had done for almost a hundred years.

"Catherine, I know you've been a cop for a long time, but how much do you know about the military?"

"You mean besides what a person learns putting the bracelets on young squids after a bar fight?"

"I mean just that it adds another element. Complicates things further."

"Believe it or not, I used to live on post right here."

"No shit?"

"Enlisted housing. Not for very long. I got married right after high school, and my husband enlisted just after we got married. He finished at Great Lakes and joined the fleet here, and I moved down from a little no-place hollow called Montebello up in Nelson County, where we were both from, in the spring of '81. You wouldn't believe it. Norfolk, Virginia. I thought it was as big as New York City. Neither of us had ever even seen the ocean outside of pictures. I'm a hillbilly, Lamar. I come from way out back of beyond."

"So what happened?"

"The usual. He goes out nights with the boys and comes home drunk as shit and wants to have a boxing match while I'm trying to do the laundry. Finally I called my daddy, and he drove straight down through the night, and he takes one look at my eye all swole shut and tells my husband to get out and starts packing my bags. You always think you want to be grown, but sometimes even now, I think I could curl up in my daddy's arms if he was living still."

"I bet he'd liked to have killed that boy."

"Could be. He was a hard man in many ways, but he worked at being a good Christian better than most. I wished he weren't right then, but we got the master-at-arms to the apartment in case Del, that was my husband, came back."

"He get chaptered out or what?"

"No. It wasn't like it is now. I think maybe he got a month extra duty, but I was gone by the time that was sorted out. The thing was, this master-at-arms who came to the apartment that night — there was something about him. He was only a couple years older than me, but boy, it seemed like he had it together. My daddy was a deputy sheriff for a time back in Nelson County, but somehow, I never saw him the way I could see that young sailor until I was older. Between him and my daddy, we got through the night as well as could be hoped for. And I had so much admiration for this MA that I decided I wanted to become a cop."

"So that's your why," Lamar said.

"My what?"

Lamar laughed. "Your *why*. In high school, I had a ball coach used to say that to us." He put on a thick drawl to match the coach's voice in his memory: "'Gotta find y'all's why, boys.'" Catherine watched the young detective drift through happy memories, then shake his head to return to the difficulty of the present. "It's cheesy, but when you're sixteen and scared of the world, that kind of thing really matters. His point was that it's not enough to know what to do. Or even how to do it. You better know why. 'Cause if you don't, and the boy lined up across from you does, he's gonna spend sixty minutes whipping that ass. So," Lamar said, "that's your why."

"It was at the beginning, that's for sure."

"And now?" he asked.

She took another drag off her smoke. "When I was a kid, I saw my daddy do the right thing when he knew he'd suffer for doing it. All these years on the job, I still don't know if I have that in me. Maybe my why is waiting to find out." She tossed the smoke on the ground and said, "Funny how things shake out, ain't it?"

"I hear you. Being in charge of your own life doesn't mean you're gonna guess right how it turns out."

"No. Probably anyone else would guess better than the person living it."

"Yeah," said Lamar. "I've got a notion about that too." He pitched his Styrofoam cup into a nearby trash can and turned toward the driver's side of the unit.

Cat noticed the black band on his wrist as he sent the cup flying toward the trash. Knew what was stamped into the metal: names and ranks and dates and the name of a place that Cat knew only enough about to be glad she'd never been there.

"Let's find out who he is," Lamar said. "Least we can do is see he gets buried with a name, right?"

"Right. Hey, did you get a pic of him?"

"Yeah." Lamar pulled the Polaroid out of his pocket. He fanned it in the air as if waiting for the image of the body to appear, but it was already there, the face serene in its own way.

Cat took the photo and looked at it for a minute. "You work enough of these, Lamar, gets hard to remember they're more than just a face and a name." She handed the pic back and got in the car.

They drove the rest of the way down Monticello, and the gray concrete dome of the arena hovered beyond the Greyhound station. They pulled into the lot and headed in. Lamar checked along the edge of the roofline and up under the awnings for cameras. Nothing. He followed Cat in, and the station's interior was indistinguishable from the inside of any other bus station on earth. The linoleum tiles reflected the buzzing over-head lights. A quartet of metal benches stood in the middle of the room.

Lamar went down the only hallway to check for lockers, and Cat walked over to the ticket desk. A young woman sat chewing gum and flipping through a magazine. She looked up at Cat, who was leaning against the desk with her badge laid out on the top.

"Can I help you?"

Cat pulled out her notepad and asked for a printout of the manifest for tomorrow's first express bus to DC.

Lamar walked up beside her. "No lockers," he said.

"I can't print it out 'cause people can walk up and buy tickets until just before the bus leaves if it ain't sold out," the woman said.

"Can you tell me if a ticket for Tom Brown on that bus has been canceled or if it's still valid?"

The ticket agent punched a few keys and said, "No changes."

"Was this ticket bought solo or did other seats get purchased with this one?"

"Looks like the only one."

"When did Mr. Brown get here?"

"A week ago."

"Any bags get left here?"

"We only hold bags for twenty-four hours."

"Just check, if you don't mind," said Cat.

Behind them, the line of travelers snaked through the board-ing lane. Lamar watched as each one paused at the podium, where the employee hardly glanced down at either the ticket or ID. Half the passengers didn't even show ID, and the man at the stand did not seem bothered in the slightest, if he noticed at all.

The ticket agent went back into the baggage area. Cat turned around and watched the boarding process.

"Well, Catherine, I'll tell you what. If you wanted to travel under the most lenient identification requirements possible, this would be the way to do it. You rent a car, you need a driver's license and insurance. On Amtrak, ID and ticket get checked on the train. Planes? Shit. Not gonna happen. But you could be anyone you want to be on a trip like this."

Catherine sighed. "Yeah. Even Thomas Brown, man of mystery."

The woman came back. "Sorry," she said. She sat down and picked up the magazine where she'd left off.

Cat spun it out to bounce it off Lamar one more time. "So you're from DC and come down to Norfolk, Virginia, for a week, ninety-nine percent under an assumed name."

"Maybe from DC or maybe that's just where he got on the bus."

"Okay. Either way, he's gotta stay somewhere, right?"

"Yeah. Maybe somewhere that checks IDs as hard as Greyhound?"

"Sure. But if you don't want people to know your name, good bet you don't want to be noticed at all."

"You're the kind of guy who wears a decent-looking suit in the middle of the night, so you're not going to a complete dump."

"Too fancy, and they want to know all kinds of stuff. Want to sign you up for rewards programs and the like. Cameras in the lobby, at least."

Lamar stood there thinking for a minute. "Okay. Sanity

check. Are we sure this dude isn't just Tom Brown from Washington, DC, who gets hammered and overdoses on the beach while he's here for some insurance conference?"

"No. We're not sure. But if he is, there's plenty of reason to think he's not expected back until tomorrow afternoon. So when they call up to DC to run our boy against missing persons, I'm betting nothing shows. But you don't believe that. And neither do I. Look, Lamar, my only rule for partnering up is that we work every angle on every case as hard as possible until it's proven unnecessary. You can't overwork a body. But you sure as shit can underwork it."

"That's not what I meant."

"I know. I'm just trying to explain why we're hound-dogging this thing even though we don't know anything yet. You have to stay one step ahead of what you don't know on a murder case, Lamar. That's rule number one. We can slow it down if we need to, but there ain't no way to play catch-up."

They leaned back and put their elbows on the desk to the barely disguised annoyance of the ticket agent.

"You know this area pretty well?" Cat asked her.

"I guess so."

"Any decent hotels nearby? Like, walking distance?"

"Yeah, there's a Marriott and a Hilton down by the water."

"Which water?" asked Lamar.

"Past MacArthur Square. On Main. Maybe Waterside."

"Any sort of boutique hotels? Not big chains?" said Cat.

"There's a small hotel, the Something Inn over on York, I think."

"The Something Inn sounds about right, doesn't it?" said Lamar.

"Worth a look," Cat said. "Can you get us an exact address,

please?" she asked the ticket agent. They went out the front door of the bus station with the address of the Square and Compass Inn, only a ten-minute walk west down Brambleton and across the tracks.

"Leave the car?" Cat asked.

"Yeah. Probably worth it to walk."

They headed west down the sidewalk on the north side of Brambleton with their eyes active. Where would this man have left a trace? Were there cameras? A bar he might have stopped in? Anything at all that they might probe further? It sometimes seemed to Catherine that the world had become more challenging to hide in over the past ten years. She'd pinged cell phone towers to close cases. She'd found high-definition videos of murders posted online in the middle of her investigations. Rarely did a day go by for most people without them archiving themselves into the world's collective digital record. The trick for her was finding the trace. A selfie on Facebook. E-mails. Texts. And at no time was it trickier than when a suspect realized that most of this was optional. The technology, the way we anchored ourselves to one another in the ether — once you chose to exclude yourself from the record, you could travel through the world almost invisibly without much effort. It required only a little attention. But the choice was what made it hard. Soon enough, people would forget they could make that choice at all.

They passed the office of the *Virginian-Pilot,* and Cat said she thought there were cameras in the lobby, but she didn't think they'd catch the street. After a few blocks, the sidewalk was shaded by trees, and the buildings spread out. They walked through an open space under the green leaves that kept them shaded from the summer sun. They crossed another block of

Brambleton, and here the buildings on the north side were set back a little farther from the road. On the south side, they stood separated by six lanes of traffic and two sets of commuter train tracks. When they saw the Hampton Roads Transit station across the street, they crossed the road, and from the other side, Lamar took in the arrangement of buildings, streets, people, and trains.

"No way he's on camera from here to the bus station," Lamar said.

"Let's see if he was even here at all."

They passed through the York and Freemason HRT station. Cat pointed to a camera high up on the exterior brick of the YMCA building that was aimed west down York.

"Maybe," said Lamar. "It's something, anyway."

They walked the remaining blocks to the end of York. New brick sidewalks and empty storage facilities. Renovated-warehouse apartment buildings rose above gravel parking lots with only gravel parking lots between. At the end of all of this, two Victorian row houses stood, untouched by progress. They were islands in a sea of identical corporate offices and desperately hip boutiques and coffee shops, the endless reproducibility of contemporary gentrifying urban American chic.

They took the steps up to the porch of the inn and rang the doorbell. They turned their backs to the door to take in the view from the covered porch.

The door opened behind them, and they turned around. A tiny woman at the boundary of old age stood in the entryway. "I wasn't expecting any new guests. But please, come in," she said. A small desk was tucked into the space next to the elegant wooden staircase. No computer. No electronic card reader. A credit card imprint machine at the edge of the desk. Cat saw the lockbox on the floor behind the chair. The woman sat down and flipped open a calendar. Cat looked up at Lamar, who gave her a slight nod.

"Ma'am, I'm sorry. We're not looking to rent a room. My name is Detective Wheel, and this is my partner, Detective Adams. We're with the Norfolk Police Department, and we were hoping we could ask you a few questions."

The woman closed the calendar and sat upright, quickly and formally. "Why, of course," she said.

"Do you have a guest named Thomas Brown registered?"

"No, I'm afraid I don't."

"Ma'am, I'm very sorry, but you didn't even check in your book," said Lamar.

"I don't have to. I only have one guest at the moment, and that's not his name."

"Could you describe him to us?" he asked.

The woman looked nervous. "Don't you need a warrant or something?"

"No, ma'am. Not to ask questions," Cat answered. "As long as you're comfortable, we'd really appreciate any help you could give us."

"Well, all right. Could you please tell me what this is about first?"

"We don't want to shock you, but we're homicide detectives, and we're trying to identify a man who was found this morning," she said.

The woman was flustered but only for a moment. She composed herself quickly. "Oh, dear. Oh, dear. You don't think Mr. Baker was involved in this, do you? He's such a nice man. I hardly even knew he was here, but so polite, you know? Oh, bless his heart."

Lamar looked over at Cat and mouthed, *Mr. Baker?*

She shrugged in answer. "Could you tell us a little about Mr. Baker? What does he look like? When did he check in?"

"It's just that, well, you see, Mr. Baker asked if I would be discreet. He said he was a private person, and I've given my word." She looked at Catherine and said, "You understand, don't you?"

"I do," she answered. "Of course I do. It's just that we want to make sure Mr. Baker, well, that he isn't the man we found."

"If you could just tell us a little bit about him, it would really help us out," said Lamar.

The woman gave them a description that matched the body. Lamar asked her if he could show her a photograph and told her it might be unsettling. He showed her the Polaroid of the dead man's face, and the woman's hand shot to her mouth to stifle any noise that she might make instinctively. "Yes, oh my Lord, yes, that's Mr. Baker."

"Can you tell us a little bit about his stay?" Lamar asked.

The woman collected herself again. "He arrived one week ago." She flipped to a page in her calendar. "The room was booked over the telephone a week before that, and he let me know that he'd be paying in cash when he arrived."

"Do many of your customers pay cash or book in this way?" Cat asked.

"Yes, I've found it rather difficult to keep up with the changing technology. I pay to have a website maintained. We explicitly inform our guests that cash or personal checks are the preferred payment methods. It's right there on the website. It can't be missed."

"You said he asked you to be discreet?" she said.

"Yes, he said that it would be a working vacation, and he

would like to be undisturbed in his room. If he had any visitors, which he did not expect to have, he asked me to please avoid giving them any information about his stay. And he said he would not need me to clean his room. I have to confess that worried me, so I did steal a look after a few days, and I was satisfied that he was keeping things up in an orderly fashion."

Lamar said, "Ma'am, is there anything else about his stay that you remember? His comings and goings. Did he keep to a schedule?"

"He went for a run every morning at five thirty and returned at six fifteen. I could hear the shower going for a few minutes after that. Then he would go out and return again about eight at night."

"No deviations from that?" asked Cat.

"Well, he didn't come back last night. And I obviously didn't see him this morning."

"No, I guess not."

"What about your other guests?" Lamar asked.

"There are only three bedrooms, one of which is mine. I live on the top floor. The room next to Mr. Baker's is vacant. We lose out to the hotels at the beach this time of year, you see."

"Ma'am, we're terribly sorry to have to inconvenience you, but we are going to need to examine Mr. Baker's room," said Cat.

"Of course," she answered.

The woman led them up the staircase holding an extra key to the room on the right side of the second-floor landing.

"May I?" asked Lamar politely.

The woman nodded.

He took the key, unlocked the door, and handed the key back to the proprietress. She went down the stairs. Catherine pulled on her gloves, and so did Lamar, and she pushed open the door to the room. The room was oriented toward a large bay window at the front of the house. Even though it was north-facing, the room was flooded with afternoon light. Against the rear wall, a double bed was flanked by wooden nightstands. They checked the drawers and found them empty. Lamar pointed to the bed.

"Hospital corners," he said.

"You think he liked Martha Stewart?"

Lamar laughed. "I bet that's it."

An armoire stood against the far wall on the right. Cat opened it. A medium-size dry bag sat at the bottom. Two suits of the same kind the man was wearing when he was found were hanging from the bar. Two white shirts. No tags. A pair of running shorts and shoes next to the dry bag. Three sets of Hanes briefs, neatly folded.

Lamar leaned down to a desk beneath the bay window. "Catherine, you got that key?"

"Yeah." She went over to Lamar, pulled the key out, and handed it to him. A wide drawer spanned nearly the length of the desk beneath its wooden worktop.

He put the key in the lock and slowly opened it. Arranged neatly in the drawer were a laptop, a six-by-nine-inch manila envelope, and a box of Fiocchi nine-mil subsonic ammo. He opened the box and counted out the bullets. Seventeen. Ran through some numbers in his head.

Cat came up alongside him and gently removed the envelope.

"Somewhere out there is a suppressed nine-millimeter with a couple of loaded mags," he said.

"Jesus Christ, Lamar. Take a look at this."

He turned toward her. She had four passports fanned out in her left hand like a magician doing a card trick. In her right hand, a stack of bills folded in half. "Euros and dollars," she said. "Who the hell was this guy?"

"I don't know," Lamar said. He put the ammo box on the desk, pulled out his flip phone, and made a call. "Yeah. Get the forensic guys down here. York, that's right. Computer guy too. And, hey, check and see if a pistol turned up at the scene at Ocean View Park. Anything, but if you find a nine-mil with a suppressor, I'll buy you a beer." He looked at Catherine. "What's the next move, Detective?"

Catherine returned the items to the envelope. "Stay one step ahead," she answered.

SIX

Sally followed Graves out into the hall and tried to linger nearby unobtrusively. It'd be good to get a quote from him. Something with a local angle would do. Anything to pin him to a verifiable statement. *Are you thinking of expanding the facility in Chesapeake if the contracts are approved?* Something like that. Maybe she'd get lucky and he'd lie. She'd like to ask him about the lawsuits, but those had been sealed and nondisclosured to hell and back, and she didn't want to waste her time just to get no-commented.

Graves took out his phone and paced back and forth along the wall outside the hearing room until the phone rang. He answered it and snapped his fingers at the man who'd sat behind him while he testified, and that man walked over and stood at the far end of his pacing. Graves stopped pacing, stood still, tucked one arm under the opposite elbow, held the phone to his ear, and bent down slightly.

Sally took her notebook out and eased her way over to Graves with her eyes mainly on the notebook. She stopped just close enough to him to hear him speaking at a conversational volume, even accounting for the ambient shuffle and hum of the hallway.

"Watch your language," she heard him say. Then, "Okay.

One? Only one?" He stood listening to the voice on the other end of the line a bit longer. "How big of a problem will this be, Harris?" he said.

Sally flipped casually through her notebook and tried to get down Graves's end of the conversation. She wrote, *Who is Harris?* and underlined it three times.

"Don't tell me it's not a problem. Tell me how you intend to mitigate." He listened to the other end for a few more moments and said, "Let me know," and closed the phone. He turned to the other man, and they stood there speaking with their voices too quiet for Sally to hear, and then they went down the hallway.

Sally let them pass and then jogged to catch up, falling in alongside them as they walked. "Mr. Graves, I'm Sally Ewell with the *Virginian-Pilot*. Does Decision Tree plan to expand the facilities—"

He stopped, turned directly to her, and raised his hand to quiet her. "Go back to Norfolk, Ms. Ewell. Our media relations team is down there. And by the way, it's rude to hover." He turned away and he and the other man walked down the corridor. She tried to ask another question, but they showed passes to a Capitol Police officer who let them into a restricted area and kept Sally from following them down the hall.

She made her way to the entrance, walked out into the sunshine, and sat down on one of the bottom steps. She took her bag off her shoulder, pulled out a pair of sneakers, put her flats in the bag, put the sneakers on, and started walking down Independence. She crossed at the Mall, walked under the shade of the interlacing crowns, and crossed over the Arlington bridge and into Virginia about an hour later. She made her way down the cemetery's shady boulevards and watched the rows of white stones march in endless formation beneath the trees. She went to the Tomb of the Unknown Soldier, stood silently as the sentinel took his twenty-one steps and snapped his rifle, and quietly listened to the sharp mechanics of the ceremony.

After a while, she shouldered her bag and went toward section sixty, where the stones were newer. Some of the trees were so young they still had their thin trunks tied and staked against the wind and their roots circled in fresh mulch. She stepped from the pavement to the grass, walked down a row of stones, stopped, and sat down in front of one. It was hot without the shade of the trees, and not far in the distance, Sally saw the green mesh fencing between the dead and the ground reserved for the dead to come.

She stared at the black letters and the stone so white. Then she tucked her face between her knees so she wouldn't have to see how black and indifferent the letters remained after almost five years of seasons of sun and rain and snow.

STEVEN J

EWELL

HM3

US NAVY

JUL 11 1984

NOV 9 2004

PURPLE HEART

SILVER STAR

OPERATION

IRAQI FREEDOM

She began to cry, rocked back and forth, and felt the sun falling on her black hair. Then she sat up and pulled a hair tie from her bag. She ran her hands through her hair a few times and cinched the tie in two loops until it was out of her face. She'd cried her nose runny like a child, and with the backs of her hands tried to wipe the tears away, and her hands came down smudged black as ash from her mascara. She looked up, and a woman about her mother's age was standing beside her.

"Are you okay, sweetheart?"

Sally tried to say yes, but her mouth began to shake, her bottom lip fluttered arrhythmically, and she could not find the breath to answer. She shook her head no and started crying again, and the woman reached down and pulled Sally up to her shoulder and held her there. The woman wore a jean jacket stitched at the shoulders in sequins, and Sally buried her face in the jacket. The sun shone on the white stones and the bejeweled denim at the woman's shoulders. Through the flood of her tears, the world danced and spun in a kaleidoscope of light and color.

"We got to take care of each other now," the woman said.

The tears stopped falling, and Sally raised her head from the woman's shoulder. The woman held Sally's face between her hands gently, and Sally nodded with her face still trembling. The woman kissed her forehead and wiped away the tears that had pooled up beneath her eyes with her thumbs.

"You're gonna be all right, girl. I promise," the woman said. Then she turned and walked down a few rows away from Sally's brother, put both of her hands on top of a white stone, and leaned over the grave the stone stood marker for.

Sally watched the woman for a minute, then pulled out a can of wintergreen Skoal and a bottle of Budweiser from her bag and laid them on her brother's grave. She heard a sound cut the quiet and saw six white horses pulling a caisson between the old oaks that lined York Drive. She watched the caisson roll, and the honor guard in their dress blues rode before it and turned the whole detail onto a dirt path that cut across the burial ground. The last row was incomplete, like a flood not yet risen to its crest.

Sally said, "Happy birthday, Stevie," and turned away from the grave and started walking back to the shade of the tree-lined drive. She made the turn back toward the exit, then heard behind her a wailing speechless grief that broke the stillness into pieces that would never fit together again. Sally wanted to turn around and go back to her, but she couldn't find the strength. Her tired legs shook. She stepped up onto the curb and put her hand on the trunk of an oak. She leaned her weight against it and closed her eyes. Then she made herself listen.

A few hours later, she was in a DC hotel room, lying on the bed and listening to the sounds from Massachusetts Avenue coming in through the open window. The hot summer breezes set the thin curtains swaying, and she watched the light filter through them and fall over her and the bed in the otherwise darkened room. She drifted into a half sleep with the television on. The insistent pinging sound of the BBC News theme wove its way in and out of her consciousness.

When she gave up on actual sleep, she sat up on the bed and looked at the phone on the nightstand but did not reach for it. She rolled her head around, trying to loosen herself up, and went into the bathroom. She took a cotton ball out of her makeup kit, wet it with astringent, removed the black streaks from under her eyes, and washed her face afterward. She looked at her watch, put on jeans and a T-shirt, and went downstairs to have an early dinner alone in the hotel restaurant in the lobby.

After she finished, she ordered a glass of white and sat there staring at it. The bartender came over and asked her if any-thing was wrong.

"Yes. No, I mean. I changed my mind. Sorry." She took out a five from her bag, dropped it on the bar top, quickly gathered her things, and left. When she got outside, she took out her phone and sat on a brick knee wall in the pink shade of a crape myrtle. She let the phone flip open and closed in her right hand absentmindedly until she scrolled through her contacts and dialed a number.

Her mother answered on the third ring. "Sal?" she said.

"Yeah."

"How are you?"

"I'm okay."

"Are you still in DC?"

"Yeah. Should be back tomorrow night."

"Are you getting work done?"

"Yeah. Hey, Mom?"

"Yeah, baby?"

"I went and saw Stevie." Sally waited for a few seconds, looking up through the paper-thin flowers at the hint of the sky above.

"I think your dad's out by the dock," her mother said. "You want me to go get him?"

"He's working on the boat?"

"You mean that hole in the water he throws our money in? I think so. He's been out there long enough to build an ark. You know it's the disease he's trying to keep his mind off, Sal. He's wondering if it'll be nothing but beds of empty shells come winter."

"Are y'all ever gonna come up here, Mom?"

"Sal. Please. Don't." She let out a long sigh. "Cal Briggs

down at the marina is talking about taking tourists out. Do you want me to go get your dad?"

"No. That's all right."

"Can you imagine that? Your daddy and some stockbroker and his fancy wife out on a skipjack? That'd be something to see."

"Yeah, Mom. That'd be something."

"I'll tell him you called, okay, Sally? Come by soon."

"Okay, Mom. Maybe I'll come out next weekend and stay a couple of nights. Love y'all," said Sally, but the line was already dead.

SEVEN

The Square and Compass Inn on York was taped off, with technicians streaming in and out of the Victorian row house, when Detectives Wheel and Adams pulled away. They arrived at the Tidewater office of the chief medical examiner late that afternoon and then made their way to Dr. Martin's office. Cat knocked on the half-open door. "Solved it yet, Pat?"

Dr. Martin, at his desk, said, "Come on in, y'all. I'm just finishing lunch."

They entered the room and sat down in two chairs facing the ME's desk. "Our guy in the examination room?" asked Lamar.

"Yeah," said the doc. "I figured he wasn't gonna walk out on me while I ate, you know?"

"Any news is good news," Cat said.

"Well, I got some broad strokes for you. Let's go see him. I'll tell you on the way."

Dr. Martin got up, and Cat and Lamar followed him out of the office. They wound through a maze of linoleum and institutionally lit hallways. The doctor lifted his glasses from a chain around his neck and then looked down at a chart he held in his other hand. "Okay. Most of this you know, but here goes. White male, age thirty-five to forty. Five foot eleven. A hundred and sixty pounds. That's a wide net. Narrowed down, I'd say he's of Mediterranean ancestry. Southern Italian. Greek. Maybe North African or Middle Eastern." He pushed open a pair of double doors, and they followed him through. "All the stuff we talked about before. Excellent physical condition, other than being dead. But here's the kicker. He's got some unique distinguishing characteristics. And while it may be a couple of weeks to be a hundred percent sure what killed him, I've got a reasonable guess."

"No shit? That's great," said Cat.

They walked down another linoleum hallway until they found themselves in the bowels of the autopsy area. Dr. Martin opened a door, and they walked into an examination room. Thomas Brown, or Mr. Baker, or whoever he had been in life lay naked on a metal table. His chest had been opened with a Y-shaped incision, and a pair of industrial shears had been used to cut through the rib cage. The skin on the back of his skull was peeled back. A portion of the skull itself had been removed to allow access to brain tissue. A pungent but indistinct chemical odor permeated the room, and Cat and Lamar were grateful it masked what it did.

Pat put on a pair of gloves and then stepped to the other side of the body. "Check this out." He rolled the body toward himself so that Cat and Lamar could see its left shoulder area. There was a small circular bruise, the outer edge of which was barely visible beyond the body's underarm hair. "Get in there and look closely," the doctor said.

They put on gloves, leaned down, and moved the underarm hair where it obscured the main body of the bruise.

"Do you see it?"

"What are we looking for, Pat?" asked Catherine.

"Got it," said Lamar. "Puncture. Here, Cat." He pointed out the small hole.

"That from a needle?" she asked.

"Yeah," the doctor said. "Looks like a run-of-the-mill hypodermic. Hard to say what gauge exactly. But the bruising is what interests me." He lay the body back down on the table. "The amount of force required to create that level of bruising is, let's say, unnecessary when someone is given an injection voluntarily."

"You ever see anyone shoot into their armpit?" she asked.

"Nope," said the doctor.

"Me neither."

"And let's say the dude's an innovator," Lamar said. "There's nothing anywhere else. No tracks. No collapsed veins. No scarring." He moved down to the body's thighs, then feet, and checked between his toes for evidence of prior injections. He looked up at Catherine and the doctor and shook his head.

Dr. Martin continued, "My professional opinion, even without the tox report, is that the likelihood this is accidental is near zero. And not to step on y'all's turf, but I think I've got a decent idea of what happened. Lamar, would you come over here a minute?"

"Sure."

"Okay. So I want you to look toward the door."

Lamar turned toward the door, and Dr. Martin came up behind him. "Lamar, I'm gonna put you in a choke hold, okay?"

"Yup."

Dr. Martin put his left arm gently around Lamar's neck. Even though the pressure was light, not even uncomfortable, Lamar instinctively reached up to Dr. Martin's forearm and grabbed it. He didn't think about it. He didn't have to. It was pure reflex.

"All right, Cat. I'm right-handed. If I was gonna inject young Detective Adams here, the puncture and bruising would be evident under his right armpit."

Catherine stood there thinking for a moment with her hands on her hips. "Let's say the two men Mr. Bajalan ran into are our suspects. Any chance it's a tag-team situation and narrowing down to lefties throws us off?"

"Lamar, let's try one more time." The doctor took a needleless syringe from a cart next to the autopsy table. This time he wrapped his right arm around Lamar's neck. Again, Lamar reached up toward the doctor's arm instinctively. Pat moved the tip of the syringe toward Lamar's now-exposed armpit and pressed the end gently but firmly into it. "If this isn't how it went down, you got me," said the doc. He let go of Lamar's neck and patted the younger man on the shoulder. "Sorry to make you the crash-test dummy, Detective."

"No problem, Doc," he replied.

"That's outstanding work, Pat. Real good," Catherine said.

"Lefties are, what, ten percent of the general population?" asked Lamar.

"Seven to ten," said Pat. "Call it ten."

"So we know the guy who actually did the deed was a lefty. That's gonna make our lives a hell of a lot easier," said Catherine.

"Though it doesn't mean we can exclude anyone from being Johnny Sidekick," said Lamar.

"True. So what else, Pat?" Catherine asked.

"Come around here next to me."

Cat and Lamar walked around the table to stand on the body's right side. The doctor pointed to a tattoo on the right shoulder: A parachute with two wings, one on either side. The inner portion of both wings was dark blue. The outer portion was light blue.

"Jump wings," Lamar said. "Not ours."

"Any ideas?" asked Catherine.

"We'll have to see what we can find online. I was just a leg. Nothing special. I wasn't really around the high-speed guys," said Lamar. "Never seen these before."

"What else, Pat?" asked Catherine. "Can you tell how long he's had it?"

"Not with any certainty. But it's not brand-new. And just behaviorally, my bet would be he's had it for a while."

Catherine leaned down toward the body. A forty-year-old man in peak physical condition. A military parachutist tattoo. "Lamar," she said, "what's the ballpark age for a guy to get a tat like this?"

"Well," he said, "jumping out of planes is a young man's game. So is getting ink done, generally speaking. Especially if this is his only one, and he's really forty. I'm gonna guess he's a vet or decently high-ranking if he's still on active duty."

"You think he might be active duty even with the haircut?" asked the doctor.

"Yeah, especially if he's foreign. They don't usually go for high-and-tights. A cut like this is well within the regs in most militaries," said Lamar.

"Pat, is there a computer I can use?" asked Catherine.

"Yeah, of course." He went over to a cabinet along the wall where a desktop computer sat among papers and boxes of latex gloves. He logged her on to the medical examiner office's internet and grabbed a stool for her.

Cat sat down and pulled up the search engine, and the

doctor and Lamar took up positions over her shoulders. "*Foreign jump wings,* Lamar?"

"Probably a good start."

She typed that in. A grid of images filled the screen. She scrolled down the page. Hundreds of images. A small number of the badges and pins had light blue wings, but none had the distinctive shape of the body's tattoo or the darker shade of blue. "I'm not seeing it."

"Try adding *blue,*" said Lamar.

Catherine went back to the search bar, added it, and hit Return. Another collection of images filled the screen. Many had been in the previous search, but not all. She scrolled down the page again. The screen's glow washed over their faces as they leaned in closer to look.

"Come on. It's gotta be here somewhere," Lamar said.

She kept scrolling. One page turned into another. And then another. And another.

"There!" said Dr. Martin. His finger shot to the edge of the screen. It hovered over an image of a patch with the exact same color scheme as the tattoo.

"The wings are angled a bit different, but the colors are right," said Cat. She clicked on the image. It led to an online marketplace where an embroidered patch was for sale. The item's description read *SAS pattern parachute wings.*

"What's *SAS* stand for?" the doctor asked.

"Special Air Service," Lamar answered. "British special forces."

Catherine looked up at him. "Would that explain what we found in his room?"

"Maybe. But it doesn't explain why he'd be here. Maybe some

kind of training exercise for the secret squirrels? I don't know. But even for these guys, my guess is it's highly unusual for a foreign special forces soldier to be solo in the U.S. with a weapon. Hey, try searching for *SAS jump wings*. The angle of the wings is still not quite right. Let's see if there's a better match, or maybe it's just the guy who did the line work on his tat improvised."

She typed the words in. Near the bottom of the first page, they saw it. An exact match in shape and color. Catherine clicked on the link. It led to another online marketplace where a patch with the wings was for sale. The item's description read *Genuine Modern Australian Special Air Service Regiment Parachute Wings.*

"The Australian special forces?" asked Cat. "What the hell is going on here?"

"I don't know. I'd see those guys every once in a while when I was over there. I know they do a lot of heavy lifting in Afghanistan too. Here's what I want to know," Lamar said. "What are the odds that all four of the people on that beach don't have some connection to Iraq?"

Cat counted off on her fingers as she answered. "Bajalan. Perp one. Perp two. And our vic."

"I'd say slim to none, and slim left town," Lamar said.

Catherine got up from the stool and said, "Pat, you are a lifesaver. I'm gonna get you a junior detective badge for this one."

"Thanks, Detective Wheel," he replied sarcastically.

Cat stripped off her gloves and threw them in a medical-waste receptacle. "Seriously. You are the absolute best."

Lamar stripped off his gloves as well and said, "Okay, Detective, what's next?"

Cat was lost in thought as they walked out of the building and into the fading daylight. She lit a smoke. "You want Bajalan or the nerds?"

"I think I can break the ice with Bajalan." He checked his watch. "He should still be at the motel. If I get there soon, I can see if there's more to his story."

"Sounds good," said Cat. "I'll head to the house and see if the techs got anything. Drop me at my unit, will you? It's still in the parking lot by the beach. And Lamar," she said.

"Yeah?"

"Pack a bag. We're going to DC in the a.m."

Lamar watched Cat drive out of the parking lot and head toward the ramp to get on I-64. He turned and looked out over the long stretch of sand to where it met the sea, low and gray but coming in again. By the time it was dark, the spray and foam would reach close to where the body lay that morning. It was not dark yet, but the shadows of the bent pines had already joined his own in stretching out across the sand.

He left his car in the lot and walked down toward Bajalan's place of employment, the Sea Breeze Motel. When he crossed the parking lot, his shoes crunched in the shell-speckled aggregate, and he looked up at the letter board beneath the faded hotel sign. THE REWARD FOR LIVING A GOOD LIFE IS LIVING A GOOD LIFE, it read. Lamar smiled and shook his head, then scanned the property before walking up to the door, one hand on his hip and the other resting casually on the backstrap of his holstered .40.

The bell dinged when he swung the glass door open, and he walked into a clean but well-worn reception area. An old man behind the check-in desk looked up from the book he was reading and eyed him suspiciously over the tops of the pair of glasses resting on the bridge of his nose. He wore a black ball cap with the 101st Screaming Eagle on the front, and he had both hands somewhere below the level of the counter.

"Help you, son?" he said.

"I hope so. Hoping I could speak with Mr. Bajalan again. We met this morning. I'm a detective with Norfolk PD."

"You got a card or something?"

"He around?"

The old man didn't say anything. Lamar rested his elbows on the counter and saw the butt end of a shotgun leaning against the employee side of the desk. A large revolver hung from a holster on the old man's tooled-leather belt.

"I don't mean no disrespect, young man, but if you ain't got a warrant and you ain't got no card saying who you are, that's likely gonna remain a mystery to you."

Lamar took out a card and handed it over to the man. He took out his detective badge and showed it to him before clipping it to his belt again. "That's my fault, sir. I should have made mention when I first came in."

The old man looked the card over and put it in the pocket of his shirt. "I'll see he gets it. Whether he wants to talk to you is up to him. Boy's grown."

"He's not in any kind of trouble. I was kind of hoping I could ask him a few questions about his time as a terp. An int—"

"I know what it is," the man interjected.

"About his time during the war."

"Like I said, boy's grown. And if it's all the same to you, y'all ought to be able to figure out that circling a man's place of employment all dang day might make him reluctant to speak if he's got any sense in his head."

"Pardon?" Lamar asked.

"I seen that same Dodge Charger go up and down Ocean View least six times. How many civilians do you think there are driving blacked-out Chargers with bull bars on the front?

Came through the parking lot couple, three times, maybe. You really want to talk to that boy, you oughtn't to be hounding him this way. He ain't done nothing."

"Sorry, sir, you mind if I step outside and make a quick phone call?"

"When I woke up this morning, it was still a free country." The man slid a yellow Post-it note across the desk to Lamar. "Didn't see the whole plate," he said, then he crossed his arms over his chest and sat there glaring.

"Okay. I'll be right back."

Lamar stepped out into the parking lot and walked a few steps away from the door to be out of the proprietor's line of sight. He dialed Cat's number, but it rang through to her voice mail. "Catherine," he said, "something weird's going on with Bajalan. See if someone at the house put a unit on him, will you?"

He closed the phone and looked out across the parking lot to the web of streets and single-story buildings shaded by the crowns of trees that rose behind them. No traffic. The air quivered in the heat. A sweat bee hovered by his ear; he swatted at it lazily. He dialed up the area office of the state police. A voice answered, and Lamar spoke in a nervous hush. "This is Detective Adams with Norfolk PD. I need to speak to someone in the witness protection program ASAP."

"Do you have the extension?"

"Sorry? No. Can you just put me through, please? It's urgent."

"Hold, please."

Breezy jazz guitar crackled over the connection. Lamar looked at his watch. After eight p.m. *Please be there.*

"Detective, are you still there?"

"I'm here."

"Sir, no one from that unit is available right now. If you'd like, I can take a message, and someone will get back to you tomorrow in the a.m."

He put the mouthpiece of the phone against his shirt and cursed. He brought the phone back up to his ear. "No. Thanks. I'll go through my department and get a direct number." He closed the phone and sat there staring at it wondering who to call. The phone rang in his hand. "Catherine?" he asked.

"Hey. What's up? I just got to the house. About to see if the tech guys have anything before they head home."

"Did you listen to the message?"

"No. Sorry."

"Do me a favor, please. Check if someone put an unmarked on Bajalan."

"All right, hold tight a sec."

Lamar scanned the landscape. Streetlights on but the sun still up. Bugs swarmed the lamplight. The first sliver of pink far out to the west had begun its journey across the sky. It was almost twilight under the trees. He thought he caught a glimpse of a black sedan pass by a cross street and then fade again, hidden by the street-side trees.

Catherine came back on the line. "Nobody's on Bajalan. Everything all right? You had a chance to talk to him yet?"

Lamar thumbed open the button of his holster without thinking. The sweat bee buzzed at the back of his neck. "No. Something spooked him. His boss ran interference for him. I don't even know if he's still here."

"What spooked him?"

"Old man at the motel says they've seen what sounds like an unmarked circling, making the rounds up and down Ocean View. I don't know. Could be he's trying to put me off, but I don't think so. Old boy doesn't seem the type to traffic in bullshit.

I called the troopers to try to get in touch with witness protection but didn't get anywhere."

"Yeah, that's a dry hole, Lamar. I tried to use it a couple of years back, and they told me the best they could do is put in an alarm system at the wit's house, but it might take a month or two."

"Jesus."

"Yup. Look, why don't you see if you can lay eyes on Bajalan, and I'll have a couple of uniforms sit on the motel if it'll ease his mind."

"Yeah. Okay. That'll work. Thanks, Catherine. Let me know what you hear from the tech guys."

"Call me back after, will ya? I'm gonna head home in an hour or two to pack for the morning."

"Got it. Talk to you soon. Hey, put a BOLO on a Charger with bull bars on the front, will you? Partial plate X,Y."

"X,Y. Okay, I'm on it."

Lamar put the phone back in his pocket and kept his eyes on the distant intersection where he thought he'd seen the sedan pass by a few minutes before. Nothing. Waves crashed against the beach across the street behind him. The wind shook the leaves of the trees, gone silver in the fading light. He turned and went back inside.

⟵⟶

Catherine dropped her bag at her desk on the top floor of police headquarters. She called dispatch and asked for a patrol unit to detour to the vicinity of the motel. She closed the phone, took her holstered pistol, and stuffed it and the phone in her purse. The city was almost dark outside the windows. Fluorescent lights hummed in a checkerboard above her. She used the card on her lanyard to access the stairwell and went to Investigative Support. A few heads popped up from cubicles when she swung the glass door open, but the unit was practically empty at that hour. She passed through the open workspace until she got to another door, behind which the forensic section worked.

Joe Parker, the department's senior computer forensic examiner, waved her over. She walked to his desk, put her hand on the back of his chair, and leaned over his shoulder to see what he was working on. The laptop they'd found at the Square and Compass Inn was open. Joe's arms were folded on his desk, and his chin rested on them. He looked up at the blank screen like a child in class who did not want to be called on.

"Joe? You all right, bud?" Catherine asked.

He didn't answer.

She patted him on the shoulder, but he kept eyeing the screen as though it might be possible for him to win a staring contest with an inanimate object. "Fort Knox, Detective Wheel. No. A bank vault inside Fort Knox inside a maximum-security prison."

Catherine straightened up and waited for him to spin his chair around and look at her. He did, then crossed a leg over his knee and took his glasses off. "I'm very good at my job, Catherine."

"I know you are, Joe."

"No one is getting into this computer."

"What do you mean? Can't you do your hacker stuff? Run some kind of program to break in?"

He laughed. "Yeah. Normally, we'd do the 'hacker stuff.'" He put it in air quotes. He turned back around and looked at the laptop. "I'm serious, Detective. This isn't like some kiddie-porn asshole who uses his high-school mascot as his password.

This is really sophisticated protection. This is like, I don't know, National Security Agency–type protection. Whoever had this laptop wanted to make damn sure whatever's on it wasn't seen without permission."

"There's really no way in?"

"Cat, it's completely air-gapped. Network ports are blocked. Get me a key and the best decryption software in the world and maybe. This thing has never been connected to the internet. It can't be. That functionality has been eliminated. Jesus, even the LAN connection is blocked. This is set up almost like a bearer bond. Whoever physically possesses the password and key, and probably an associated thumb drive, gets in. Everybody else can kick rocks."

"Who uses this level of security?" she asked.

"I wasn't kidding. NSA. Foreign equivalents. Maybe some of the top multinationals. The thing is, security like this is implemented only when you know someone wants it bad enough to violate a bunch of different laws. Security like this means you're willing to physically guard the information. I don't know who you've got on the other end of whatever case you're working, but they're serious."

"Yeah," she said. "It's looking that way. Thanks, Joe."

EIGHT

The kids wheeled their oversize beach cruisers through the hot night, pumping the pedals, then standing with their chests at the curved handlebars as they glided down the sidewalk along Ocean View Avenue. Four wide, they turned into the sandy parking lot of Red's Beachside Bar and Billiards. One by one, they dismounted, the oldest standing with both feet on one pedal until the bike rolled to the back corner of the building, where he hopped off and leaned the bike against the cinder blocks.

The four of them, none older than fourteen, huddled in the darkness outside the reach of the parking lot's lights. "Ante up," the oldest boy said. The other three reached in their pockets and brought out dollar bills and half rolls of quarters that they turned over to him. He stuffed the money in the pocket of his board shorts and said, "I'll be right back."

They watched him slink toward the open screen door just around the rear of the building, from which they could hear a country band distinguish itself from the more common collective noises of a dive bar at that hour. The boy went into the kitchen, which was hot and loud, the cooks sweaty and swearing and tipping back cans of Natural Light from an open case that sat on a wire shelving unit behind them. They worked the fryers in their stained aprons, and as they tossed wings in pans, they hardly noticed or cared to notice the boy's figure passing behind them. He stepped carefully across the slippery red tiles and peered through the window of the swinging door that separated the kitchen from the hallway that went past the dirty restrooms and led to the bar and sawdusted dance floor. The music was now louder than any thought in his head, and by habit, he eyed the lit-up cigarette vending machine sitting at the end of the hall and pushed the swinging door open just enough to slide through.

When he got in the hall, he slowly inched his way along the wood-paneled wall, and a man and a woman stumbled out of the ladies' room, she buttoning up her cutoff shorts and the man with his arm around her shoulders for support. He could see them both laughing but could not hear it as the band pushed a honky-tonk number till the bar's sound system reached its limit and stayed there, the pedal steel guitar wavering and the bass and drums thrashing out a wall of noise that had the crowd in a frenzy of sweat and beer and movement.

The woman looked at the boy, smiled, and tousled his hair as they passed him and went back to the dance floor. The boy knelt down by the vending machine and loaded up quarters and dollars until he had enough to pull the knob on a pack of Kools, and as he did, he looked over his shoulder and made eye contact with the barman. He saw the man point and his mouth formed the shape of a shout, and the boy grabbed the smokes and ran out through the kitchen, taking four beers from the open case meanwhile.

The other boys watched him come around the corner running with an armful of beer cans, shouting, "Go, go, go!"

"Oh, shit!" said one, and the boys grabbed a beer each from

him, stuffed them in their pockets, slung their bikes toward the street, hopped on, and began to pedal furiously. They were laughing, and a cloud of sand white as the moon rose from their back wheels in the sodium-vapor lamplight as they scrambled out of the parking lot and turned down the sidewalk toward Ocean View Beach Park. The oldest boy looked behind him and saw the barman come out of the building. He lingered in his looking, the boy half believing he saw grief or sadness in the barman's expression. The barman stayed too and watched the figures fade into the night as if they had been ghosts come to visit from his own distant youth.

Not even a quarter mile down the road, the boys turned off the sidewalk again and coasted through the parking lot to the far corner of the park's seagrass, gray and waving in the welcome night breeze. They stashed their bikes one by one in the depths of the grass and crested the small dune and slid down its backside. They sat all in a line watching the low white-caps fall over the gray shore. The older boy opened the pack of Kools and handed out five smokes each to his companions. One said, "Fucking score, Dougie," and another was the first to open his beer and take a giant slug, which he nearly spat out, shaking his head against the bitter taste of it.

Dougie pulled a Bic out of his pocket and lit one of the smokes awkwardly, holding it between his thumb and forefinger. He puffed on it a few times and passed the lighter down the line. His friends lit their own smokes and took turns coughing as they inhaled. Dougie feigned experience, and he looked upward and watched as a colony of gulls circled the moon. A few clouds rolled in, and the beach and the boys resting at its edge went from dark to faintest light to dark again in a slow hypnotic rhythm. Terns ran up and down the waterline, racing against its rise and fall, stippling the wet sand with their beaks and retreating when the waves broke and rushed in, erasing the pockmarked record of their hunger.

Dougie reached into the grass behind him for the beer he'd set down. His hand brushed against some other metal before he found the beer. He ran his fingertips across the metal surface, almost stroking it. Dougie felt a pattern like that of a rasp from his father's woodshop but without the bite. He closed his hand around the object and pulled it out of the grass and brought it out before him in the darkness. He held a pistol with a longish pipe on the business end, which he guessed from the movies was a silencer. He had grabbed the thing around its grip naturally and automatically as if he would never have picked it up by any means other than the way it was meant to be held. As if its maker had considered a young boy's wonderment while grasping it as the most crucial element of its design.

⌒

Lamar stood in the reception area and watched the clock on the wall behind Mr. Peters. "I really think you ought to close for the evening, sir. I've got a patrol unit coming to sit in the parking lot. You don't have to worry about the motel. It's almost nine thirty. Surely anybody coming in off the street can find another room."

Arman sat on a stool behind the reception desk next to the old man. "I think it's a good idea, Mr. Peters. Like the detective said, if it's nothing, it's nothing. If it's something even a little dangerous, why stay?"

"So lemme ask you something, Detective."

"Shoot."

"You're saying this Charger I seen might be the two fellers did the crime you think Arman here was witness to?"

"Might be."

"But you don't know for sure."

"I don't know for sure. Might could be a couple of kids cruising on a Friday."

"But you don't think so."

"No, sir, I don't."

The old man looked at Arman and settled his eyes on the young man as if he might want to tell him something, but he did not.

Arman said, "Really, Mr. Peters. Don't worry about me. I'll be okay."

"Sir, I promise you the commonwealth has resources for situations like this," said Lamar. "I'll take Mr. Bajalan to his apartment. We'll pack him a bag, and he can stay with me tonight. State troopers will put him in another apartment tomorrow morning, and we'll have a detail on him until the trial's over. A little inconvenience. No skin off your back at all."

The old man leaned against the wood paneling and looked at the ceiling's popcorn surface. He looked back at Lamar. "Son, what trial?" he said. "Don't sound to me like you have a goddamn clue what's going on out there except Arman here might be in some kind of danger. And for the record, it ain't my skin I'm worried about." He put one of his big hands on Arman's shoulder and squeezed. "I never did think these sons of bitches would have the onions to hunt you up all the way across the ocean."

Arman patted the old man's hand and stood up, holding on to it for a moment. "It'll be all right, Mr. Peters. Probably just kids out cruising. Probably the whole thing has nothing to do with me." He stepped through the door separating the employee section from the reception area and stood on the opposite side of the desk.

"You ready, Mr. Bajalan?" Lamar asked.

"Sure."

"You're gonna have a unit sitting in that gravel there in just a minute, sir," Lamar said to the older man.

"All right, then," said Mr. Peters. "I'll get to locking things up. Be out in a jiffy." The furtive circling of the cars made sense now. If it wasn't police patrols, it was one vehicle on a scouting expedition. Mr. Peters felt he now had a more complete picture of what was happening than the two younger men did. Whoever was in that Charger was coming for Arman. They all knew that. And while Mr. Peters understood that Arman and the detective had each felt the adrenalized atmosphere of combat, he did not think they could read the situation the way he could. They were conversant on the subject of men trying to kill each other, but Mr. Peters was fluent. He'd spent the better part of his life speaking that language. With all other plausible explanations exhausted, he could now read the signs the strangers in the Charger had left as clearly as he could read the pages of his Westerns.

The motel had been scouted by professionals. That much was obvious. But there was no reason to think the scouts knew they'd been discovered. In moments like this, Mr. Peters reverted to an instinctive practicality in his thinking. As long as Arman and the detective were away from the motel, Mr. Peters could solve the problem the men in the Charger presented by himself. He looked them over a last time before he decided. Whatever was coming, he planned to be the one waiting for it.

Lamar and Arman started walking toward the door. Mr.

Peters pulled the heavy Colt Python from its holster and held it below the level of the reception desk. He opened the cylinder, turned it until he'd confirmed it was loaded with six .357 cartridges, then put it back in the holster.

Lamar pushed the door open, and Arman turned around and said, "Thank you, Mr. Peters."

The old man looked up. "For what?"

Arman smiled. "I'll see you Monday morning."

"I'll have a want ad in the *Pilot* on Tuesday if I don't. Now y'all get out of here so I can close this place down."

The two younger men let the door shut behind them. Mr. Peters watched them through the glass and kept his eyes on the door for some time after they'd passed from view. He opened a drawer and put two speed loaders on the desk and walked over to the door Arman and Lamar had just gone through a minute before. He looked out over the parking lot, the white-shell aggregate seemingly aglow in the moon's light. Mr. Peters watched the taillights of Lamar's unmarked car disappear down the street, then locked the dead bolt and turned the placard over on its chain until it read CLOSED on the outside. He went back through the employee-only door, grabbed the 870 from where it leaned against the wall, and worked the action to confirm it was loaded. He set it down across the desk, the barrel pointed toward the reception area.

⟵

At 9:20, the radio in the patrol car en route to sit on the Sea Breeze Motel crackled with the usual Friday-night summer traffic: 10-12, vandalism at the Piggly Wiggly on Princess Anne; 10-43, drunks outside the clubs on Granby; 10-44, disturbance from an off-campus house party near Old Dominion University.

Officers Sherwood and Washington from the Second Patrol Division kept their unit pointed north down Chesapeake Boulevard toward the water. It felt like getting over, being tasked to sit in a motel parking lot in the comfort of their patrol car with the AC running.

They pulled into a gas station at Little Creek Road, and Officer Sherwood ran in and came back out in under two minutes with a six-pack of High Life tucked under his arm. Second of the evening and three hours into the overnight shift. He jumped back in, put the beer down on the floorboard, and pulled one out for Washington, who expertly worked the twist-off cap with one hand and with his other wheeled the unit around quickly. Sherwood took a big swig and blipped the light and sirens as they passed through the intersection, and they were back on their way.

When they took the curve by the golf course, Officer Sherwood put the window down and took another pull on his beer and silently waited with childlike anticipation for the first glimpse of the ocean to come into view. He focused on a small patch of blackness at the end of the divided boulevard, tunneled down its length with leafed-out oaks and covered in its own lesser darkness.

Officer Washington took the call at 9:27. "Unit two-seven-one, what's your twenty?"

"En route Sea Breeze Motel on Ocean View. Northbound Chesapeake Boulevard."

"Two-seven-one, bypass that code one. Respond code two, ten-twenty-nine. Call came in from Red's Beachside."

"Ten-four, code two, person with gun, two-seven-one en route."

They hit the lights and sirens, and Officer Washington

punched the gas. Sherwood took both open beer bottles and flung them out the window, where they smashed against the curb and left shards of blue and red light glimmering in the gutter.

They flew through the light at Chesapeake and Ocean View, the heavy cruiser listing like a storm-blown ship. The sirens wailed, and the pulsing lights pushed against the dark as they floored it up the beachside strip of pavement. They blew the light at Granby too, and a few seconds later, they pulled into the parking lot of Red's and skidded to a stop. Washington called out, "Dispatch, two-seven-one is ten-nine."

"Ten-four, two-seven-one on scene."

With his gun drawn, Sherwood exited the passenger door and slowly walked toward the building through the cloud of still-rising dust, the cruiser's lights pulsing rhythmically off the cinder blocks. Washington killed the sirens and exited as well, and the two men approached the front door, from which music still spilled. The barman had his hands up when the officers entered. He turned his head away from the wall of light emitted by their flashlights, knowing the barrels of their pistols pointed at him in the darkness. "You can put your guns away. Boys here said it was an accident."

At ten p.m., the two officers sat on the hood of their patrol car in front of Red's giving their statements to their lieutenant. The parking lot was full of police vehicles, the bar shut down, and the customers gone. Evidence techs and a couple of uniforms were down on the beach. They watched the ambulance's spinning lights disappear up Mason Creek Road.

"So, accidental discharge?" their lieutenant asked.

"The kid?"

"Yeah."

"That's what it looked like, LT. Other kids said it was an accidental discharge too."

"That right, Officer Sherwood?"

Sherwood sat there with his arms crossed, chewing his bottom lip. He stared at the gravel and the tips of his boots.

"Sherwood?" their sector lieutenant said again.

He looked up. "Yeah. Something spooked him and it went off."

Lieutenant Billings scratched down the last bit of the statement in his notepad. Then he looked up. "All right, kid, it's a shitty deal, but it was always gonna go this way. Kids like that, it was just a matter of time before the commonwealth put them on paper. This one's just ahead of schedule."

"Yeah, LT," Sherwood said quietly. "That's the way it goes."

"Hey, sir?" Washington said. "What about that babysitting job at the motel? We got detoured off that to come here."

"Don't worry about it. Priorities, am I right? I'll get someone over there. And one more thing, Officers," Lieutenant Billings said as he walked back to his car, "find a fucking breath mint. I can smell the Schlitz on you two from ten feet away."

Washington looked over at Dougie, hooked up in the back seat of their cruiser. Sherwood seemed lost in thought. "What's up, partner?"

"What're we doing out here, Wash?"

"What do you mean?"

"One in the back of the cruiser and another in the back of a bus. Look around. No one cares. Shouldn't we be... I don't know... fucking alarmed?"

Lieutenant Billings put his notepad in his shirt pocket and slipped the pencil beside it. He took his cell phone from his belt, flipped it open, and dialed. "Yeah. Lieutenant Billings here. Tell Detective Adams we found that gun he was looking for." He pulled out a cigarette and waved at another cop to give him a light. "Yeah, the James Bond–looking one. You won't believe what it's been up to."

NINE

"Where to, Mr. Bajalan?" asked Lamar.

"Do you know Boissevain Ave.?"

"In Ghent?"

"Yeah."

Lamar put the car in drive and took the backstreets behind the Sea Breeze toward Granby at a crawl, keeping his eyes moving down each cross street, hoping to catch a glimpse of the Charger. He checked his rearview when he turned to head southbound on Granby. He saw only an empty road until a patrol car tore ass with lights and sirens through the traffic light to where the street dead-ended at Ocean View.

Lamar kept his eyes moving, but the long straight road was otherwise quiet for a Friday night. He looked over at Bajalan in the passenger seat with his arms crossed and his head leaning against the roof pillar. He looked out the window without interest, and if any aspect of the little bungalows and run-down brick commercial buildings caught his attention, he gave no indication of it. They stopped at a light, and Lamar said, "Arman, you mind if I ask what Mr. Peters meant when he said he didn't think anybody would come looking for you over here?"

Arman leaned back in the passenger seat and looked out

the windshield now. The light turned green, and Lamar stepped on the gas and let the silence sit between them for a minute.

"I saw something," Arman said.

"You saw something?"

"Yeah."

"Okay. Something like what? Terrorists? What?"

"Yeah, maybe something like that."

"That why they fast-tracked your SIV?"

"Someone did me a favor. Platoon leader I was interpreting for."

"You trade what you saw for the visa?"

"That's not how I would put it."

"Well, Arman, that's what I'm trying to figure out. How you would put it," Lamar said.

Trust had not served Arman well in his interactions with Americans. There were exceptions, of course. Mr. Peters. The lieutenant whose platoon he'd worked with. But they only reminded him what trusting the rest had cost him, and it had cost him everything. He looked at the detective sitting next to him. There was nothing to distinguish him from the men who had killed his wife and son. And there was nothing to ensure that he'd be like Mr. Peters. He was just a man. Unpredictable. And like all men, there was no avoiding the fact that he was dangerous. "I don't know who they are," he said quietly. "I just know they were looking for me over there. The lieutenant got me out. He knew they were trying to kill me, so he got me out."

"How'd he know they were trying to kill you?"

"They'd already tried. He started the paperwork for me."

"These guys?"

"I don't know if it's the same exact guys, but it's the same guys, if you know what I mean."

"Arman?" Lamar looked over at him. His face had gone gray except around his eyes, which were red and welling up with tears. "Did you have American forces after you?"

"Contractors."

Lamar exhaled hard. "Did your LT try to help?"

"You're relieved."

"I guess so."

"He couldn't prove anything. I couldn't prove anything. But I know what I saw."

"What did you see?"

"They opened up on a crowd at the university."

"In Mosul?"

"Yeah."

"Jesus. I heard about shit like that when I was there, Arman. But I don't know. Guys say they took fire, and that's the end of it."

"They didn't take fire."

"How can you be so sure?"

"Detective, I was there."

"With your unit?"

"No. I was a graduate student. I didn't run missions all the time."

"Can your PL corroborate any of this?"

"You don't believe me."

"Arman, I'm a cop now. It doesn't matter what I believe. It only matters what I can prove."

"He can't."

"He can't, or he won't?"

"He's dead."

Lamar drummed his fingers on the steering wheel. He looked over at Arman again. "How?"

"Car accident. Last year."

"Single vehicle?"

"Yeah."

Lamar stared out the windshield. "Do you know where?"

"I think he was home on leave. He'd been in Afghanistan."

"Where was home for him?"

"Texas."

"You remember where in Texas?"

"No. I might have an e-mail from him. Maybe he mentioned it."

"So y'all kept in touch?"

"Yeah. A little."

"He must have had a company by then."

"I guess he did after I got to Virginia. I didn't hear much from him on his last tour."

Lamar dug in his pocket, pulled out a notepad and a pen, and flipped them over to Arman in the passenger seat. "Start writing, will you?"

"What do you want to know?"

"You want me to catch these bastards?"

"Yeah."

"Then write down everything. Everything that happened. Everyone you told. Everyone they told. I don't care how irrelevant you think it is. Write it down."

He started writing. After a few moments, he paused and said, "I gave him my camera."

"Your LT?"

"There was a video on it."

"Of?"

"The massacre."

"You have the camera?"

"No. I never got it back."

Lamar went quiet and listened to the scratch of pen on paper. Five minutes later, they crossed the Lafayette River, and Arman watched the doghouse lights of a big motor sailer slowly work toward the Elizabeth and the open water of the bay beyond. Lamar swung the unmarked onto Llewellyn. Another five minutes, and he had the police cruiser moving at ten miles per hour through Stockley Gardens toward Arman's street.

Arman glanced at him. "What are you looking for?"

Lamar didn't answer. His eyes scanned every car parked on the street. He drove past Boissevain and took a left down Onley to come at the road from the other side. They passed Arman's building on their left, and Lamar asked him which apartment was his. "Other side. I've got an attic studio."

"You need to go into the building to get to your door?"

"You can get in from the fire escape. The stairs go down to the alley."

"All right. Tell me if you see anything out of place."

"Like what?"

"Anything you're not used to seeing."

They parked the car on the street half a block from Arman's building. A few lit windows broke the darkness. Lamar said, "Stay a half step behind my right shoulder." They walked down the sidewalk on the other side of the street from the apartment. Arman looked down and saw Lamar had his pistol out, half hidden, with his arm extended down to his thigh. If the Charger had been there, it was gone now.

When they stood across from the apartment building, Lamar

scanned the alley. It was lit up by a single weakly flickering streetlamp. "Okay. Let's go." They crossed the road, and Arman headed toward the front door of the building, but Lamar stopped him. He looked over at the alley and the fire escape. "You got your keys?"

Arman nodded.

"Come up behind me."

They slowly made their way to the fire-escape landing outside Arman's apartment, and Lamar stuck his hand out for the keys. He stood off to the side of the window and looked into the darkened studio. He saw a bed pushed against one wall. A small love seat and coffee table and bookcases full of books. A galley kitchen ran most of the length of another wall. "What else? Bathroom?"

"Yeah. That door next to the couch. Front door all the way across."

Lamar put the key in the lock and turned the tumbler as slowly and quietly as he could. He pushed the door open gently and grimaced as the rarely used hinges creaked. He held up his hand for Arman to wait, then he pulled the pistol close to his chest and entered the room. Arman watched him keep to the room's walls until he reached the bathroom door. It was slightly ajar but dark. With the toe of his shoe, Lamar flipped the door open and thumbed his high-powered flashlight on. Nothing. A bachelor's bathroom. Cleaner than most but empty. Lamar took a deep breath and felt the adrenaline flood out of his system. He went to Arman's door and looked through the peephole. Just the staircase landing. His was the only apartment on this floor. "All right, Arman. Get a couple things."

"For how long?"

"I don't know. Pack for two or three nights."

Arman flicked the light on, and Lamar shot his hand over to the switch and turned it back off. "Use the light in the bathroom," he said.

Arman walked over to the bathroom and turned the light on. He left the door cracked a little, and enough light came into the studio to see by, but only just. He stood there looking at his things for a minute and crossed his arms. "Who was the man on the beach, Detective?"

"We don't know."

"You don't know anything?"

Lamar holstered his pistol and stood there rubbing the back of his neck. "We think he's Australian SAS. Do you know what that is?"

"I think so."

"Maybe former. He had fabricated passports. Some money. He'd been here about a week."

"Was he coming for me?"

"I can't say for sure. All we know is you were a half hour late, and something went down when you didn't show at the beach at your normal time. Maybe he was trying to warn you. Maybe you had a guardian angel, and the two guys you saw stopped him from...I don't know. I'm still trying to work it out. There's just not enough to know for sure. But my guess is this guy wanted to find you. Could be they were on him and hoping that would get them to you. Maybe he was on them hoping for the same. After what you told me, either way would fit."

"So what now?"

"They're gonna make a mistake, Arman. We just gotta stay one step ahead. Come on. Get your things and we'll head to my place and get some sleep. It's been a long day."

Arman looked at the alarm clock next to his bed: 10:01 in

digital red. He started packing a small duffel with a few changes of clothes, a couple of books, and toiletries. Arman's world had shrunk down to almost nothing once, and now he had to leave even the tiny piece of ground he had made a life on.

Lamar watched him take a five-by-seven-inch photograph of a young woman and child out of a picture frame on the bedside table and slip it between the pages of one of the books. Lamar knew what it meant. He turned to look at a bookshelf while Arman finished packing in order to give him something like privacy. Lamar read a few titles in the dim light from the bathroom and ran his fingers across the books' spines. *Supernovae and Supernova Remnants.* Kant's *Universal Natural History and Theory of the Heavens. The Diversity of Neutron Stars.*

"I think I'm ready, Detective," Arman said.

Lamar nodded. "All right. Let's go."

They went out the front door. Lamar started down the stairs at a trot and heard the keys fall to the old wood floor of the landing behind him. He turned around and looked up at Arman, who stood trembling at the door, his hand shaking as if he were still about to use the fallen keys to lock the door behind them. A word in Arabic script had been spray-painted in red across the door. "Arman?" Lamar called. He went back up the stairs and put his hand on Arman's trembling shoulder. "What does it say?"

"Khayin," Arman answered quietly. " 'Traitor.' "

Lamar reached down, picked up the keys, and locked the door. He handed the keys back to Arman. "They're trying to scare you. Don't let them. These guys aren't even Arabic. It's for show, all right? We're looking out for you. We'll protect you. Trust me."

Trust. Arman felt sick to his stomach. His life depended

again on something so fragile. But he had no other choice. He looked up toward the ceiling and closed his eyes against the light falling over the landing from the dirty flush-mounted fixture above them. He mouthed a silent prayer, then said, "You don't understand, Detective. They're not trying to scare me. They already know I'm scared."

"So what is it, then?" asked Lamar.

Arman lowered his head and opened his eyes. "They're trying to remind me."

TEN

Three blocks away from the carousel of police lights spinning in the beachside bar's parking lot, Harris and his partner sat in their Charger, watching. One by one, each vehicle left the lot and turned up or down Ocean View, headed toward other scenes of distress and cruelty scattered throughout the Norfolk night. When the last lights faded, Harris turned the key in the ignition and put the transmission into neutral. They sat for a minute, the two of them confirming the stillness and quiet that the police had left behind, looking out the windshield for any sign that it might yet break. The tuned Hemi rumbled in its cradle and then came to life when Harris dropped the shifter into drive and rolled on the gas.

They did a U-turn and approached the Sea Breeze from the maze of surface streets that spread out behind the motel, the tinted windows reflecting the passing scene under the street lamps as they drove. They pulled into the motel's parking lot and turned the vehicle around to point toward its exit. Harris's partner pulled out a notepad and wrote down descriptions and plate numbers of the cars in the parking lot. The lot was nearly empty. Besides Mr. Peters's beat-up Chevy pickup, there was a minivan with West Virginia tags, an SUV from Jersey, and a battered Civic with Virginia plates.

Harris eased the shifter into park and cut the engine. His partner reached up and turned off the dome light with his left hand. When they opened the doors to exit, they did so in darkness. They met at the trunk of the Charger, pulled out their pistols, and eased back the slides until each one saw the glint of brass casing in his chamber. They holstered them again and headed toward the door and the darkened reception area behind it.

The CLOSED sign faced them, and the interior was lit only by a fire exit sign and a sliver of light passing through the cracked-open motel office door. They saw a breezeway around the side of the entrance that led to the courtyard the rooms themselves opened onto. The two men turned around and one pulled on the glass door gently, but it quickly bumped against the dead bolt. He waved his hand at Harris, and he passed him an electric multi-pick and a thin metal tensioner, and he placed both in the lock. The multi-pick buzzed for a second, and he put pressure on the tensioner until they heard the sound of the tumbler as it backed out of the bolt. He passed the locksmith tools back and nodded. Harris opened the door, and they both entered and dead-bolted the door behind them. They stood there silently, listening, with their hands on their pistols, but there was no sound except their slow, regular breathing. They went through the employee-only door and found themselves on the other side of the reception desk. Harris opened drawers and shuffled through their contents while his partner eased open the door to the manager's office.

When the door was less than halfway open, the man saw the shotgun barrel and tried to dive out of the way, but three of the nine pellets hit him and shattered his shoulder blade. In the enclosed space, the noise was overpowering. Mr. Peters's ears filled with a harsh tone that drowned out all other sounds.

He racked another shell into the chamber and swung the barrel toward the desk. Harris had rolled over the desk and dropped out of sight. Mr. Peters looked down at the injured man, who reached for his pistol and rolled toward his uninjured shoulder, attempting to bring the barrel up to fire. Mr. Peters let the barrel of the shotgun drop and fired point-blank into the man's face, then racked another round and fired through the desk just above the floor. The buckshot tore a hole through the chipboard, and Mr. Peters moved right and fired again. He dropped the shotgun and pulled out the Python, and just as it cleared the holster, Harris rose up from the other side of the desk.

Mr. Peters got a shot off but missed, the bullet passing over the man's shoulder and smashing into the red glow of the exit sign, extinguishing it. The two men were no more than six feet apart, their pistols never more than four. Harris fired his pistol a fraction of a second after Mr. Peters, and their muzzle flashes in the darkened room nearly met as they exchanged fire. A bullet hit Mr. Peters just below his left clavicle, but he did not know it yet. By the time Mr. Peters emptied his cylinder, he had hit the other man twice, one round grazing his forearm and another hole-punching the cartilage of Harris's right ear.

Eleven seconds after firing the first shot, Mr. Peters lay on his back, soaking the cheap carpet behind the reception desk with his blood. Harris's .45 held two more rounds than Mr. Peters's revolver, which had been the difference. The first had buzzed past Mr. Peters's ear like a hornet, but the last had hit him just above his right eye, shattering the orbital bone and darkening the back wall of the reception area with blood and brain matter. Mr. Peters was merely a body then, a slave to gravity, and he slumped down dead. He lay on the floor with one leg trapped under him due to the awkwardness of his fall.

The light from the open office door fell over the old man's face and onto the dead eyes staring into nothing.

Harris came around through the employee door again. He dropped the magazine from his pistol and put it in his pocket. He pulled another from his belt, slammed it home, and pulled the slide back, loading a round into the chamber. He looked down at what was left of his partner and at Mr. Peters lying dead and twisted up by gravity. He thumbed the safety on and returned the pistol to his holster. He looked at his watch: 10:45. He grabbed his partner's gun from where it lay on the floor and went through his pockets, removing the locksmith tools, a small wad of cash, and the keys to the Charger. He went through the drawers again more methodically and then through the papers and file cabinets in the office but didn't take anything from any of them.

He left through the glass door at 10:47 and used the tools to lock the dead bolt again. He opened the driver's-side door, sat down, and started the engine. He pulled the Charger out of the parking lot four minutes after he'd pulled in and drove away.

At a quarter to midnight, Harris pulled into an empty power substation parking lot, eased the car behind a row of trees, and killed the lights. He opened the glove box, took out a first aid kit, and rolled up his sleeve, torn where the bullet from the old man's gun had streaked across it, carving a narrow channel into his forearm. Slowly, he patted a cotton ball soaked with alcohol along the length of the superficial wound, grimacing at its sting. He took another cotton ball and pressed it against his ear, the inside of which was caked with dried blood. The bloody cotton balls went into a zip-lock bag, and he wrapped his forearm with a spiral of gauze.

He exited the car, went to the trunk, and opened it. He unfolded a duffel bag and placed the zip-lock in it. He removed a plate carrier and an M4 from the trunk, put them both in the duffel, and slung it over his shoulder. He closed the trunk and leaned against it, took out a map, and unfolded the map over it. He worked out his eight-digit grid coordinates, folded the map back up neatly, unzipped the duffel, and slid the map inside. Then he took a cell phone from his pocket and dialed.

"Harris?" the voice answered.

"Yeah. I need exfil and a wrecker."

"Grid?"

He read the coordinates off to the voice.

"Status?"

"Solo."

"Three-two?"

"Down."

"You clean?"

"Yeah, I'm clean."

"Move to the following grid." The voice rattled off a series of numbers.

Harris repeated them back.

"Exfil will be waiting for you. Torch the vic."

"Tracking."

"And Harris?"

"Yeah."

"That was strike two."

Harris spun the Charger's wheels pulling out of the sub-station's gravel lot. He headed into deeper darkness, surrounded on all sides by the impenetrable blackness of the swamplands through which he drove. Two hundred yards past an intersection of rarely traveled two-lane roads, he turned left onto dirt and found himself going down a single-lane causeway ridge. When he was a mile deep into the swamp, headlights flashed at him. There was barely room for one car on the causeway road, and the vehicle that had high-beamed him was a silver four-door dually pickup. He eased the Charger up alongside the truck, and the driver pointed to a small break in the trees about fifty yards farther down the causeway.

Harris pulled off to the side, retrieved the duffel from the trunk, and walked back toward the pickup. Two men hopped down from the pickup and started walking toward him.

"They told me to torch it," said Harris.

"Gotcha. You okay?"

"Little dinged up. Nothing major."

"What about Dempsey?"

"Dempsey's dead."

"You sure?"

"Yeah."

"How sure?"

"Twelve-gauge-to-the-face sure."

"Goddamn it, Harris. How'd this get so fucked?"

"Old man went fucking Audie Murphy on us."

"Retrieval?"

"If Bajalan has it somewhere, it's not anywhere he's been since we've been on him. Apartment's clean, place of employment's clean. Whatever he knows is in his head."

"All right. Torch the vic. Stuff's in the bed."

Harris went to the truck's bed, reached over the side, and pulled out a gas can. He turned around and started walking back toward the Charger. "You know," he said to the two men behind him, "I thought that old bastard was gonna—"

He was interrupted by a pistol shot. The sound echoed over

the black water and ricocheted among the cypresses and tupelos. The two men walked over to where Harris lay facedown in the dirt.

"Pop the trunk, Jimmy," the first man said.

Jimmy went to the Charger, opened the driver's-side door, and hit the trunk latch. "Come on, Chris. Let's get this done. It's past my bedtime."

They stood at either end of the body. Chris reached into the dead man's pockets and pulled out a roll of cash and an ID card. He put the roll in his back pocket and handed the ID card to Jimmy. In the light of the moon, Jimmy made out Bajalan's face on it. They carried Harris to the trunk by his hands and feet, his stomach dragging along the dirt. They folded him up in the trunk, and Jimmy went back around to the driver's side and torqued the steering wheel as far over as it would go. He threw the column shifter into neutral and called back to the vehicle's rear, "You ready?"

Chris closed the trunk. "Go."

They began to push. Jimmy kept the wheel turned, and they pushed together until the heavy sedan started moving under its own weight. When both front wheels had gone over the side of the causeway, they gave the car one last shove and watched it roll down into the water until the swamp closed in over the roof, and it was gone. They grabbed the duffel, tossed it in the back seat of the dually, and got in. They started up the motor. When they turned the truck onto the hardball, the swamp behind them was quiet again, once more an indifferent witness to the works of man.

ELEVEN

Lamar pulled into the Sandbridge RV park not quite an hour after leaving Arman's apartment. He parked his unit in the driveway in front of a single-wide, looked over at Arman, and said, "Home sweet home."

They went out to the porch, and Arman sat down in one of the plastic-banded loungers, and Lamar followed him out with two beers. Arman shook his head and said, "Thanks." Lamar sat down next to him, kicked his feet up onto the cheap glass table, and looked out into the darkness of the back bay. He swigged the beer, and they sat there, each imagining the other saw something different in the night.

"They killed my wife and my son," said Arman.

Lamar paused, not knowing what to say. "I saw you grab their picture. What happened?"

"Four contractors pulled up in an SUV and blocked us in an alley in the old city. The two on the passenger side fired without saying anything. They knew it was me. They must have thought they'd killed us all, but I was still alive. One of them got out and spray-painted *khayin* on the wall above us."

"They didn't say anything at all?" Lamar asked.

"No."

"Do you think you could ID them?"

"They wore kaffiyehs."

"Arman, I want you to know that I believe you, but how can you be sure? You worked as a terp. I don't have to tell you—"

"You don't. And maybe that's what I would have thought. That's what they wanted me to think. I mean, Detective, that's what everyone told me to think."

"But you don't."

"I don't."

"Because?"

"Because when they got out to spray-paint the wall, I watched them step in the blood of my wife and child as it ran into the gutter. They were wearing Merrells. I never met an Iraqi who wore Merrells."

Lamar's silence was an acknowledgment. He took a big pull on the beer, finishing it, then set it down and opened the other. "You were hit bad?"

"A Stryker platoon was patrolling and heard the gunfire. They took me to Diamondback and stabilized me and put me on a Black Hawk to Balad."

"What happened to your wife and child?"

"Their bodies? I don't know. I never saw them again. I didn't get to bury them. They were left like trash in the street. The last thing I remember is watching those Merrells. I woke up in the trauma tent once, I think, for just a few seconds. I think I remember the lights. I was in Balad for two weeks. They were going to kick me out once I'd recovered enough to walk. I managed to get a message to Lieutenant Taylor."

"That's your LT?"

"Yes. He got me on a flight back to Diamondback, and they picked me up. That's when I told him what I'd seen."

"At the university?"

"Yes. And the Merrells."

"Did he have any idea who they were? What company they were with?"

"I don't know. He told me the ones who attacked me probably weren't even in-country anymore, but I think he was just trying to reassure me. Keep me from being scared."

"You kept running missions with them? After, I mean?"

"Believe it or not, the only time I've ever felt safe since the attack was when I was surrounded by an infantry platoon. Do you remember what companies were there? You were in Mosul then, right?"

"Arman, I was just a twenty-three-year-old E-four. I didn't know shit about shit. This was '04?"

"Right."

"I was back by March of 2005."

"But you don't remember?"

"I remember a lot. But all I remember about contractors is what they called us soldiers in the DFAC."

"What was that?"

"Ten-percenters."

"Ten-percenters?"

"Yup."

"Why that?"

"Because we got paid ten percent of what they did. Assholes." They sat quietly in the mothy light on Lamar's porch. "You know Detective Wheel, Arman, she's gonna figure out what's going on here."

"Don't say 'I promise.'"

Lamar laughed. "I'm not that dumb. But we're gonna do

our damnedest, I can tell you that. You sure you don't want a beer?"

"I'm sure."

"You want a Coke or something?"

"Thanks."

Lamar stood up and stretched and went through the slider to the fridge. He reached in his pocket for his phone to fill Catherine in on everything Arman had told him over the past couple of hours. He flipped it open, but it was dead. He went into the small bedroom and plugged the phone into the charger on his nightstand, then he sifted through his closet and grabbed a pair of gym shorts and an old Virginia Commonwealth University basketball T-shirt he'd had since college. He flipped the clothes over his shoulder, went back out to the kitchen, and turned over the convertible dining benches to make a sleeping area. He found a set of sheets and a pillow in a cabinet and laid them out on the bunk as neatly as he could. He grabbed a Coke and another beer from the fridge, went back out, tossed the shorts and T-shirt into Arman's lap, and put the drinks down on the table between them.

"I don't know what you packed, but those are yours if you need them. Got the rack set up for you in there too. It ain't much, but it's what I got. Help yourself to whatever you need. Mine is yours and all that."

By the time Lamar sat down, Arman had stretched the T-shirt out in front of him, looking at the logo. "I'm more of an Old Dominion guy," he said.

Lamar popped open the beer, took a long pull, and put it back down. "Everybody's got jokes," he said. Lamar looked out toward the bay, the whole world a void beyond his porch light. "It's all right, Arman," he said. "Nobody's perfect."

———

Catherine had fallen asleep with the television on. The show slithered into her dreams. It was one of those news programs that had devolved into almost exclusive coverage of the tawdry, small-town murders that keep the country entertained. She sat upright on her couch in the dream and watched the victims walk by one by one. They were almost all women. Catherine kept trying to ask them where they were going, but she couldn't speak. She turned her head in the dream and saw that the line of victims seemed to extend forever. One of them turned to Catherine and said, "Why couldn't you stop it?" She felt a hand on her shoulder and looked back. Her father stood behind her in his old Nelson County sheriff's deputy uniform and watched with her as the parade of victims went by.

She woke to her phone ringing, disoriented, unsure if it was night or day, if she was herself or some version of herself haunted by the remains of the half-remembered dream. "Wheel," Cat said. She ran her fingers through her silvered red hair, and the television came into focus as the caller spoke.

"Detective Wheel, it's Lieutenant Billings. You know that body on Ocean View this morning, one with the wit worked at the Sea Breeze down the street?"

She rubbed her eyes, looked up, and saw the host of a late-night show and two guests laughing together. She grabbed the remote and turned the volume down. Only the glow of moving light remained. "Yeah. What's up?"

"You should probably just come down here."

"Where?"

"The Sea Breeze. Place is the fucking OK Corral."

"Sorry, what? My partner had me put a unit on it. Everybody all right? What the hell is going on?"

"Yeah. I'm sorry, Catherine. It's been a proper goat-fuck around these parts tonight. That unit got diverted to a code one. Good news is we found the nine-mil your partner put a BOLO on. Bad news is we got two bodies in the motel lobby."

She thought of Lamar. She looked at her watch. "My partner was there two hours ago. Is he there now? Is he all right?"

"He's not here. It's the owner and a John Doe. I tried calling Detective Adams, but it went straight to voice mail. We need someone from Homicide on scene, and I figured you'd want to know."

"I'll be there in fifteen."

She tried to call Lamar while she drove, but the phone went straight to voice mail, just as Billings had said. When she pulled up to the motel, the lot was so full of city vehicles and flashing lights that she had to park on the street. She ducked under the tape and passed uniforms taking witness statements from the few guests of the motel, a tech team placing evidence markers along a blood trail on the crushed white shells, and a vehicle she recognized as belonging to the office of the medical examiner.

She approached the building and saw Lieutenant Billings standing in front of the glass doors at the entrance, which were propped open and in the process of being dusted for prints.

"Come on," he said. "In here."

She followed him in and saw dowel rods sticking out of the wall to mark the trajectory of bullets. The reception desk had had its lower portion torn apart. "Where are the bodies?"

Billings waved her toward the entrance to the area behind the desk. She saw the man who had been hit with the shotgun blast first and then the old man's body lying bent and twisted like a marionette that had been carelessly dropped to the ground. The shotgun was off to the side where the old man had dropped it. The Python lay where it had fallen, next to him.

"These boys could have had this shoot-out in a phone booth, close as they was," Billings said. "You ever seen anything like this?"

"Can't say that I have."

"Gonna be some closed caskets, I can tell you that much."

"Nothing missing, I guess?"

"Don't look that way. Money in the till. Safe in the office is closed. My guess is old-timer here gets the drop on them before they had the chance to get to robbing him. Shithead number two catches a couple but drops the old man and skedaddles."

"You call the hospitals?" asked Catherine.

"They got their eyes open, but nothing so far."

Cat knelt over the John Doe. "Where's his piece?" she asked.

"Come again?"

"He wasn't holding the shotgun, seeing how he got the wrong end of it. I don't think that big-wheel gun was his either, considering it ended up next to the old man. So where's his?"

"I don't know. Shithead number two grabbed it before he left, maybe?"

"Lieutenant, you ever heard of an accomplice who, after he's been shot in the course of an attempted robbery, stops to collect his partner's shit before he hauls ass?" she asked.

"No, I guess not."

"Me neither."

"So, you got some inkling as to what set this thing off if it wasn't a robbery?" Lieutenant Billings asked.

Catherine stepped over the two bodies, careful to avoid the bloodstains as she made her way to the office. She looked inside. Papers were shuffled about, but she'd seen messier offices at headquarters. "Yeah. I've got an inkling. Pretty sure we can rule out love. Not much left if we rule out money. I'm gonna guess my case has three bodies on it now instead of just the one." She came back and looked down at the old man's face, broken and mottled. The one vacant eye drying out as she stood over him, lightless and wide enough to think she might fall into it. The other eye peeked through a circle of blood that had settled in the socket like a tide pool. "LT, can you have all the reports sent to the Homicide section? I've got to follow up on something tomorrow, and I need to get some rest."

"No problem, Detective. Smoke?"

"Sure."

They went outside and stood next to a concrete urn filled with sand, a half dozen cigarette butts already poking out of it. Catherine opened her pack and held it out to him. He grabbed one, and she handed him a lighter. They stood there quietly for a few minutes, processing the scene in the privacy of their own minds. Billings finished half the smoke, tossed the butt on the ground, and put it out with the toe of his shoe. "I'll tell you what, Detective. You got to give the old man credit. Son of a bitch went out with his boots on."

She looked up at the motel sign and the letter board beneath. "Yeah, LT, he sure did," she said dryly. "Now he gets to be the toughest man in the graveyard."

———

Just before midnight, Lamar heard the phone buzzing softly from his bedroom. "One sec," he said to Arman and went inside. He unplugged the phone, answered it, returned to the porch, and stood by the table.

"Lamar, where the hell have you been? I've been trying to reach you for damn near an hour," Catherine said.

"Phone died. Hey, we got a lot to catch up on."

"Me first."

Lamar went quiet and stayed that way.

TWELVE

Sally woke the following day to the buzz of her cell phone. She rolled toward the hotel nightstand and felt for the phone, grabbed it, and rolled back and opened it. "Yeah," she said.

"Sal, it's Matt."

"Hey, Matt."

"Can you get down to Ocean View Ave.?"

"I'm still in DC."

"Shit," said Matt.

"What's up?"

"There's been bodies piling up within a few blocks of the park down there."

"What?"

"Yeah. Two gun deaths and an undetermined. Undetermined was first."

"I thought you'd want Will or Lisa on something like this."

"Will's on vacation in Sarasota, and Lisa's father is in the hospital. I just need somebody to bang out some copy on it, Sal. 'Rash of Violence in Ocean View.' Something like that."

"I'm not writing 'Rash of Violence,' Matt." Sally felt pressure in her chest, her body beginning to rebel against the bender's end. She sat up in the bed, but the weight remained.

"Come on, Sal, you know what I mean."

"I'm following up on that tip I got. I'll be back this after-noon. I can make some phone calls on the way home. This for tomorrow?"

"Yeah. Just give me fifteen inches for Metro, will ya?"

"Who's lead?"

Sally heard Matt shuffling through papers on the other end of the line. "Detective Catherine Wheel had the first John Doe on the beach early yesterday morning." More rustling. "Second was...Billings. Second Patrol. Blue-sector lieutenant. Looks like a robbery gone wrong at the Sea Breeze Motel. They were still working the scene a couple hours ago, so no one would talk to us. You know what to do. I just need something meta. One of the interns already cribbed the blotter for the website."

"I got it. You want me to come in?"

"I don't care, Sally. Just file something, please."

"Okay."

"Where are you with the hearing?"

"He told me to go to Chesapeake and talk to PR."

"So, 'Go fuck yourself.' What a dick. Any fireworks?"

"At the hearing?"

"Yeah."

"No. Almost seemed like they'd rehearsed it, they had their lines down so well."

"World's a stage and all, I guess."

"Overheard him talking about a problem after. Nothing specific, though." She reached for her notebook and flipped it open. "You ever hear of anyone named Harris in the Decision Tree C-suite?"

"No, but I'll put out some feelers for you, see if I can find a Harris he's connected to. You want to poke around a bit more on that? Maybe see if you can put something together from the congressman's side? Congressman Wright is an asshole, but he's at least a principled asshole."

"I've heard. An ex from college is on his staff."

"No shit? Look at the cub reporter with a source in Congress."

"Matt."

"Sorry."

"Unless you want to print the transcript, I'll need a little more time. I'm supposed to meet the guy on his staff for lunch."

"Okay. Sounds good. So fifteen inches on the 'Rash' and keep digging on Decision Tree."

"How are the cops?"

"Who, Wheel and Billings?"

"Yeah."

"Billings is an asshole, but he'll talk if he thinks you'll owe him a favor. Wheel is tougher. She won't bullshit you, but some people she likes and some she doesn't. If she doesn't, well..."

"Gotcha."

"And, hey, Sal?"

"Yeah?"

"If your mystery man shows up at Union Station, do not go anywhere with him, okay? I'd feel more comfortable if you talked to him in a public place."

"I'll be fine, Matt."

"Sally, I'm serious."

Sally hit End and sat there looking at her reflection in the phone's black screen. For a moment, she thought she was getting another call, the way the phone was shaking. Then she realized it was the hand holding it. She reached over with her other hand and grabbed her wrist, trying to still the tremors. She was drenched in sweat. She dialed a number and pulled the covers over her head as it rang.

"Carter West."

She didn't say anything for a moment. "Trey, it's Sally."

"Sal, it's six in the morning. If you're calling to cancel, you could have waited until I was awake."

"You're awake now. And I'm not canceling. I wanted to ask you a favor."

"Do I owe you a favor?"

"Don't be a dick, Trey."

"Sorry, what is it?"

"I'm supposed to meet a potential source after lunch. Will you come with me?"

"You want to bring a source to meet another source?"

Sally closed her eyes. Her head fell to her chest. She waited before answering, hoping he'd somehow hear the words without her having to say them out loud. "I don't want to be alone," she said.

"Are you worried about this person, Sally?"

Sally sat there listening to Trey's breath cut through the soft buzz of the line.

"You're drinking again," he said. It wasn't a question.

"Not today . . ."

"Jesus, Sally, it's only six a.m."

"No. I mean I won't today, Trey. I just need . . . I don't know who the guy is. Someone left me an anonymous note at the paper. Wants to meet at Union Station at one fifteen this afternoon. My assignments editor gets creeped out by stuff like this."

He took some time to answer. "Okay," he said finally. "I'm there. You want to tell me what we're looking for?"

"He also sent a thumb drive. Note said 'Air gap only.' Also 'Union Station, Saturday, July twelfth.' And 'Under Themis.'"

"Air gap only? Sally, are you serious?"

"Yeah. I had to ask the IT guys at the paper what it meant."

"What'd they say?"

"They asked if I was secretly in the NSA."

Trey didn't respond.

"Trey, they were joking."

"No, Sal. They weren't. Not really."

"You know what it is?"

"Air gap only?"

"Yeah. You sound weird."

"Well, it's just a high level of information security. People send stuff over thumb drives all the time. Air gap only is . . . it's just not something you see every day, even in my job. Can I call someone about this?"

"Are you trying to kill my story before I even know what it is?"

"I'm trying to make sure you don't do something illegal, Sally. I work on the National Security and Foreign Affairs Subcommittee. I have a duty to report."

"So now you're a Boy Scout?" she said, regretting it before the last word was even out of her mouth.

"Hey, fuck off, Sally. I take this shit seriously. We've got American troops getting killed—" Trey stopped. He felt the silence on the other end of the line. "Oh Jesus, Sally, I'm so sorry."

She didn't answer right away. She wasn't trying to punish him. It just took the same amount of time to collect herself as if she had been. "No. You're right. I shouldn't have said that," Sally said.

"Maybe it's nothing. It could be someone wants to pass you corporate books or something. If it's nothing, I won't even look. I can have somebody come with us and keep an eye on the meet."

"Can you get me a safe way to open the files?"

"You really haven't tried?"

"No. The IT guys acted like it would melt the paper's entire network. I don't know. I figured I'd wait to see if the person who sent it was a kook."

"Yeah, I can, but the risk is real. I can figure something out."

"Okay. You and me look together. No one else. Nobody watches the meet. You can be the representative of the U.S. government if you want. But I'm not giving up the story if there's something there, okay?"

Trey thought about it for a minute. "Did you go see Stevie?" he asked.

"Yeah," she said.

"Are you okay?"

"It looks like they're opening another section. Are you?"

"Don't be mad at me because a war started three months before graduation and I didn't drop everything and go. It's not fair. We can't all be like Stevie."

"I'm sorry, Trey. It's not you."

"It's all right. Shit, I loved the guy too."

"I know."

"I'll call you with the address for lunch. Someplace close to the station. Sound good?"

"Yeah. Sounds good."

Sally closed the phone and caught her distorted reflection in the minibar's glass, then looked down at her hand balled into a fist and unfurled it flat as it would go. She studied the almost imperceptible tremors and left her hand there, flexed and shaking, for how long she did not know but until its strain began to seep up her forearm, and she shook her hand loose from her mind's unthinking grip on it.

She changed into running clothes and took the elevator down to the lobby. Her mind fixated on the unnamed pressure that pushed in and out of her chest with a pulsing, frictious heat. She stood inside the front entrance, watched the rain come down over the small triangular park across Massachusetts Avenue, and listened to the thunder quietly rattle the sky someplace far away. The trees there in the park were half shrouded in fog and mist. The light of the early-morning sun fell weakly as though in a losing competition with the pattering drizzle. The city in this weather seemed low and gray and a likely place in which to lose oneself. She preferred to run in the predawn twilight, that in-between time when late nights had ended and early mornings were yet to start. It was the only time when solitude felt different from loneliness. But loneliness would do for now.

When Arman woke, he peeled himself off the cheap vinyl mattress Lamar had laid over the converted booth. He lifted himself up onto his elbows and felt the sweat matting his hair to the sides of his head. George Jones belted out "The Door" from the clock radio in Lamar's bedroom, and Arman heard the shower going through the accordion bathroom door. He stood up and went to the small stove and put a kettle on the burner and poked through a couple of poorly stocked cabinets until he found a jar of instant coffee. He looked through the slider and out beyond the porch. The back bay sparkled in the

126

sun as if something sifted through it for diamonds. When he heard the kettle whistle, he spooned crystals and sugar into two cups and poured the hot water in. Arman took one cup onto the porch and left the other on the counter for Lamar.

He sat there drinking the sweet coffee, and Lamar came out onto the porch behind him with his own cup.

"You sleep all right?" he asked Arman.

"No. Not really."

"Yeah. The bed leaves something to be desired in terms of comfort."

"It wasn't that."

"Oh."

"Well, it was a little that."

"Detective Wheel is on her way."

"I thought you said she was going to DC."

"She is. She's gonna want to ask you some more questions."

"I wouldn't think there are any more questions."

"No. Me neither. But she'll have thought of some. She'll ask some of those, and she'll ask some of the same I did. Partly, we need to figure out what to do with you."

Arman looked down into the coffee cup, brooding. "I don't know that I like being something that something needs to be done with."

Lamar sat down at the table with Arman. "I don't blame you. Nevertheless."

"Okay."

They were both drinking a second cup of coffee when Catherine walked around the side of the trailer and came up the porch steps. "Any more of that?" she asked.

Lamar nodded toward the slider, and Catherine came out with a cup, the instant, and the kettle after a minute. She laid a dish towel on the table, poured herself a cup, and put the kettle on the dish towel. She leaned against the porch railing, stirring the coffee with a spoon and looking at Arman, who was staring at the bay. When Arman felt her eyes on him, he glanced up, and she said, "I'm sorry about your wife and child, Arman."

Arman looked away from her and over the sparkling blue bay and said, "Thank you." He hoped she was the kind of person who knew it was enough to say it once.

"There's never a good time for questions like this, but I need you to think," she said. "Anything that's ever felt strange or unusual since you been here?"

"In America?"

"Uh-huh."

"It's all felt strange, Detective." He wondered if she could ever understand. Or Lamar. Maybe because of their work, they might. But how do you explain the strangeness of surviving? It's more than guilt. It's a kind of torture to wake every morning to the deaths of your loved ones as if they were happening for the first time. How do you explain the cruelty of those first few seconds awake, when you shut your eyes and pray that it was just a dream, only to realize you've been born again into a world without them?

"I don't doubt it. But I mean anything unusually so."

"No. Nothing that comes to mind. I have a simple life. Regular. I go to work. I go to the water to swim. I go home."

"And the info you gave to Lieutenant Taylor?"

"The sworn statement about the massacre at the university?"

"Right. That went up the chain not long after the incident?"

He put his hands in his lap and looked them over as if to remind himself of what they'd once held. The hand of his dying son. Three black strands of his wife's hair that he'd managed to touch before losing consciousness. He looked up at the detective and nodded. "I wrote the statement the next day," he said. "My family was killed a week later. A month after I got back to Anaconda, he pushed the SIV through. I bounced around a bit. Down to Kuwait, Doha. A few months later, Mr. Peters picked me up from the bus station. I stayed in one of the motel rooms until I saved up enough for my apartment."

"All right. That's something. You know if that video you took made it into the report?"

"No."

"No, it didn't, or no, you don't know?"

"I don't know."

"If these people are just now coming for you all these years after what you witnessed and swore to and all, I'd guess there's something brought you to their attention. Might have caught the attention of our mystery man as well. If we can figure out what it is, maybe we can also figure out why everyone and their cousin is so interested in keeping you quiet."

He put his head in his hands. "You're not going to find them before they find me."

She went over to the table and sat down on the empty chair. She took Arman's hands from his face, held them for a second, then let his hand down in his lap and leaned back. She pulled out her cigarettes, took one out, and started tossing the butt end against the tabletop from an inch or two above it, like a dart. She looked over at him and lit the smoke. She took a long draw, and they let the quiet settle in over them. "I've been a cop almost twenty-seven years, Mr. Bajalan," she said. "More than half my life. Homicide for damn near twenty. I've worked, oh, probably a hundred and fifty murders in that time. I do the best I can. Sometimes there's failure. I'm not gonna lie to you about that, because you're smart enough to know it if I tried. But I'm a good detective. And I'm responsible for you and your friend Mr. Peters and that man on the beach."

That's what she said. But she wanted to tell him how hard those failures were, that there weren't enough Red Onions or needles in Greensville to make up for even one of them. That there was a debt she'd never be able to pay. She'd tried so hard to accept it. And sometimes, she could. But most days, she thought, *We're all wrecked in the same vessel, aren't we?* It wasn't just about the job anymore, not after all this time. So she'd ask herself fairly often, *Are we supposed to stop bailing water even if we know the ship is gonna sink?* No. It was a responsibility. *Every second we get to keep our heads above the water, well, if it ain't a victory, it's something else.* She knew she wasn't ever gonna win. She knew the last murder wasn't getting solved on her watch. Not on Detective Adams's either. She wasn't even sure they ought to be trying to win. They were up against some darkness of the human heart. You'd just as well try to stop the tide coming in. She wanted to say, most of the time, *I'm just hanging on compared to what we're up against,* but she didn't. Now she just said again, "I'm responsible for y'all. And it's the only thing in the world I care about. I don't know what else to tell you."

"That's what David said too. Lieutenant Taylor."

"What'd he say?" she asked.

"That I was his responsibility. That he was gonna look out for me."

"And he died anyway, is what you're saying?"

"Yeah."

"I'd say that's a man who held up his end, Arman."

"I'm not sure I should be putting anyone else in that position, Detective Wheel. My wife and son. David. Mr. Peters."

"I don't think you put them anywhere. We think we have that kind of power over people, but most of the time, we don't. People put themselves where they want to be, that's all. Sometimes they know what they're doing. Sometimes they don't."

"So what's your plan?" asked Arman.

"The three of us are gonna get in that unmarked police car out front and take an all-expenses-paid trip to our nation's capital, courtesy of the city of Norfolk, Virginia. That man you found wasn't planning on ending up dead on Ocean View Beach. We're gonna go see if anyone is there waiting for him to come back. And you're gonna tell us if you recognize anyone. It's a roll of the dice, Arman, but if there is someone waiting for him, it just might be someone you've seen before. You up for all that?" she asked.

"I think so," he said.

Catherine looked over at Lamar. He nodded at her. She stubbed out the cigarette, slapped her knees, and said, "Get your shit together, fellas. If we hurry, we can stop for breakfast and still get to Union Station on time."

They rode over the Potomac near noon, and the traffic slowed on the bridge. From the back seat, Arman saw the white stone of the Washington Monument loom through gray summer weather. Lamar looked over the river and said to Catherine, "What do you carry in the trunk?"

"You worried?"

"You aren't?"

"There's an 870 back there."

"Okay."

"You want to tote it through the station?"

"No. I guess not."

"Did you find anything about Arman's lieutenant, David Taylor?"

"The accident?"

"Yeah."

"I found some articles online. Single car out by Johnson City, Texas. I asked the LT to see if they'd send us what they had."

"Whose jurisdiction?"

"Blanco County sheriff. Texas Department of Public Safety."

"You think you ought to go out there?"

"Do you?"

"Depends on what's in the accident report, but yeah, to be thorough, you probably should."

"His old man still lives out there."

"In Johnson City?"

"Somewhere out in the country."

"Be worth talking to."

They caught a hint of the Tidal Basin through the trees, and the white cupola of the Jefferson Memorial seemed to glow in the rain as they curved toward the Mall.

"What about Metro PD?" asked Catherine.

"I called Transit."

"They okay with us being up here?"

"Took them a minute to figure out why we're waiting for a guy we know isn't coming."

"But otherwise?"

"Fine."

"They sending anyone?"

"No. Once I told them we aren't expecting to make an arrest, they lost interest."

"I guess they don't respect seeing what's what as an investigative technique."

"I guess not."

They went down through a series of tunnels, dark and humming with the sound of steel belts on the blacktop, and came up the other side of the Mall and took a right toward the station.

"You ever been up here, Arman?" she asked.

"Once. Last year. Mr. Peters took me. He wanted to see the Korean War memorial. He'd never been."

Catherine looked at him in the rearview. "What'd he think?"

"There was snow on the ground. Where the statues march. He said at least they got that part right. He talked about how cold it was. He said there was a time he thought he'd never get warm again in his whole life."

"I guess they don't have wars where the weather's good anymore," said Lamar.

Catherine wheeled the unmarked around Columbus Circle and up the ramp to the garage. Taxis on their way to the stand in front of the building passed in the other direction. She parked in the deck, and they got out, and rain still fell over the city around them. They took an elevator down to the bus terminal, and Lamar walked over to the arrivals and departures screens in front of the ticket office and checked his watch. "We're still good," he said. "Another half hour."

They walked down toward the station proper, and Lamar tilted his head back to take in the intricacies of its architecture. "Looks like a damn church in here," he said.

Catherine and Arman joined him in looking. The ceiling arched and vaulted and arched again and again. The scale was not proportioned for people but for people's ideas of themselves. "What do you think you're meant to pray for in a place like this?" Lamar asked.

"Getting there," said Detective Wheel, "and getting back."

They went down another level, bought lunch from a dimly lit Sbarro's kiosk, and then went back to the bus terminal at the parking deck. Rain fell near sideways and pooled up on the concrete at the garage's edges beneath the low walls. There were probably forty buses from the three lines that used the terminal in various stages of coming and going.

Lamar asked them to hold on for a minute, and he went in and asked the ticket agent if there was a good place to watch arrivals. She looked over the rims of her glasses at him suspiciously and pointed toward a small bench in the interior of the ticket office. "Thanks," he said. He walked out into the open garage again and checked his watch. "All right, let's walk down this way." They sat on a bench at the top of the stairs to see disembarked passengers heading toward the station and the H Street exit closer to the ticket office.

"Mr. Bajalan," said Catherine, "I want you to look at every single face that goes by. If you think you saw them at the grocery store, you tell us. If you think they maybe halfway look like someone you once saw in a dream, you tell us. If you think maybe you seen them somewhere but don't know where or when?"

"Tell you," said Arman.

⟵

Trey stood up from the table when she walked into the pub on F and shook out her umbrella. He reached out to her hand, and his other went to her shoulder, and he leaned in. Their lips could have met out of habit, but he only kissed her politely on the cheek and pulled out her chair for her.

"It's good to see you in the flesh," he said.

Sally laid her napkin across her lap and took a sip of the ice water waiting for her on the table. She smelled the pungent odor of generations of spilled beer on the floorboards, looked Trey in the eye, and smiled. "You too."

"I—you know, Sal…"

"I know. You've been worried about me. I'm sorry. I just… I'm trying. I want you to know how much I appreciate you meeting me today. You didn't have to, especially after…"

"I wouldn't be here if I didn't think you've been trying. And I would have been hurt if you'd come up and didn't call. So don't worry about it now, okay? Whatever you need to say, you can say when you're ready."

Her body felt as tight as coiled rope. She nodded quickly as if she might get the acknowledgment of what she'd done out of the way, as if the gesture might prevent her from unraveling. She thought of the morning he'd found her, of waking in a hospital bed, his father standing there talking to Trey like she was merely a problem to be solved. She forced another smile and said, "Thanks."

"Before we go up to the station, maybe we could narrow down who might be waiting for us there. Sound good?" The waitress came by, and Sally ordered an iced tea. Trey already had a beer on the table. He held the glass up in front of Sally. "Is this okay?" he asked.

She gave him the same quick nod. "I haven't really been doing any major stories. Mostly local human interest. Kid from Young Terrace gets an Ivy League scholarship. That kind of thing. The only big story I'm working on is Decision Tree. The hearing, possible growth. I mean, it's potentially national, but I'm mostly working it from the local angle. Jobs, land-use stuff. They're trying to expand their facility into a Wildlife Management Area."

"It's got to be that."

"But Trey, I haven't published a word on them yet."

"You've talked to people, right?"

"Sure. So far just on background."

"That's all I am to you?"

"Ha-ha. Very funny. Seriously, though."

"If you're working it, that means people know you're working it. Maybe even people who know you were formerly in a relationship with a congressional staffer on the very committee looking into the details of this contract."

Sally put her elbows on the table and dropped her head into her hands. "Oh my God."

"Yeah."

She looked up at him, her hair splayed wildly between her fingers. "I'm a cutout?"

"If it's what I think it is, the person who passed along this info knew you were working the story. There's no way the fact that we dated all through college would be a surprise to them. It's not an insult, Sal. It's just the game. In a weird way, it's a compliment."

"Even so, why come to me? Why not the *Journal* or the *Times*? You take their phone calls, don't you?"

"Yeah, of course. I don't know the answer to that one. Maybe they figured whatever they've got would get lost in the shuffle at a place like that. But it'd go to the top of the pile at your paper. Maybe they thought we, or I, would take it more seriously coming from you. I really don't know. Remind me to ask your mystery man."

"So what have you got so far on them?" asked Sally.

"What have you got?" he answered.

"You really do think this is a game, don't you, Trey?"

"Of course it is," he said. "You want to find out what I know, and I want to find out what you know."

Sally folded her arms across her chest and stared at him for a few moments before beginning. "Trevor Graves, a scion of one of the First Families of Virginia, enrolls at Princeton in 1986. Army ROTC. Accepts commission as a second lieutenant in the army just in time to deploy to the Middle East during the First Gulf War. Executive officer of a Ranger company in Somalia. Highly decorated for his actions in Mogadishu. On the fast track until '98, when he retires at thirty as a major. Takes a C-suite position at a small investment—"

"No."

"Which part no?"

"I'm not telling you this. You're hearing things, but you'll have to find another way to confirm what the voices are telling you."

"Okay."

"You ever hear the term *sheep-dipped*?"

"Um, no."

"Department of the Army Special Roster?"

"No."

"He didn't retire."

"So what'd he do?"

"Hypothetically, let's say you've got a real high-speed guy, Seventy-Fifth or SF or whatever. Maybe someone wants a look at him for Special Activities Division. Or special operations units that don't get publicly acknowledged. They can't just transfer him over. Can't have his promotion to E-8 or CW4 or major posted in the *Army Times*. So he gets sheep-dipped. He disappears. Retires. Whatever. But he's put on a separate track. Comes out with a new identity. Consultant, State Department attaché, or some other BS. Sometimes with a new name and passport. But these guys are still soldiers. Only now, instead of doing company-level maneuvers with the joes, they're fighting the forever war in back alleys in Malta or with a suppressed five-seven living in a shitty hotel in someplace Joe and Jane Six-Pack couldn't find on a map for all the money in the world."

"This is Graves?"

"This is a hypothetical. Where do you pick up Graves next?"

"He spends six years at Mini-Goldman and quits to found Decision Tree in 2003. Gets his first big contract guarding KBR convoys in Northern Iraq in 2004. Now, just a few years later, the government wants to give him two billion dollars. It's too quick, right?"

"He was never at the bank."

"What? Trey, get the fuck out of here."

"He was never at the bank. In 2001 and 2002, he's doing some highly classified shit in Afghanistan."

"He was never at the bank?"

"There never was a bank. If there was, we can't find it. It was paper only. Cover."

"Okay."

"So these guys, Sal, to a man, are exceptional. They're dedicated, brave, intelligent, and deeply committed to our country."

"That doesn't sound like Graves."

"No. And people don't get kicked out of these units because they are so unbelievably good at selecting the right people."

"But he did?"

"Not officially."

"How about unofficially?"

"These guys don't talk."

"Do you hear voices when you're around them? Like I'm hearing now?"

He smiled. "There are hints. It may be that some people wanted him prosecuted for something that happened over there."

"But?"

"But if you prosecute this guy, what was once in darkness is brought into the light," Trey said theatrically, raising his hands in the air. "A group of these guys said if he wasn't removed, they'd kill him themselves. That's what the voices told me. We don't really know what he did. I saw the report, but they blacked out everything except the articles. The *blank*. A *blank*. An *blank*. Oil and gas exploration, maybe. It's shell company over shell company under shell company, forever and ever, amen. We've got some of the best forensic accountants in the world working for our committee, and we're still not sure where the money came from."

"For Decision Tree? What do you mean? He's from one of those First Families of Virginia. Those are your people, Trey. Y'all have more money than God."

"Well, I like to say I grew up comfortably." He smirked but quickly remembered Sally was not the type to find it funny. "But seriously, they're just names now, mostly. It might help you get into Princeton, but his family ran out of money a long time ago. That land in Chesapeake, where the Decision Tree facilities are? That's it. That's what he received from his father's estate, a thousand acres of swamp. Sal, you'd have to pay someone to take it from you."

"Have you seen their books?" she asked.

"We've subpoenaed a lot. And they've complied. But there's definitely more we don't know about the business than we know."

"So you've got nothing."

"Nothing actionable," said Trey. "And even if we find something, it's got to be solid enough for a U.S. attorney to take on. These people all have careers, and they don't want to risk them by going after soldiers."

"They aren't soldiers, Trey."

"The public can't tell the difference. Or they don't care."

"So what's the next step?"

"Throwing darts? I don't know, Sal. The forensic accountants the committee hired think a SPAC fills in a lot of blanks."

"What's a SPAC?"

Trey took out a pen and began diagramming loosely on a napkin. "Special purpose acquisition company. It's basically a blank check. Investors buy shares for the company to use to acquire another business, but you don't know going in what the SPAC will use the money for. You can hit big, but if they don't make an acquisition in two years, they have to give you your money back."

"So you think Graves is financing Decision Tree's expansion with SPAC money?"

He shrugged. "It's possible. It would fit. But we can't prove it. Our best guess is he needs the contract to go through for Decision Tree to be legally acquired."

"And if they don't get the contract?"

"They have to send the money back to their investors."

"What if they don't have it?" asked Sally.

"That would be a problem. A good way to end up broke. Maybe in jail. These companies can be super-shady. A lot of the time, people use them to circumvent the IPO process. Keep the SEC from digging around."

"Jesus. Can you imagine people putting war in their retirement portfolios?" she said.

"Sal, c'mon. It's already there. Raytheon. Northrop Grumman. Lockheed Martin. General Dynamics. Nobody cares because they've been around for a while. But if this is what we think it is, what could it be? We're talking about war start-ups. Thirty-year-old billionaires looking for a niche in global conflict. The need to innovate."

"Invention being the mother of necessity and all," she said.

"That's right. And the thing no one wants to admit, not on the news, not in my boss's office or any other member of Congress's office, is that borders as we've always known them are essentially meaningless. The borders that matter now aren't between countries. They're between tax brackets. Global citizens. Ultra-high-net-worth individuals. Someone's from Iraq. You're from Virginia. So what? Theater. The real countrymen are the guys with fifty million, a hundred million in assets. Doesn't matter if they're in London, the Emirates, Hong Kong. They don't give a fuck about nations. We're talking about a tech billionaire with a battalion-size element of special forces–trained contractors on retainer. He can't get extraction rights to a lithium mine in Chile? Fuck it, he can fund and arm a coup. You're gonna make him pay taxes? He has to follow your laws? Sal, we can't even imagine what the world would look like after twenty years of that. I mean, a wealth gap? Try fucking feudalism." Trey polished off the beer and held up the glass to signal for another. He caught Sally looking at him. "You mind?" he asked.

"No," she said half-heartedly. "Go ahead." She sat there pushing a lemon slice down into the bottom of her glass with her straw. "Well, at least your boss is trying to stop it."

"Yeah. Trying."

"What, you don't think it will work?"

"I don't know if it's gonna go exactly how I said, but no one is gonna stop it. It's too late. At this point, I think we just have to hope for the best."

"Jesus, Trey. When did you get to be such a cynic?"

"You know how they say it takes a lot of room to turn a battleship around?"

"Sure, I guess."

"Try reversing the orbit of planet Earth. That's what we would be up against."

"If no one is really trying to stop it, what's the point?" asked Sally.

"It gives you a reason to put your hand out."

Sally crossed her arms and looked away from him. "Don't tell me it's about money."

"It's about human nature. People figure they might as well get paid if everyone else is. Contributor on cable news, kickbacks from lobbyists, taking notes for your memoir—at a certain point, they're just different positions in the same industry."

"Trey, you don't believe that."

"It would still be true even if I didn't, Sal. Don't be naive."

"No," she said, slapping the table hard enough to surprise herself. "What's naive is thinking there aren't any conse-quences for anyone."

"I'm sorry," he said, trying to lower the temperature. "Really. I don't want to fight."

She glared at him. "Fine," she said. "So if Graves is in the oil and gas business after he gets the boot from the secret unit, why does he go back into security work?"

"It was seed money, best guess," Trey said. "Even if he did

enough for a multinational or a foreign government to give him a payday, he's not dumb. He must have known he wasn't going to disrupt the oil and gas business. So he finds another niche more suited to his skill set. It's impressive if you think about it. Mercenaries have existed for millennia, but governments got spooked by all the cowboy stuff that went on in Africa in the sixties and seventies. Too high-profile. Too messy. Too many people like you writing about it."

"So Graves corporatizes it. Puts on Brooks Brothers instead of a boonie hat."

"That's right. Takes a PowerPoint filled with business-speak and pitches private military corporations to the U.S. government as if it's some brilliant innovation, but underneath, they're no different than they were. The bottom line is some people think Graves has done things that ought to prevent him from receiving a single cent of taxpayer money. Frankly, I think he should be in prison, but I can't even tell you what crime he committed, let alone provide any evidence that he's guilty of one."

Sally sat there thinking. She looked at Trey, but his eyes revealed nothing to her. "You know Themis?" she asked.

"Divine justice?"

"You looked it up."

"Of course I did. I'm not as smart as you. But hey, at least we know your blind date has a sense of humor. Come on, it's quarter to one."

They left the pub, walked up F, and crossed over Massachusetts to the station in the rain. They stood there looking at the grand facade. Sally pointed to Themis, and they went and stood at the center of the three arches at the entrance. They looked back toward the street and the cars going by. There was a glimpse of the Capitol dome behind the trees as if behind a waterfall.

"What now?" she asked.

"I guess we wait. He must know what you look like."

A reflexive shiver went through Sally's body. "Yeah," she said. "I guess he must."

THIRTEEN

Tom and Lester Yancey watched the green Blazer come around the corner through the trees and a slanted curtain of morning light and head toward them on the causeway. There was a light bar across the top of the Blazer. Without even seeing it, they both knew that CONSERVATION POLICE was stenciled on the sides of the truck and that its driver was Eugene Marshall, the man responsible for enforcing all the Department of Game and Inland Fisheries regulations in that area.

Lester spat on the ground and tilted his head, listening for the dogs. The boxes in the bed of the old Toyota were wide open, and Tom had the GPS unit in his hand, looking at the four points of light moving across the map screen. Lester heard the dogs baying faintly to the west, farther into the depths of the swampland, and he swatted away mosquitoes and turned his head back up the road to watch the warden as he came.

Gene pulled the Blazer off to the side of the causeway, a little shy of the Yancey brothers' truck, where the ground got a little wider. He stepped from the SUV and looked into the trees rising from the black water as if they'd been made by a god who worked only in shade, shadow, and silver leaf. He left the door open and the motor running and walked over to say hello to the Yanceys.

"Y'all aren't running your dogs on no bear or deer, are you?"

"No, sir. That would be illegal, won't it," said Tom.

"It would indeed. How they shaping up?"

"They all right, Gene," Tom said. "They still dumber than a bag of hair put together, but they're right interested in putting their noses in the dirt. They're interested. That's something."

Lester spat tobacco juice off the side of the causeway as if to close that portion of the conversation. "What brings you out here, Gene?"

"Heard a couple of poachers was out here last night. Someone drove by said there might have been spotlighting going on around these parts. You fellas heard anything about it?"

"No, sir," said Tom. "Last night me and Les wet a couple lines and smoked a few doobies out by North Landing."

"That's your alibi?" asked Gene. "You were smoking weed and fishing?"

"Shit," said Lester. "You know our licenses are good. We ain't the types to break more than one law at a time."

Gene laughed. "That's fair. Y'all hear anything about poaching in the Wildlife Management Area, you let me know, all right?"

"Yeah, sure," said Lester.

"I'll see y'all later."

"Oh," said Lester. "They's tracks up the causeway 'bout a half mile. Put down last night would be my guess."

"What kind of tracks?" asked Gene.

"Damn, son. Tires," said Lester. "Ain't you the one asking about folks spotlighting? They ain't ours, and we ain't seen a soul all morning except for your sorry ass."

"Huh. Much appreciated. I'll go take a look. Y'all take care now." Gene turned toward the Blazer and heard the Yancey brothers' dogs' yawping.

"Love you too, Officer Marshall," the brothers said together, and Gene laughed and put his hand up behind him and flipped them the bird. A breeze snuck in through the morning's heat, and Gene took off his mesh ball cap and fanned himself with it to encourage the breeze to keep on blowing. He got back in the Blazer and put the windows down. He drove by the Yanceys slowly, keeping his eyes on the sides of the causeway for the hound dogs that might dart out of the swamp's darkness and into the road. As Gene went farther up, he stuck his head half out the window, looking at the ground for tire tracks. He did not travel far before he picked up two sets of them preserved in the fragile dust where the swamp had closed in on the causeway once again and kept the wind back, preventing their erasure. Gene stopped the Blazer so as not to disturb the tracks any further than he had already. He got out and looked around. When he glanced back at where he had come from, he saw the Yanceys as indistinct blotches of color at the end of the thin line the road carved through the trees and black water. Heard the dogs howling closer still. A tunnel of shimmering heat in the otherwise still of the swamp.

He squatted down and looked at the dirt road's surface and what he saw perplexed him until he realized the tracks were made by a dually. Tracks on one side of the narrow surface seemed to go four wide and cloverleafed where the truck had turned around and went back out toward the road. He followed the other set on the other side a little farther up until he saw blood in the middle of the road and drag marks that paralleled the tracks and more blood here and there along the way. "God-dang poachers," Gene said aloud without thinking.

He went forward with the tracks. The drag marks stopped, and the blood pooled a bit where the animal must have been loaded into a vehicle. Whether it was a deer or a bear taken, he could not say. He was puzzled that there seemed to be no track marks turning to leave the way there had been with the other set behind him, and there were none advancing farther into the swamp. He keyed his handset and waited for a voice on the other end. "Go ahead," it said.

"That call by the WMA last night, did they say anything about dogs?"

"Wait one."

Gene turned back to the tracks. This was some hellacious country to take an animal without dogs, even if you were spotlighting. Something had to get them out from cover. And it seemed curious to Gene that there'd be two vehicles out poaching. He'd have to ask the Yanceys if they'd ever heard of folks bringing two vehicles spotlighting.

"Negative. Someone on the hardball saw lights through the trees and heard a gunshot."

"This was around midnight?"

"That's what the caller said. You find anything?"

"Well, sure does look like someone took an illegal animal. Beyond that, I can't say."

"You want to sit on it tonight?"

"Not really," Gene said. "Do you?"

"Very funny." The radio crackled, and the voice on the other end of the line signed off.

Gene turned to the tracks again and saw where the tire tracks curved off and disappeared but could not figure for the life of him how the vehicle had left the swamp afterward. He looked down at the Yanceys a half a mile away, just shapes in the heat. He walked to the Blazer, turned around, and drove back down the causeway. When he had covered the ground, the Yanceys were loading the dogs in their boxes, and Lester was sweetly scratching behind the ears of one beautiful hound and making baby talk to it and letting it lick all over his face.

"You out of here already?" Tom said.

"No. Not just now. Wondering if I can ask y'all a favor."

"Ask away, Gene," said Lester.

"How's y'all's tracking?"

"Better than yours, I'd bet."

"All right, get on in the truck. I got a puzzle for you up the road a piece."

They shut the dogs in their boxes and shrugged at each other, and both went to get in the Blazer's back doors.

"One of y'all sons of bitches get in the front seat, will you? I ain't your chauffeur."

Lester opened the back door and got in, and Tom went around to the front passenger side. He made a big show of getting comfortable and said, "Sorry, Gene, we just don't have much practice riding in the front of law enforcement vehicles."

Gene tried to hide his smile but could not. He drove the truck down to where he had parked previously and they all got out.

"So what is it?" Lester asked.

"I don't know. You tell me what you think, and let's compare notes after."

Tom and Lester seemed to have an unspoken plan for how to proceed. They each took a side of the road and followed the tracks slowly, pausing every ten feet or so to ponder some aspect of the scene. Once in a while, one of them spat tobacco juice into the dust, and Gene finally said, "Come on with the dip spit, fellas. This might be a crime scene."

"You really gonna get all *CSI* out here on account of someone bagging an animal out of season?" replied Tom.

Gene leaned against the hood, crossed his arms, tilted his ball cap back, and rubbed the sweat off his forehead with the sleeve of his uniform. It took the Yanceys about ten minutes to cover the ground from where the tracks started to where the drag marks began.

"Hey, Gene?" said Tom loudly, his eyes fixed on the road.

"Yeah," he answered.

Gene watched Tom wave him up and then started walking toward him. By the time he got to Tom, Lester had joined them, and all three stood bent over the drag marks and their accompanying blood trail.

"You ever hear of someone going for headshots when they out spotlighting?" asked Tom.

"What do you mean?" Gene asked.

"Well, look it, you see how the blood trail is all off to one side? Ain't no overlap at all between it and the drag marks."

"Okay."

"Seems to me whoever was toting this end had the hind legs, and the other fella had the fore. I'd expect blood, such as there would be, to be laid down more or less where they drug the critter. Pretty close to the center, right? Give or take a few inches."

"Right," said Gene.

Lester looked up at him. "Everybody I ever met aims to put it behind the shoulder, generally speaking. Don't see how you'd even consider a headshot, especially at night."

"Not unless you don't have a lick of respect for the animal," added Tom.

"Funny how I don't see a single track of either in the road," said Lester. He looked at Tom and then at Gene. "You say they was spotlighting?"

"That's right. Someone driving by reported a gunshot and lights back down the causeway here."

"You putting it together, Tom?" Lester asked.

Tom straightened up and walked over to the end of the tracks, tires and footprints both. He looked around at the shuffle of boot prints in the dust. He looked back to where three sets of tracks terminated in a pool of blood, but only two continued, now joined by drag marks and a blood trail. "Yeah, Les. I believe I see what you're seeing."

Les was standing at the edge of the road, looking out over an unremarkable stretch of open water, black as wet coal on the surface and still as ice. It was not black all the way down. When Lester looked carefully, he found the water's transparency. Where it turned from black to brown, the light broke through and lit the depths like darkened honey. He saw particles and all manner of microbes and insects for which he had no names suspended in it. His heart pounded. He pulled the dip out of his mouth and tossed it to the ground. With shaking hands, he took a pack of smokes from the pocket of his Wranglers and knocked one cigarette free from the pack along with a lighter.

"Les?" Gene asked. "You okay?"

"Somebody got killed out here, Gene. Weren't no poaching."

"What?"

"Les said them tracks is two fellas dragging a third. More than likely after they shot him in the head," said Tom.

Lester took a long pull on his cigarette and waved Gene over to him. When Gene stood alongside him, Lester pointed down to the murky water of the swamp. "You see it, Gene?"

Gene looked down Lester's arm, following it to the hand, the finger, and what it pointed to. "I can't see shit in there, Lester."

Lester pulled his hand away. "Keep looking. You'll see it."

Gene focused and looked past and through the swirling blue-gray smoke from Lester's cigarette as it dissipated. "Is that —"

"The roof of a car?" said Lester. "Sure looks like it to me."

"About three feet down?" asked Tom.

"Yup."

Gene stuck his hand out to Lester. "Gimme one of those butts, Les, will ya?"

Lester handed him a smoke. "Hundred dollars says old boy's down there too."

"Goddamn," said Tom. "It's a hell of a place to get killed, ain't it?"

Lester brought the smoke to his lips and tilted his head back, closing his eyes to the bright sun above them. He exhaled and blew the smoke skyward. "Ain't they all, little brother? Ain't they all?"

An hour later, while Lieutenant Billings was in the break room trying to sleep away the double at the Sea Breeze he'd finally come off of a few hours before, he heard his Nokia buzz. Behind him, the sizzle and boil of the ancient percolator sent the smell of tar-dark coffee wafting under the Casual Male XL sport coat he'd wrapped his head in to make something close to darkness for himself. He didn't move toward the phone, letting it buzz itself in erratic arcs across the table. Finally, he said, "Will somebody get my fucking phone?" to whatever creature was shuffling through Second Patrol's break-room drawers somewhere to his left.

"Lieutenant Billings's phone," he heard a disembodied voice say, then a few seconds later he felt a tap on his shoulder. Billings pulled the sport coat off his head and sat up, blinking through the unnatural yellow light at one of his uniforms, who was mouthing, *Are you here?* with the phone held to her chest. He gave her the give-it-here motion, mouthed, *Thank you* to the patrolwoman, and closed his eyes again. He kicked his chair back, put his feet on the table, and sighed "Lieutenant Billings" into the mouthpiece.

"Hey, LT, your name came up on a BOLO for a Dodge Charger, partial plate XY, bull bars on the front."

"No, that's Detective Wheel, Violent Crimes. Or her partner, what's his name. New guy, whatever."

"Sorry, LT, I called the number in the system."

"Don't worry about it." Billings dug around in his inside jacket pocket until he found his notepad and pen and shifted the phone to his other ear. "I didn't ask—who's this?"

"Gene Marshall, Conservation Police officer."

"No shit. Okay. What happened, someone, like, run over a fucking deer or something?"

"No, sir. Chesapeake PD search and recovery team is about to hook the vehicle up to a wrecker and pull it out of the water."

"Thanks for the heads-up. You first on scene, then?" Billings started scratching info into the notepad.

"That's right. Chesapeake PD took over when they got here, but dispatch told me about the BOLO when I called it in. Figured you'd want to know."

"Give me...shit, I don't know where it is."

"You're an hour out, give or take."

"Okay. Walk me through it when I get there?"

"Of course. Sir, you mind if I ask what's the Charger mixed up in on your end?"

"Double homicide."

"Well, we'll find out once the car comes out of the water but pretty sure there's a dead guy in the trunk."

"Thanks, Gene. I'm on my way." Lieutenant Billings wrote *+1* in the notepad, slung on his sport coat, and headed for the door. When he reached his unmarked, he clipped his phone to the dash and pulled out a card from his wallet. He punched in the number for Matt Jacobson, assignments editor, *Virginian-Pilot,* put it on speaker, and pulled out of the parking lot toward the military highway.

"Matt Jacobson," said the voice through the speaker.

"Matt, Jack Billings."

"What can I do for you, Lieutenant?"

"I was wondering if I could interest you in buying me dinner at Mizuno?"

"Pretty pricey spot, Jack."

"Twenty dollars says your next call is to make a reservation."

"Okay. You're on. Let me hear what you got."

FOURTEEN

Cat looked at her watch, then over at Arman, with his eyes darting around the terminal. Quarter after one. Too many faces moving too fast. She was about to wave him and Lamar over and call the whole thing off when her phone buzzed in her bag. She pulled out the phone and walked over to the bench where the two men sat and held up two fingers.

Lamar leaned over to Arman and said, "Two minutes, and we're gonna bail." He reached over and awkwardly patted Arman on his shoulder and then said, "We tried."

Arman nodded, took a deep breath, and let his eyes fall to the dirty concrete. "Okay," he said. "Okay. What now?"

Lamar just nodded toward Detective Wheel, flipping her phone open.

"Wheel," she said.

"Hey, Wheel, Lieutenant Billings. Game warden found your Charger in some swamp or some shit way out in Bum-Fuck, Egypt."

"No shit, Jack? Jesus. Who's on it?"

"Chesapeake PD. I don't know who. I got it from...hold on a second...Gene Marshall, Conservation Police."

"You know I'm in DC right now. Can we get anybody out there?"

"Detective, I am your knight in shining armor. I'm gonna drive out to this mosquito-swamp motherfucker myself."

"Are you bringing the reporters with you or what?"

"Wheel, I'm insulted. You know how much I just love police work."

"What's-his-face is buying you dinner, isn't he?"

"Mizuno."

"Well, at least give me something before you give it to him, will ya?"

"I'll call you when I know what's what. Right now looks like one dead guy in the trunk with a GSW to the coconut. I don't know how they'd know that yet. That's just what the game warden told me."

"Let me know. And get me this game warden's info. I'm gonna want to talk to him."

"You got it. Oh, yeah, one more thing. Guy at the *Pilot* is gonna have one of his reporters call you."

"About the Charger?"

"I don't know. I think he's got her on the John Doe at the beach. Anyways, Sally something. She's gonna call you when she gets back from DC."

"Jack."

"What?"

"Come on, Jack. Any chance you asked what she's doing in DC?"

"He said she's meeting some tipster up there."

"Did he say where?"

"Hold on a sec, Wheel. Jeez Louise. So pushy. I do outrank you, remember?"

Arman and Lamar both looked at Catherine's foot tapping

impatiently on the concrete, wondering what had her so worked up.

Cat heard Billings's weight shifting in the driver's seat, digging through his pockets and the console. "Tell me she's meeting someone at the bus station, Lieutenant."

There was silence on the other end of the line as Billings stopped looking for his notes. "Yeah," he said quietly. "Yeah, Cat. Meeting a source is supposed to come in on a Greyhound. Jesus. Sherlock Holmes got nothing on you."

"Compared to you, Jack."

"Fuck yourself."

"Get me her number, will you? ASAP?"

"Of course. Hey, Wheel, now that I think of it, he sounded a little worried about the kid. Said he didn't like the meet. Y'all watch your six, okay?"

"Yeah. Hey."

"What's up?"

"Thanks, LT," she said.

"Seriously, Catherine. Sounds like Important Police Shit," he said, and ended the call.

Arman and Lamar just looked at her, waiting. "I think we got something," she said.

Sally and Trey stood on the steps of Union Station, not knowing they were waiting for a dead man to appear. They checked their watches and then each other's faces to see if either thought it was worth staying longer.

"What do you think, Sal?"

"You'd think whoever it is would be on time, at least. What time you got?"

"Quarter of two."

"Yeah. Me too. Can we give it five more?"

"Probably better to wait until the rain lets up a little before you head back anyway."

Sally scanned the faces swirling around her, but most of them dashed to the waiting taxis. Not many lingered, and those who did seemed unlikely candidates for a meet like this. A handful of tourists in red, white, and blue shirts and hats. A few Acela riders left over from the previous workweek. Two young boys drummed a steady go-go beat on upturned buckets just under the awning enough to clear the rain.

"Maybe it's not—" Sally's phone rang. She looked at Trey and let it ring three more times.

He said, "Sally. Answer it," and mimed pulling it out of her bag.

She took the phone out and flipped it open, her throat suddenly dry, her voice shriveled up in her mouth as she said, "Sally Ewell, *Virginian-Pilot*," twirling underneath the arches as if she might spot the caller on the other end of the line.

"Sally, this is Detective Catherine Wheel, Norfolk PD. Tell me where you are right now. We need to talk."

Trey asked, "What is it?"

Cops, she mouthed.

"Sally, this is very important. You were supposed to meet a source at Union Station. He's not coming."

"How do you—"

"Sally, I'm here at the station with another detective. The man you were supposed to meet is dead. Those bodies piling up at Ocean View, the ones your editor told you about? They're related."

"How do you—" Sally whispered, leaning down and into the stone wall at the arch's base.

"I just got off the phone with Matt Jacobson. One more time, Sally. Please listen carefully. I need you to tell me where you are, and we'll come to you."

"Okay...okay. We're out front under the awning, center arch."

"Who's with you, Sally?"

"A friend."

"Sal, I can't—" Trey started.

Sally lifted her hand to cut him off. "You trust him?" Catherine asked.

"Yeah, of course."

"All right, hon," said Cat. "Stay put, keep your eyes on. We'll be there in a minute."

Sally closed the phone, took a deep breath, and shut her eyes tightly. She opened them again and looked up at Trey.

"Sal, what the hell is going on?"

"We're waiting for a dead guy."

"What are you talking about?"

"I don't know. I don't know," said Sally. The words came out so quickly that Trey had to chase them down to keep up. "Norfolk police said my source is dead."

"Sal, I don't know if I can get mixed up in this." He put his hands on his hips and looked away from her. "Fuck. I'm a congressional aide."

Sally glared at him and jabbed a finger in his chest. "Carter fucking West the Third, if you bail on me now, I'll never forgive you." She wasn't crying by the time she finished the sentence, but she was about as close to it as you could get.

Trey looked down at her finger still pressing against the front of his shirt, then put his arm around her. "All right," he said. "All right. I'm here, Sal. I'm not going anywhere."

A few minutes later, a blue Caprice pulled down the road and cut into the taxi lane. Catherine jumped out of the front passenger seat and left the door open. Hunched against the rain, she jogged toward the entrance with her badge held above her.

Sally saw her and waved and began to head toward her, but Trey grabbed her arm and said, "Wait."

Catherine walked up to them, and Sally saw her face beneath the rain-dampened curls. Cat removed her hand from her holstered revolver and held it out to Sally, not yet acknowledging Trey. "Sally, I'm Cat Wheel. I'd really like you to come this way, please, ma'am."

Sally was still holding her hand when she nodded. "Okay." She felt the detective's hand on her back starting to gently guide her out into the rain.

Catherine looked back at Trey with a squint and said, "You're the friend?"

"Yes, ma'am," he said.

"Well, c'mon if you're coming."

Trey followed and watched the detective hold the rear passenger door open for Sally. Another passenger, a dark-haired man, was already in the back seat. Trey tried to slide in behind Sally.

"No," she said. "You ride up front with Detective Adams."

He stood there letting the rain fall on him for a moment and watched the detective get in after Sally, sandwiching her in.

"Why?" he asked.

"'Cause I'm the police, and I said so."

Then the front passenger window rolled down, and he saw

the other detective lean toward it from the driver's seat and say, "Get in the car, chief."

"Fuck," he said. He opened the door, slid into the seat, and buckled up. He met the eyes of the black-haired man in the rearview and then looked over at Detective Adams, who threw the shifter into drive and peeled out toward Columbus Circle, water fishtailing behind them. "You said it, brother," Detective Adams said. Then into the rearview, he asked, "Where to, Cat?"

FIFTEEN

Early that morning, the two men who'd pushed the Charger into the Great Dismal Swamp the night before walked out onto the breezeway of an EconoLodge just off North Carolina Highway 17 where it passed through Elizabeth City. One packed two duffels with the sun coming up while the other went down the stairs and across the parking lot to the lobby and grabbed two big Styrofoam cups of coffee. They looked like half the men of a certain age in the South did, more or less. Oakley sunglasses and steel-toe ropers. One wore a T-shirt with an eagle perched on a Panhead chopper, and the other was in a billowy fishing shirt with a visor on above his shades. Jimmy had a thick beard while Chris was shaved clean and deeply tanned by years in the sun. They both had medium-reg haircuts and gave off the air of being veterans without trying to.

Jimmy finished packing the duffels, slung each one over a shoulder, and walked down the open staircase to the silver 3500 Duramax parked in the spot just below their room. He saw the other man walking toward him with the coffees and shouted, "Chris. Bed or back seat?"

"Put them in the bed, Jimmy. We ain't going that far."

Jimmy dropped the tailgate, slid the duffels just behind the truck's cab, and closed it again. Chris put one of the coffees on the back bumper, leaned against the tailgate, took out a can of cherry Skoal, and offered it to Jimmy.

"Your boyfriend know you dip cherry?" Jimmy said.

Chris snorted and put a lipper in. "Fuck you, Jimmy. That title work squared away?"

"Yeah. All good. Let's dump this bitch and go home."

They drove a mile up 17 to its intersection with 158 in Elizabeth City and pulled the dually into a circular gravel driveway. A small converted shipping container functioned as the office for Marty's Auto-Rama, six cars of various makes and models flanking it on either side and bordering the driveway.

They both got out and walked back to the tailgate. Each man picked up a duffel, and they walked to the two pallets that made a small porch in front of the office and dropped them to either side. Chris banged on the door and stepped back. A man opened it, gave Chris the hairy eyeball, and nodded toward Jimmy. "Who's this *Roadhouse*-looking motherfucker?"

"Nobody. How you doing, Eunice?" Chris asked.

Eunice dapped him up and gave Jimmy another nod, this one halfway toward an acknowledgment. "Can't complain, can't complain."

"Ain't a damn soul listen if we did," Chris said.

"I know that's right. We talking paper or what?"

"Come check the goods," Chris said.

Eunice stepped out onto the pallet and did a little half jog toward the truck. Jimmy took in the man's three-piece, five-button suit and alligator shoes and said, "You gonna get hot in that suit, brother."

Eunice stopped and took in the Silverado. "Chris, you gotta shut this cracker up," he said. "Giving me fashion advice looking like he buys his shit from the clearance rack at Walmart."

Chris smirked at Jimmy and got a shrug back. "He's cool, Eunice. Swear to God."

"He might be cool, but he ain't *cool*-cool." He started circling the truck and rubbing his hands together. "All right, we got a '06 Silverado thirty-five hundred. What's the miles on it?"

"Seventy-five," Chris answered.

"Kind of a lot for an '06."

"Work is work, brother."

"What do you want for it?"

"Gimme a swap?"

"What with?"

Chris pointed to a '96 Camry. "How's the motor on that one?"

"Fucking Toyota, man. Like it just rolled out the factory."

Chris reached in his pocket, pulled out the keys, and tossed them to Eunice. Jimmy stood behind him with *What the fuck* written on his face.

"All right, gimme just a second," Eunice said and turned toward the office.

"Hey, Eunice, it's clean, no bullshit?"

"I'm insulted you think I'd do you like that. But yeah, clean as a motherfucking whistle." He went inside and came back out with the keys to the Camry and placed them in Chris's palm. He held on to Chris's hand and gently pulled the other man close to him. "You getting too old for this soldier-of-fortune shit, my guy," he said quietly.

"What am I gonna do, sell cars?" Chris answered.

"You always were a no-good rat mother—" He laughed, and they slapped hands and gave each other a pound on the back.

"Love you too, bro," Chris said and then nodded toward Jimmy. "Come on. Get the bags, and let's go."

They rode in silence until they were on a bridge over the

gently rippling blackness of the Pasquotank. "Chris, what's that Chevy worth, like four or five times this piece of shit?"

"Trust me. It's a bargain. That truck'll be sold on three or four more times by next week. Not only will it never get back to us, but it also won't ever get back to Eunice."

"Weird name for a dude, ain't it?"

Chris laughed. "You should have told him that."

"How the hell did you hook up with him anyway?"

"He was my platoon sergeant in Mogadishu."

"No shit?"

"Baddest motherfucker alive."

"No shit."

Not long after, they turned the Camry north in Barco and headed toward Currituck to catch the nine a.m. ferry to Knotts Island. They loaded up the car with a few minutes to spare and leaned against the railing as the ferry pushed off the terminal and into the Currituck Sound. Jimmy watched the land recede behind them and the water shimmering in the morning sun out to the horizon. He saw Chris walk over to the pilothouse and talk to the ferryman, and then he came back and put another lipper in and waited, turning over his own view in the privacy of his mind.

After a while, Jimmy saw the ferryman signal to Chris, and Chris nodded to Jimmy. They walked over to the trunk of the Camry and pulled the duffels out. Chris looked back up to the pilothouse, waited for a moment, then dropped his duffel over the side. "Go ahead, Jimmy."

Jimmy dropped his too, and they leaned back over the railing. "What's with all that?" he asked, looking toward the pilothouse.

"Deepest part of the sound."

"Seems like a lot of extra steps. They ain't never gonna find that dude."

"Maybe. Maybe not. But I'm gonna make it hard for them if they try."

Jimmy went back to contemplating the water. The breeze picked up a little salt spray as the ferry went.

"And Jimmy," Chris said.

"Yeah."

"You're not supposed to talk about this shit out loud."

Jimmy took it in silently, intelligent enough to grasp the gravity of his error.

"Last night, we watched a thirty-five-lap Sportsman race at the Dixieland," Chris said. "Had too many pops and slept it off at the EconoLodge. You tracking?"

"Tracking."

"Someone asks you about Harris, the correct answer is what?" Chris asked.

Jimmy thought for a moment before he said, "Who is Harris?"

SIXTEEN

The gate at the WMA was closed when Billings arrived. He got out, unwrapped the chain from the entrance, pushed it open with his foot, walked back to the car, and got in. He didn't make it all that far up the causeway before a uniformed Chesapeake PD officer flagged him down and waved him over to the side. When he got out, he put his hand up to shade his eyes and, looking down the causeway, saw half a dozen or more emergency vehicles lined up ahead of him: An ambulance. Three patrol cars. Gene Marshall's Blazer. A couple of unmarked cruisers, the crime scene tech's van, and a big converted panel truck from the search and recovery team. He showed his badge to the uniform, got a hat tip back from him, and walked up the clear side of the causeway to the show.

When he got to the end of the line, he saw a group of men, most of them uniformed, circled around a body on a gurney. Behind them, a wrecker was already loaded with the Charger on the back. The wrecker driver ratcheted the vehicle by its wheels to the flatbed, and Billings noticed water still trickled out from the undercarriage. About half the men turned around at the sound of his approach, and he lifted his badge up casually just in case.

Gene Marshall put his hand up and said, "Lieutenant Billings?"

"Yeah. Marshall, right?" He stuck his hand out, and they shook.

Gene waved him over and introduced him to the assembled group. "This is Lieutenant Billings, Norfolk PD. They had the BOLO out on the Charger."

Nods and hellos all around. They made space for him in the circle, and he gave the body on the gurney a once-over. Caucasian male. Maybe thirty-five, forty. Discolored and goosebumped from being submerged overnight. He knew without looking that the hands and feet would be wrinkled too, as if the dead man had merely been in a bath too long. "ME?" he asked. Some shrugs. He recognized one of the suits from Chesapeake. "Martinez, right?"

"Yeah, LT. Good to see you. ME is on the way. Cause of death is a no-brainer."

"Jesus Christ, Martinez." Someone chuckled.

"Hey, come on, I didn't even mean it like that," he said.

Billings looked down at the bloodless void of an exit wound at the center of the dead man's brow line. "Any ID on him?"

"Not a thing," said Martinez. "Car's completely empty. We'll process it, of course, but I'm not gonna get my hopes up."

"Doesn't look like the critters got to him, at least," Billings said.

"So how's this victor hooked up on your end?"

"Guy reports a suspicious vehicle creeping around his motel, couple hours later him and the perp both are perforated."

"Oh, damn. That was down at Ocean View, right? I heard that was some cowboy shit," one of the uniforms said.

"Yes, sir. Guns blazing."

"Is it true the old man went out like Audie Murphy?" someone asked.

"Audie Murphy lived, dumbass," one of the paramedics shouted. "That's how he went all Hollywood movie star and shit." He got the bird back in reply. "I'm just saying, dudes who get smoked don't get famous."

"You think this is Thing Two laid out?" Detective Martinez asked Billings.

"Could be. We think the other guy got hit, maybe. You check the old boy for injuries?"

"No. Like I said, cause of death—"

"No-brainer. Right. You mind?" Billings asked.

Martinez looked at his partner and shrugged. "Hey, no sweat, LT. Just tell the ME you wanted to do his job for him."

Billings looked down at the dead man, hunching over close enough that his tie skirted along the side of the gurney. "Who's got gloves?" He looked up just in time to see one of the paramedics toss a pair over to him, and he snatched them out of the air. He put them on, and the men circled behind him casually, curious to see if he'd find something interesting.

Because of the way the killing wound had an undeniable pull on one's attention, they had overlooked the circle Mr. Peters's Colt Python had hole-punched through the dead man's earlobe. Billings used his pen as a pointer and indicated the wound to his audience. An argument began behind him over who should or shouldn't have seen it. It had been easy enough to miss, the hole tucked discreetly in the cavity just below the top curve of the ear. Billings stood up. "That's not where those weirdos put the fucking...you know those..."

"Gauges?" one of the paramedics answered.

Billings turned around to point at him. "Exactly," he said

enthusiastically, then noticed the paramedic staring at him coldly had a big cork wheel in each earlobe.

He turned back to the cops with a half shrug and a look that said, *What are you gonna do?*

The other men in the circle leaned in to get a good look at the bullet wound. "Good catch, LT," said one.

"That's one lucky motherfucker," said another. "A couple more inches the other way—"

"You are such a fucking moron," said his partner. "Do you not see the giant hole in this asshole's face?"

"You know what I mean. The principle of it."

Billings moved on to a careful examination of the man's wet clothes. He took the pen and stretched the work shirt out flat in a couple of places, looking for additional wounds. After a minute, he made it to the sleeves, where he saw the torn fabric near the forearm. He began to roll the sleeve up and saw that a bandage had come undone but was still wrapped loosely around the man's arm. One of the crime scene techs rushed over with a bag, and Billings dropped the bandage in. He got the sleeve up to the elbow and looked down at the raw streak of the graze.

"That your guy?" Gene asked.

"Dollars to doughnuts," he said. He looked at the others. "At least tell me you checked his pockets."

"Sorry, LT. We didn't strip him down, but no ID. Promise."

Billings peeled off the gloves and looked for somewhere to toss them. The paramedic who'd eyeballed him before put his hand out, took the gloves, and dropped them in a biohazard bag. "Thanks, kid. I...you know..."

"No problem."

"Gene, you mind giving me the rundown?"

"Sure thing, Lieutenant Billings."

Officer Marshall steered the lieutenant away from the circle and farther up the causeway to the crime scene location proper. They sidestepped cones marking out tire tracks and yellow number plates indicating different sets of footprints. Gene stopped them when they stood over the beginning of the dried blood that continued along the center of the causeway. "So you got the drag marks to either side, sir. You can see where the three sets of footprints stop right here, and the two go on out wide of the blood yonder."

"That's some *Walker, Texas Ranger* shit right there, Officer Marshall."

"What's that?"

"Tracking. Laying out the scenario just so. Not even knowing it's a crime scene. That's some good-ass police work."

"I can't really take credit for it. Believe it or not, it was just a couple country boys who owed me a favor."

"Uh-huh," Billings said absentmindedly, kneeling down and taking in the scene. "So these aren't penny loafers leaving these footprints."

"No. Definitely some kind of boot. Maybe hiking or hunting."

Billings took out his pad. "Throw some brand names at me."

"Oh, top brands are probably Danner, Vasque, Merrell. Go to any REI or Bass Pro, and they'll have a hundred boots could have left these tracks."

"All right, that's a good place to start. And the vic?"

"Well, your techs will tell you for sure, but it's a dually, no doubt. I'd guess an F-350 or Ram. Maybe Chevy. Can't think of any others off the top of my head."

They walked back to the gurney just as the medical examiner arrived.

"Doc," Billings said.

"Hey, Lieutenant. Yours?"

"Martinez's," Billings said, nodding in the direction of the young detective from Chesapeake. "I'm sitting in for Wheel. She's gonna want to stop by and say hello to John Doe here."

"She always does," said Dr. Martin.

He went over to Martinez, and they shook hands. "You work with her a lot?" Martinez asked.

Billings looked down at the dead man's shoes and back up at the younger officer. "We've both been in the department a long time." He took his thumb and ran it around the outsole, taking off a film of muck and grime, trying to find the make.

"How is she to work with?" Martinez asked.

Billings felt raised lettering on the outsole and rubbed a little more firmly. Merrell. He knew what the detective was asking. Hadn't missed the subtle stress on the word *she* in Martinez's question. Billings probably would have asked it himself in the younger man's position if he hadn't known her so long. He took one boot in his hand and turned the foot up to get a good look at the sole, closed his eyes, and compared them in his mind to the tracks he'd just seen. He opened his eyes, backed away from the body, and stood there with his hands on his hips, pondering. "Well, Martinez," he said. "If someone killed me, I'd want Catherine to catch the case."

SEVENTEEN

Twenty minutes after Lamar pulled the unmarked out of Columbus Circle, he hit the exit off the Leesburg Turnpike. No one spoke as he pulled the car into a garage at Tysons Corner and slowed down to a crawl. The motor echoed through the cavernous parking deck, and the wheels *thump-thump*ed over the metal seams in the concrete surface as they ascended in corkscrews to the top. Lamar stopped the car. "Well?" he asked.

"Someone's gotta tell me what the hell is going on," said Trey. His phone buzzed, and he pulled it out, checked the rearview mirror, and flipped it open. His thumb hovered almost imperceptibly over End but then punched it.

Cat thought she caught a glimpse of a 757 area code and filed it away. "I need to stretch my legs," she said. She opened the door, and Lamar cut the motor.

They piled out of the car and took up various positions around it. Sally leaned against the trunk and rubbed her forearms with her hands like she aimed to smooth some wrinkle out of them. Arman stuck his hands in his pockets and stared at the ground. Lamar hung on the driver's-side doorframe with his foot up, looked toward Trey, and said, "You first."

Trey put the phone back in his pocket and pointed his finger at Lamar. "Listen here, goddamn it—" he began.

Sally interrupted him, still rubbing her arms like Virginia in July had a chill no one else could feel. "Okay. So someone left an envelope with my name on it at the *Pilot*," Sally began. "There was a note asking for a meet today at Union Station and a thumb drive. The note said the thumb drive was 'air gap only,' so I run it by the tech guys at the paper, and they're freaking out."

Cat leaned against the railing and lit a cigarette. "Say that one more time?" Cat said.

"What?"

"Air gap only, you said?"

"Yeah, that's what it said in the note."

Lamar looked over at Cat, and she held up her hand as if to say, *Not right now.* "Okay, sorry. Keep going," said Cat.

"So the tech guys don't want me to put it in our system. They're worried about a virus, acting like this is some super-top-secret stuff. My editor wasn't even sure about the meet. So I call Trey and ask him to come."

"And you're like—what? The boyfriend?" Lamar asked Trey.

Trey ignored him and turned to Catherine. "I'm an old friend from college. We think the mystery man wanted me involved."

"Why?" she asked.

"I'm a congressional aide. Sally's been doing some digging on a company my boss is interested in."

"And that company would be?" Catherine asked.

"Decision Tree," Trey said.

"Okay, so what's Decision Tree?"

"PMCs," Lamar answered.

"That's right," said Trey.

Arman looked at Catherine. "Private military contractors," he said.

"Jesus," she said. She took a deep drag off her smoke and briefly closed her eyes.

"Detective," Sally said. "You said the guy who set up the meet with me is dead. How? How do you know?"

"You know that John Doe on Ocean View Beach Matt Jacobson asked you to look into?"

"Yeah?"

"We think he was looking for Mr. Bajalan here. He had a return ticket to come back on a bus so we figured we'd see if anyone showed up thinking he'd be there."

"Jesus," Sally said. "And there we were."

Arman looked at Sally. "These guys, contractors, they're trying to kill me. They think I have something I don't have."

"What are they looking for?" she asked. She looked at the man standing across from her. It was hard to imagine a person more different than her, but she could see a sadness in his eyes that mirrored her own.

"A video," he said. He felt the younger woman's eyes on him. He thought she was looking at him with pity, but when their eyes met, he knew that it was recognition.

"Arman witnessed a massacre in Mosul," Lamar said. "He got it on video and gave it to his LT."

"You were a terp?" Trey asked.

He nodded.

"So why not have your LT send it up the chain?"

"I don't know. Maybe he did. Maybe no one cared."

"I remember that," Trey said. "You're talking about the university attack?"

"That's right."

"I thought that was investigated by the Coalition Provisional Authority. They said it was AIF."

Arman shrugged. "I was there."

"Did you give testimony?"

"I was going to. I never got the chance. I was attacked after I reported it. Everyone thought I'd been exposed as a collaborator, but I know it was the same men."

"So what's your boss's angle on this?" Catherine asked Trey.

"Decision Tree is up for a multibillion-dollar government contract. My boss wants to make sure they don't get it."

"Why?" said Lamar.

"They've got a reputation. Let's just say people might be more receptive to Arman's story now than they were a few years back."

"And so?" Arman asked.

Trey shrugged. "It's not about whether they'd believe you—"

"It's about what you can prove," Arman finished.

"Arman," Trey said, "I have to ask. Do you have any animosity toward the U.S. government?"

"The fuck, man?" Lamar said.

"My people are going to want to know," said Trey.

"I don't know how to answer that," Arman said.

"It's simple," he said. "Friend or enemy?"

Arman sighed. "Mr. West, my people have no friends but the mountains," he said. "But you are not my enemy. All I've given, I would hope that much is clear."

A cold silence settled over them, one that needed to be broken. Sally spoke up. "Detective, if Mr. Bajalan is in danger, why isn't he in some kind of protective custody?"

"I can see you haven't had much experience working with

the commonwealth," Catherine said. "There aren't the resources for it on the local level, and the state might give us some half-assed window dressing at best. I don't think half-assed is gonna cut it under these circumstances."

"Besides," Lamar said, "the SIV he got was supposed to get him out of danger. It works in Iraq if there's a bounty on you for collaborating. It doesn't do anything once you get to the States. Right now, we're Arman's protective custody," said Lamar.

"What about us?" Sally asked. She regretted it immediately. "Arman," she said, "I'm sorry. I didn't mean to make it about myself."

"It's okay," he said.

"I'm afraid we don't have an answer on that yet," said Catherine.

"Are you gonna bring on the FBI?" Trey asked.

"For what? A John Doe we don't even have a cause of death on? We don't have the first bit of evidence except this John Doe is more than meets the eye."

"The one who sent me the envelope," said Sally.

"He's got four passports and a suppressed nine-millimeter," said Lamar.

"Yeah, that sounds like something the FBI might be interested in. Anyway, a lot of bad shit went down after the university attack," Trey said. "Coalition casualties spiked to the highest levels of the war."

"Lotta bad shit going down now," said Lamar.

Sally turned away from the group and stared at the ground. "When was this? The university attack?"

"Late October or maybe early November 2004," said Trey.

"November second," Arman said. "A week later, they killed my wife and son."

"November ninth?" Sally asked. Tears welled in her eyes. She took a few deep breaths to hold them back. The bitterness of her own loss receded and left a space for her to grieve for his.

Arman looked at Sally. He saw that the mention of the date had sent her reeling and that she was trying to collect herself. "Yes," he said. He wondered what had happened then. The rain was long gone, the clouds to the west gray and drifting toward the northern Shenandoah. The blue sky the drifting clouds revealed sent the sunlight steaming up from the rain-soaked parking deck. A breeze whistled by and passed through their silence.

Trey was the first to break it. "God, I'm so sorry, Arman," he said. "That's probably how they buried the attack on you. There was such a high level of insurgent activity around then."

"But the spike was just around Mosul?" Sally asked.

"No. Whole country," Lamar said. "I even heard the argument that it set off Fallujah."

Cat noticed Trey's eyes shoot toward Sally when he heard the word *Fallujah*. She studied Sally, but it didn't seem as though a single word could send her deeper into the well of her thoughts than she was already.

"So this John Doe, he's, like, from one of the intelligence agencies or something?" Trey asked.

"Well, I don't know if he was a spy, but he was damn sure something," Catherine answered.

"Former Australian SAS, most likely," said Lamar.

Trey tucked his chin down to his chest, thinking. "The Aussies took part in the invasion in '03 and didn't stick around. They didn't come back until '05. Even when they came back, they were down south. Nowhere near Mosul."

"Keep talking," said Cat.

"He's wondering why the Australian government or our mystery man acting solo would be so interested in Arman when they probably had an entire ocean between them and what went down," said Lamar. "And, hey, man," he said to Trey, "sorry for busting your balls. I didn't clock you as a vet."

"He's not," Sally said.

"Well, you sure know a lot about what was going on for someone who wasn't there."

"I worked for the Coalition Provisional Authority out of college."

"Doing what?" Arman asked.

Trey tried to look away, not wanting to meet anyone's eyes at that moment, but he found himself more or less surrounded by the assembled group. He looked down at the tops of his shoes and said quietly, "I helped secure bids for outsourced services. KBR, cooks, laundry. A huge amount of the war effort had already been privatized at the outset. Logistics. Support. Pretty much everything besides the individual soldiers, the weapons they carried, and the vehicles they rode on."

"But contractors too?" Cat asked.

"Yeah, them too. The process my boss wants to stop had already started by then."

"That why the congressman wanted you on staff?" Cat asked delicately. She sensed his discomfort and knew there was a fine line between probing and accusing, so she walked it lightly. "Because you had existing connections to these guys?" She made a mental note to ask Sally who he'd call with a 757 area code besides her once they were alone.

"I think so. He needed someone who knew how that stuff worked."

"Goddamn, are you trying to tell me a congressman didn't know how it worked?" Lamar said.

"Congressmen don't need to know. They just do what the whip tells them."

Lamar walked over to Cat and held his hand out. "Lemme get a butt, Cat." She gave him one and lit him up, and he leaned back against the car and blew the smoke from the first cigarette he'd had since he'd separated from the army into the sky. He stood there quietly for a minute, then said, "I gotta be honest with y'all. I find that super-disappointing."

Catherine knew people were always trying to find some big conspiracy to explain all the bad things that happened in the world, but she didn't believe that was the way things worked. Some people took what they wanted. Most people didn't even get what they needed. There wasn't anyone trying to hide it as far as she could tell.

She glanced over at Sally again. Saw her nervously look off across the low skyline. Beige and green and black asphalt below squat glass towers, industrial rooftop air handlers, and gleaming white department-store entrances. "We can't stay up here forever," said Cat. "Why don't we head over to the Marriott and get a couple rooms for the night. Regroup. Figure out our next move." She went to the unmarked car's trunk, pulled out an overnight bag, set it on the quarter panel, and unzipped it. She pulled out a large plastic evidence bag that held the laptop they'd collected from the dead man's room at the Square and Compass Inn. "Sally, please tell me you've got that thumb drive on you."

Sally seemed to refocus her attention. She patted her handbag. "Yeah. I've got it."

Cat dropped her butt on the ground and toed it out. "I

don't know about y'all, but I sure would like to know what this man came halfway around the world to tell Ms. Ewell here."

An hour later, Arman looked out the window of their hotel room: the skies gray with the coming evening; the lights in the corporate office buildings scattered randomly above the nearby highway cloverleaf. They'd gotten two adjoining rooms, and the heavy door between them stood open, propped in place by a luggage stand. Sally sat at a small round table in the corner of the room. Cat had her hands on the chair back, looming like an angel on her shoulder. Lamar sat on the corner of the bed and tapped his foot absentmindedly. Trey stood behind him with his arms crossed.

"So," Sally said. "I just put it in?"

"Yeah," Trey said. "Maybe there's more encryption."

"Or maybe he bet on himself," said Lamar.

"There's only one way to find out," Arman said quietly.

Sally picked up the USB drive and turned it over in her hands for a moment. Then she put it in the port and powered on the laptop. A file image popped up on-screen against a plain blue backdrop and immediately opened documents. Not just a few but hundreds, each popping open and stacking on the screen until the first seemed to disappear into a distance given depth and shape out of the two-dimensional screen. Sally moved her finger across the trackpad. She ran the arrow along the opened files as if flipping through the pages of a book.

There were Excel files and .doc files and JPEG images and PDFs and file extensions that no one recognized. They watched the screen populate for what seemed like an eternity but was, in actuality, closer to fifteen seconds. Sally leaned back in her chair. "What now?"

"Click on something," Trey said.

She clicked on the first document, which was hundreds of pages. She scrolled through a series of articles of incorporation and corresponding certificates from various states: Wyoming, Nevada, Delaware, Wyoming, Wyoming, Nevada, Delaware, Nevada...

"What's up with that?" asked Lamar.

"Secrecy. You can incorporate in Wyoming with a registered agent. No one ever has to know who the actual owners are. You can stack shell corps too. Tax-haven stuff," Trey said.

"How about liability?" Sally asked.

Trey shook his head. "Unlikely."

"Click another," said Catherine.

Sally moved the arrow to the middle of the stack and clicked on the edge of a file. A series of sentences appeared, nested beneath each other like digital Russian dolls. "E-mails?" she asked.

Trey leaned over for a closer look. "Jesus Christ. These are dot-mil addresses."

"What?" asked Catherine.

"Guys, we can't read this stuff," he said. "Seriously. We need to shut this down and take a step back."

Lamar stood up from the bed. "Look, man, we're working murders. This is evidence. We're gonna read whatever the fuck we want."

Trey glared at him. "These are CENTCOM e-mails, Detective."

"Is that who'd have jurisdiction over Arman's report?" asked Catherine.

"Yes," Trey said. "But we can't let this go public without some kind of...goddamn it, some kind of review."

Sally turned around. "So they can come back from Central Command completely redacted? Bullshit, Trey. I'm not giving up my story."

"Story? Are you serious, Sal? You think they're gonna let you write about it?" he said, gesturing to Catherine and Lamar. "And no offense, Mr. Bajalan, but you're not even a citizen. You shouldn't even be in this room in the first place."

"No," said Arman. "I think that was the plan all along."

Trey's chin sank to his chest. He raised his hand as if to ask for a time-out. "Arman, I'm sorry."

"I think you'll find I have a good working relationship with the fine reporters at the *Virginian-Pilot,* Mr. West," said Catherine.

His head shot back up. "Are you people fucking serious? Do you understand the words *national security*?"

"Go ahead and keep on popping off like that, man," said Lamar. "Keep doing it—"

"Listen," interrupted Catherine, "we'll figure something out. If you two want to have a dick-measuring contest, go find a fucking ruler. Now, calm down. Sally, close out of the e-mails, please."

Sally closed the file and pushed the laptop back across the table. "Do we even know what we're looking for?" she asked.

"Is there any search function?" asked Arman.

Sally pulled the laptop back toward her. There was no search function for the totality of the data, but some of the files were individually searchable. "A little. It might be weeks of work going through it all instead of months."

Trey looked at his watch. "I've got hearings to prep for. If we're gonna figure something out, let's do it now."

"I need a minute," Sally said.

"Why don't we all take five. Cool off and come back with a way forward. Sound good?" Catherine said. She looked around, and everyone else nodded.

"I need to make a call," Trey said. "I've got to give some kind of indication that there's been a security breach. I can't just pretend I didn't see hacked CENTCOM e-mails."

"Yeah, roger that," Lamar said.

"Okay, that's fair," said Catherine. "Just be careful what you say. This isn't theoretical. If one hair on Arman's head is disturbed, Mr. West..."

"I understand," Trey said.

Sally stood up and looked at Catherine. "You want to take a walk with me?"

"Sure," said Cat. She turned to Lamar. "Y'all okay up here?"

Lamar looked at Arman. "Room service?"

Arman nodded and took Lamar's place at the corner of the bed and put his head in his hands. He looked up and said, "If they're coming, why don't we let them come? If these people are who you say they are, even if I run, they'll find me. I'm six thousand miles from home, and they found me. What if I don't want to run anymore?"

Lamar put his hand on Arman's back. "We can't just give you a rifle and say, 'Good luck, Arman,' even if you've earned that right."

Trey opened the door and looked back into the room. "When we get back..."

Sally looked over at him. "Trey," she said. It was enough. Trey nodded and closed the door quietly behind him.

A few minutes later, Trey walked out the hotel's front doors and into the bright hum of streetlights in the parking lot. He looked over his shoulder, took his phone out of his pocket, and dialed. It rang three times before a man answered. "Go," the man said.

The voice was unfamiliar. Trey hesitated, then asked, "Where's Harris?"

"Who is Harris?" the voice replied.

"He's the one who answers when I call."

"Now it's me. Talk to me."

"Fine," Trey said. "You have a problem."

As Trey made his way to the parking lot, Sally and Catherine found a pair of comfortable chairs in the lounge area next to the bar. A waitress came by and asked them if they wanted drinks. "Iced tea. Unsweet," said Catherine.

Sally looked up at the waitress. "Same," she said.

Catherine eyed Sally as the waitress walked away. "Should have stopped somewhere and got you a sweatshirt."

"What?" Sally asked.

"You must run cold, the way you've been rubbing those arms."

"Oh," she said. "It's not—"

"I know," Catherine said. "I don't mean to pry. I just notice things. Curse of the detective, I guess."

"Is it that obvious?"

"No. The scars are barely there. You must have had a good surgeon."

Sally laid her arms in her lap with her forearms up. "I feel like I'm walking around with a neon sign around my neck that says, like, I don't know, *Head case* or something."

"I don't doubt it feels that way, but you don't. You don't have to tell me anything if you don't want to."

"But you'd like to know."

"I would. There's a lot of moving parts and people who need me to figure out how they fit together," said Catherine.

"Trey's dad knows the head of plastics at Johns Hopkins. He came down and helped me out."

"Well, it's good to have those kinds of resources."

"I don't have them. Trey does," said Sally. She laughed. "He just lent them to me because he was getting in my pants at the time."

"Is he from Norfolk too?" Catherine asked, thinking of the 757 number she'd seen Trey ignore on his phone.

"No. He's a NOVA kid. We met at UVA. Sophomore year. Dated until..." Sally trailed off.

"Oh," said Cat. "Right. All the same."

"Yeah. You know what's funny? I remember coming out of it, didn't even know where I was, and there's Trey's father and the surgeon and Trey standing over me. They saw I was awake, and they just kept on talking about me like I wasn't even there. It was the pity. That was the crazy thing. It wasn't any different from before. A suicide attempt didn't make it worse. It was like they'd already found me maximally pitiful. You know what I mean?"

"Yeah. I do," she said. Catherine knew there were times the world sent so much trouble your way, there wasn't much that could be done about it. You either get out from under it, or you don't. She didn't believe you ought to judge a person either way. Most folks understand, but they also act like pain is a sickness that only spreads if you admit it's real. Nobody wants to be reminded how fragile a thing a life can be while you're trying your level best to live your own, she thought. She didn't blame them for it. Cat knew most people were scared of the part of themselves that knew it was true. She probably was herself.

"You know, a while back," Catherine said, "I was thinking about this older lady waitressed up at the country store near Vesuvius when I was young. This was after we lost Mama. When I went down to the diner, she'd say hello and ask after my daddy and me and give me a little smile. It didn't seem like much, but it meant a lot to me at the time. I tried to remember if she was just that way with everyone, but I couldn't. Then I thought maybe it didn't matter if her kindness was because she felt I needed it or if she just had enough of it to go around that she never felt the need to be greedy with it. I used to think about her a lot when things got hard in my life, the way they do for everyone.

"Anyways, I went home for my twenty-fifth high-school reunion not too long ago. So I'm back home and think, *Let me ask after her at the diner.* I hadn't been up in Nelson County since I left with Del other than once or twice, maybe. And to bring Daddy down to Norfolk before he passed. I don't know what I expected to hear. I figured she'd be old by then, as she must have been about the age I am now when I left. I don't even know what I wanted to say to her. Maybe I wanted to hear the kindness in her voice just once more.

"But it took me a long time to find someone to talk to me about her. I don't really blame them. Turns out, a couple of years after I left home, she went up to Crabtree Falls with her husband's old .410 snake charmer and took her life. He was ate up with cancer the year before, and after he passed, folks said they'd go out to check on her and bring her a plate or something, and her mind would just drift about like an old balloon a child gave up on. She got tired of waiting, I guess. I don't know. Truth be told, it scared me a little trying to put myself in her shoes.

"Point is, I remember telling someone about this when I got back to Norfolk. About how much her kindness had meant to me as a girl. But they seemed to think what she did at the end of her life should change how I felt about her. As if I ought to be suspicious somehow. But that seems like a terrible thing to me. To take something good in the world and decide it ain't good enough." She looked over at Sally, lost in thought. "I'm sorry," Catherine said. "Probably not your favorite subject."

"No. It's fine. It feels... it's good to talk," Sally said.

"You ever do that?"

"What?"

"Talk about it."

"I went to AA. Couple, three times. Maybe I'm working up to it."

"I heard a lady tell this fella once on a case I was on, long time ago, you never have to be alone if you don't want to. She was in AA. That's where she got that idea."

"How'd it work out for the guy?"

"Some people want to."

"Be alone?"

"Yeah."

"I guess that's true," Sally said. She sat there for a minute until the waitress came by and shook her out of her trance. The waitress put the two iced teas down on the cocktail table and then a little to-go cup with lemon slices and a small container of sweetener packets.

"Thanks," Sally said to the waitress and then asked Cat, "What was it about? The case."

Catherine leaned back in her chair as if the mention of it took something out of her. "Neighbor calls us on account of gunshots, and we get to this house and find a woman with ten .380 holes in her on the living-room floor. You see something strange in that?"

"Besides, you know, the obvious?" Sally asked.

"No. Why would you? Thing is, most .380s hold six or seven in the magazine, plus one chambered," Cat continued. "Follows that ten shots meant he almost certainly reloaded. Guy in a brownout buys a pistol from the pawnshop used to be on Granby Street. Drunk as Hooter's house cat. All accounts, he's a decent enough guy sober. But he's on a run and shoots his old lady down for nothing. Didn't put the dishes away or something. He reloaded. Couldn't come up with a reason when we got him. For the shooting or the reloading. 'But you got to know folks are walking around like that' is what my partner at the time said. And I said, 'You mean drunk as hell with a pistol in their pocket?' And he says, 'Well, yeah. That too. But I mean with that inside them.' This guy was a banker. Accountant. Something like that. Went to work in a suit and tie. 'But everyone's a killer under the right circumstances,' my partner says. 'You gotta know it even if they don't.' Anyway, I guess he'd tried to quit drinking a couple times before, and those same folks tried to help him after we locked him up."

"Even after? They tried to help even after?"

"They did. Went and visited him during the trial and everything."

"Weren't you, like, I don't know, angry?"

Cat leaned forward again in her chair. "That they didn't give up on him? It surprised me. But no, I wasn't angry. He did what he did. I put him on death row where the Commonwealth of

Virginia said he belonged. If I had to hate everyone who deserved to be there with him, I wouldn't have the energy for anything else. Besides, one thing the world's got plenty of is people giving up on each other."

Sally looked down and realized that Catherine was holding her hand across the small table, patting the back of it the way her mother sometimes did. "You ever lose anyone close?" Sally asked. Tears welled up in her eyes, and she took her hand back and wiped them off where they'd begun running down her cheeks.

"Close like your brother, you mean?" Catherine asked.

Sally nodded.

"He died in the war?" Cat asked.

"Yeah, how'd you know?"

"Like I said. Professional noticer."

"I loved him so much. All these years and I can't stop thinking about how scared he must have been. It hurts so damn bad."

"My father died, but not like that. I was grown. I loved him to pieces, but it wasn't like your brother."

"No?"

"No," said Catherine. "It wasn't. I don't know. It tore me up, but it didn't seem unfair. My mother died when I was pretty young too. Hurricane Camille. Before your time. But to tell the truth, I don't think I remember her enough for it to hurt the way I know it should. I don't know. I've been around a lot of hurt and a lot of unfairness doing this job. But I've seen people come back from all sorts of heartache. You're not alone. That I can promise you." She nodded toward the ceiling. "Mr. Bajalan lost his wife and child. People lose each other all over the world in every way you can imagine."

"And they just get over it."

"No. I don't think they do. I'd say they never do. I think it's like..." She looked around the room as if the fitting analogy might be tacked up on a wall. "You know what a tumbler is?"

"What, the rock thing?"

They both laughed a little. "That's right. The rock thing," Cat said. "I think maybe it's like that. You get this pain handed to you. It's all sharp edges. You feel like it's gonna cut you open from the inside out. And you carry it in you. It's always turning over, hurting. You feel like that's all there is, just that hurt and the emptiness it rolls around in. Then one day, you feel the weight of it, and you know it'll always be there, that weight, but the edges are all smoothed out somehow. Just a pebble left. That pebble is always gonna be with you, but it doesn't hurt the way you thought it always would. The only thing left is to decide what to do with it."

"I know what you're saying, Detective. And I know it's true, but..."

"You don't believe it."

"No, I guess I don't."

EIGHTEEN

Billings walked into the morgue just after eight p.m. Dr. Martin looked up from the examination table and saw the take-out bag swinging from the lieutenant's hand, smiled, and said, "I never did believe all the shit they say about you, LT."

Billings laughed and put the bag down on the counter, pulled out a sub, took a bite, and started talking with his mouth full. "This is officially the midnight oil you're burning, Doc. I hope you get a shitload of overtime."

Pat Martin shrugged. "Salary. What are you gonna do?"

"I bet you wished you'd paid attention in med school now, huh? Could've been making real money like me instead of cutting open shitheads like this guy," the LT said, nodding toward the body on the table.

"No, this is better. I never did get the hang of all that bedside-manner stuff."

"Anything interesting?"

"That's the joy of the job, LT. It's always interesting."

"So you know if this is our guy?"

"From the motel?"

"Yeah."

"Won't be able to say definitively until we get the blood

work back, but his injuries are consistent with the story you laid out. Hell of a thing, though."

"What's that?"

Martin took off his surgical gloves, tossed them in a biohazard bag, and tried to rub the urge to sleep from his eyes. "Well," he said, "generally speaking, murder vics don't go around collecting gunshot wounds throughout the day."

"Yeah, usually get them all at once," Billings said. "But it's consistent?"

"Sure. Nothing I can see that says this ain't the guy. Timelines all work. But you've got a doozy on your hands."

"You mean beyond the fact that you've been adding to your inventory of stiffs all weekend?"

"He's a cop, Lieutenant."

Billings nearly choked on the sub he'd just unwrapped. "What?"

"Or was, anyway. We put him through the usual ID checks. Got a pop on IAFIS just like that." He snapped his fingers for emphasis.

"Not here he wasn't a cop," Billings said. "I'd like to think one of those assholes out at the swamp would have recognized him."

"Not here. Texas."

"Texas? What the fuck, Doc?"

"I'm just the messenger. Our guest here is...was"—he grabbed a document from a stack of papers on the counter—"Michael Harris, date of birth March fourteenth, 1974, Fredericksburg, Texas. White male, six three, one hundred ninety-five pounds. Prints came from a background check for an Austin PD hiring in 1998. Here. Take a look at this." He showed

Billings a printout. Two reference photos at the bottom, both younger, smiling versions of the man laid out on the table.

Billings took the paper and leaned back against the counter. He looked up and seemed to stare past Martin.

"Lieutenant?" Dr. Martin said. "LT?" he said, waving to get the lieutenant's attention.

Billings shook the printout in front of him absentmindedly. "Military too."

"I saw that."

"How's a guy like this end up mixed up in this shit?"

"Lieutenant Billings, we both know a uniform doesn't change a man. Lots of guys wearing them who don't deserve to."

Billings junked the half-eaten sub in a biohazard receptacle. "Maybe it's...I don't know. Maybe he was—"

Martin held his hands up. "LT, you tell me we're looking for a guy mixed up in a double murder. Guy turns up dead. Bingo. Now I tell you he had a shield, and all of a sudden, you go looking for alternative theories of the case?"

"Ah, fuck," he said. "Computer?"

Martin pointed to the desktop.

A minute later, Billings punched a number into the morgue's landline. A voice on the other end said, "Austin Police Department."

"Hey, this is Lieutenant Jack Billings, Norfolk Police Department. Can I talk to someone in personnel?" He looked over at Martin and covered the mouthpiece. "Worth a shot, right?"

The person on the end of the line said, "I'm sorry, sir, you said—"

"City of Norfolk, Virginia. I'm police. I need to talk to someone about one of your officers' records."

"I'm sorry, sir. There's no one available until Monday eight a.m. central."

"Okay, how about this. Right now, at this very moment, I'm in the office of the medical examiner of the Commonwealth of Virginia. I'm looking at a dead guy. Right in front of me, like. Homicide victim. Suspect in multiple homicides in our fair city. Guess what happened when we ran his prints?"

"Sir, I'm sorry, but—"

"You guys got Internal Affairs out there? Anybody I can talk to who isn't gonna ask me to call back when I tell them there's a dead Austin PD officer shot in the head a thousand miles away from home?"

"I'm sorry, sir, this is just...wait one."

"Sure." Billings listened to the hold music, some kind of smooth jazz crackling over the line. A click, and then the music cut off.

"This is Sergeant Blankenship, Austin Police Department."

"They didn't tell you anything, did they?" Billings asked.

"No. Who am I speaking to?"

"Jesus Christ," Billings said.

"I doubt it, sir."

Billings sighed. "Sorry, Sergeant. Long day. I'm a Norfolk, Virginia, cop. Lieutenant Jack Billings. I'm looking at one of yours in the morgue, and I'm trying to figure out what's what." Silence followed on the other end of the line. "Holy shit, right, Sarge?" Billings said.

"Sorry, LT. I'm just the duty officer."

"Do you have access to personnel records?"

"Sir, I just need to confirm—"

"How about this—I'll tell you I've got Mike Harris, hired

by Austin PD in 1998, who is now in Virginia with his head blown half off, and you tell me if any of that info makes more sense to you than it does to me. Fair?"

"Fair. I'm gonna keep you on the line. Just give me a sec, sir."

Billings heard typing on the other end. The quiet shuffle and buzz of after-hours activity. Phones rang. Voices back and forth in the background.

"Sir?"

"Go ahead, Sarge."

"He's no longer with us."

"Yeah, that part I figured already."

"No, I mean—"

"Sorry, bad time for jokes."

"Fired for cause in 2003. Huh."

"Huh what?"

"Not many people make SWAT and get shitcanned in the same year."

"Anything else you can tell me?"

"Sorry, LT. If you need the circumstances, you'll have to talk to someone in IA."

"Gotcha. Number?"

The sergeant gave him a list of contacts in the Internal Affairs office of the Austin Police Department. He scratched the info down in his notebook and stuck it back in his jacket pocket. He hung up the phone, looked at Martin, and then walked over to the body. Billings had never gotten used to seeing the dead in this setting. Bright lights. The clinical nature of it. Their humanity was by this point wholly erased and what was left transformed into a mere specimen. Out on the street or back when Billings was an eighteen-year-old kid in Vietnam, a body somehow stayed a person. Some connection to the life he'd just stopped living was retained in the eyes. Even now, when he came upon a victim, he could feel the echo of that person's life still ringing, fading into the distance beyond the boundaries of yellow crime scene tape. But whoever Mike Harris had been, whatever choices he'd made that led him to that cold table, had long faded. Billings stood there looking at the body, listening for that echo. But it wasn't there.

NINETEEN

The lobby had emptied out by the time Cat and Sally finished their dinner. Yacht rock was quietly drifting from the hotel PA system. They walked to the elevators without speaking. They got in, and Cat kept her hand floating in circles near the small of Sally's back. When the bell dinged for their floor, Cat reached into her bag, took out a Kleenex, and stood there while Sally wiped mascara smudges from her cheeks. Sally gave Cat a quick, uncertain smile, tossed the Kleenex in a garbage can, and said, "Okay."

They saw the three men huddled over the laptop when they opened the door. Room-service trays lay on the beds. Beers from the minifridge had been emptied and lined up on the windowsill. Arman held a paper cup of coffee in two hands, transfixed by a still image from a video on the screen.

"Is that it?" Catherine asked.

Arman nodded, then looked at the floor. Cat and Sally stood behind the men. "Just watch," said Lamar. He spun the video back and looked at Arman. "Arman, you don't have to watch it again if you don't want to."

"No," he said. "Play it."

Even though the video footage from Arman's digital camera was grainy, the woman on the laptop's screen was unmistakably beautiful. Her dark eyes squinted as bright near-winter light washed over the lens. When the image returned, she held up a young boy and cooed at him. She turned toward the camera and spoke to the man behind it in a language no one in the room but Arman understood.

Sally picked out his name from the conversation on the video, and she clearly heard Arman's voice on one end of it, though he had not made an appearance on camera. Sally guessed correctly that he was the one filming. She looked away from the video and back to Arman. His head was down, and his eyes were closed. She watched him silently mouth every word of the conversation he'd filmed that day with his wife, as if by moving his mouth into the shapes of the words she'd once said to him, he might remember what it was like to feel her lips against his own.

Sally turned back to the video. The background was unclear, as Arman's wife and son occupied most of the frame. But you could make out young people casually passing by in twos and threes, a vast lawn behind them crisscrossed with pathways between institutional buildings. Between the grounds and the buildings, a narrow road was fringed with willow and tamarisk trees, and Sally watched as the woman on the screen turned her head to look at something approaching behind her.

The noise of speeding engines drowned out what had been the relative calm of an ordinary afternoon in an occupied city. Arman said something to his wife, and he pulled her out of the frame but kept filming. They continued talking, more urgently now, and none of the people watching the video in the hotel room needed a translation for the fear that had entered their voices.

With his wife out of the frame, the scene became clearer.

A convoy of dark SUVs roared down the narrow street and stopped haphazardly in its middle. The twos and threes casually passing by became a rush as the young men and women scrambled to leave their places on the wide lawn and duck into nearby buildings. It was not a stampede, not yet, just a crowd moving with purpose away from the collection of SUVs.

The camera backed away from its previous position. It turned toward Arman's wife and son sitting behind a concrete wall. She spoke to him again, and she swallowed her breath as she talked. The camera turned back to the vehicles. People still exited buildings and came around corners. Some went on their way, but bolder students cursed the SUVs in Arabic and Kurdish. A man stepped out of the passenger side of each of the first two SUVs, and they stood together at the rear of the front one. They wore kaffiyehs and had rifles in three-point slings ready at their chests. One of the men began to speak. It wasn't loud enough to be understood, but it was clearly English. They went back to their respective vehicles, but just as they were getting in, the man from the lead SUV shouted to the man in the second. It was the first word recorded by the camera that everyone watching the recording understood.

"Harris!" the man shouted. "Harris!"

"Stop," said Sally. "I think I know that name."

Lamar held his hand up. "Just wait," he said.

A group of students formed a ring around the vehicles. It was not an organized protest. They didn't chant slogans or make demands. They were angry, that was all. Then one stepped in front of the lead SUV and sent a plastic water bottle cartwheeling toward the windshield.

Lamar paused the video, looked at Arman, and waited until he saw him look back at him. The two men didn't speak, but at that moment, they came to an understanding. Arman stood up, tossed his coffee cup into the garbage, and left the room.

"Should someone go with him?" Sally asked after he'd closed the door behind him.

"Give him a minute," Catherine said.

Lamar pressed Play again. The bottle continued its flight toward the SUV's windshield, bounced off it pathetically, and cracked on the ground. The video lasted only fifteen more seconds, the first five of which recorded close to thirty rounds being fired from the SUVs. When the shooting stopped, all that was visible was a single blade of grass, an old cigarette butt, and a small portion of the wall Arman huddled behind with his family.

Sally felt sick. She'd never seen anything like it. How quickly the victims fell. How shockingly efficient it had all seemed. She'd expected something alien. More chaotic. In fact, she'd expected something incomprehensible. But instead, she'd watched something brutal in its clarity and simplicity. The rifle barrels went out the SUVs' windows. They jumped in harmony with the sound of gunfire. The bullets passed through half of the students who'd been shouting at the men a few seconds before. "I'm going to find Arman," she said.

Catherine, Lamar, and Trey went through those last fifteen seconds of the video frame by frame. They looked away from the screen and listened. They played it in slow motion and at full speed until Catherine stopped the video for good and turned it off.

"One more time, Detective Wheel," Trey said.

"It's not there," said Lamar. "I've been looking for it too. But it's not there."

"What's not there?" Trey asked.

Lamar went back to the minifridge, pulled out another beer, and tipped it back.

"A reason, Trey," said Catherine. "A reason why they did it."

It took Sally almost ten minutes to find Arman; he was sitting on a bench on the patio at the rear of the hotel. She watched him through the glass double doors. He was very still. He seemed to be looking for something invisible in the darkness, but Sally knew he was not looking anywhere but inside his own mind. She pushed the door open, walked out, and stood beside the bench. She tried to look where she imagined he was looking, but it led her only to her own mind. She thought she ought to say something to him but didn't.

There was room for her on the bench, but Arman slid closer to its end and made more. She sat down and waited to see if he would say anything. She didn't want to talk. The night was hot and quiet. She reached over and put Arman's hand between both of hers. Some time passed before she noticed her hands weren't shaking anymore.

Half an hour later, they were all back in the room discussing how to proceed. "I need to take the laptop and thumb drive, Detective Wheel," Trey said.

"I'm sorry, what? Why the fuck do you think you can just big-time us like that, my guy?" Lamar said. "This is our case."

"Yeah, your case, my hearings, Sal's story. The fact of the matter is I have to turn this stuff over to the congressional investigators. It's not gonna disappear. You're gonna have it to make your case, but I could get in a lot of trouble if I know this information is out there and don't do anything to secure it."

"Cat," Lamar said, "this is our first real lead on finding

these guys." He put his hands together and pleaded with her. "We cannot let the only hard evidence we've got get out of our hands. We've got no chain of custody. We haven't done any deconfliction. The laptop shouldn't even be here. It should be in an evidence locker at Violent Crimes. We're talking about both our careers."

Catherine looked at Arman and then Sally. Lamar was right. She wasn't one to cut corners, but she was usually solving murders, not trying to prevent them. She'd taken risks she knew she wouldn't have in any other situation, and it wasn't like her. She nodded. "All right, Lamar." She looked at Trey. "When we get back to the house, I'll have it sent through the proper channels. I know Congress is a recognized authority. But I can't give it to you now. It's my ass if something happens to it, not yours."

Trey put his hands behind his neck. "Fuck," he said. "Fine. But I want a sworn statement saying you refused to turn it over to me."

Lamar stepped toward Trey, but Arman gently put his hand up to keep him from taking another. Lamar pointed at Trey and said, "I swear to God, if you fuck us, I'm gonna find you. And we're gonna move some fucking furniture, you understand me?"

Trey's face flushed, but he was smart enough to keep quiet.

Catherine's phone rang. She picked it up. "Detective Wheel," she said. She sat there listening, nodding occasionally. The others watched her, hoping they might read what was being told to her from the expression on her face. She motioned for a pen, and Lamar handed her a hotel stationery set. She started scratching down notes. Names, phone numbers. "Yeah," she said, and "Uh-huh," and "Really." After a few minutes, she said, "Thanks, Lieutenant," and hit End. She looked at the rest of the group and said, "That was Billings. We got one of the shooters at the Sea Breeze."

Lamar gave a silent fist pump.

"Under arrest?" Trey asked.

Catherine shook her head. "No. Dead."

"Were they able to identify him?" asked Arman.

"Ex-cop named Harris. Game warden found the Charger in a Wildlife Management Area. Sunk in a swamp. Chesapeake PD rescue divers pulled the guy out of the trunk."

"Harris," Sally said. "That's the name from Arman's video."

"That's right," said Cat.

"I was trying to tell y'all before. Graves was on the phone with someone named Harris after the hearing. No way it's a coincidence."

Lamar reached over to squeeze Arman's shoulder. "These assholes are gonna get the bracelets. We're almost there, okay?"

Arman took a deep breath and allowed himself half a smile.

Trey paced in front of a window. "Don't suppose Chesapeake PD knows who put Harris in that trunk?" he asked.

"No, but whoever it was put a hole in Harris's head first." Catherine rested her chin in her hand for a moment. "Arman, your lieutenant was from Texas, right?"

"Yes," he said.

"Johnson City," Lamar said.

"Make a pit stop in Austin on your way to Johnson City. This guy was former SWAT. I want to know why he was former. I've got a contact for you with their Internal Affairs."

"When should I go?"

"Dulles is just down the road. Get the first flight out in the a.m."

"What about me?" asked Arman.

"They're gonna e-mail me some pictures. I want you to see if you recognize the man. But I think you ought to stick with me for the time being, regardless. Might be tricky following up on some of these leads, but we'll make it work," said Catherine.

Arman looked out the window but saw only himself lit up against the night. He caught Sally's eye in the reflection.

"I've got an idea," said Sally. "It might sound a little crazy, but hear me out."

An hour later, they were racked out in separate rooms, Sally and Cat in one and the three men in the other. Sometime in the night, Arman woke up. He looked at the twin bed next to him and saw Lamar splayed across it. He got up and went to the minibar to grab a water bottle. He looked out the window at the empty night, tipped the bottle back, and turned around. He saw blankets tossed haphazardly on the floor next to the sofa Trey had crashed on. He was gone. Arman went to the table, fumbling in the darkness. The laptop was gone too. He turned on the light and shook Lamar awake. It was all gone.

The sun was down beyond Richmond's skyline when the Camry crossed the bridge over the Shockoe Valley. Chris turned the radio on and cranked the window down. Jimmy watched the lamplit signs and billboards slip by from the passenger seat. The highway then curved northwest around the city. Before long, the checkerboard of crumbling buildings and abandoned lots was far behind them, and Chris pointed the car north toward Washington.

"He's gonna ask about Harris again," said Jimmy.

"I don't think so," said Chris.

"No? His only contact disappears and he's just not gonna worry about it when he meets us?"

"My experience," Chris said, "guys like this only worry about themselves."

By midnight, the Camry sat on Thirty-Third Street NW between O and P with its engine idling and the dome light off. There wasn't much activity on the block. One-way traffic all around them. The sidewalks were mostly empty. A dog walker went by on the opposite side of the street. A light blinked on in a town house. There was a streetlight at each end of the block, but only there. Along the sidewalks, leafed-out trees blocked most of the light that would have made it down from the buildings on either side.

The two men sat in silence for a while. A young couple walked by on their side of the street. Chris and Jimmy looked away, fully aware that eyes have a tendency to meet if you let them. The couple continued down the block. Their conversation hadn't quieted as they passed the Camry, and the two men relaxed. They might have been seen, but they'd been overlooked. A wealthy American neighborhood is as much a wilderness as anywhere else. The same rules apply if you understand that fact.

A yellow cab stopped in the middle of the road at the north end of the block. They watched the door open. A man got out and leaned toward the front to pay. Then he hopped up on the opposite sidewalk and headed south. A leather messenger bag hung from his shoulder. His head was down. His hands were stuffed deep in his pockets.

"Him?" asked Jimmy.

"Maybe. That's the address," said Chris, pointing to a stately gray town house. "Come around behind?"

"Yeah. Gimme two minutes." Jimmy opened the passenger door, got out, and closed it gently. He walked north until the man had passed him going south on the other side, and then he crossed the street quickly. He paused behind a mature oak and then came up behind at a brisk walk. He was twenty yards behind the man, then ten, and then almost on top of him. He couldn't believe the man hadn't sensed his presence.

Trey had the messenger bag pulled close to him. He slowed down as he approached his town house, hoping the figure behind him would continue down the sidewalk, but he didn't. Trey turned around and gave the man an awkward smile and nod.

When Jimmy saw his face, he approached him and said, "Carter! What's up, buddy?" He wrapped him in a hug and pulled him close. Jimmy whispered in his ear, "Walk with me to the car. Get in the passenger seat. Don't be slick." He backed off the hug and looked at Trey again. "Man, what's it been, like three, four years?"

Trey nodded nervously. The man put his right arm around him and, with his left hand, put something against his rib cage and guided him into the street and then across it. They walked back up to the Camry, and from the driver's seat, Chris pushed the passenger door open. Trey got in, and Jimmy closed the door, opened the rear passenger side door, and got in. Chris pulled out with the lights off. When they took a left on P, Chris turned the lights on and swung south. They crossed the Francis Scott Key Bridge back into Virginia, the Potomac below them a mirror of the moonless night. Trey looked at his watch as they passed through Rosslyn. Not yet one a.m. He reached into his pocket and felt around for the buttons on his phone.

Chris looked at Jimmy in the mirror and gave the nod.

"Phone. Keys. Wallet," Jimmy said.

"What the hell is going on here, guys?" Trey started, but Chris cut him off.

"You called us, remember?" he said.

"Look, I don't—"

Chris lifted one hand from the wheel. Trey caught the gesture's meaning and stopped talking. He took out his keys, his wallet, and his phone and passed them, one by one, over his shoulder. The car went quiet again.

Trey looked out the window and watched as they crossed back over the Potomac, northbound now on 395. When they picked up the Southeast Freeway, he asked, "Where are we going?"

"We need to debrief you," Chris said. "We're not gonna do it in your house."

Trey was nervous, but he tried to calm himself down before continuing. "I told you what I know. That was the arrangement: I call the number. Give you guys a heads-up. That's it. That was the agreement I made with Graves."

"Okay, buddy," said Jimmy. "If you say so."

Then they crossed the Anacostia River. Trey knew most of the city well, but not Southeast, not this side of the Anacostia. He started looking for landmarks. When they took the exit off the freeway, Trey saw a sign for Minnesota Avenue. They turned right at the end of the off-ramp, passed beneath the stone piers of the Metro tracks, then swung left on Minnesota. Buildings went by. Streetlights. A gas station. A light-industrial facility lit up like a ballpark. The God's Good Fortune Church. And then they were on a street he'd missed the name of. Overgrowth on one side. Ghetto palms, trees of heaven. A tidy white house on the other. The car pulled beyond it. Trey looked back. There. A street sign: Forty-Fourth and Lee NE.

Chris cut the lights and stopped the Camry just beyond the bend in the road where one street turned into the other. No intersection. No streetlights. He left the motor idling. "We need the rest of the materials, Carter."

"Hey, man. That wasn't part of it. Do you know how much trouble I can get in just for telling you this shit? All I agreed to do was give you information. This stuff has to go to the committee."

"Carter, you don't understand what's happening right now," Chris said.

Trey handed the bag back to Jimmy. Jimmy put it on the floorboard behind the seat. "Out," Jimmy said.

Trey got out of the car. Jimmy followed him, tense, waiting for him to turn and swing at him or take off running. He visualized hitting a moving target with a stolen, poorly maintained, small-caliber pistol in almost total darkness. But Trey mustered only one final act of resistance. When Jimmy lifted the .32, Trey raised his hands and said, "Come on, man, you can't shoot me. My dad will pay. Please."

Jimmy snorted. "That's not how it goes," he said.

Trey looked up at the sky, at its dull electric glow above the brush. Power lines spanned the street above like the strings of an instrument. He took a deep breath. "Just leave Sally out of it, you son of a—"

He fell into the overgrowth when the first shot struck his head. Jimmy stepped up to him and dumped the rest of the mag into his body. Chris joined him and they dragged him farther into the brush before his nerves stopped sending and receiving signals and the spasms ceased. They were almost clear through to the gravel ballast beneath the seven rows of railway lines when they dropped his legs unceremoniously. They made their way back through the brush, and Chris popped the trunk, took out a gas can, and put it in the front seat.

"You'd think he'd have at least tried something, right?" Jimmy said. He didn't know how rare it was for people to actually fight back or run.

"Yeah, well, fight-or-flight is a misnomer," Chris said. He put a dip in and spat emphatically into the brush, falling comfortably into the role of instructor. "I mean, at best, at *best*, it's an incomplete description of the human body's reaction to threat." He placed a rag in the mouth of the gas can and lit it with a Zippo. "*Freeze* is a lot more common as a physiological response, and it has to be trained out of you. What do you think the point of basic is?"

"Maybe. I just don't get it," Jimmy said.

"I know it seems like cowardice, but it's not. It's just programming."

"Well, you can bet your ass I'm going out swinging."

"Why?" Chris asked.

They cut through the brush and hopped the fence separating the tracks from a tow yard. "Seriously? What do you mean, *why*?" Jimmy scoffed. They crossed the pedestrian bridge over the Kenilworth Avenue Freeway.

Chris picked up his cell phone and dialed. "Hey, we're good," he said, then turned to Jimmy. "What was that name he dropped?"

"Sally," Jimmy said.

"Right." He put a finger up to his other ear and said into the phone, "Can you work up the name Sally as a known associate of Carter West?"

A voice on the other end of the line said he'd work the name, then gave him an intersection nearby. Chris closed the phone and looked over at Jimmy. "I mean, what's the fucking difference? Dead is dead. You think you're gonna take your pride with you?"

"Did you hear that shit he said, though?" Jimmy asked.

"What?"

"That 'my daddy' stuff."

"You hear all kinds of things when they aren't ready to admit it's over," Chris said. They started walking down the dark streets toward Kenilworth Park.

A small pavilion stood in the grass beside the blacktop not far down Deane Avenue, a playground behind it. Chris pointed toward the pavilion. "There you go," he said.

Jimmy walked over to a garbage can, pushed the lid open, and tossed in the stolen .32. "No, I guess I'm just saying the whole thing doesn't make any sense to me. Did you see the dude's crib? Guy definitely didn't need more money. Rich daddy. Working for Congress and all that." They continued through the park, the street a tunnel beneath the overhanging canopy. A fire engine blared its siren back across the Anacostia.

"You don't read the *Times,* do you? Great Recession?"

Jimmy waved him off. "Get the fuck out of here, Chris. Dude's rich as shit."

"This is America, big guy," Chris said. "Everybody needs more money."

TWENTY

Lamar landed in Austin at noon the next day. He deplaned and made his way to the airport exit, down the escalator, and into the stale heat below the elevated arrival ramp. He crossed the street, dodging lifted pickups and shuttle buses, and entered the rental-car area. He found his car, opened the trunk, and put his day bag in the back. When he pulled onto 71, he picked up his phone, dialed the number Catherine had given him, put it on speaker, and dropped it into the seat next to him. With his left hand, he steadied the wheel and held the MapQuest directions.

"Garza."

"Hey, this is Detective Lamar Adams, Norfolk PD. I was told you'd be expecting me."

"Yeah, sure thing. What's your schedule looking like?"

"I'm out to Johnson City later today. Fly back tomorrow."

"Meet now?"

"Sure."

"You eat yet?"

"Not yet. I'm at the Super Eight on the interstate."

"I'll pick you up in an hour."

Less than half an hour later, Lamar pulled into the parking lot of the two-story motel. The rooms all horseshoed around

a neglected pool, still and a few days away from being tinted
Jell-O green with algae. He checked in at the desk, dropped
his bag in his first-floor room, and went out by the pool. He
kicked a Coke out of a derelict vending machine, sat down in
a plastic-banded lounger, and put his feet up and his hands
behind his head. The hot sun washed over him, and he sat
there sipping at the room-temp fizz. He saw a man in a custodial uniform come out of one of the second-floor rooms.
Lamar put his hand up over his eyes to shield them from the
sun. He thought about Arman and wondered what the man's
story was. A few college-age kids walked by him, eyeballing
his dress shirt and tie and the pistol on his belt. Looking back
out toward the interstate, he saw the corner of a parking lot.
Three men leaned against a pickup drinking beers. The pink
swoop of a bingo-hall roof. Tejano music sprawling out the
open doors of a cantina.

An unmarked Crown Vic pulled up the steep motel entrance
and parked sideways over two empty spots. The driver's door
opened. A man got out, put his forearms on the car's roof, and
looked out across the pool. "Adams?"

"Yeah."

"Your department must hate you, bro. What a fucking
shithole."

Lamar stood up, walked over to the car, and hopped in the
passenger seat. Inspector Garza stuck his hand out, and Lamar
took it and shook. Garza pulled up to the red light before the
highway overpass and rolled his window down. He shouted in
Spanish to the men in the parking lot, and they turned up the
radio in their pickup. Garza started drumming on the wheel
and looked over at Lamar. "You know Shelly Lares?"

"Naw, man. Can't say that I do."

"The fucking best, bro."

The light turned green, and he crossed the overpass and swung left to get back on the highway. They went over a big, slow-moving river. "That the Colorado?" asked Lamar.

"Town Lake."

Lamar looked at him sideways. "Who named it that?"

Garza shrugged his shoulders. "Who knows?"

"They must not have ever seen a lake before."

A few minutes later, the unmarked pulled into a parking lot. They got out, and Lamar looked up at the sign. POLVOS. Around them a few billboards. GET YOUR ASSOCIATE'S DEGREE. 1-800-GET-BAIL. Scraggly live oaks lined the streets, 1970s paint-by-number architecture. Behind them, a *panadería* with bars on the windows had a swirling pink mural of a dancer painted on the wall. They walked through the door, and Garza kissed the cheek of one of the owners, who sat them at an out-of-the-way table in a corner.

They ordered food, and when it came back sizzling, Inspector Garza moved two manila folders he'd put down out of the way and bowed his head. He made the sign of the cross and looked up at Lamar and smiled and took a slug of his michelada. "Okay. Now we can talk."

"So, did you know this Harris personally?" Lamar asked.

Garza pushed his plate to the side and slid one of the manila folders to the center of the table with his fingertip. "Not exactly. That's the write-up on him. Clean as a whistle in uniform."

Lamar took the file and started to read as Inspector Garza continued.

"Everyone likes him. A little aggressive, but you know how it is. We ain't out here playing cops and robbers. So he gets a couple excessive-force complaints from citizens. Nothing major.

Maybe a guy bumps his head getting in the ride on the way to lockup. Nothing we felt the need to highlight in our shop. Dude makes SWAT, and all of a sudden, he's king shit. Free-lancing on the dealers at Twelfth and Chicon. Starts out he's just working the street. Finding CIs, that kind of thing. Pretty soon, it's shaking guys down. Then he's using department intel to plan fucking stickups. You believe that shit?"

"I don't know, Inspector. You hear a lot of stories when the cuffs go on."

"No doubt, bro. But how many of those stories all have the same main character? Every other arrest on the east side, dudes start saying, 'Motherfucking Harris jacked me,' Harris did this, Harris did that. But nobody from patrol or SWAT clues us in, you know? Nobody wants IA digging in their sandbox. But you can only ignore it for so long."

"What made them stop ignoring it?"

"Guy from the *Texas Observer* comes up to me one day. I see him at this lunch spot on Congress, and he says to me, 'Hey, Garza, why y'all sitting on a dirty cop?' And I'm like, '¿Qué onda? What the fuck, bro? You know me. I arrest bad guys. You know about bad guys I don't know about, you gotta tell me so I can do my job.' So this dude buys me lunch and starts dropping knowledge on this piece of shit. So I go back to work. I tell my lieutenant, 'You know about this asshole?' And he looks at me like I just told him I kicked his dog or some shit."

"He knew already."

"Of course he did. If you're a politician, bad cops are bad politics. One side thinks we're all fucking gangsters. The other side would blow you after they caught you fucking their fat-ass wives. You make rank, you start to care about that shit. Start fucking juggling so no one hates you long enough for it to count. Me? I'm the police. I wanna catch bad guys. And bad cops are bad guys."

"So what's he say, your LT?" Lamar asked.

"What's he gonna say? He knows I'm gonna work it, so he says, 'Work it.' I start digging. I'm out in Fredericksburg talking to people he grew up with, that kind of shit. He's peacetime army, mostly, in the nineties. Gets a CIB in Somalia as a private. You know what that is?"

"Yeah. Combat Infantryman Badge."

"You were in?" Garza asked.

"Army. Nothing special."

"Marine Corps. Right on. So anyway, Harris. I mean, respect, you know? Dude did the shit. But he's one of those dudes with all the bumper stickers and shit. Fucking punisher and this and that. All I see is a dude with a sign that says *Free Gun* on his truck for any homeboy with a slim-jim walking by."

"This is when he's in uniform?"

"When he gets to SWAT. For some reason, my guy starts acting like East Austin is fucking Al-Anbar Province. He wasn't scared of getting caught or nothing. I go out beating the bushes, and I got ten homeboys willing to testify against him in an afternoon, I shit you not. A bunch of straight-up civilian witnesses too. If I would've had a week, there'd have been a line from the highway to the courthouse wanting to swear on a Bible against Harris's ass. But hey, you know they're gonna make it hard to lock up a cop. DA ain't taking the word of some dude slinging dime bags of dirt weed over SWAT. You know how that shit goes."

"But you had him," Lamar said.

"Straight up, I had that motherfucker cold."

"I'm surprised they wouldn't charge. I thought this was some hippie paradise."

"Shit, man," Garza said, then lifted his empty glass and shook the ice noisily to ask for another. "It's a hippie paradise as long as my people stay on our side of town."

"East Austin is, what, like the immigrant neighborhood? So no one really cares that a cop is terrorizing them, that's what you're saying?"

"Immigrant neighborhood!" Garza laughed and slapped his hand on the table. "I'm Tejano, my man. We ain't the immigrants. We're more Texan than ninety percent of these fake-ass buckaroos. Ayyy, bro. These dudes move here from wherever. All of a sudden, they're wearing hundred-X Stetsons and two-hundred-dollar Ralph Lauren pearl snaps. It's a joke." He sighed and leaned back in his chair. "And then these bongo-playing white folks out Windsor Road know it's the cops keeping the lines, the lines. Pearls get clutched over that shit for real. So he gets canned. Not even a misdemeanor."

"So that's it?"

He spread his hands out wide and looked up toward the ceiling. *"¿Quién sabe?"*

"And you were okay with that?"

"I mean, I checked up on him. Time to time, you know. I wasn't trying to catch a harassment case, but I wanted him to know I was out there. Like, 'You used your get-out-of-jail-free card all the way up, homeboy. You're a civilian. You fuck around now and get the bracelets, no question.'"

"So he stayed clean after? You know what he was doing?"

"I don't know, man. Like six, eight months, I'm letting him know I'm out there. Once or twice a week. Next thing I know, there's some hipster couple moving boxes into his apartment.

217

I came back a couple times just to make sure he's *gone*-gone, and the new dude is playing, like, a fucking Dobro or some shit out on the porch. Tattoos and whatnot. Thinks he's the next Townes Van Zandt or whatever. He ain't no relation to Harris. No forwarding address. I heard Harris got on with a contractor. Some funny-ass name."

"Lacedaemon?"

"Could be. Sounds right. Had a connection from his army days. Did six months in Iraq on the private side. Some shit like that. I never heard his name again until last night. I get a call at the crib from someone in the shop. 'Harris got popped.' I'm thinking he got picked up for some dumb shit. Assault, bodily injury, or something. Then my guy says, 'No, bro, he got popped in the melon.'" Garza mimed a gun with his thumb and forefinger and put it to the side of his own head. "Boom. Welcome to Valhalla, *güey*. Forwarded me the crime scene photos you sent. Laid out on the slab. There he is. I couldn't believe it." He looked past Lamar and flagged the waitress down. "So how'd he get on your radar?" he asked.

Lamar put his knife and fork down when the waitress came by and asked for a beer. "You gotta understand, Inspector. I just made detective. We got a John Doe on the beach. At minimum, suspicious circumstances, we're thinking. We got a witness. Apparently, Harris and another guy are looking for the witness too. Used to be a translator in Iraq. Gets an SIV, now he works at a motel. So Harris and an accomplice pop the lock on the motel office after hours. Owner, this old-timer, he's in there waiting. Lets an 870 go on the one guy's face. Ends up on the losing end of trading shots with Harris."

"How close is the motel to the place he got fished out of?"

"Not close enough. Someone put him there a couple hours later."

"Damn. So an unidentified accomplice, then Harris gets it from another unknown subject at a completely separate crime scene? That's a real-life murder mystery, Detective. Some *Columbo* shit."

"Yup."

Garza put his finger on the folders and moved them absent-mindedly around the table in a small circular motion. "You think this will help?"

"Yeah, this is great. You're a lifesaver. Now we got a real dude with a trail. Gotta have known associates. Seriously, man, I really appreciate this. I don't feel like we're even over the fifty yet, but this is huge."

"Hey, no sweat, my man. We gotta look out for each other, right?" He took the photo from the morgue out of the folder, Harris laid out post autopsy. "Your witness out of the woods or what?"

"We got the ball, but I don't think the other side's gonna forfeit."

"That's the game, right?" Garza said. He looked down at the body in the photograph—the proverbial one who got away. He sat there taking in the image for a few moments, then said, "*Dios tarda pero no olvida,* motherfucker." He looked up at Lamar. "I hope you catch all these vultures, man. Put their asses under the jail."

"I'm gonna try," Lamar said. "You able to get that other file for me?"

"Yeah, no problem." He peeled off the top folder and passed the one beneath it across the table to Lamar. "Got curious and looked it over. Why are you interested in a single-car accident in the sticks?" asked Garza.

"Victim's connected to my witness. Could be nothing. Just want to check."

"Cars end up in those arroyos all the time. You get tired. It's dark. Corner sneaks up on you."

"Like I said, just want to dot my i's," Lamar said.

Late in the day, Lamar headed west on the two-lane road that curved off into the rolling landscape like a white ribbon. The sun leaned down and beat on the windshield of Lamar's rental. On either side of the road, the low hills fell and rose in gentle waves. Mountain cedar here and there in thick brakes on the steeper slopes. A scattering of Bigelow oaks gave shade to skinny cattle in the parched fields. He reached the Pedernales, pulled the car to the side of the road, stepped out, and walked down to the crossing. More a ford than a bridge; there were no rails, just a series of low concrete castellations as the boundary between the road and the water beneath. A yellow flood gauge to mark the river at high water. He looked out over it, clear and shallow and almost gray. The limestone bed layered beneath the slow water like peeled mica. Above him, the sky was shot through with slender clouds and blue as patterned china.

Lamar took out his map again, moved his finger up the ranch road highlighted on it, and got back in the car. He turned off onto a dirt track hidden in the brushy cedar along the road. A hundred yards through the dark scraggle, the land opened up around him. The wheels buzzed over a cattle guard. He crested a hill, and the dirt road turned back to parallel the river, and he watched the river flash reflected sunlight through the scrub. Another minute and he came to a fence around a modest stone ranch house. There was no gate, but Lamar eased the rental into the grass before he passed the fencing and got out. He wiped the sweat from his forehead and walked up to the porch. He looked around. *Lieutenant David Taylor,* he thought. *What happened to you, bud?*

The front door swung open when he got about ten yards from the house. An older man stepped out onto the porch. He was thin and lean, and his hair grayish blond and wispy above his ears. When the man took the steps down to the dooryard, he put a hand over his eyes to block the sun, and Lamar saw that his arms were liver-spotted and taut as halyard line.

"Something I can do for you, mister?" the man asked.

"My name's Detective Adams. I came out from Norfolk, Virginia, this morning. I was hoping you might give me a few minutes of your time. I'm sorry, I tried to leave a message."

The man put his hands at the small of his back, stretched unhurriedly, and rolled his head around. "I don't have no machine," he said.

"But you are Mr. Taylor, aren't you?"

"I am."

"I was hoping I could ask you some questions about your son," said Lamar.

"He's been dead a fair bit now."

"Yes, sir. I know it. And I'm sorry. I've heard he was a good man."

"Do you have kids, Detective?"

"No, sir."

The man stood there considering Lamar's answer but didn't address it. After a few moments, he said, "You carry a badge on you or something?"

Lamar pulled it out of his pocket, walked over, and gave it to him. The man turned it over in his hand. "All right, well, come on in the house," he said and went back up the steps. Lamar walked up behind him and entered the living room. There was a woodstove off to the side on a small brick pedestal and a little mantel over it. They passed it, and Lamar took in the pictures lined up on it. Family portraits. David in his uniform at West Point. He and his father holding shotguns with bobwhites lined up at their feet in a gray autumn field. An in memoriam picture of a woman in her thirties wearing clothes from twenty years before.

They got to the kitchen and Mr. Taylor cleared off a few dishes from the table and asked him to sit. "You want some tea, Detective?"

"Please."

He brought out a big plastic jug from one of the cabinets and unscrewed the lid. He took a spoon, dipped it into a Crystal Light container, and turned the spoonful over into the jug. He ran the jug under the sink and let it fill, then he screwed the cap back on and with both hands sloshed the water around in the jug until it bore a resemblance to tea. He put two cups out on the table and poured the tea. "I ain't got no ice," he said.

"That's all right," Lamar said and took a sip of the lukewarm sweet tea.

Mr. Taylor sat at the head of the table and looked at Lamar. "Well, you brought your questions a long way. Go ahead and ask them."

Lamar took out his notebook, laid it on the table, and pulled a pen from the chest pocket of his shirt. "Do you mind?"

"Not a bit."

"Did your son ever mention a man named Arman Bajalan?" Lamar asked.

"Not that I recall. What sort of name is that?"

"Kurdish. Where was he stationed when he had the accident?"

"He was deployed. Home on leave."

"Afghanistan?"

"I think so. He went all over the place. Sometimes didn't tell me where. Sometimes couldn't."

"What was his duty station stateside?"

The man drummed his fingers on the table and looked up at the ceiling, thinking. "Let me see. He was last at Fort Belvoir."

"You said he sometimes couldn't tell you. Do you know why?"

"Yes."

"Do you mind filling in the blanks for me?"

Mr. Taylor looked at him until Lamar set his pen down and turned his notebook over. "I don't suppose there's any harm in it now. What're they gonna do, send federal agents out here to arrest me for revealing classified information?"

"I don't think it's likely."

"No. Some sumbuck probably got it in a spy novel as we speak. He was in something called Intelligence Support Activity. Task Force Orange, he called it once."

Lamar leaned back in his chair, thinking of the video they'd watched in the hotel room the night before, and tried to connect the dots to it. The dead man Arman found on the beach had been Australian Special Air Service. Probably in both Iraq and Afghanistan at one time or another. David Taylor, captain in a classified U.S. military unit and Arman's former platoon leader, also in Afghanistan. The likelihood that they crossed paths was considerable. Not guaranteed, of course, but those circles were nothing like the army Lamar had served in, where you might not know anyone in your battalion who wasn't in the same company as you.

"When he...passed, sir. Did the army send you his personal effects?"

Mr. Taylor got up from his chair and headed toward a hallway. He looked back at Lamar. "Come on, son," he said. Lamar got up and followed. Mr. Taylor opened the door to a bedroom and held it so Lamar could go in first. Lamar stood in the center of the room, preserved just as David Taylor had left it when he'd gone to join the long gray line almost ten years earlier.

A twin bed stood neatly made with plaid sheets at the far corner of the room, a Delbert McClinton concert poster thumbtacked to the plain white wall above it. A wooden desk and chair were up against the other wall. Lamar walked over to it and looked at Mr. Taylor. He nodded, and Lamar opened the drawer. Inside there was a three-ring binder with *LBJ Eagles Seniors!!!* handwritten in Sharpie on the cover. Beside it, a graphing calculator and rows of sharpened pencils and Bic pens lined up ruler-straight. Lamar turned to the dresser by the door and once again looked over at Mr. Taylor, who raised his hand and walked over to the bed and sank down onto it. Lamar ran his finger along the top edge of the dresser. A Texas 2A Baseball Regional Playoff MVP plaque next to a framed photo of the young David and the woman from the in memoriam picture in the living room. He opened the top drawer, saw crisply folded underpants inside, and closed it again. Lamar set both hands back on the dresser and hung his head.

"Gear's in the closet," Mr. Taylor said.

Lamar walked over to it and opened it up. Two pairs of creased jeans and three Wrangler button-downs lined up on hangers. Beat-up high-top Nike Air Force 1s and a pair of boots with the leather so worn the shafts spilled over to the side. Under the hanging clothes, Lamar saw a duffel bag standing in the corner and two Pelican hard travel cases of different sizes stacked on top of each other. He knelt down on the carpet and opened up the first case.

"He had an apartment off post, but he was hardly ever there. Not much to it. I asked one of his buddies to help me out and send back his stuff and square away the gear that needed to be turned in. This here was his personally owned stuff. Uniforms, that sort of thing."

Inside the first, smaller case, a military-spec Panasonic Toughbook sat in a foam bed. Other compartments carved into the foam held cords and other accessories. Lamar closed it and set it to the side. He pulled out the larger of the two and opened it. A .40-caliber Glock with two magazines was tucked into the side of the case. The main compartment held an assortment of electronics. Lamar wasn't sure what all of it was. Maybe a compact Wi-Fi router. Two nondescript black boxes each about the size of a pack of smokes. A short tube with a pistol grip. He looked back up at Mr. Taylor, who now sat on the bed with his face in his hands, quietly crying. Lamar turned around to the closet, pretending not to notice. He stayed there on one knee, looking into the closet at nothing in particular, until Mr. Taylor stopped crying, got up, walked over from the bed, and touched him on the shoulder. "I'll be out back if you need anything, son," he said.

Lamar looked at the electronics piece by piece. He guessed it was some kind of signals intelligence equipment or surveillance gear. Lamar pulled out the Glock and worked the slide back to confirm it was unloaded, then let it go forward again, put it back in the case, and closed it. He pulled both cases out of the closet and set them on the end of the twin bed. He saw a child's rendering of the ranch house in flat-fired clay on a wooden stand on the night table next to the bed. He looked around some more but didn't see anything in particular that he thought would have knocked Mr. Taylor back into his grief. After a moment, he shook his head, feeling guilty he'd assumed he'd ever come out of it in the first place.

Outside in the back, Mr. Taylor leaned against the far fence and looked out toward the horizon line. Lamar walked up, and when he was about ten feet behind Mr. Taylor, he asked if he needed privacy.

"No. That's all right. Get plenty of that," Mr. Taylor said.

Lamar came up next to him, put his arms on the fence, and joined him in taking in the view. "It's quite a spot you've got here, sir," he said.

"I been here all my life. Expect I will be too. I ain't tired of it yet."

They were looking west as the day began its slow retreat toward the bluffs above the river in the distance. The red ball of the sun was half hidden. One long ribbon of cloud splashed a golden light across the sky.

"When I was a kid, I turned over a tractor right there," Mr. Taylor said, pointing to a spot where the field sloped down toward the knotty wood line and the low river beyond. "Got myself properly pinned under that sumbuck. Thought I was done for. Knew it, in fact. Probably should have been." Lamar listened to the crickets and katydids as the man spoke. "Come nighttime, I hear someone close by and I try to call out, but it's just wheezing. Felt like breathing through a dang coffee stirrer. Half my ribs busted. Arm broke all to hell. And I hear someone calling my name. It's my brother, but I don't know it's him. Just my name on the wind, it sounded like. Before too long, there ain't nothing but darkness, darkness, and my brother calling my name into it. When I tell you I was afraid, I mean that's all there was. Just it and the dark. After a time, I knew what was coming, but I wasn't scared of it the way folks get now. Not that I say I'm any better for it. I was scared shitless, but in the same way my daddy used to scare me. Not like folks now."

"Can't say it's a thing you get used to, being that close to it and all," Lamar said. "Don't know that I'd want to."

"Used to didn't be that unusual," Mr. Taylor said. "I don't know if it was better. I don't pretend to know much about the world anymore." They stood there for a while, letting the whirl and buzz fill the silence sitting there between them. "Had to be about a year on the mend after they got that tractor off me. One day I give my daddy that old 'Why me?' number. You know what he said?"

"No, sir."

"He said, 'Why not you?'" The old man, almost whispering, repeated it: "Why not you?" He looked over at Lamar and went on. "Two years later, I turn eighteen and I head down to Austin. I'm gonna sign up for the army and go to Vietnam. Well, I got one arm can't hardly raise above my head." He raised it while speaking and moved his elbow out in a circle, mimicking a broken wing. "Couldn't go. Wouldn't have me."

"My mother always said God don't make mistakes," Lamar said.

"Yeah," he said. "My brother found me pinned under that tractor? He turned eighteen few years after me, in 1969. Fit as

a fiddle. Got himself killed in someplace called Fire Base Rip-
cord the next year. Never did turn nineteen. But God don't
make mistakes. After David died, I used to like to tell myself
that if my daddy carried on, I could too."

"I could see how that'd help."

"I don't know. I fought with him. David, I mean. You
know that? Before he went to West Point. I can tell you served,
so don't get me wrong. I love my country. Love this little bit
of it in particular."

"You don't have to explain to me, Mr. Taylor."

"I guess you can tell I don't have a chance to talk to folks
much."

"I don't mind a bit. Part of my job is letting folks talk, sir."

"I wrestled with it, being older. His mother gone. You think
the world's just wearing your ass out. I know it sounds silly to
young folks, but you try to find a way to take it. So before he
went, I tell him the Good Book says, 'Thou shall not kill.'
Don't say *unless* nowhere in it."

"Not something I'd argue with."

"Well, I laid that on him. 'Don't go,' I said. 'You'll put your
soul at peril.' But of course, your son is gonna do with his life
what he thinks is best. Anyways, after David died, I was out
here one evening, and I got to thinking about my own father.
Occurred to me, I don't actually know what the hell he felt
about losing my brother. I didn't know a darn thing about the
man my daddy was, you understand?" Mr. Taylor started digging at the ground beneath the fence with the toe of his boot
and sighed. "I only knew the man it happened to. What was
left of him, anyway."

Lamar never asked about David's accident. They walked
back up to the house a few minutes later as afternoon drifted

into twilight. Pink became purple while it waited for dark. Mr. Taylor wrote down the name and number of the officer who had helped him sort out his son's apartment after he died. Lamar asked if he could take the two Pelican cases if he promised to bring them back, and Mr. Taylor said it was fine. He walked Lamar out to the porch, and Lamar reached up and put his hand on the older man's shoulder. Mr. Taylor patted him on the back and said, "Go on, son. I'll be all right."

Lamar walked to the rental, got in, and backed it out. He looked in the rearview and saw Mr. Taylor standing there with his hands in the pockets of his jeans. A shroud of moths swirled around him in the porch light. The sun's last rays slanted toward him. When Lamar turned back onto the ranch road, it was silver with twilight. He looked down at the phone on the passenger seat and saw he'd missed half a dozen calls from Detective Wheel. He picked it up to call but couldn't get a signal. He put one hand on the wheel and rubbed the metal band on his wrist with the other while he drove. Lamar had spent a lot of time trying not to think about it, but he was pretty sure he didn't know what *all right* was.

TWENTY-ONE

After they dropped off Lamar at Dulles and after Sally collected her things from her hotel, Catherine turned the cruiser onto 95 South and headed toward Maryland. Before long, they crossed the bridge over the Potomac at Dahlgren back into Virginia. From the top of the bridge, the view spiderwebbed through crisscrossed iron beams, she looked out the window toward the river's mouth and the bay beyond.

Sally, Arman, and Catherine rode together in silence. Sally, in the back seat, dialed Trey's number every five minutes for the first stretch of the trip, letting it ring through to voice mail without leaving a message. The silence broke only when they passed the Rappahannock and then Port Royal, where Sally leaned between Arman and Detective Wheel sitting up front and said, "Here. Take this left. On this till Saluda."

"All right," Catherine said.

"Please, Catherine," she said. "Give him a chance to make it right."

"I get back to Norfolk, and he hasn't called, Sally..." Cat said. She'd known something was off about Trey. The 757 number he'd ignored; the way he'd kept his eyes down when he talked about working for the Coalition Provisional Authority. Two qualities had made Catherine a good detective: her attention to detail and her ability to put those details into a story that made sense. She'd built a career relying on instinct and experience, and both had failed her last night. She looked over at Arman. He'd been paying for other people's mistakes for a long time. More than any man ought to be called on to pay. She wouldn't ask him to pay for hers.

Sally sat back in the seat and redialed the number.

Another hour and another turn into deeper, less traveled country. As they drove along the river and then over the Piankatank, fields went by, hardwood stands like tall fences in between. Tractor Supply and Dollar General. A Fas Mart where they tried to stop for gas was closed. A handwritten sign in the window read *Billy no-showed I quit.* After leaving 17 at Saluda, they passed Middlesex High School. Next to it, the courthouse and the Middle Peninsula Regional Jail loomed with institutional brutality as if to remind the students that the short distance between the two was more than a metaphor.

Soon enough, the hardwoods thinned. Loblollies lined the narrowing road, tall and thin as ships' masts. Another gas station. Manufactured homes. A country church restored to its original humble beauty sat across a traffic light from a shuttered NAPA Auto Parts store. Marinas appeared around the bends in country roads as they neared the bay. One or two flat-bottom bay boats and walkarounds at anchor surrounded by empty docks. Bowriders perched on trailers abandoned in parking lots. "If you switched out this water for mountains, it'd be just like home," Catherine said.

They passed a red-and-white sign for the Milford Haven U.S. Coast Guard Station and a hundred yards farther reached a swing bridge with its candy-striped barrier pole stretched out across the road. They were first in line, and the bridge had just started to open, so Cat cut the motor. Arman got out of the passenger side, and Sally and Cat both got out and joined him. They walked to the edge of the land. Beside the bridge, they looked across the narrows toward Gwynn's Island.

A two-masted ketch was the first boat through, and Arman stood transfixed by the wind in the bright white sails, the sun on its fine rigging casting shadows like black lace across the green water. A deck boat followed in the ketch's graceful wake, powerboats behind that headed south toward the hole in the wall and out to the deeper waters of the bay. Soon the seventy-year-old mechanics of the bridge swung into action again and awoke the turning span.

They got back in the car, waited until the barrier pole rose, and went out onto and over the grated surface and down the other side. "This is it," Sally said. "Welcome to Gwynn's Island."

"This is where you grew up?" Arman asked. He surprised himself with his desire to know more about her. When she'd come to keep him company outside the hotel the night before, he could sense her hesitancy. Most people are afraid of other people's pain, but she was not. Sally's generosity at that moment required a rare form of courage, and he admired her for it.

"That's right," she said.

"How many people live here?" asked Catherine.

"Six hundred, give or take, full-time. A bit more now that it's summer. But basically, everybody knows everybody. The bridge is the only way onto the island except by boat. My dad's real tight with the chief of the Coast Guard station at the other end of the bridge. And besides, I figure if there's one place on earth a person wouldn't think to go, this place would be a contender."

"Home sweet home," Catherine said.

"Something like that."

Late in the afternoon, they pulled down the gravel drive at Sally's childhood home, a small white Cape with gray shutters just up Barn Creek on the southern part of the island. The low ground around it in an uneasy truce with the bay in calm weather. The dirt road they'd come in on ran behind them along the front of the dandelion-speckled yard. Out back, not far beyond the little white Cape, a long dock with a covered boat lift at the end of it jutted out into the creek's brown water. Her father's boat, a twenty-five-year-old dead rise, bobbed in the shade of the boat lift's roof.

"C'mon," Sally said. They walked to the house. Arman started to veer toward the front walk until Catherine and Sally both said, "Round back," more or less in unison. Sally stepped across the small slate patio and opened the door. Out of habit, she pushed open the frilly curtains on the back-door window, then held the screen door open to let the others in.

"Mom," Sally called out. They were in the kitchen, and from a room in the front of the house, they heard a news program and a shuffle as Sally's mother got up from her seat. She turned the volume down and came through the cased opening and into the kitchen. She kissed Sally on the cheek, went over to the sink, and washed her hands.

"You know you got to call before you bring company, Sally Anne," she said. Then to Arman and Catherine, she said, "Y'all must be hungry. I'm so sorry. If I'd known, I'd have had something ready for you. Lemme fix you something to eat." She walked over to Arman and said, "What's your name, young man?" and without waiting for an answer, she went on, "I think I've got some sausage pinwheels. Is it too late in the day for those, Sally?"

"It's fine, Mom."

"Or how about some ham biscuits? What was your name again, son?" she asked Arman. He opened his mouth to answer, but Sally's mother went on, flitting about the small kitchen like a hummingbird, getting ready to cook for three times their number if necessary. "And you," she said to Catherine, "you snuck up on me, dear." She put her hand up to her forehead and feigned exasperation. "Sally, really, you make me look like I don't know how to treat company." She stopped for a moment, hovering in the center of the kitchen. Tupperware and plates with plastic wrap stretched out over them appeared as inexplicably as if she had pulled them out of a hat and were spread out on every available surface. She looked at Catherine and Arman. Catherine stifled a smile, and Arman swayed in the wake of Sally's mom's activity. "I'm so sorry, dears. Just run y'all's names by me one more time?"

"Mrs. Ewell, my name's Detective Catherine Wheel. I just wanted to tell you, you have a lovely home here."

"Oh, Catherine, aren't you sweet," she said and looked at Arman.

He put his hand out nervously. "Arman, ma'am. I'm very pleased to meet you."

When she said his name back it sounded like "Armin," and though he'd never heard it said that way, he didn't object because she said it as if she'd been saying it all her life. "Arman, dear, you look like you haven't eaten in days. Sally Anne, why don't you take them to the living room, and I'll bring in something for you to peck at, at least."

Sally smiled. "Come on," she said and led them into the other room. She came back and stood at the cased opening. "Where's Dad?" she asked.

"Cal Briggs called from the marina this morning and asked him to work a charter with him. Bunch of lawyers down from Richmond."

"What? Bluefish? Jesus."

"Sally."

"Mr. Briggs doesn't pay. And what's Dad doing working as a mate for that asshole anyway? Cal's an idiot."

"Well, it's nice to know you're too good for a hundred dollars. Might be two hundred if they tip."

"Yeah. They tip if they catch. Richmond lawyers don't catch. Dad and Cal will put them on fish, but Mom. C'mon. A hundred bucks to be a glorified bartender? He's better than that."

Sally's mother put her head down and turned away from her. "No, Sally. He's not better than that. You're the only one worried about who's better than who. He's doing what it takes to pay the bills." She lowered her voice to a whisper. "Who are these people anyway?"

"I'm working on a story. They're helping me out, and I owe them a favor."

"A big one?"

"Story or favor?"

Her mother shrugged. "I don't know, Sally. Both? Either?"

Sally watched her mother look out the kitchen window toward the dock. "Both," she said.

Her mother had managed to put together a platter while they talked: Deviled eggs and ham. Cornichons in a jar. Crackers and sliced apples with soft cheese smothered in red pepper jelly. She composed herself and passed the tray to Sally. "Get in there and offer something to them before I die of embarrassment."

"Loaves and fishes got nothing on you, Mama," Sally said.

She stood there for a moment, waiting for a reaction. "Hey," she said. Her mother was at the sink with her back to her. "I'm sorry I said that about Dad."

Her mother waved her off. "I'll bring drinks in in a minute." Sally turned to head into the other room.

"Sally Anne?" her mother said.

Sally stopped without looking back.

"Is everything okay?"

"I think so," she said. "I'll let you know when Dad gets home."

She joined Arman and Detective Wheel in the living room. Her mother had left the television on with the volume down, but they ignored it. A ticker ran along the bottom of the screen. Stock prices down. Record temps up. Somewhere someone was suffering. Somewhere someone else was inflicting suffering on others. The clock ticked forward.

Sally's mother was in and out of the room, filling glasses and clearing plates. Arman looked up and smiled and thanked her for her hospitality. When she left the room again, he said, "I won't stay here, Sally. Not while your parents are here."

"I know," she said. "I just need to talk to my dad. I can get him to take her to my uncle's place in Tappahannock. It'll only be a couple days. Detective Adams is gonna get something off the Harris ID. We're almost there, right, Catherine? It's almost over."

Catherine listened to them both, staring at the floor. "I don't know, Sally. I've got to talk to the commonwealth's attorney to see where we're at. Hopefully there's enough to get a warrant for Decision Tree's personnel files. Photographs Arman can ID. Something, anything, so we can get this mess on the commonwealth's radar. If Trey gets something from the laptop, that would surely do it. But after what he did, I'm not ready to rely on him. And I don't like the idea of leaving y'all here without protection."

"I don't like it either. But you said the state wouldn't do anything worthwhile, especially not before there's an actual crime they can charge that he was witness to. So in the meantime—"

"Do I get an opinion?" Arman said. "Or am I supposed to wait wherever you tell me until it's safe? Detective, you seem a lot more confident than I am that it's going to be safe anytime soon."

"Let me call Lamar. See where he's at with everything." She took her phone out and dialed. Sally took hers out and tried to call Trey again. Arman watched as they listened to their calls ring through to voice mail.

Catherine looked at Arman as she closed her phone. "Okay, Arman. What do you think we should do?"

Sally closed her phone and looked at him too.

"I don't know," he said. He looked up at the two women. "Let me go. I told Lamar. Let them come after me. I'm not scared to fight. How do you think I got my visa?"

"No one thinks you're scared, Arman. I sure as hell don't. But I don't see the point of looking for a fight if these sons of bitches won't give you the chance for one." Catherine sat down next to him. "What you've gone through to be here? There ain't a right-thinking person on earth who'd say you owe us anything. Far as having the right to live here in peace, you're as paid up as any man ever walked the planet. But you might be the only person who can put these bastards in prison. I can't make you, though. You got to decide."

A long time seemed to pass before he spoke. "Go talk to the commonwealth's attorney, Detective Wheel," he said. "Sally, you get your parents off the island."

"I can get us on that boat and into the bay in five minutes if it comes to it," Sally said. "There aren't twenty people in the world who know these waters better than..." She trailed off, then fell silent.

Arman looked up at Sally and found her staring at the television, the anchorwoman mouthing words without sound. A few seconds of video of a burned-out car on an urban surface street. An aerial shot of railway tracks followed. A white canopy obscured an active crime scene to the side of the tracks. A dozen people in white protective coveralls moved through the tall grass. Three people in suits stood just outside the canopy. One was on the phone. Another took notes. The last stepped out of the way as a body bag was carried into the aerial camera's view and toward an opening in a chain-link fence where an ambulance waited in a wrecker yard. The ticker along the bottom read *Congressional aide found murdered near Kenilworth Ave.* They watched the scene unfolding in silence until Arman said, "Sally, I think we should turn the sound up."

"Right." She went to the couch, got the remote, and stood back in front of the television. She turned the volume up just as a picture of Trey appeared on the screen. The anchorwoman said, "The body is believed to be that of congressional aide Carter West the Third, twenty-eight, of Great Falls." Sally didn't hear anything else. She dropped the remote on the floor and fell back onto the couch. Her body began to tremble. She tried to hold herself still but could not. Her mouth opened, but she choked on the words before they formed. Catherine sat beside her, pulled her close, and held her tightly. Sally looked up at her and repeatedly said, "No," until she accepted that the truth does not depend on being believed.

Arman hung his head, desperate to find the correct answer

to a problem without one. As they sat together in the quiet living room, the back door opened, and they heard Sally's mother going to it and talking at a quick whisper. A minute later, Sally's father turned the corner into the room.

He looked at them, trying to make sense of the unlikely trio. "Sal, baby," he said. "Aren't you gonna tell me who your friends are?"

Butch Ewell was a small man with an outsize presence. His hair was black and fine even though he was in his early sixties. His eyes were almost black, and his face always seemed ready to fall easily into a smile. Or it had been until a few years before. Now he looked tired. Confused. A little sad. He had a potbelly that stuck out over his belt, and when he reached over to shake Arman's and Catherine's hands, they saw the faded green eagle, globe, and anchor tattooed on his forearm. When Sally stood up to hug him, she was taller than him by a good two inches. She buried her face in his shoulder and began to cry again.

Mr. Ewell stroked his daughter's hair until the sobs stopped, and she cried silently into the crook of his neck. He held her out in front of him with both hands, and she looked at him, grimacing. "Sal, what's going on?" he said. Arman and Detective Wheel stared at each other and listened as Sally told her father what had happened. When she finished, Mr. Ewell looked over at Catherine and said, "Detective Wheel, I'm gonna drive my wife to Tappahannock. I'll be back in two hours. I know you've got business to attend to, but I'd appreciate it if you'd stay till then. I'm sorry, but it's the only way I'll participate."

"Understood."

He looked at Arman. "Son, you know how to use a firearm?"

Arman nodded. "Yes."

"All right. Y'all c'mon." They walked through the kitchen and out into the backyard. The fading day was heavy with the summer heat. Gnats floating above the ground stippled the air with white clouds. Mr. Ewell waved his hand in front of his face to beat the bugs back, and the three of them followed him to a shed between the house and the dock. He opened the door, and they just barely managed to fit inside together. A workbench was along one wall. Woodworking hand tools hung on a pegboard mounted between the naked studs. Pink batten insulation had been laid on the walls but never covered. On the other wall, a row of fishing rods of various lengths and sizes hung one above the other from floor to ceiling. Tackle boxes and coolers were stacked in a corner. He walked to the back of the shed and pulled a chain, and a bare lightbulb lit up between the joists. Mr. Ewell stood in front of a safe about the same size as he was and turned the dial on the combination lock. He jerked the handle up, and the heavy door swung open. He pulled out a shotgun and two boxes of no. 2 steel shot and handed them to Arman. He pulled out another shotgun and gave it to Sally, then turned back to the safe. He took out a .30-.30 and a box of ammo for it and slung the rifle over his shoulder. "All right," he said.

They walked back out into the yard, and Sally's mother was standing on the patio with a suitcase in her hand, crying noiselessly. Mr. Ewell went into the house. Sally leaned the shotgun against the cruiser, ran up to her mother, and hugged her. Her father came out of the house with a 1911 and stuck it into the waistband of his jeans. He looked at Catherine and said, "What do you got in the trunk there, Detective?"

"Twelve-gauge."

"How do you feel about using that?"

"I feel like I hope it doesn't come to it."

"But it might, you think?"

"I don't think it will."

"But it might."

She nodded.

"Better to have it and not need it, right, Detective?"

She nodded again.

"I don't mean to sound like I'm bossing."

"This is your house, Mr. Ewell. Under the circumstances, I'd say you've got a right to," said Catherine.

"All right, then," he said. "I want y'all sitting right beside that boat. I want those shotguns pointed, one toward the water, one down toward Cockrell Point, and one back up toward the house. Sally, you get her ready so you can take her quick, need be." He walked over to where Arman casually held the shotgun by the receiver. He looked him in the eyes and squeezed his shoulder. "These shells are made for bringing down waterfowl, okay? I don't keep no slugs nor buckshot, but these'll damn sure ruin a man's day if you hit him, you understand? If it comes to it, you keep shooting till they drop." He took the shotgun from Arman and a handful of the no. 2 shells and started loading them into the tubular magazine.

Arman nodded. He took back the now-loaded shotgun and worked a shell into the chamber. He pointed the barrel at the ground and let his cheek rest on the buttstock. He found the bead and tried to keep it steady. "I never thought I'd have to do this again," he said, then looked back up at him.

Mr. Ewell forced a smile. "I know, son. Me neither. But it sounds like we all passed 'want to' some time ago. We in the land of 'got to' now." He walked over to his two-tone Ford and got in the driver's side. Mrs. Ewell threw her suitcase in the bed and then got in on the passenger side. He backed up the truck, leaned out the window, and said, "Two hours."

They watched the truck kick up gravel dust and then turn up the dirt road. The sky above the trees was a darker blue but not yet twilight. Late afternoon, the air hazy, the trill and rattle of life hidden in the grass along the island's wooded banks.

Detective Wheel went to the trunk of her cruiser and took out the shotgun. She loaded it and leaned it against the car, then took Sally's out of her hands. She racked the pump action and checked the function of the safety button. She handed it back to her. Sally held it stiffly, upright in both hands. "You see this little bead on the end of the barrel?" Catherine said.

"Yes," said Sally.

"If you have to, you put that little bead smack-dab in the center of someone's body and squeeze the trigger. Don't go jerking on it."

She moved her finger toward the trigger guard. "I'm not helpless, Detective," she said softly as if trying to convince herself.

"I know, Sally." She put Sally's hand in her own and guided her finger back outside the trigger guard. "Not yet, okay?" said Catherine. "Don't put your finger on the trigger until you're ready to shoot. Don't point it at nothing you don't want to shoot. See this button?" she asked, pointing to the safety. Sally nodded. Catherine pushed it in until it showed red. "That means it is ready to fire. You have to reload, you pull that wooden bit all the way back, then push it all the way forward. Bead on the target. Squeeze the trigger."

"Okay," she said.

Arman stood to the side, watching. "You got it?" Catherine asked him.

"I've got it," he said. "It's just been a while."

"Me too," she said. "Let's go get our stuff and get down to the dock." The other two followed her toward the door.

"Detective Wheel?" Arman asked.

"Yeah."

"You ever have to shoot anyone?"

"No. Been lucky, I guess."

TWENTY-TWO

Lamar was back in his room just as it was finally getting dark. He walked across the street to the cantina and asked if they had a cigarette machine and walked out with a pack of Winstons a minute later. Men and women came and went. Music lifted out of the building and into the evening sky as the doors opened and closed. He went over to the wall out front, kicked one leg back against it, lit up a smoke, and took a big draw in. He watched the women come twirling through the night heat, and the men with their silver-tipped boots glinting like sparks from the dull yellow streetlights scattered around the parking lot. The doors closed and opened again. The music rose and fell. After a while, he tossed the butt on the sidewalk, toed out the cherry, and walked back to the motel.

He sat down in the same plastic-banded lounger from earlier in the day and took his shoes off and then his GoldToe socks and put them inside his shoes. He rolled up his pants legs, went over to the pool, sat on the coping, and let his legs dangle in the water. On one of his legs, surgical scars shot down from his calf to his foot in the green water and seemed to glow in the pool's dim white light. *Maybe Mr. Taylor was right. Why not me?* Lamar rotated his reconstructed ankle and extended his salvaged foot out in the water. He imagined he still felt the shrapnel in them, but it was only the screws and plates with which the salvage and reconstruction had been done. The bones of his midfoot and ankle had now healed permanently around the hardware. Sometimes he wondered if the weight of what had been put in was close to the weight of what had been removed. He didn't know why it mattered, but for some reason, it was important to him that he came out even on the deal.

He took out his phone and notebook and flipped back a few pages until he saw the name and number Mr. Taylor had given him. He punched in the number, set the notebook beside him, and lit another cigarette.

The phone rang four times and then a voice on the other end picked up and said, "Miller."

"Chief Miller?" he asked. The line went quiet.

"Who am I speaking to?"

"Chief, my name is Detective Lamar Adams of the Norfolk Police Department. I was hoping I could take a few minutes of your time to discuss a sensitive matter."

"I'm retired, Detective. I'm not sure how much help I could be."

"It's about David Taylor. His father gave me your number. Said you'd been a big help to him and might be willing to help me out too."

Lamar heard the man sigh. "Shit. Fucking Davey. Captain Taylor was the best company-grade officer I ever worked for. But look, Detective, I'm guessing if you talked to his father, you know there are limitations on what I can discuss, civilian now or not."

"No, I get it, Mr. Miller. I know how it is. If you can't color outside the lines, I won't push."

"You were in?"

"For a minute. Got out in '05."

"You overlap with Taylor? He was there around that time. Shit, I was too."

"No, I never knew him. Different units. I was just a joe. Got an early trip to Brooke anyway."

"You all right?"

"Sure. Some trauma ortho decided I should keep my foot. Ain't much to look at, but beats the alternative. So what about you? What's a retired chief warrant officer do with himself these days?"

"A little of this. Little of that. Corporate consulting. That kind of thing. So what can I help you with?"

"Any chance you're still near Belvoir?"

"Yeah."

"I've got some personally owned equipment David had at his father's house. I was hoping you'd be willing to walk me through it. The other thing is a bit trickier. I think he was collecting evidence of a crime committed while he was in Iraq."

"What kind of crime?"

"Civilians and contractors. You heard of Lacedaemon?"

"Sure. They were...around. Until a couple years ago, right?"

"Yeah. How about Decision Tree?"

"Sure. I've worked with those guys."

"Same guys?"

"You know how it is, guys sign a contract for six months. Next one is with another outfit. I might know faces. Not names."

"How about Captain Taylor?" Lamar asked.

"I'm only guessing, but I bet he would have said the same."

"And at the top?"

"Who, Graves?"

"He connected to Lacedaemon?"

"I don't know, Detective. I'm not his accountant. Sorry."

A door opened on the second story. Billy Joel spilled out onto the breezeway. Two young men came out onto it with bottles of Lone Star in their hands, their arms wrapped around each other's shoulders, belting out "The Piano Man" at the top of their lungs.

"Where are you, Detective?"

"Sorry. At a motel. Someone is having a good time," Lamar said. He put the mouthpiece up to his chest and shouted to the partyers, "Hey, y'all mind keeping it down a little?"

"Fuck you, Gramps!" one of the guys slurred at him; the other shouted, " 'Now, John at the bar is a friend of mine. He gets me my drinks for free!' "

Lamar reached into his pocket, pulled out his badge, and held it above his head. They scurried back into the room and shut the door. Lamar chuckled as he imagined dime bags of dirt weed circling the drain and the poetic recriminations of the hammered drunk at twenty-two.

"Well, look, Detective. I'm happy to meet up. Talk on the phone. Whatever. Let me know where you're at, and I'll come to you." Lamar heard the distinct slapping sound of someone packing a can of dip. The voice returned, and Lamar could hear the lipper the former chief warrant officer had put in when he spoke. "If you think there's evidence of a massacre that Davey wanted out there, I definitely want to get eyes on it."

"All right. Thanks, Chief. I really appreciate it. I'm flying into Richmond tomorrow in the a.m. I should be back at the house sometime in the afternoon."

"I can probably do that. What time does your flight get in?"

"Let's see. I'm into Richmond at ten minutes of two."

"I'm in DC right now, but I've been meaning to go see

some friends in Little Creek for a while. Why don't you let me pick you up in Richmond? I'll drive you down, and we can chop it up on the way."

"That sounds great. Hey, I really appreciate it."

"No problem. Happy to help. And, Detective?"

"Yeah, Chief?"

"Call me Chris."

———

They'd been waiting on the dock for an hour and a half when Lamar finally called Catherine back. When she picked up the phone, Lamar could hardly hear her over the din; the night had come alive with insects. "Catherine? Cat? I can't hear shit," he said.

She held one finger up to Sally and Arman and said, "One minute. I'll be right back." She walked toward the house until the noise receded a bit. "Where the hell have you been, Lamar? I've been calling half the day."

"I went out to the sticks to see David Taylor's father. Not much in the way of reception out there. What's up? Everybody all right?"

"Well," she said, looking back down toward the darkness of the creek and the dock sticking out into it, "we're at Sally's parents' house. Sitting on the dock with shotguns like *Wagon Train* until her father gets back."

"I'm sorry, what?"

"Trey's dead, Lamar."

He set the phone down at his side on the pool's coping and put his hands behind his head. He watched the underwater light dance across the white stucco bottom. He picked the phone back up as Catherine was calling his name. "I'm here. I'm here," he said. "How?"

"We don't know. It's only a preliminary ID, but Sally tried his phone all day and couldn't get through. Pulled out of the brush next to some train tracks in DC. It's all over the news."

"Jesus. I...I don't know what to say. Tell Sally..."

"Yeah. I know."

"So what's the plan?"

"Sally's father is going to be here in a few. I'm gonna head back to Norfolk and meet with the commonwealth's attorney in the a.m. Pitch protective custody for Arman."

"And what about the laptop? The thumb drive? Damn it, Cat, I'm not trying to criticize, but—"

"We've got to assume they're gone."

"So do we have any actionable evidence?"

"I'm open to ideas. You got anything better than we had yesterday?"

Lamar's head was spinning. "Harris was in on all of it," he began. "That's almost a certainty. Fired from Austin PD and deployed to Iraq with a contractor six months later. He was in Somalia before he was a cop. Sally said Graves was too. The timeline adds up. I ran the name Lacedaemon by the guy from IA, and he said that could have been the group he went with. But it's all circumstantial. If they're connected to Decision Tree, we need something solid."

"To charge them," Catherine said.

"Right," Lamar said. "If we want to hook them up."

"Yeah."

"Cat? What are we talking about here? Do we want to hook them up?"

"Did you get anything else?" she asked without answering him.

Lamar reached down and hooked a thumb into his belt. He found himself flicking at the floor plate of one of his magazines with his finger, lifting it out of the leather holster and pushing it back down again. "I'm meeting someone who served with Taylor in Afghanistan when I land in Richmond tomorrow. I got some equipment from Taylor's father's house. There's a laptop. Maybe this guy can get us somewhere with it."

"Who is it?"

"Retired warrant officer named Chris Miller."

"You trust him?" she asked.

"I don't know. What choice do we have? We've got, what, four murders? I'm out of ideas. The old man said this guy was a friend of Taylor's. If you've got a better idea, I'm all ears."

Catherine looked back toward the creek again. The sky was dark enough to see the Milky Way, a slash of stars above the trees. She had sweat through her shirt. Her curly hair, now wet and stringy, clung to the sides of her face. "I know it's Graves, Lamar," she said. "I know it. It's the only thing that makes sense. If he's connected to that video, he can say goodbye to that contract. And I don't think Arman is gonna be safe if Graves thinks he's a walking stop-payment on a two-billion-dollar check."

"So we prove it," Lamar said. "Come on, Catherine, we prove it."

"I've been sitting out here thinking, Lamar, and I can only see two ways this goes if we do this by the book."

"What do you mean, *if*?"

Catherine looked toward the dock where Arman and Sally huddled against the dark. "First way, we make the case," she said. "Get Arman in protective custody before Graves's guys get to him, and he spends the rest of his life hoping Graves don't hold a grudge. The second way—"

"We don't make the case," Lamar said, finishing her sentence.

"And you know what that means, right?" she asked.

"Yeah," he said.

"So I'm thinking, if we can't stop them from going after Arman, maybe someone ought to start going after them instead."

"Jesus, Cat."

"You don't have to be a part of it, Lamar. I won't hold it against you."

"It's not that," he said.

"What is it, then?" she asked.

"I shouldn't have left y'all back there."

"We'll be all right."

"I'm serious, Catherine. Ninety-nine percent of the time, we know cops are off-limits. But these guys killed a congressional aide in the middle of an investigation."

"Metro thinks he got rolled in a dope buy."

"What did you tell them?"

"I told them he'd been with us last night. Consulting on a homicide investigation possibly connected to his work in Congress."

"God, they aren't even gonna investigate it, are they?"

"They said they found works on him. Seemed to lose interest in alternative theories of the case. Maybe they'll call after they get through tearing up the projects."

"Shit. Seriously, though, you think Sally's old man can handle himself?"

"They've got a boat ready to go out in the bay at the first

sign of trouble. He's been around the block. Knows his way around a firearm."

"But do you think he can handle it?"

"I don't know."

Lamar thought about the first time he'd been shot at. He'd been in the turret of a Humvee, manning the 240. He couldn't get his head up above the roofline to aim the weapon, let alone return fire, he was so scared. He remembered realizing his legs were shaking with actual cartoon-knees-knocking fear. He didn't know how long he stayed like that or what made him come out of it. He just remembered the weight of his body as he willed it into position behind the machine gun. He'd felt so impossibly heavy, as though he'd had to fight against some figure from another plane of existence trying to pull him back down into the vehicle's relative safety. There were flashes of noise and light in his memory. The singular sound of a bullet breaking the sound barrier as it unzipped the air beside his head. The absurdity of a rocket-propelled grenade skipping down a Mosul street like a stone across water, him turning to watch it go by. *Do you think he can handle it?* he'd asked her. It had seemed like a perverse miracle when he understood he was prepared to kill another man. Prepared to get killed trying to do it. But that couldn't be right. It was too common to be miraculous. "Catherine," he said. "Take them with you."

"Who?"

"I don't know. All of them."

"Lamar."

He looked out over the water rippling in the light. His feet kicked in it gently like a child's. Music again from the room upstairs, but quieter. He wondered what kind of twenty-year-olds listened to music like that. It sounded like a dirge for the end of the world. One more round before the lights go out. "Arman, then. Take Arman. Put him in a holding cell at the shop. Shit. Just put him in an interview room until we get this figured out. Tell Sally to lay low. They're after Arman after all, aren't they?"

"Get some sleep, Lamar. Call me when you land."

He listened to her breathing on the other end of the line, a static pulse every few seconds interrupting the insects filling the night with sound. He was twelve hundred miles away. Powerless. And they both knew it. "Catherine," he said. "Please be careful."

"I will. Now go get some sleep."

He closed the phone and set it down. He took the pistol out of his holster, unwound the belt through the loops, and put them beside the phone. He emptied his pockets. The door opened up on the catwalk above him. The song still played but louder now through the open door. He turned his head toward the room, closed his eyes, and listened to the words rolling over a slow dance between two minor chords.

He pushed himself off the pool's edge and into the water and stood there in it with his clothes still on. A young woman came out of the room, lit a cigarette, and leaned on the iron railing. She looked down at him. Their eyes met. They didn't say anything. A guitar soloed through the doorway and into the night, bright and melodic. Lamar let himself fall back into the water, floating, listening.

———

Two headlights in the distance cut through the dark and lit the unsettled dust along the road. They watched from the dock as the vehicle approached the house, went behind it, emerged again, and turned down the gravel driveway. They could see the silhouette of a pickup, and Arman said, "Is that him?"

Sally put a finger up to her lips, and the three of them turned to face the driveway with the shotguns pointed toward it. Her father called out to them, "Sally! Y'all all right?"

"C'mon," said Cat. They stood up and walked toward him.

"Anything?" he asked.

They all shook their heads. "You get Mom to Uncle Timmy's all right?" Sally asked.

Mr. Ewell leaned over and kissed her on the forehead. "Yeah, she's fine. She's scared, but I told her it'd be all right. Just being extra-careful." He turned to Catherine. "Detective, I appreciate you staying here. I know you've got business to attend to."

She stood there thinking about her conversation with Lamar. "Thank you, Mr. Ewell. And I'm sorry all this happened to you. To Sally too."

He looked over at his daughter. "It's a mess, that's for sure. But it ain't happening to us. It's just happening. We get a say in how it turns out."

Arman looked up at the porch light, his thoughts adrift, only half listening to the conversation around him.

"Arman," Mr. Ewell said. "I know you didn't ask for any of this. But I want you to know you're welcome to stay with us until Detective Wheel gets it all sorted out. We'll look out for you just like you're one of our own."

He didn't know what to say. His thoughts tangled into an impossible knot. Arman closed his eyes, and in the darkness of his mind, he saw pairs of boots in a gutter, sticky with blood. His father and mother stood before a sandstorm that walled off the world. He bounced his baby on his knee. The child's hand explored his face and then reached for the unruly pages of his dissertation on his desk. One by one, his son flicked sheets of paper off the pile and watched with glee as they floated like white leaves down to the floor. He heard his wife's laughter from another room. "Light Echoes of Collapsing Stars." "Asymmetry in Supernova Remnants." "Reconstructing the Explosion of Cassiopeia A." He realized he had not gazed with wonder at the night sky since he'd lost them.

"Arman?" Mr. Ewell said.

He looked over at Detective Wheel and held up his hands with his palms out. "Tell me what to do," he said.

"Mr. Ewell, Sally said you are friends with the chief of the Coast Guard station just off the island."

"Sure. Chief Rawls and I go way back. He's a good egg."

"Call him up. Tell him to have someone call you if anyone comes across that bridge that they don't recognize. Tell them Sally's got a stalker. Tell them anything. Just get their attention, okay?"

"You got it." Mr. Ewell walked to the house to make the call.

"Arman," she said. "We're gonna sleep at Violent Crimes tonight. I'll set up the break room for you. You're gonna stay there until I say you can leave."

He nodded. "How long?" he asked.

"I don't know," she said. "As long as it takes. Lamar says he's maybe got another lead. I'm gonna beg and plead for real protection."

"Call me when you know something, okay?" said Sally.

Arman and Catherine took turns giving Sally hugs. "Will do," said Catherine. "And don't you go sending in this story yet."

Sally's eyes had begun to well up, but a laugh broke through anyway.

"Take care of your dad," said Arman.

She held his hand in hers and said, "I will. Y'all be careful, all right?"

Arman and Detective Wheel walked to the cruiser and got in. Sally's father called from the back door, "C'mon, girl. I don't want you out there by yourself."

TWENTY-THREE

Jimmy leaned against the motel's second-floor railing and watched Chris pull out of the parking lot and take the Jeff Davis Highway toward I-95. He reached in his back pocket, pulled out two quadrants from a U.S. Geological Survey large-scale topo map, and unfolded them. He walked back into the motel room and laid them on the bed so one was situated just above the other and the boundaries met.

Now he had a detailed map that depicted the eastern tip of the Middle Peninsula from Deltaville south to Mathews County, including Gwynn's Island and the various waterways that separated them. He followed the depths of the Piankatank just north of the island with his forefinger. He paid particular attention to the complex bathymetry of Milford Haven, which ran between the island and the mainland. He took out a fine-point red Sharpie and made some markings at the mouth of Barn Creek, then traced the road's path from its end on the bank opposite Cockrell Point back to the bridge over the narrows. He circled stretches of land exposed at low tide and compared them to a printed tide table.

He leaned over the bed, grabbed the motel phone, dialed 411, and asked to be connected to the Mathews County Sheriff's Office. He looked at his watch while waiting for someone to pick it up. It was ten o'clock, and the phone rang for forty-five seconds before a tired voice answered.

"Sorry, wrong number," he said and hung up. He guessed they had only a handful of full-time deputies for the entire county. He guessed they were understaffed, even for a small department. He'd guessed correctly.

Jimmy looked at his watch again, then folded his hands behind his head and stretched out on the bed. The tide chart showed sunrise at 5:55 a.m. That put astronomical twilight at about 4:00. Nautical at 4:45. He needed enough light to operate but not so much as to be exposed. He'd give himself thirty minutes to get on and off the island—4:15 to 4:45 a.m. It would take two hours to get there, plus fifteen minutes more if he had to wait for the bridge. Add a half-hour cushion. He needed to be in the truck and moving by 1:15 a.m. Plenty of time.

He picked up the phone and called a number from an online classified service. He gave the address and room number. "Half an hour," the woman said. He reached under the bed, pulled out a duffel bag, unzipped it, and pulled out a suppressed nine-millimeter submachine gun with a collapsible stock. Two dots of lubricant went into the action. A plastic Walmart bag was on the nightstand. He pulled out a new package of lithium button batteries from it and peeled open the cardboard backing. He replaced the battery in the red-dot sight and turned it off and on, then got up and turned the light off in the room and adjusted the red dot's brightness. He flicked the light back on, placed the submachine gun back in the bag, zipped it up, and slid it under the bed.

At 11:00, Jimmy heard a knock at the door. He got up and opened it and looked out at the girl standing on the second-floor walkway. His shirt was off, and he caught her staring at the tattoo across his chest that read *Infidel* in a barely legible, intricate cursive. She looked up at him and forced a smile and, in her best attempt at a sexy voice, said, "Hey, baby, are you John?" but she couldn't hide the fear in it, and she knew it.

"You're late," he said. "Don't talk."

She felt like he was staring past her when he looked at her, as if she either wasn't there or wasn't worth considering. He grabbed her by the forearm and pulled her slowly toward him and fully into the room. He shut the door behind her and leaned against it.

She had a brief moment of clarity, seeing herself in the motel-room mirror. The ratty fishnets. The dark mascara and eyeshadow she'd used in a vain attempt to hide the remnants of the black eye her dope dealer had given her a few days before. She thought she caught a glimpse of her double in the mirror, the girl she might have been, who she had been the year before, a fifteen-year-old who partied and smoked a little weed but had never shot up.

There would still have been the hunger. One meal a day. Maybe a six-piece chicken nuggets if her mom remembered after finishing her second shift. There would still have been an unbearable shyness, the paralyzing anxiety of showing up to school knowing she was the poorest kid among a thousand poor kids. Her clothes always worn for at least two weeks before being washed because even if the washer in the common area wasn't broken, who had quarters for the laundromat? There would still have been heartache, wondering why her father had never come back, lying in bed with her little sister late at night, searching for memories of him that had never formed. There would have been all that and more yet to come. More pain. More hardship. More hiding in closets in tears while her mother's next new man beat the shit out of her in the other room. More uncomfortable hugs from her gym teacher when they were alone in the girls' locker room after PE. More, more, more. But there wouldn't be this.

She flicked her bangs out of her eyes, and the moment passed, like sea glass exposed by one wave and washed away by the next. The fear came back, and then the desperate, relentless need for that first rush of escape the point of a needle brought. The feeling that the whole universe pressed down on her with its immeasurable weight, daring her to draw another breath. So she surrendered. She didn't fight it. Couldn't fight it. Running had only brought her here. She lay down on the white sheets, a doe frozen in a winter field, the whole world a wolf.

An hour later, he stood up from the bed, walked into the bathroom, and wrapped himself in a towel. He threw one at her. "Clean up. Be gone when I get out." He left the bathroom door open, turned the water on, and she sat there and watched the little alcove with the sink and bathroom mirror fill up with steam.

She put her clothes on as quietly as she could. Her arms hurt where he'd torqued them behind her. She thought for sure he'd pulled out a clump of her hair. Blood ran down the inside of her thighs. She used both hands to pull open the drawer of the nightstand. A Bible. A pad and pen. She knelt down on the carpet and ran her fingers between the mattress and box spring but found nothing. She saw a black nylon strap peeking out from under the bed and pulled on it gently. The bag was heavy, and when she got it out, she walked over to the sink and turned on the water, splashed her face, and checked out of the corner of her eye that he wasn't about to get out. She went back to the bag, unzipped it, pushed the two sides open, and saw the submachine gun and a heavy, bulky vest with a pistol shoved into a holster affixed to its front. She saw the two sheets of paper and unfolded them. She wondered what the map led to, but then she heard the water shut off. She coughed loudly, zipped the bag back up, and pushed it under the bed before she realized she was still holding the map pages. She stuck them in the open cubby above the nightstand drawer and sat up on the bed.

He walked out with the towel wrapped around him and saw her. "I thought I said be gone."

"You didn't pay me," she said quietly.

"It's sitting right there," he said brusquely and pointed to the envelope tucked under the room's rotary phone. He paused, and she could see that he was processing something, that he had noticed the map pages were out of place. She grabbed the envelope and tried to run to the door, but he took one hand off the towel and shoved her into the television cabinet. She crashed into it, and the corner bit into her side and cracked a rib. Her head hit the television and smashed the screen. She slid down to the floor and tried to catch her breath. He let the towel drop to the floor, walked over to the bed, and pulled the bag from underneath. The girl rolled over on her side and shrieked with pain as lightning emanated from her broken rib and pulsed through her body.

"You trying to rob me?" he said. He knelt down, opened the bag, and quickly inventoried the contents.

Still lying on the floor, she shook her head, her top lip swelling from the impact with the television. She rolled onto her back and looked up at him standing over her, seemingly seven feet tall, completely naked, his face utterly expressionless.

She saw the black void of the pistol barrel pointing down at her. The way he held the gun and the angle he stood over her made it look like he was trying to cover his privates with it. She couldn't help it. It made her laugh.

He reached down, wrapped one hand around her throat, lifted her off the ground, and slammed her against the closed door. He started to choke her. She felt herself drifting. She heard him say, "Funny?" and then she felt the tip of the barrel smash into her mouth. She swallowed at least one tooth. She didn't know how long it would last. She started to choke again but didn't know if it was from him squeezing or her trying not to breathe in the blood filling the back of her throat. Finally, he dropped her.

He walked over to the bed and sat down facing away from her. He had his hands at his sides, pressing down on the bed, even the one that still held the pistol. His whole body trembled with rage. She stood up and grabbed the envelope, went to the door, and pulled it open to run, but it bounced against the security chain. She started sobbing uncontrollably and leaned back against the door. She didn't want to die. For the first time in as long as she could remember, she was sure she didn't. She wanted to live.

He stood up and walked over to her. She covered her head with her arms, her whole body now the one trembling, but with an animal terror. He reached past her and flicked the chain from its socket. "Look at me," he said.

She was too scared to move.

"Look at me," he said again.

She pulled her arms down and met his eyes.

"No one will believe you. Even if they do, no one will care," he said. Then he shoved her out the door.

She stood on the second-floor catwalk, shaking, the shock fading and the pain coming in to take its place. She looked up and down Jeff Davis for someplace she could go where the employees wouldn't kick her out as soon as they laid eyes on her. There was an Exxon station where she'd scored before. Two eighteen-wheelers were parked lengthwise along a chain-link fence in the parking lot. She didn't know what time it was, but the gas station's small convenience store had its lights off and looked closed. Midnight at least. Probably closer to 12:30. She walked toward the exterior stairs and slowly limped down them and into the motel's parking lot. She looked around, walked to the street, leaned against a telephone pole, and opened the envelope. Fifty bucks. Jesus. She knew she needed something, but it had gotten to the point that she often couldn't tell if she was starving or fiending. She didn't have a coin to flip, so she looked up and down the highway again, saw the yellow sign of a Waffle House lit up about a mile to the south, and started walking toward it. Halfway there, she saw an old Tacoma drive by with a kayak ratchet strapped in the bed. The man from the motel was behind the wheel. He didn't look at her. She stopped for a minute and watched the truck shrink into the distant dark. She took the envelope out of her pocket. She didn't have a pen, so she reached up to her face. She grimaced, took her hand from her face, and wrote the plate number down as best she could with her blood.

———

Master Trooper Charmayne Hendricks pulled her patrol car out from the highway underpass and turned north on Jeff Davis. She was three hours into a ten p.m.–to–six a.m. shift, and the night had been quiet. They usually were. A couple of tickets, a disabled vehicle, an accident every once in a while. Rarer, but not entirely unusual, an accident with fatalities. A month earlier she'd held the hand of a drunk who'd turned his F-150 over in a tobacco field out by Chancellorsville as they waited for EMS to cut his body from the truck's cab. The metalwork was so mangled it looked like someone had balled up a piece of paper and tossed it into the field. He'd still been breathing when she'd arrived, pinned between the wheel and one of the twisted roof pillars, a spray of blood misting the air every time he tried to exhale with his broken lungs. He'd stared at her those last few minutes of his existence, but she didn't think he actually saw her. An arm dangled out the pick-up's window, so she took his hand in both of hers and knelt in the dirt beside him. She'd felt the man's fingers fluttering against the palm of her hand, and then he died.

In her sixteen years in the Virginia State Police, she had never really felt in danger. No one had ever pointed a gun at her, let alone fired one. She'd taken a lot of verbal abuse, but even the worst DUIs she'd locked up had never raised a hand against her. She'd drawn her service weapon five times in the line of duty, each time to put down an animal that had been hit by a vehicle. Three deer, a dog, and once, when she worked out by Big Stone Gap, a black bear that had been wounded by a hunter and limped down to a gas station on Highway 23, where it lay down between the pumps and waited to die.

As she headed north on Jeff Davis, her eyes scanned the roadside. Up ahead, she saw the sign for a Waffle House and figured it was as good a time as any to take a meal break. She parked in the lot, walked to the front door, and looked through the glass windows. A typical crowd for a weeknight. All members of the upside down, as she thought of the world of the night. A couple of workers getting off a B shift. The lone traveler headed who knew where. A girl in the back turned her head away as Charmayne walked up. She figured she was probably a working girl from how she'd reacted to her uniform outside the window. Still, Charmayne's philosophy toward that profession was that if they weren't causing trouble for anyone else, she wouldn't add to theirs. Lord knows they had enough to deal with.

She opened the door and nodded when the shift workers looked up at her, made a mental note of the traveler's studious avoidance, and saw that the girl in the rear now had her back turned to her. She sat down at the counter and ordered the All-Star breakfast. When the waitress came to pour her coffee, Charmayne said, "How's everybody doing tonight?"

The waitress clicked her tongue and said, "Well, I'm doing fine, but somebody's had a rough night," nodding her head toward the girl in the back.

Charmayne took a sip of her coffee. Before long, the plate was in front of her, but she let it sit while she looked out of the corner of her eye at the girl. A half-eaten plate of bacon and waffles was in front of her. She still had her back turned. When the waitress came by again, Charmayne asked, "How rough?"

The waitress set the coffeepot on the counter and put her hands down on either side. "She looks like I did every Saturday night of my first marriage. Twelve rounds and didn't win a one."

Charmayne kept her eye on the girl and tried eating but she'd lost her appetite. She put her knife and fork down, wiped her mouth with a napkin, and stood up from the counter. She took her coffee and walked over to the girl, and when she got to her table, Charmayne realized she was passed out against the back of the cushioned bench with her knees tucked up under her chin. She walked around to the side to get a look at her. She was a lot younger than she'd first thought, and the waitress was right—some bastard had taken out his problems on her face.

She sat down in the chair across from her, folded her hands on the table, and waited. After a minute or two, the girl stirred. She squinted at the light through her swollen eye. When Charmayne got a good look at her face, she said, "Sweet Jesus."

The girl turned her head and saw the uniform first, then Charmayne's eyes, and she started to cry. She still had her knees tucked up under her and said, "That bad, huh?"

"Yeah, baby," Charmayne said. "That bad."

"Are you gonna arrest me?"

"Do you want me to? As far as I can tell, you ain't the one committed the crime here."

"Like you don't know."

"Sure, I know. I been around the block. All the same, if I was gonna arrest somebody, it would be the piece of shit that did this to you."

The girl relaxed ever so slightly, but Charmayne noticed. She turned her whole body toward the table again. She looked out the window and saw only herself reflected in it. "Is it always gonna be like this?" she asked.

Master Trooper Hendricks shifted in her seat. She took the question seriously. "If you want it to be different, it can be different. That don't mean easy, now. But you gotta want it to be different."

"I do."

"Do you want to tell me who did this to you?"

"I don't know his name." She took out the envelope and

slid it across the table to Charmayne. "He was driving a truck. Here's the plate number. Had a map of someplace."

Jesus Christ, thought Charmayne. *She wrote it in blood.* "Short? Tall? Black? White?" she asked.

The girl closed her eyes and saw his face again. His eyes stared through her. "Tall. White. Kind of biker-looking guy."

Charmayne took out her notepad and started to write. *White male. Late twenties to early thirties. Brown hair. Short brown beard. Tattoo in cursive script across his chest. Six feet to six two.* "Anything else?"

"He had a bag with guns in it."

Charmayne looked up from her notepad. "Guns? How many?"

"There was, like, an Uzi-looking one or whatever, I don't know, and a pistol. The pistol was in a big heavy vest. Like the ones the army guys wear."

Charmayne leaned back in her chair and took a sip of coffee, looking at the girl. "This map, do you remember anything about it?"

"I don't know. It was a map. Two pages. He'd marked some stuff in red."

"A name of a town? Street names? Anything?" Charmayne saw the girl put her head down and pull her knees back up under her chin. "Hey, what's your name, sweetie?"

"What?" the girl asked.

"Your name. You got a name, don't you, baby?"

"Ashleigh."

"Ashleigh, I'm Charmayne. You're doing really, really great. I want you to think real hard, just one more time for me, okay?"

She nodded. "Deltaville? Something like that. At the bottom of the page, there was an island. I don't know the name."

"That was the first page?"

"Uh-huh."

"What about the second?"

"The second one was less water. Mathews, I think? There were a bunch of words. I think I remember Mathews."

Charmayne held up her hand and said, "Give me just a sec, okay, hon?" She stood up from the table and turned away.

"Charmayne," said Ashleigh.

The trooper turned back around.

"Please don't leave."

"I'm not, Ashleigh. I promise. I'm just going to get something out of my car. It's right there." She pointed out the window to the blue-and-gray patrol unit. "You can see me the whole way, okay?"

"Okay."

Charmayne walked out to the parking lot, reached under her patrol car's passenger seat, grabbed a Virginia Department of Transportation atlas, and brought it back inside. She sat down at the table and ran her finger down the index, then turned the page to the map that depicted Hampton Roads, the Eastern Shore, and the southern half of the Chesapeake. She turned the map toward Ashleigh. The girl had gotten clammy. She was sweating and started to grimace. She held her knees up against her tightly.

"Ashleigh," Charmayne said. "Are you okay?"

"I feel sick to my stomach."

Charmayne took the radio handset from her shoulder, keyed it, and said, "I need EMS at the Waffle House, Route One, north of Business Seventeen."

"No," Ashleigh pleaded. "I don't want to go."

"Send a female tech." Charmayne hooked the handset back

to her uniform and said, "Sweetheart, you need a doctor. I can't let you sit here suffering."

The girl threw up on the floor. The waitress saw it and hollered, "Oh, Lord have mercy!"

Charmayne moved to the bench beside Ashleigh, took a napkin, and wiped the vomit off her chin. She looked up at the waitress and said, "Don't worry, I'll take care of it." When she ran the napkin across Ashleigh's face, the girl cried out in pain. Charmayne dipped the napkin in ice water and gently dabbed at her face a second time. She put the napkin down and wrapped her arms around the girl.

Charmayne closed her eyes and rocked the girl. She felt like the two of them were floating on some small boat out on the water far from shore, small peaks of waves bobbing them from side to side. Ashleigh leaned against her, and Charmayne ran her fingers through the girl's hair. She whispered to her over and over, "You're gonna be okay. You're gonna be okay," then prayed to God that He would not make a liar out of her.

They stayed like that for only a minute more, and then they heard the sirens arriving out of the night. "They're almost here, Ashleigh. You're gonna be okay."

"Charmayne?" the girl said.

"Yeah, baby."

"Here."

Charmayne opened her eyes. The girl pointed to an island on the map. "It looked a little different on the one he had, but it was here." She gestured to the southern part of Gwynn's Island. "It was here. Where all the writing was."

The ambulance pulled up in the parking lot. Charmayne waved to the techs when they got out. She looked down at Ashleigh and said, "You ready?"

The girl nodded. The trooper helped the girl stand up and supported her on the short walk to the parking lot. The techs had the gurney out, and when Ashleigh got to the techs, one took her by the hand and gently helped her lie down on it. The female tech started asking her questions. Ashleigh closed her eyes without answering them. The techs rolled the gurney into the back of the ambulance. Charmayne took one of the techs aside and said, "She's dope-sick, and someone beat the shit out of her."

"Roger," he responded.

Before they closed the door, Charmayne took one of her cards and put it in the girl's hand. "Ashleigh," she said.

The techs had put a cardiac monitor on her and an IV in her arm. "Yeah?"

"When you get to the hospital, I want you to call your mother."

The girl's top lip started to tremble, and she shook her head. "She doesn't want me, Charmayne. I'm just a worthless piece of shit."

"That's not true, baby. That's not true."

The tech reached out to shut the doors, and Charmayne saw Ashleigh's face a last time through the narrowing gap. She said again, "Call her," just before the doors closed. The girl nodded and said, "Okay."

The ambulance hit lights and sirens as it pulled onto Jeff Davis and headed to Mary Washington Hospital. Charmayne watched until the glow from the swirling emergency lights had faded from the sky. *You're not worthless,* she thought.

She went back into the restaurant, dropped forty dollars on the counter, and got back in her patrol car. She ran the license plate the girl had given her. It came back to a '91 Tacoma stolen the day before in Woodbridge. She radioed to the state police office in Gloucester and then put out a statewide BOLO on the truck with the description the girl had given her. She made a point of advising any officer who saw the vehicle to approach with extreme caution. The suspect was armed and dangerous. *Armed and dangerous,* she thought. Men like this one were more like rabid animals. *Dangerous* was an insufficient descriptor. Master Trooper Charmayne Hendricks blipped the lights and pulled out onto the highway. It was two a.m. She knew he'd had a head start, forty-five minutes, maybe more, so she put the pedal to the floor.

TWENTY-FOUR

Detective Wheel and Arman arrived at Violent Crimes just after midnight. They stepped off the elevator, and she led him through the maze of cubicles. She took him into the break room and pointed to the couch against the wall. "Let me go get you some blankets," she said.

Arman sat down and looked around the room. There was a small kitchenette in the corner. Three round tables with four chairs at each. Two coffeemakers percolated on the counter. Even at that hour, the place was alive with activity. Detectives went in and out. Stood over the microwave, waiting for whatever meal their body clocks called for. He felt as though he'd been awake for a year. Thoughts of his wife and son were always near, but over the past few days, that nearness felt threatening, as if he might be overwhelmed by seeing their faces in his mind, by saying their names softly to himself. As if his grief might make him more vulnerable than he was already.

Catherine came back into the room and two detectives gossiping over microwaved Hungry Man TV dinners gave her a nod. She brought the stack of linens over to the couch and sat down next to Arman. "I guess I didn't think this through," she said. He didn't answer. "C'mon," she said to Arman. To the two detectives, she said, "I'm taking interview three, guys."

One of the detectives gave her a thumbs-up and returned to his Salisbury steak. The other leafed through a two-year-old *Sports Illustrated* Swimsuit Issue and never looked up. She led Arman down the hall and unlocked the door to the spartan room. It contained a small table and three chairs. There were hooks in the wall and on the floor a suspect could be hand-cuffed to. The two-way mirrors of old had been replaced by audio/video observation, so the walls were blank. Arman sat down in one of the chairs, and Catherine sat on the other side. "Do you want me to try to rustle up an air mattress? A cot?"

"Yes," he said. "Please."

She returned five minutes later, unfolded a cot against the wall, and laid the linens on it.

"You're not going to lock me in here, are you?"

"No, Arman. Of course not." She sat back down in the chair opposite him. "This is gonna be over soon," she said.

He looked at her blankly. "Over?" he asked. "How could it ever be over? I can't stay in here forever, Detective. What if he never stops coming after me?"

She looked at the man across from her. His shoulders slumped. His eyes were heavy and red with exhaustion. She'd seen him startle at sounds, at shadows. She thought of her father taking her into the mountains above the Tye River as a child, hunting black bear or the small, sturdy bucks that lived their lives at dawn and dusk, hidden in morning mist and thickets of mountain laurel. *Patience, Cat,* he'd say. *Just walk 'em down. All you gotta do is walk 'em down.*

That's what these men were doing to Arman. Walking him down. "They aren't ghosts, Arman," she said. "They aren't shadows. They want it to feel that way, but they all have faces. They all have names. They all have addresses and birth certificates. They live in the same world we do, and no one walks through it without leaving a trace. We'll find them."

"Find them? And do what? What did Trey say? The people these guys work for aren't citizens of a country, they're citizens of a tax bracket."

"All I know is some things were crimes a long time before anyone thought to make laws against them, and we had ways of setting things right a long time before anyone wrote the first punishment down. Arman, I'm trying to tell you I'll do whatever needs to be done."

He looked at her across the table. Tried to read on her face if she meant what he thought she did, if she understood what it could cost her. "Why?" he asked.

"I don't know, other than it needs doing. Someone hurts somebody. I catch them so they can't do it again. The sort we're dealing with, you gotta break like you'd break a hot horse. Not because they're bad. Not because they deserve it. You gotta break them because they won't stop kicking unless you do. That's the only thing that matters, far as I can tell. Paying for what they done already? That's the lawyers' job. The judge's. Making them stand up before God and everybody, I think that's to make us feel better about the fact they need breaking in the first place. I don't know that there's a higher meaning waiting at the end of it. I won't pretend to believe in closure. And I won't pretend you'd believe it if I said you'll find it."

"I wouldn't even know where to look for it."

"I know. I'm sorry. I can't do anything about that, Arman. If I could fix what was done to you . . . but I can't. My job, my only job, is to stop them."

"And if you do stop them? What then? I just get on with my life?"

"You think that's the choice you have, Arman, but it isn't. Your life's getting on whether you want it to or not." Arman sat there with his arms folded across his chest. She got up and went to the door. "I'm gonna call Sally. Check up on them. You need anything else?"

He shook his head.

"All right, then, I'll be in the break room." She opened the door and got halfway out before looking back at him. His elbows were on his knees, and his hands held the back of his head. He felt her waiting there and looked up at her.

"You know, Arman, you don't have to do it by yourself," she said.

"Do what?" he asked.

"Get on with your life."

———

Sally and her father stayed up long past midnight. They sat at the kitchen table with a pot of coffee on the gingham table-cloth between them. They'd laughed a lot more than they had over the past few years of visits. The last time she'd felt like this at home was during Hurricane Isabel. Stevie home on leave. The four of them with too much stubborn pride to evacuate. She remembered the house all candlelit. The roar of the wind outside. The rip of black waves through Milford Haven. She wondered what it was about that time and this one that made her feel a desperate, giddy joy woven into her fear. She could not remember ever having loved anyone as much as she'd loved her family then and her father now. She'd almost forgotten about her father's lever gun lying across his lap. The .45 tucked in his belt. The twelve-gauge leaned against the counter by the back door. She didn't remember nodding off at the table. Her father nudged her awake. It was two o'clock when she checked her watch. She looked up at her father and said, "Daddy, why don't you get some sleep? I'll sit up and keep a lookout."

He laughed. "Yeah, right. Go upstairs. Get some rest. I'll be fine. Detective Wheel called while you were asleep. Just checking on us."

"You want me to set an alarm?"

He looked down at his own watch then. "Quarter of five? If the boogeymen ain't stormed the beaches by then, maybe we'll take the boat out. Watch the sunrise."

"Dad," she said. "Don't joke about that."

He drummed his fingers on the table. "I'm sorry, Sal. I didn't—"

"I know. The jokes don't make it less scary, though."

He waved her up the stairs. He was surprised at how easily what happened with Trey had slipped his mind. He'd liked the boy well enough. Knew that Sally loved him, or had at one time, anyway, which was sufficient for him. But he'd forgotten how easily you could move between death and laughter once you knew how. He hadn't considered that Sally hadn't learned that lesson yet the way it had been beaten into him at her age. He hoped she never would.

She walked up the stairs and heard them creak as she went. She stood at the top step and opened the door to her bedroom. She emptied her pockets on the nightstand and changed into sweats and a T-shirt. She looked back through the open door into the hallway. Down the hall, directly opposite her room, was Stevie's. She went back out and walked across the landing and opened his door. His room looked empty. Unlived-in. It was certainly no shrine to the departed the way parents who outlived children sometimes left their rooms. In fact, she wasn't sure if the door had been opened since Stevie was last home. She saw a few cardboard boxes stacked in a corner. She went to the nightstand, turned on a lamp, and brought one of the boxes to the bed. She opened it, set it down, and took out a framed picture from their childhood. The two of them with middle-school cross-country medals around their necks. Stevie smiling with a front tooth missing from a four-wheeler accident the week before the meet. She chuckled to herself. Who the heck had let him run, as beat up as he was? And he'd almost won.

She took out another picture of the four of them at his graduation at Great Lakes. Another with Stevie smiling goofily, helping her move into her dorm room in Charlottesville. He'd written her letters when he was deployed, and she somehow knew when reading them that she'd never see him smile that way again. She'd never thought he'd be killed in combat, but she was sure the child who had been beside her for her entire life would be. She put the box back in the corner. She walked around the room slowly, running her fingers across the top of his writing desk. Looked into his dresser mirror, hoping to see him somehow staring back at her. She lay on his bed and stared up at the ceiling. She thought about saying a prayer for him but wasn't sure what to say. So she told him she loved him. That was all. It seemed to Sally like it ought to count. Then she fell asleep.

TWENTY-FIVE

Jimmy had the Tacoma's speedometer needle hovering over fifty-five miles an hour the whole way down the Middle Peninsula. Two times on 17, someone had driven by and flashed their brights at him, but he didn't respond with flashes of his own. Each time, he had passed a county patrol car tucked into a roadside tree line a minute or two down the road. He knew they had hit him with the radar gun, but as long as he didn't get pulled over, he was positive they wouldn't ID the make, model, or plates as he went by in the dark.

At 3:45, he was a half a mile from the bridge to the island. He came around a slight bend in the road and saw the faintest blue glow of lights in a distant gap between the trees. He immediately flicked off his headlights and downshifted into second. A gravel two-track was fifty yards ahead on the right, barely visible in the moonlight. He stood on the brakes, turned onto it, and fishtailed the back end, spraying gravel over a trailer home's yard. He slowed the truck to a crawl and took the two-track farther into dense woods. He stopped, pulled out the topo map, and found his location on it with a mini–LED flashlight.

Up ahead, the two-track split. It circled back to the main road to the right, and he could take his chances backtracking to try another way. He put his elbow up on the door and rubbed his beard. If the police were already at the bridge, they were undoubtedly behind him now as well. He would have driven right into them if they'd left their lights off. And then there was the girl. He didn't know how, but he was sure she'd been the one to tip off the cops. At six a.m. Chris would be sitting in a Motel 6 by the Richmond airport, waiting for him to call. He knew he had to call with good news or not at all.

He took the left turn on the gravel two-track. Soon enough, it turned to dirt and then a barely used path through the trees. After about a mile, the trees opened up to the left, and he stopped the truck. The trees continued along the right side of the path. On the other side, an old farmer's field had given way to the early stages of succession. He pulled out the map again and looked at it. The path dead-ended in the woods a little farther down. A half dozen large houses fronted a cove two hundred yards beyond those trees. He didn't need to worry about being seen by their occupants. Maybe on the way back. Only a few stands of pines stood between his location and Milford Haven at the far edge of the field. He'd be directly across from Barn Creek and a little under a mile to the house if he put in right there.

Jimmy put the map in his shirt pocket and got out of the truck. His eyes were already adjusted to the dark night. The field was covered in blue sedge up to his waist, dotted here and there with blackberry. He worried about getting the truck stuck in the soft ground, so he walked along the path at the edge of the trees until he found a gap big enough to park it in. Once the truck was out of sight, he put the vest on and slung the submachine gun to rest in the low ready position. He tucked the dry bag under the seat and pressed the door closed quietly. He walked to the back, loosed the kayak's ratchet straps, double-checked that the paddle was still tucked into the hull, and lifted it over his head.

It weighed forty pounds, and at nine feet long, it wasn't easy to keep balanced. In a few minutes, he crossed the field and worked his way through the trees down to the water. There was a small white ribbon of sand below the trees, so he put the kayak down and slid down the bank. Once he had his feet in the sand, he pulled the kayak off the ledge, put it half in the water, took his time getting both feet into the cockpit, and sat down. He took the pole, pushed off the sand, and slid into the water. He could see the far shore in the starlight and paddled into the channel toward the indistinct mass of the island.

As he approached the far shore, docks came into view. Just starboard off the bow, he saw the land fall back where the water of Milford Haven ran inland up a creek. Unless he'd drifted north, which Jimmy was reasonably sure he hadn't, he needed to follow this creek past the first riprap breakwater and put in somewhere on its right bank. He checked his watch: 4:30. He was fifteen minutes behind schedule. He couldn't believe he'd let the girl do this to him. He put the paddle in the water and got into a rhythm. Nautical dawn was fifteen minutes away. He knew that the deep blackness of night would soon bleed into gray on the low horizon off the island's far shore. If he didn't get the job done quickly, he'd have to find a way back in the plain light of day.

As he reached the mouth of Barn Creek, he looked over his left shoulder and saw the twirl of blue lights still going above the tree line. A few minutes later, he pushed the kayak toward shore. The whole bank of the creek was steep riprap. He pulled up alongside the rocks and saw a covered boat lift a hundred yards downstream. He clambered onto the rocks and pulled the kayak's bow along the bank by the tow rope until he found a suitable place to tie off. He reached down to the red-dot sight and turned it on, checked its brightness, and began to jog in a crouch toward the house in the grass just above the riprap.

Jimmy arrived where the dock met the bank and looked up at the house. One light was on in an upstairs room. He reached under his vest, pulled out the map, and checked his notes against his surroundings. This was it. He looked down the dock and saw the boat in the water. He lowered his body to shrink his silhouette, trotted down the weather-beaten planks, and hopped aboard. He went into the pilothouse and reached under the wheel. He opened the housing, grabbed a handful of exposed wires, and pulled as hard as he could, snapping enough to render the boat useless. He went back up to dry ground and circled the house as he approached it, looking for any sign of activity. He found the box where the phone and cable lines entered the house, pulled out a knife, and cut them. He circled the house one more time, pausing at the leading edge of each window to look inside.

He closed his loop of the house at the back door. A pair of frilly curtains were shut over the glass. He tried the door. Locked. He checked the windowpanes to see if any were loose. None were. With the buttstock of the submachine gun, he broke the pane of glass just above the doorknob. He reached inside, unlocked the knob, and slowly pushed the door open.

Butch Ewell stood at the open door of his son's old room and watched his daughter sleep. The feeling he had when she was like this had not changed since the day they'd brought her home from the hospital. Something like awe and terror mixed together. Maybe it was reverence. That this child could be so vulnerable and yet have enough faith in him to lie down and sleep in a world like this. Whatever it was, he didn't feel equal to it. Never felt like he'd genuinely earned that trust. And after Stevie...well, he hadn't made it that far yet. Didn't know if he ever would.

The lever-action hung loosely by his side, the foregrip in his right hand just in front of the lever. His fingers drummed along the worn wood. His eyes hadn't moved from where Sally lay on the bed. Off to the side of the room, he saw a picture of himself and Stevie out on the boat. The boy, not yet ten, holding a big red drum out in front of him. Butch closed his eyes. Remembered the sound of the line as Stevie cranked and pulled. Remembered the feel of the spray against his face and the June wind. The dark water flashed in the sunlight and beat a gentle rhythm against the hull. He heard glass break.

It took a few seconds to register in his mind. Butch knelt down quickly, brought the rifle to his shoulder, and turned toward the stairs. He heard it again. Shards splashed across the floor. He kept the gun at his shoulder and backed into the room. He knelt down next to the bed and laid the rifle down with the barrel pointed out the bedroom door. He put his hand over Sally's mouth and held his finger up to his lips. She struggled against his hand until she fully woke. He pointed to the dormer in the back of the bedroom and whispered, "Out the window, girl. Get to the boat and get to the Coast Guard station."

"Daddy, no," she said.

He gritted his teeth and barked at her, "Now!"

She rolled off the bed and opened the window. A small arc

of the yard behind the house was lit by the glow coming from the upstairs room. Darkness lay beyond it. She hooked one leg through the opening and looked back at her father. He was on one knee with the rifle up, his cheek on the stock. He kept his eye over the iron sight and waved at her to go. "I'll be there soon, baby. Promise."

Sally crawled out onto the low roof and glanced down. Ten feet? Twelve? She looked for a place to hang and drop but saw only the gutters running along the end of the roof. She knew she couldn't hang from them, so she sat down and scooted toward the edge. She looked down at the back of the house and saw that the kitchen door was open. She looked up to the bedroom window again, then dropped to the ground. She hit hard and rolled onto the lawn. Her left ankle throbbed from the impact. She took off across the backyard toward the dock. Her ankle hurt and felt a little unstable, but it wasn't far. She turned her head and looked back up toward the house in time to see the light go out in Stevie's upstairs bedroom. She started crying.

At the end of the dock, she jumped onto the boat without breaking stride and opened the pilothouse door. She went to the wheel and pushed the starter button. Nothing happened. She tried it again. And again. And again. Nothing. She started to shake. Tears streamed down her cheeks. She got down on a knee and checked the starter button in the dark. Saw the tangle of wires in the busted-open housing. She looked through the windshield at Barn Creek. Lights burned at a few of the houses on the other side. Three hundred yards. If she ran along the creek a little more inland, a breakwater from the opposite shore would cut that distance in half. But what if they found her in the water halfway across? She'd be completely helpless.

She hopped over the side of the boat and looked up toward the house. Beyond it, the island was practically uninhabited. A hundred acres of deep woods that she knew every square inch of. A few houses lined the beach on the other side of the woods. An RV park anchored the dwellings, and beyond them, the island thinned until it was not much more than a sandbar. *We're going to be okay,* she told herself. *Get to the RV park, Sally. Get there and scream bloody murder.* She took a deep breath and started to run.

Jimmy stepped into the house and tried not to crush the glass at his feet. He made his way through the kitchen and into the living room. He moved fluidly, the submachine gun an extension of his body, his torso swiveling slowly as he scanned the room. He saw the front door and the staircase landing at the far end. He circled toward the stairs like a boxer, keeping his distance from them until he could lean out ever so slightly and look toward the second floor. He leaned back so he'd be blocked from the line of sight of anyone at the second-floor landing. There had been lights on upstairs when he had approached the house, but now there were none. He crossed the landing to the far side of the staircase and pointed the submachine gun up to the second floor. He placed his right foot down on the far side of the first tread as close to the wall as he could get and put his weight down on it slowly. No sound. He did the same with his left foot on the step above. And the next. And the next, until he found a pace that let him gather momentum without making noise. He checked the angles as he went. Even in the low ambient light, he saw a hallway extending in both directions at the top. Jimmy knew that taking stairs like this solo was hardly different from suicide if anyone was waiting for him. He paused one step from the second-story landing and leaned out to look down the hall to the left.

Sally ran across the dirt road and into the woods. She'd twisted her left ankle on the drop from the roof, but her adrenaline pushed the pain away. She ran through brambles, hurdled downed limbs, and tore her feet up on the forest floor, but she didn't slow down. She ran, and after a minute, she looked back and had already lost sight of the house through the trees. She wouldn't stop running. Not until she got help. But then she heard it. Three sharp cracks of a rifle. Impossibly loud even at this distance. The shots broke the steady concentration of her stride. Her foot caught on a bittersweet vine and she twisted her ankle and fell to the ground. She looked down. It was the same ankle she'd hurt jumping from the roof. A wave of nausea came over her. She felt dizzy. She stood up and turned to run again but could hardly even walk.

Butch was down on the floor in Stevie's room in the prone position. He'd set up on the stairs and could see only slightly more than an inch of the landing through the bedroom door. The darkness moved in his narrow field of view. He didn't hesitate. He fired the rifle, and the muzzle flash lit the second floor quick and bright as lightning. The gunshot roared, and his ears rang instantly. He couldn't see if he'd hit his target. He worked the lever and fired again. Worked the lever and fired. He popped up to a knee and leaned out into the room to see down the hall.

A muzzle flash blinded him from ten feet away. He heard the sound of a jackhammer as the action of a suppressed submachine gun sent five subsonic rounds into the bedroom. He shut his eyes against the flash and circled left to the corner of the room. He got down on a knee behind the dresser and peeked out the side toward the bedroom door. He couldn't see to the stairs anymore, saw only about a foot of the far wall of the hall outside the room.

How many times had he fired? He thought he still had three shots in the rifle. He tried to shake the ringing out of his head. His right arm was wet. Butch looked down and saw blood dripping onto the floor. He'd been hit through the right biceps. He gritted his teeth. He was breathing fast now, and he forced himself to slow down, take deep breaths, and exhale slowly.

Jimmy was hit too. The first round Butch sent down the hallway found its target. It struck squarely in the center of the ceramic plate tucked into his vest and knocked the wind out of him. He fell back against the wall and slid down until he sat on the top step. The second round hit the pistol holstered on his vest and exploded into a shower of fragments. One of the fragments hit Jimmy's right eye, blinding it. By the time the third round hit the wall over his head, he'd brought the submachine gun up to his shoulder. Blood poured out of his eye. He couldn't aim properly. He held the submachine gun out in both hands away from his body and looked through the red-dot sight with his left eye. He saw movement and squeezed the trigger, but he couldn't hold it steady against the recoil. He scooted down two more steps so he'd be out of the other shooter's line of sight and gasped for air. He caught his breath after a few seconds and examined the situation.

An armed man with a rifle was barricaded in the bedroom. Jimmy would have heard radio traffic once the shooting stopped if it was the cops, but he'd heard nothing. He hadn't heard anything at all since he'd returned fire. It could be the guy was down. Jimmy thought about taking down the room. He figured it was even odds that he'd be killed as soon as he crossed the bedroom doorway if the guy wasn't dead already.

He and Chris both knew trying to take the house solo was a bad idea. But when the cop had called, Chris said somebody had to meet him. They flipped for the house. *Fucking tails,* Jimmy thought.

His head hurt so goddamn bad. He knew the eye was gone. Bet your ass the cops at the bridge heard the long-gun fire. He had maybe five minutes to put them down, get to the water, and then what? Find an emergency room? He would have to drive another five minutes inland when he got to the truck to get cell service. Maybe get Chris to have one of the company docs meet him on the down-low in a motel somewhere. He took a deep breath.

It dawned on Jimmy then that he wouldn't make it out. He'd been a good soldier once. He knew when a situation was salvageable and when it wasn't. He'd been a good soldier until he took a thousand bucks a day on a ninety-day contract when he was twenty-six. Now he was wounded in a gunfight, totally alone, not knowing what he might be dying for besides a paycheck. He didn't know what to do, so he yelled, "You're gonna have to come out sometime."

The ringing had subsided just enough for Butch to hear the man call. He'd been in this house since he got back from Vietnam. Had never lived anywhere else. In all those years, he figured he'd heard a voice call to him from just about every square foot of the house. The man was still on the stairs, near the top. It was a stick-built Cape, the home. Plain drywall. Studs sixteen on center. Butch didn't know from ballistics, but he figured he had a pretty good bead on the guy even through three walls. He rose up from his knees and circled out from behind the dresser but stayed out of the doorway. He brought the lever gun up to his shoulder and aimed it at the wall two feet in front of him. It would have to clear that and both walls of the hall to make it to the stairway. He fired three times, working the lever as quickly as possible while keeping the rifle stable at his shoulder between rounds. Deaf as a post again. The gun empty. He had six more .30-.30 rounds in his shirt pocket but left them there. He ducked behind the dresser and pulled the .45 from his hip. "My god-dang house. I ain't going nowhere!" Butch yelled back.

Jimmy never heard him. Studs stopped the first and the third round Butch fired. But the second had passed through the gypsum board without resistance and entered Jimmy's side just in front of his right armpit. It exited through his back, shattering his scapula into tiny shards of bone that ripped into the muscles around his shoulder. He tried to use his right arm to push himself off the ground, but it was useless. A black wave of pain broke over him. He faded in and out of consciousness. Sweat poured down his face. He pushed himself off the stairs with his left arm and got up. A bone fragment had nicked his subclavian vein. He was already bleeding to death. Another wave, and he slumped against the wall. He staggered toward Stevie's bedroom like a drunk going to the wrong front door. His right arm hung limp against his side. As he approached the doorway, he reached into the room with the submachine gun in his left hand and fired erratically, emptying the magazine.

He turned around and hugged the wall all the way down the stairs. He dropped the submachine gun on the floor, opened the front door, and sat down on the brick steps. He looked at his watch. He wondered how long it would take him to die. The sun was not yet up, but the darkness was lifting.

When Sally heard the second set of shots, the strange dull *thump-thump-thump* of the submachine gun, she stopped and leaned against a tree. She hardly even reacted to her tears, and, with her jaw set and her face now awash in them, she started to limp back toward the house. Before she'd even gone halfway, she fell to her knees. Her ankle was already grotesquely swollen. She crawled. And when she heard another set of rifle shots and then more of the strangely muffled firing, she kept crawling. Ten yards from the dirt road, she looked between the tall pines toward the house. She saw a figure sitting on her front steps. A man with a beard. She got closer. His right arm hung awkwardly by his side. Half his body was soaked in blood. She got close to the road and stopped before dragging herself out of the woods. He looked in her direction. One of his eyes was a bloody mess. She didn't think he'd seen her. A fragment from the video they'd watched together in the hotel room flashed through Sally's mind: The man who'd exited one of the SUVs and shouted back to Harris before the shooting started. It was him.

Just across the bridge, Master Trooper Charmayne Hendricks leaned against the hood of her car on the side of the road next to the Coast Guard station. Another trooper and a Mathews County deputy blocked the entrance to the swing bridge with their cars. Senior Chief Rawls, commander of the station, leaned against the hood beside her. They both sipped at Styrofoam cups of coffee and let the quiet of the fading night and the soft blue spin of the police lights wash over them.

He looked at his watch: 0450. "Maybe he's not coming. If he was, he ought to have been here."

Charmayne thought about the girl. She had to be sedated in a room at Mary Washington by now. Charmayne was so sure she was gonna get the bastard when she'd pulled out of the Waffle House and took off after him. But maybe the chief was right. Should have been here by now. Wasn't another way on the island. Not unless he meant to swim or paddle. Maybe she'd mixed up how bad she wanted to put the bracelets on him with how likely she was to be the one who did it. Still, if this wasn't worth the trouble, she didn't know what was.

"You said your friend called, right? Said to watch for anyone you don't recognize?"

"Yeah, but he was worried about trouble with his daughter's ex-boyfriend or something. Besides, no one came across before y'all got here. Had one of the seamen keep an eye out. Not really authorized to do more than that anyway."

A few more minutes passed. Charmayne walked up to the barrier pole and looked out past the narrows toward the open water of the Chesapeake. She could feel blue sky below the horizon even though she couldn't see it yet. A sense of the light rising, particle by particle, like candles being lit in a church. She closed her eyes.

Three shots rang out in quick succession. She turned back to the other trooper and the deputy. Chief Rawls ran up. "Rifle fire," he said. "South of here, I think. Across the narrows."

"Chief, where did you say your friend lives?"

"Shit," he said. "Just up Barn Creek. Could have come

from there." He got on his radio. "Get a small response boat in the water, now! I'll be there in one minute."

"I'm driving," she told him.

"Main road about three miles, then hang a right on a dirt road. They're at the end."

Charmayne signaled to the other trooper and the county deputy to follow her. She got in her car and cranked the engine. The two officers got in their vehicles and backed them out of the bridge's path. A seaman from the Coast Guard station threw up the barrier pole manually, and Charmayne hit the sirens and punched it. The big Crown Vic buzzed across the bridge. She hit seventy-five miles an hour down the two-lane road and a hundred where it narrowed, farther from the bridge. She heard another round of rifle shots. Two minutes after she cleared the bridge, she braked hard, slung the car around the right-hand turn, and gunned the motor again as the back end straightened out. She saw a white Cape at the end of the road and checked her rearview mirror. The trooper and the deputy were right behind her. She pulled the vehicle broadside across the dirt road, got out, and took a position behind the front fender. A man sat on the steps. Bloody. Had on a military plate carrier.

The other two police vehicles pulled behind her, and the trooper and deputy got out and posted up behind the rear fender of her car.

"A tactical team is on the way," the trooper said.

She looked over the hood at the man, turned back, and ducked behind her front wheel. "Pistol holstered on his vest."

"Roger. Who's in the house?"

"I don't know. But we aren't waiting for the tactical team. Let's go." Charmayne guided the two junior officers to the side of the house with hand and arm signals. She left the cover of the engine compartment and came out in front of the man with her pistol raised. "Virginia State Police!" Charmayne yelled and moved toward him. He didn't respond. She could see that he was close to death. His right eye was disfigured and bleeding, and his arm hung at his side, drenched in blood.

Sally pulled herself up using a sapling when she saw the blue lights flying down the road, the sirens seeming to come screaming in behind them. The officers quickly got out of their vehicles and moved toward the man on the steps from two directions. The female officer who had gone toward the front of the house was in her line of sight. Sally tried to call out to them, but she was so out of breath and her throat was so dry she could only croak.

In his mind, Jimmy was somewhere else. He felt like he'd sunk into deep water. He remembered a strange sunrise. *Was that the muezzin call?* He felt like having a smoke. Where had he left them? *Oh, yeah, shirt pocket. Who's that? Maybe she wants one.*

Charmayne kept the pistol in her right hand aimed at the man on the steps. She reached behind her back to her utility belt to take out her handcuffs. There was no doubt it was him. A rabid dog. He reached up toward the vest and smiled at her. "Gun! Gun! Gun!" she yelled.

Sally gathered herself, leaned against a tall pine, and watched the officers close in on the man. One of them yelled out, and they all fired. She threw her hands against her ears at the sound and fell to her knees. They were too quick to count. To Sally, it sounded like chaos incarnate.

Of the twenty-two rounds fired at the man on the porch, fifteen hit him. She looked up again with her hands still over her ears. For the briefest of moments, the man lingered upright as if suspended in the air. But then he slowly fell over onto the brick steps, his head awkwardly trapped between two spindles of the iron railing.

She didn't know what she yelled when she broke from the woods. Her voice came from deep within her, calling out from the seat of desperation—for mercy. For her father. For help. She tumbled over and crawled across the road, pulled herself up off the ground, and tried to run again.

Charmayne turned and saw the young woman emerge from the trees with her arms waving wildly above her head, screaming for her father. She realized she was looking at her down the sights of her pistol when the other trooper yelled out that she was unarmed. She holstered the gun and ran over to the woman and caught her as she fell once more. She helped her to the ground. The woman kept screaming for her father. She had cuts all over her arms from diving through thorns. She reached down to her ankle, and Charmayne saw it was ballooned and bruised an ugly purple. "Where's your father?" she asked.

"He's in the house," Sally said. "Please help him."

"Is he armed?"

Sally pointed to the dead man on the steps. "He was trying to kill us!" she screamed. Charmayne waved over the deputy and told him to stay with Sally.

"Okay," she said to the trooper. "We're going in to find her father."

But they didn't have to. Butch Ewell came down the stairs and pushed open the front door. With his good hand, he held his wounded arm at the elbow. His shirtsleeve was bloody. He paused at the top step and sat down on the bricks next to the dead man. Sally saw him and tried to run to him but almost fell; the county deputy caught her and guided her to the brick steps.

"I'm all right," Butch said. "Just a little out of breath. I'm all right." He tried to wave off the two troopers as they approached.

Charmayne saw it first: Blood soaked his shirt from the right breast pocket down to his belt. Three bullets had stitched the fabric up and down his right side like wayward button-holes. She looked over at the other trooper. "Get on the horn. Tell dispatch we need a medevac to MCV."

The young trooper looked at the old man on the porch struggling to breathe. The uninjured eye of the dead man slumped on the railing stared back at him, cold and blue, what-ever spark it had once held extinguished now, absolutely and forever.

Charmayne snapped her fingers and barked, "Trooper! Now!"

He ran off to his car and called it in. A boat roared up the creek behind the house. Sally limped over to the brick steps and knelt in front of her father. He had an elbow on each knee and his hands together. Her father took short, sharp stabs at breath as if he were drowning and might find a drop of air in the water. He sipped at the air shallowly but couldn't seem to find any. "Sal, I just can't catch my breath," he said. He reached out for her hands. Sweat beaded on his forehead. He looked up to the sky: A band of pink above the trees. Heron blue across the dome of the heavens. He looked at her and smiled. Gri-maced against the pain.

A trio of Coast Guard seamen ran up from the dock and around the house. One knelt beside them with an aid bag at her feet. She looked at Sally and said, "What's his name?"

"Butch," she said.

The other seamen had already started to cut off his shirt when she said, "Butch, my name is Petty Officer Clark, but you can call me Sarah, okay?"

He didn't answer.

The petty officer talked calmly and quietly to the seaman who had taken up a position on the other side of her. "Get me a chest seal and a hemostatic bandage."

She took the occlusive bandage out of its packaging and placed it over the highest of the three bullet holes in Butch's torso. "Hey, Butch," she said. She took a hemostatic bandage and wrapped it around his body, trying to cover the other two entry wounds and stop the bleeding. She kept talking to him, walking him through what she was doing. "Butch, I'm gonna wrap this bandage around you so we get that bleeding under control, okay?"

The other seaman said, "One in the arm too, Clark."

"Got it," she said. She took another bandage and lifted the wounded man's arm to get the dressing around it. Felt the weight of the injured limb in her hands, not resisting, not helping. She got the bandage around his arm. She looked at him. His head was down. "Butch," she said. "I want you to listen to my voice. Butch, can you hear me?"

He didn't answer.

TWENTY-SIX

Detective Wheel sat on a bench in the cemetery of St. Paul's Episcopal across from the courts buildings in downtown Norfolk. A few white-cupped flowers still bloomed on the magnolia trees. Their fallen leaves blew across the grounds in the morning breeze. The thin headstones stood, set off-kilter by time and gray-greened by weathering. She looked at her watch and lit a butt. Eight thirty. A groundskeeper pushed the leaf litter around the graveyard with a rake, not interested in collecting it.

She waited a few more minutes until she saw Demetrius Byron, the head of the Violent Crimes section of the commonwealth's attorney office. He pushed open the iron gate in the brick wall surrounding the churchyard. He was a big man, gray at the temples, wearing a double-breasted suit and a metallic-blue tie. He walked up to Catherine and stood in front of her with his hands on his hips. "I had to come down here, Wheel?"

She held up her lit cigarette, and they shook hands. She could hardly get hers around his with the big Prince Hall Masonic ring he wore on his pinkie. He sat down beside her. Spread his arms over the back of the bench and cocked a foot up on one knee.

"I need your help, D.," she said.

He put his hand out in front of her, and she pulled a smoke from her bag and lit it off her own. She passed it to him, and he took a deep drag and said, "Unless you can beat the four teenagers who got killed on Alexander Street last night, you ain't making the top of my list of shit to worry about today, Cat."

"You know the body turned up at Ocean View Beach the other morning?"

He sat up on the bench and looked over at her. "Yeah."

"I might have let some evidence out of my custody."

"Hold up. What?"

"The case is a mess, Demetrius. We're on the right track, but we can't connect the dots. I asked a congressional aide and a reporter from the *Pilot* for help."

"You gave evidence to a fucking reporter, Catherine?"

She put her cigarette out on the ground and put her face in her hands. "Not exactly. Information sharing."

He looked at her sideways. "Information sharing?"

"Don't bullshit me, D. You do it too."

"When I do it, I share the information, not the actual evidence. Jesus, Wheel. How long have you been a fucking cop?"

"Long enough."

"Can you get it back?"

"Problem is the aide tried to big-time me. Said there were national security concerns. He wanted to use his resources to go through a laptop. I told him we had to go through proper channels. Figured I'd get probable cause, and you'd get me some subpoenas. He waited until I didn't have eyes on and he just...he just took it."

"He took it? Are you fucking bullshitting me, Wheel? He fucking took it? You must be fucking with me."

"D., I've busted my ass my entire career," she said. "Damn near three decades. I color in the lines. I keep my shit squared away. I keep my people squared away. You know I do. And you know why? It's not to close cases. It's not to get promoted. It's because we both know if you do this job long enough, there's gonna come a time where you need the benefit of the doubt. And I'm telling you I need it now."

"Okay, Catherine. So where's this laptop?"

"I don't know. The guy got shot. DC Metro is working it as a stickup gone sideways."

"And they didn't recover a laptop."

She shook her head. "They did not."

"Don't tell me your partner let you do this."

"No, he didn't know anything about it."

"Cat, why didn't you loop me in once you knew Congress was involved?"

"I swear to God, I got here as fast as I could."

"So now you want the benefit of the doubt and a favor too?"

"Look, I've got a wit camped out in an interview room at the station. I need to get him protection. And not some security camera on his front door three months from now. Like, actual round-the-clock guys with guns."

He snapped his fingers. "I know," he said sarcastically, "why don't I buy this motherfucker a round-trip ticket to the Bahamas? That way, he can sit and drink strawberry daiquiris while I wait for you to tell me who to charge, what charges to bring, and what actual case I need this motherfucker as a witness on."

"They got four bodies in less than a week, Demetrius. It's not funny. If I don't figure something out quick, my guy is gonna be number five."

He leaned forward and started rubbing his face. "Okay, you say you got the dots but can't connect them, right?"

"Right."

"So tell me what I'm gonna see when you do."

She pulled out another cigarette and lit it. Sat there quietly smoking for a moment. "I want the CEO of Decision Tree to spend the rest of his life in Red Onion for conspiracy to commit murder. And I want his shooters in Greensville until they get the needle."

He looked at her with his mouth wide open, then said, "Detective Wheel, Trevor Graves was at a fundraising dinner for the commonwealth's attorney two weeks ago. I sat across the table from him."

"I don't tell you who to break bread with, D. I just need his personnel files and financial records going back to 2004."

He stood up and looked past the brick wall at the traffic down City Hall Avenue. He turned back around. "Fuck you, Catherine."

"You're not my type."

He put his hands behind his head and looked up through the crown of the trees at the morning sky. "Catherine, this ain't the time for jokes." He sighed deeply. "All right. Give me a couple hours. I'll call in some favors and get some protection for your guy." He looked at her again, stuck his finger out at her, and said quietly, "But you better not even speak that name again until you bring me something better than what you got now, which is fucking nothing. And by the way, you're putting in your papers as soon as this closes. See this through, but let the kid take lead. After that, you're done."

She sat there on the bench, thinking about what he'd said, but she couldn't wrap her mind around the idea of not being a cop anymore. "Demetrius. My papers? You're gonna retire me? Are you fucking serious?"

"Am I serious? You're telling me you want to lock up one of the most influential donors in the commonwealth based solely on evidence you removed from custody without authorization and then fucking lost! How could I possibly prosecute a case with those facts? If it was anybody but you, I'd consider bringing charges. You've been a good cop, Catherine, and a friend. But you know you fucked up. So this is what it looks like."

"This is what *what* looks like?"

"The benefit of the doubt."

Catherine watched him walk across the churchyard and then slam the iron gate behind him as he stepped onto the sidewalk. She knew there were only two choices when you felt something slipping from your grasp: you could hold on to it tighter, or you could let it go. She took out her phone and called Lamar, knowing he hadn't landed yet. Had probably only just taken off. "Lamar, it's Cat," she said. "I think we're at a dead end. Commonwealth's attorney wants more than we got. More than we're gonna get, maybe. I hope you've got an ace up your sleeve. Call me later."

She stood up from the bench and started walking back to headquarters to check in on Arman. The sky was almost white in the morning sun as she left the courts buildings behind her. Cars going up and down the four-lane road, passing every minute with a hundred lives in them. Lawyers on the crosswalk brushed past mothers on their way to hearings at the juvenile and domestic courts. Cops and criminals argued on the corner about Phoebus and Hampton and who looked better for state champ with two-a-days still a month away. Someone needed two dollars because he ran out of gas, he swore. Pigeons pecked through the gutters. The world went by as it always had, she thought, as it would continue to whether she locked these bastards up or not. And it broke her heart.

———

Lamar woke up as the plane circled Richmond. He looked out the window and watched the James River slither west up the Piedmont and toward the distant mountains. They touched down, and he waited until the plane disembarked, then walked down the concourse and took the stairs to the baggage carousel. Another five minutes, and he had his own small bag slung over his shoulder and the late David Taylor's equipment on a luggage cart. He opened the lockbox where he had checked his service pistol and tucked the holster back onto his belt. He took his shield out of his bag, clipped it to the front of his belt, and began to push the cart out the automatic doors into the pickup area. He looked up and down the roadway shadowed by the elevated one above it and spotted an older blue Chevy Cavalier with government plates. A man leaned against the hood wearing a navy polo and khakis. Lamar waited until the man looked up at him, and he waved and pushed the cart toward the Cavalier. "Chief Miller?"

The man walked over to him and stuck his hand out. "Come on, Detective. It's Chris."

"Right," Lamar said.

Chris went to the trunk, opened it, helped Lamar load the cases, and pushed the cart back to the airport doors. He walked around to the driver's side, stood by the open door, and said, "Ready?"

Lamar nodded and got in the passenger side.

Chris pulled out of the loading zone and turned onto the airport exit lane. They passed a decommissioned fighter jet on display like a trophy as they left the airport grounds and headed through Richmond's far east end toward I-64.

They traded war stories for the first hour of the drive, with Lamar mostly listening. Personally, Lamar hated talking about the war. Half the time, it was chicken-hawk assholes trying to live vicariously through you, saying, "I would have gone if...," and the other half it was people acting like you were one bad day away from the psych ward. But he played the game.

When they passed Williamsburg, Lamar said, "Anything ring any bells after we talked last night?"

"Like what?" Chris asked.

"How much work did y'all do with the Aussies?"

"Who's *y'all* in this scenario?"

"I don't know," Lamar said. "Taylor. You. In general."

Chris kept his eyes forward the whole time they talked. Hands on the wheel at ten and two. "Special Air Service Regiment guys were around. Four Commando. Some ASIS guys. Look, Detective. It isn't like Big Army in a lot of these places. Guys come and go. You call each other by your first names. Dudes wear Chuck Taylors on patrol because who gives a fuck as long as the job gets done? So, yeah, Aussies were around. I'm sure Taylor worked with them, but I couldn't give you details beyond that."

"What about you? You willing to look at something for me?"

"Like what?"

Lamar reached into his bag and pulled out a Polaroid of the dead man's face a tech had taken on the beach the morning Arman found him. Chris took it, looked down, then handed it back. "No. I don't recognize him."

"Look again, Chief. If you don't mind."

He took the picture back from Lamar. His eyes darted between the road and the Polaroid. He shook his head again and handed it back. "Like I said."

Lamar tucked the picture into his bag. Took a long look at Chris. "We've got a video—" he said, then stopped himself. What had Chris said the night before when they'd talked on the phone? A crime. Civilians and contractors. Was that it? He tried to remember if he'd been more specific. What had the chief said back to him? *If you think there's evidence of a massacre that Davey wanted out there . . .*

"Detective?"

"We've got a video," Lamar said. "American contractors that we need to identify." Lamar looked out the window. Chris said something to him, but he didn't hear it. Kept asking himself if he'd said *massacre* on the phone to Chris the night before. It wasn't exactly a leap. Pretty easy to connect the dots, especially for someone who was there. So the chief made an inference when Lamar told him a crime had been committed. It wasn't that hard to believe.

They rolled across the interstate through Newport News and on toward Hampton. Trees flashed by like the world was nothing but a repetition of itself. Electronic billboards lit the day: POWERBALL AT $200,000,000. They passed abandoned warehouses. Manicured fairways. White stucco condos lined up on inlets of the bay.

"Do you still have the video?" Chris asked.

"What?"

"Do you still have the video?"

Lamar looked over at him and saw that Chris was waiting to read his answer on his face. The bay came into view on the right, and they approached the tunnel that would take them into Norfolk. Pretty easy to connect the dots—*especially for someone who was there.* "Chief," Lamar said. "How'd you know I was talking about a massacre?"

"What?" he asked.

"When we talked on the phone last night."

"You told me."

"I don't think I did."

The Cavalier entered the tunnel. Sank beneath the earth. Dull lights lined the tunnel walls. Lamar kept his eyes forward. He felt like he was staring into an overhead light at the dentist. Traffic zipped by. Chris kept the Cavalier in the right lane. Lamar slowly let his hand move toward his right hip.

Chris looked over at him and smiled. "I mean, probably wasn't credit card fraud. All you ever hear about is trigger-happy contractors. Jesus, Detective. I know you have to work your case, but not everyone is a suspect, are they?"

Lamar let himself relax. His hand drifted away from his holster. He looked over at Chris again. He thought he saw daylight from the tunnel exit out of the corner of his eye. Chris had his left hand on top of the steering wheel. His right hand reached into the gap between the center console and the driver's seat. Lamar saw the knife blade flash in the dull artificial light. The Cavalier thumped across the road sections, and the lights blinked by them in time with the sound. Lamar threw his left arm up to block the knife as Chris swung it backhand toward him. He caught Chris's arm at the elbow, but that only deflected the blow, and the blade sank into his chest. Chris pulled it out and swung backhand again into Lamar's chest, this time puncturing his lung. Lamar reached down for his pistol, but the blows came too quickly, one after the other. He tried to block Chris's arm as he swung, but he only flailed at it. The blade came at him again and again until Lamar only moved his hands as if absentmindedly swatting at bees. Chris kept stabbing. Lamar stopped trying to fight it. He leaned back in the seat with his hands by his sides. He got the pistol out of his holster, but it was all he could do to lay it across his lap. The blows kept coming until they were out of the tunnel.

Lamar stared at the sun when they emerged. A gull kited in the wind above the slate-gray bay. The speck of a fighter jet left contrails across the sky as it broke free of the continent and headed out over the Atlantic. He looked out the window at the water below them on the bridge. The Norfolk skyline was a mirage on the far shore. He lifted his right hand weakly to his shirt and rubbed at it as if he might wipe away the blood, but it was all blood. He looked over at Chris. His hands at ten and two on the wheel. Sweat dripped down his face from the exertion. He didn't look back at Lamar.

Lamar was dead in the seat beside him when Chris pulled the Cavalier off the first exit and drove into the Willoughby Harbor Marina parking lot. He parked the car as close to the slips as possible and got out. He boarded a thirty-year-old forty-foot motor sailer named *Seas the Day* and came back to the car with a twelve-foot-by-twelve-foot blue tarp. He'd parked the Cavalier so that the passenger side faced the water and was otherwise hidden from view. He unfolded part of the tarp on the asphalt next to the passenger door. Only someone on one of the boats in their slips could have seen him pull Lamar's body out and lay it on the tarp. He rolled the tarp up and went back to the boat. He came back with a dock cart and muscled the tarp three-quarters into it. He pushed the cart down the dock, up the ramp, and onto the boat. Chris grunted at the weight, managed to shove it into the pilothouse, then came out a few minutes later wearing flip-flops, shorts, a long-sleeved rash guard, and a sun visor, looking every bit the sunburned charter captain. He went back to the trunk of the Cavalier with the now empty cart, took out the cases Lamar had brought with him from Texas, and loaded them onto the boat.

Chris went back up to the dock, went to the fish-cleaning station, and sprayed the blood out of the dock cart. He pulled a black towel from the back seat of the Cavalier and tucked one end under the passenger headrest and the other where the seat and backrest met. He got in the Cavalier, drove it away from the boat slips, and parked it in the lot. He got out and looked the car over. Someone would notice it eventually. Maybe tomorrow. Maybe six months from now. But he didn't care. He knew he was never returning to America, let alone this particular marina in Norfolk, Virginia.

He walked back to the boat and boarded it. He took out nautical charts in the pilothouse and laid them across the small dining table. He opened one of the cases and took out David Taylor's Panasonic Toughbook. He plugged it in and inserted the thumb drive he'd taken off the congressional aide in DC. The screen populated with hundreds of files. Documents, videos, photographs. PDF scans of witness statements. Bank records. Enough evidence to put both him and Graves in prison for the rest of their lives. More likely, they'd give him the needle. But Taylor was dead. And so was the Australian. There was no one left to implicate him and Graves in the university shooting except the word of an immigrant janitor. If the government didn't have the information that Chris was now in sole possession of, he didn't think he was at risk. All he had to do was convince Graves it was safe to let the transaction go through on schedule and wait for his payday.

He charted a course for Coxen Hole off the coast of Honduras. It took him the better part of two hours to prepare the boat for the first leg of his journey. By the time he was out in open water, the sky was a violet flame on the horizon off his starboard side. He pulled the tarp out of the pilothouse, wrapped a spare anchor chain around it, and pushed Lamar's body over the side. He got a satellite phone from his cabin, took it out onto the deck, lit a cigar, and opened a beer. He dialed a number, and the phone rang through. Graves answered.

"I aborted the mission," said Chris.

"Excuse me?"

"It's done, sir. Jimmy never made his call this morning. He's either dead or locked up. Better for both of us if he's dead."

"It's not done until I say it's done. I want confirmation that this is over. You don't understand what's at stake here."

"There's nothing left for them. They know it was us, but they'll never prove it. I got the last of the incriminating materials off the cop a couple hours ago."

"What about him? What does he know?"

"Not gonna be a problem anymore."

"Jesus Christ," he said. Chris heard him sigh. "Sorry about that. You need to come in, Chris."

"Listen, Trev. It's over. I'm gone. We're the only two people alive who know you hit the terp and his family, okay? We're in the clear. I want to be done. Put my last paycheck in my account and send my bonus when the SPAC makes the acquisition."

"Please don't tell me this was all about money for you. I thought we were building something important," said Graves.

The ocean's endless waves spread out before him off the motor sailer's port side. Chris laughed. "Of course it's about the money. What the fuck else would it be about, sir?" he said.

There was a long pause on the other end of the line before Graves spoke again. "The money is for people who are part of what I'm building, Christopher, and it sounds like you aren't part of it anymore. I'm sorry, but this isn't something you'll be allowed to walk away from."

The line went dead. Chris stared at the satellite phone and then threw it into the water. He took a big puff on the cigar and drained the beer. Then he went to the cabin and turned the boat around.

TWENTY-SEVEN

A nurse woke Sally up at ten a.m. She'd been asleep in her hospital bed at MCV since a couple of hours after arriving with her father on the medevac flight. The nurse sat in a chair next to the bed and waited for Sally to remember why she was there. Sally looked down and saw the IV line taped to the inside of her forearm. "What's the IV for?" she asked.

"We were worried you were going to hurt yourself," the nurse said. "You'll need to stay off that ankle for a while."

"What is it?" she asked again.

"We gave you some midazolam. Just to keep you comfortable."

Sally felt her skin tingling. A warmth emanated from the center of her being. She remembered fragments of the flight in the helicopter, holding her father's hand as they raced the rising sun to the helipad atop the high-rise hospital. She couldn't remember much of anything else. Not the breakdown she'd had when the trauma team wheeled him off to the OR and wouldn't let her come. Not her screaming with rage, trying to tear apart the nurses' station. Not the orderlies holding her down while she was injected with a sedative. There was only the whirl of the helicopter's rotor blades cutting through the fog of her mind, a vague recollection of running through woods, but she attached no distress to any of it.

"Do you remember why you're here, Ms. Ewell?" the nurse asked.

Sally looked around the room. "My father?" she said uncertainly. "Where is he?"

The nurse took one of Sally's hands in her own. Sally looked down and smiled. The nurse's eyes filled with tears that spilled over onto her cheeks from time to time. "Let me go get the doctor," she said. She patted Sally's hand, then got up and left the room.

Sally watched her leave. After a few minutes, she noticed the tingling had begun to fade. A few minutes more and she was alone in the windowless room with a sense of immense sadness. She knew that some of it belonged to her, but not all of it. Her memory of the night before began to come back. Not the part after they'd arrived at the hospital, but her father at daybreak on the steps of her childhood home saying, *Sal, I just can't catch my breath.*

At ten thirty, a small, dark-haired woman in blue scrubs came into Sally's room. She sat down in the bedside chair and looked at Sally but didn't say anything. Sally turned her head away and began to cry. The doctor allowed her to cry quietly for a few moments before she reached out and touched her arm. "No, Sally. It's not what you think."

Sally stared up at the ceiling. She let her already fallen tears run down her cheeks and down her neck and dry up on the way. She looked back at the doctor and saw the ID badge clipped to her scrubs. The same woman's face. Less tired. Maybe a few years before. No strands of gray in the hair. Long enough ago that the smile had come easily when the picture was taken.

Sally read the text below the photograph on the badge: DR.
BHAVANI MANAJWALA, FACS. TRAUMA AND CRITICAL CARE. VCU
HEALTH SYSTEMS.

"Your father was very seriously injured," said Dr. Manajwala. She watched the young woman fight back tears, then
give in to them again. The surgeon was an anomaly in her
profession—fifteen years of treating trauma patients and dealing with their families had not made her cynical. She respected
the gravity of these conversations and understood that they
were always life-altering. Sometimes she had to communicate
the irrevocability of death; sometimes she had to give the news
of permanent disability. And sometimes she had to admit that,
despite the hospital's world-class technology and her own
medical expertise, she didn't know what would happen. Dr.
Manajwala tried to be as honest and thorough with her patients'
loved ones as her training and experience allowed. She waited
until Sally turned her head back to her.

She was still crying but she'd managed to fight the breakdown to a draw, at least for now. Sally nodded at the doctor.

"He is still in very serious condition, Sally," Dr. Manajwala
said. "There were multiple penetrating thoracic and abdomi-
nal wounds. They caused extensive bleeding in his pleural cavity, and he has spleen and kidney lacerations. He was fortunate
the Coast Guard medic arrived so quickly. She saved his life."

"Is he going to be okay?" asked Sally.

"He's stable for the moment. He's not getting worse. I know
that might not seem like good news, but it is." Dr. Manajwala
let Sally take that in before continuing. "We have resources
available," she said, "if you want to talk to someone. You've had
a very traumatic experience. And frankly, I see strong indica-
tions of substance abuse in your history." She tried to give Sally

a reassuring smile, but she'd treated enough alcoholics and addicts to know that Sally would have a tough time handling this. "I want you to know we haven't forgotten about you," she said finally.

"Where is my mother?" asked Sally.

"She's on the way. It took us some time to find her."

"Does she know?"

"Yes. A trooper came on the flight. She got word to her."

"What would I talk about?"

"I'm sorry?"

"You said if I want to talk to someone. What would I talk about?"

It was a fair question. Dr. Manajwala leaned back and stared at the far wall as if an appropriate answer might be written on it. "I don't know, Sally. But I think sometimes it boils down to knowing that you're not going through something alone."

"Do you think it will help?" she asked. Sally thought of the conversation with Detective Wheel in the hotel lobby in Tysons Corner. Carry the stone until it's worn down to a pebble.

The doctor asked herself what she actually believed before answering. She didn't want to lie to this young woman. "I don't know. Why don't we start with trying and see what happens?"

The benzo had worn off enough for Sally to feel its absence. For the want to be replaced by desire. For the desire to become the chrysalis of need. Her skin wasn't tingling—it crawled. She felt a familiar discomfort, like she'd stepped through a spiderweb that she couldn't shake off. The warmth at her center became the pit of a rotten piece of fruit.

The doctor watched her as it happened. She figured she had seen most, if not all, of the possible manifestations of human emotion: An infant's first animal wail. The alien strangeness of puberty. The irrepressible joy of survival. The humiliation of the bedpan. The addict's suicidal rejection of everydayness. Regret. Determination. Acceptance. But somewhere underneath it, she thought, there was a first cause. The source of this young woman's pain. Perhaps even her own. At its root was the fundamental and impenetrable terror of believing you have been sentenced to the solitary confinement of yourself. The worst part of that belief, the doctor thought, was that it wasn't true. "Your father is going to need your help," she said to Sally. "It's okay if you need some too." Dr. Manajwala stood up and touched Sally on the arm. "I'll have a nurse bring in a wheel-chair and take you to see him if you think you're ready."

Sally nodded. "I'm ready," she said. The doctor started for the door. "Dr. Manajwala?" Sally said.

"Yes?"

"I want to try."

TWENTY-EIGHT

Catherine and Arman sat across from each other at a small table in the Tidewater medical examiner's break room. Neither one spoke for a little while. She tried calling Lamar, but his phone didn't even ring anymore. Straight to voice mail.

"Nothing?" asked Arman. She shook her head and sat there in silence, wondering if what she knew to be true was actually true. There was no other explanation. He'd boarded the plane in Austin. Unless he'd disappeared midflight, he'd landed in Richmond. She looked at her watch. Almost four p.m. *Please, God,* she thought, *let him be okay.* Eventually, Catherine said, "It'll be a team from BCI looking after you. You'll be out in the mountains."

Arman sat there thinking about it. "BCI?"

"State troopers. Bureau of Criminal Investigation special agents."

"You trust this guy? The assistant commonwealth's attorney?"

"I do." She drummed her fingertips on the table, then reached across it to hold his hand. "It's what I would want in your shoes."

He nodded. "Okay," he said. "When?"

"Later today. They're making arrangements now. They'll send a car. It's a long way, but by morning you'll be safe."

"Promise?" he said.

She leaned back in her chair. "Yeah, Arman. I think I do."

Dr. Martin opened the door and held it for a man in a conservative charcoal suit, then followed him in. "Cat, Mr. Bajalan, this is Mr. Kelly from the Australian embassy in DC."

They both stood up to greet him, but he raised his hands and said, "Please. Sit." They sat back down, and Mr. Kelly pulled a chair out and joined them at the table. He looked up at Dr. Martin and said, "Thank you, Doctor. For all you've done."

Dr. Martin nodded and said, "I'll leave y'all to it. There are just a few more forms to fill out before we can officially release Mr. Leventis to you, Mr. Kelly." He closed the door behind him as he left.

Mr. Kelly looked at Arman and said, "It seems Mr. Leventis came a long way to find you, Mr. Bajalan."

"You knew him?" Arman asked.

"I did. Nick and I have known..." He smiled at his mistake. "Nick and I *knew* each other a long time. We served in the army together, and then in the Department of Foreign Affairs. He was a good man. An honorable one."

"How did you find him?" Catherine asked. "We haven't even sent out any formal ID requests yet."

"Nick was a careful man, Detective. When he came to look for Mr. Bajalan, he set up...do you know what a dead man's switch is?"

"I think so," she answered.

Mr. Kelly pulled a watch from his inside jacket pocket and laid it on the table. Catherine recognized it—the vintage Adina

Oceaneer that had been on the corpse's wrist. "He had a GPS locator put inside the case. Nothing happened as long as it signaled movement during a twelve-hour period."

"But if it didn't..." she said.

"That's right. I received an e-mail from an anonymized account two days ago. It took some time to verify that Nick was the sender and to collate the data the e-mail contained. But one of the items allowed us to receive the GPS signal."

"And it led here," Arman said.

"It did."

"I'm sorry, Mr. Kelly. I don't understand why he wouldn't just tell you what he was doing here," Catherine said.

"It's complicated, Detective." The man paused. He had a calm demeanor, but it broke, almost imperceptibly, for a fraction of a second. "He wasn't supposed to be here. He would have been in heaps of trouble if we'd known. In fact, I could get in heaps of trouble for telling you this."

"No offense, Mr. Kelly, but if you want to compare troubles, Arman's got the nuts."

"I know," he said. "And I'm so sorry for your loss."

"Do you know why he was looking for me?" Arman asked.

"I do now. The information in his e-mail clarified the situation immensely. We know it started last year, when Nick was sent to Afghanistan—"

"With the Special Air Service?" Catherine interrupted.

Mr. Kelly gave her a searching look.

"The tattoo," she said.

"Right. No, he was with a different organization at the time." Mr. Kelly took four photographs from his jacket pocket and placed them in front of Cat and Arman in a neat row. Names were written across the bottoms of the photos. "These are not current.

Nick...retrieved them from the U.S. Army's Official Military Personnel Files."

"Retrieved?" Arman asked. He and Catherine looked at the pictures as Mr. Kelly continued.

"Our countries share intelligence. We aren't supposed to gather it about each other, but sometimes, if a situation is delicate..."

"Him," Arman said. "From the video. He was there. Remember, Catherine?" He pointed to the name below a photograph: Staff Sergeant James Grabowski. He was younger than the man Arman had captured on video at the university, but it was him.

"There's Harris," said Catherine.

"The one who killed Mr. Peters," Arman said. "He was in the park that morning."

She nodded. The third picture was of Sergeant Patrick Dempsey. Catherine was fairly sure he was the accomplice Mr. Peters dropped at the Sea Breeze, but she'd have to wait for forensic identification to be certain.

"Nick met these men in Afghanistan. They were all working for Decision Tree International. He didn't like them. He said they were ruthless and unprofessional. And they were sloppy. One night Nick heard that their boss was coming close to securing contracts with the Australian defense forces. He requested permission to create a target profile on Decision Tree but was ordered not to. Our bosses were concerned about upsetting the relationship between U.S. intelligence and our organization."

"So how did he know all this?" Arman asked.

"He quit. That was six months ago. I never heard from him again. But he was an exceptionally good intelligence officer, Arman. There's still a lot to learn from the information he gathered, but we know he had been in contact with David Taylor, your platoon leader. We know that each of the men in these photos served under one of Trevor Graves's commands while on active duty. We saw the video. We know what happened to you. Nick knew what they were doing. He was trying to protect you. He wanted to help."

"Trying to help me has been trouble for a lot of people."

Mr. Kelly smiled. "I know that too. And I suspect I know what Nick would have said about that."

"What?" Arman asked.

"He would have said he had to try."

Arman looked at him skeptically. "Did he have a wife? Children? Is that what they'll say?"

"He did. He was married last year. He has a baby girl. And no, they won't say that today, I reckon. Not tomorrow either. But someday they might. She knew who she married. And I think part of the reason she married him was that he was the kind of person who would do something like this. I know it's part of the reason I loved him."

Catherine said, "What will happen to his body now?"

"I'm going to take him home," said Mr. Kelly. "Because of the nature of his activities since he left the service, he won't have any official recognition. But he'll be buried in a military cemetery in Adelaide. It's not far from Somerton Park, where he grew up. A few people will be there, but even fewer will know what happened to him. Those of us who do, we won't forget it." He looked over at Catherine, who was holding the last photograph. The picture was trembling in her hand. "Detective Wheel?" he asked. "Is everything all right?"

Arman looked at her. Her jaw was clenched, her face

expressionless. Tears spilled silently down her cheeks. "Catherine," he said and put his hand on her shoulder.

She put the picture down and slid it across the table to Arman. She wiped the tears from her cheeks with the sleeve of her blazer and tried to collect herself.

Arman read the name: Chief Warrant Officer 2 Christopher Miller. "Catherine, I don't understand," he said as he handed the picture back.

"It's okay, Arman," she said. "Mr. Kelly, this man picked up my partner from the airport this morning." The tears started again. "He won't answer his phone."

Mr. Kelly took an envelope from his jacket and slid it across the table to Catherine. "This is for you."

She put her hand over the envelope. She stared at the table until her vision blurred. She had to accept it. Lamar was gone.

"There's information you may find useful inside. Of course, I won't tell you what to do with it. Officially, as a representative of my government, I'm limited in my ability to help you. I would have to deny ever speaking to either of you if I were questioned. And none of this material has evidentiary value due to its method of collection. But you should know you have an advantage, Detective. He won't see you as a threat. Not immediately."

"Graves."

"That's right."

"Because I'm a woman," she said.

"I wouldn't presume to tell you how to feel about it. But in situations like this, it's advisable to use every advantage you have. I know what I would do if the circumstances were different. He was my best mate, after all." Mr. Kelly stood up and buttoned his suit jacket. To both of them, he said, "I'm afraid it's a terrible thing we have in common. These men have taken someone from all of us now." He said goodbye and left the room. Catherine and Arman understood that they would never see him again.

Catherine knew he was right. Of course, some women were dangerous, and Graves was too experienced not to have encountered them. But he'd be on guard against a threat from a man first. What would it give her, five seconds? Maybe ten? Was that enough time? *Enough time for what?* Catherine asked herself. What was she considering? Whatever it was, she'd have to control as many variables as possible. Even then, she knew what she'd be up against. Using a weapon was part of her job. But using a weapon was the *only* job of the men in the photographs. She qualified with her service weapon once a year. She practiced with it every quarter. She fired maybe two hundred rounds annually. Catherine guessed that Decision Tree contractors typically fired two hundred rounds a day, and they had fired their weapons when other people were shooting back, something she had never done.

"What's in it?" asked Arman.

His voice brought her out of her thoughts. She opened the envelope and took out a sheet of paper. Handwritten in black ink was *Tomorrow, 19:00, Dec. Tree private event, downtown Hilton, Graves in pres. suite, exec. floor.*

"Well?" Arman asked.

Before she had a chance to reply, her phone rang. She answered it, held it to her ear and stared at Arman while the voice on the other end of the line said, "Detective Wheel, this is Master Trooper Charmayne Hendricks."

"Go ahead, Trooper. I'm listening."

"I'm at the hospital in Richmond with a friend of yours."

Catherine hung her head. "Who is it?"

"It's Sally Ewell. She asked me to call you. We've all had a hell of a night. She wanted me to fill you in, let you know she's all right."

"Is her father with you there? Can I talk to him?"

"He just got out of the OR, Detective."

"Oh God. What happened?" she asked.

"How much time do you have?" asked Trooper Hendricks.

Catherine looked down at the paper before her, then at Arman. "I've got until seven o'clock tomorrow night," she said.

"Oh, well, I—"

"Sorry. I've got time, Trooper," said Detective Wheel.

Arman watched Catherine as she listened to the voice on the other end of the line. He couldn't hear everything that was said, but he didn't need to. Catherine's face told him the story well enough.

"Is he gonna be all right?" Catherine asked.

"He took multiple nine-millimeter rounds to the chest. The doc won't make any promises, but she seems optimistic."

"And Sally?" asked Detective Wheel.

"She's okay. Busted up her ankle pretty good. She doesn't have to stay in the hospital, but she won't leave her father's side. Anyway, I'm gonna sit with her for a while. Keep an eye on her," the trooper said. "The doc is hoping we can talk Sally into a treatment center."

"What about the shooter?"

"Mr. Ewell hit him in the exchange. Guy tried to draw on us when we arrived on scene before he bled out. No ID yet, but Sally told me she recognized him from a video. Said you'd know what that meant."

Catherine picked up one of the pictures from the table. "I do. Trooper, your shooter is gonna be a James Grabowski, formerly a staff sergeant in the army. That's all I've got on him right now."

"Okay, thanks, Detective. More than we got."

"Will you tell her I'll come to see her soon?" Catherine asked.

"She'll be glad to hear it."

Cat closed the phone.

"Sally?" Arman asked.

"She's gonna be okay."

"Mr. Ewell?"

Catherine shook her head. "He got one of them," she said. "He's in the hospital. They don't know for sure, but they think he'll make it." She stood up, walked over to a counter in the back of the break room, and fished around in a cup of pencils and pens until she found a Sharpie. She came back, sat down again, picked up the picture of the man Butch Ewell had killed, and put an X across his face. She drew another X across Michael Harris's face, then another over the face of Patrick Dempsey. She picked up the photograph of Chief Warrant Officer Christopher Miller and turned it over. She wrote Graves's name on the back and tucked the picture in her bag.

"What are you going to do?" asked Arman.

Catherine leaned back in her chair and closed her eyes. She rolled her head left to right, trying to loosen some of the tension in her muscles. "I'm going to stop them, Arman."

⌒

At two o'clock in the morning, Arman stepped out onto the balcony of his room in the Old Mill Inn in the tiny town of Damascus, Virginia. A pair of special agents from the Wytheville division of the Virginia State Police Bureau of Criminal Investigations occupied the rooms on either side. In four-hour shifts, the agents took turns sitting in an armchair in the lobby, letting the other agent know if anyone took the stairs to the upper floor. It was a simple and effective way of keeping Arman safe, but it had no fundamental difference from imprisonment.

He looked out over the flat black water of Laurel Creek. Farther up, the creek disappeared into the spine of the Blue Ridge, a wilderness of jagged shadows in the distance. One of the agents had told him there was hardly anything in a fifteen-mile radius that had changed in the past twelve thousand years except the residents, and he suspected that the little that had changed would have long since turned to dust twelve thousand years from now. Go a couple hundred yards off the pavement, he'd said, and the land was as undisturbed by human presence as it had been a hundred thousand years ago. Arman didn't know if it was true or even what to make of it, but he did have the sense that the world was somehow more expansive here, and he a much smaller part of it, than he could remember feeling before.

The elevation wasn't all that high down on the flat grassy banks of the creek on which the Old Mill had been built, but there was still a premonition of autumn in the cool night air. He realized he was wearing Detective Adams's VCU basketball T-shirt. The thought of Lamar vanishing the way he had sent a chill through Arman that not even the coldest winter could have caused. He thought of his wife and son, Lamar, and Mr. Peters. And Sally's father in the hospital. What if he were to be lost in a place like this? He closed his eyes. Imagined a bend in a trail. A promontory looking west, the ridges rolling like waves above an ocean of mist and fog. Another turn, another overlook. He saw Arcturus, Vega, and Altair piercing the same darkness they had when his father took him to the mountains near Zawita to stargaze when he was a child. He opened his eyes and leaned against the wooden railing. The night was silent. The world was black beyond the meager yellow lights of the inn.

Sally's phone rang at quarter after two in the morning. She'd been wide-awake in her hospital bed for hours. She reached an arm out from under her covers and grabbed the phone. It was Arman.

"Sally?" he said.

She pulled the phone under the covers with her. "Are you okay?" she asked.

"Yes. I'm in southwest Virginia. I have guards. I feel like I'm away from...I don't even know what it feels like I'm away from."

"Yeah. I know what you mean," she said.

"You know, Sally, I just wanted to say—"

"I know," she said. "I know." They listened to each other breathe for a while. "Do you need to go, Arman?" she asked.

"No," he said. "Not if you don't want me to."

"I don't want you to," she said. "Can I ask you something, Arman?"

"Yes. Anything."

"What were their names?"

He realized he had not said their names for a long time. He saw them always, felt them always, but he had not said their names, not even to himself. "My wife was called Naza," he said. "My son was Haydar, like my father."

"They're beautiful names," she said.

Neither of them needed to say anything else, so they shared their silences instead.

———

By noon the next day, Catherine had driven out to Second Patrol. When she arrived, she walked through the lobby to the back of the building, where she knocked on Lieutenant Billings's office door.

"Yeah!" he barked and smiled when she let herself in.

"Wheel, you old such and such," he said, leaning back in his chair behind his desk. "I heard you got the mother of all ass-chewings from the commonwealth's attorney."

"Something like that," she said. She nodded toward the laptop open on his desk. "You got a second or is that Important Police Shit?"

He turned it toward her to show her the game of solitaire he was in the middle of. "Getting my ass handed to me," he said. "Why? What's up?"

"I need a favor," she said. "And Jack, it's solitaire."

"Well, I guess I'm kicking my own ass then." He took off his glasses, leaned forward in his chair, and spoke in a near whisper. "Doing you favors might not be the best career move, what I hear, Cat."

She stared him down, then said, "Did you think they were about to make your fat ass chief or something? They should have retired you five years ago."

He looked at her and cocked his head to the side to evaluate her dig. "You make a good point, Detective," he said, then cracked a smile. "What can I do for you?"

"Will you check if we've got anybody moonlighting security at the Hilton tonight?" she asked.

"What am I, your secretary? Look it up. Ask the duty sergeant."

"Do I really have to spell it out for you, Jack? I'm asking if cops are gonna be there. I don't want any cops there."

"Well, you're still a cop, aren't you?"

"I'm being offered retirement."

"What's behind door number two?" he asked.

"Charges."

He put his glasses back on. "Seriously, Catherine. Usually, in this type situation, the goal is to get out of trouble, not get in more of it."

She looked down at the floor. "I'm not getting out of it, LT. You don't get out of the kind of trouble I'm in."

"It's about the kid, isn't it?" he asked. "It hasn't been that long, has it? He'll turn up."

She looked up and shook her head. "No, Jack. He won't."

Lieutenant Billings put both of his hands on top of his head, rocked back in his chair, and let out a huge sigh. "You owe me one, Catherine."

"I owe you more than one."

"I'll find out. I'll call you in an hour."

"I was never here, Jack."

"Yeah. I know."

"Thanks, LT." She got up and turned toward the door.

"Detective," he said.

"Yeah?"

"It's worth it? Whatever you're doing?"

"I'll let you know," said Detective Wheel.

She stopped by the evidence room on her way out. Twenty minutes later, she was in her car in the parking lot of Second Patrol. She looked down at the pistol in her hand, at the suppressor threaded into the end of the barrel. It still had the evidence tag looped through the trigger guard. Catherine knew it wouldn't be processed for some time. The odds were it wouldn't be missed. She wasn't sure she'd be able to get away with it, but it gave her another edge. Maybe not much of one, but an advantage nonetheless. The pistol wouldn't be any louder than a nail gun, even in an enclosed space. She set it down on the passenger seat next to the Fiocchi subsonic nine-mil ammunition box. She grabbed one of the magazines, flipped open the ammunition box, and thumbed the first round onto the follower.

TWENTY-NINE

It was not yet night when Catherine walked down East Main Street toward the lobby of the downtown Hilton. Fading light fell over the Elizabeth River and down in the canyons between the waterside office buildings and high-rise hotels. The valet out front was parking cars for guests. The Decision Tree event hadn't been publicized, but it wasn't a secret either. She'd considered wearing clothes to blend in with the other attendees but figured you'd need to be on a list to access the event. A list she certainly wasn't on. Instead, she wore her usual clothes: Jeans. A white imitation-silk blouse. A blue blazer. She kept her badge inside her shoulder bag next to the nine-millimeter and her service revolver. She saw a plain-clothes security man scanning the arriving vehicles by the door. She knew there would be more inside. A few scattered throughout the ballroom where the event was going to occur. Probably at least two on the executive floor where Graves had a room. Lieutenant Billings said no cops were working it. She hadn't thought so. She assumed they'd be in-house guys, Decision Tree contractors, but if there had been other cops on scene, she would have thought twice about what she planned to do.

She gave herself one last moment to decide while she stood

on the other side of East Main from the hotel. She knew that there would be no turning back if she crossed the street. She checked both ways. The road was clear. She walked across it and up the steps to the hotel entrance. When she got inside, she looked for signage leading to the event. On a metal stand near an escalator, a black letter board read DT INTL. PRIVATE EVENT. ROOFTOP BAR, 7–8, BALLROOM 8–10. Next to the first row of letters, an arrow pointed to the ballroom. She went down the hall to the ballroom and peeked inside. Caterers and hotel employees were preparing the room for dinner. One hundred people, at least, thought Catherine. A band set up equipment on a stage at the far end of the room. A man in a dark suit came up behind her and gently placed his hand on her shoulder. "Can I help you, ma'am?" he said.

"Is this the wedding reception?" she asked.

"No, ma'am. This is a private event. That must be in another room."

"Thanks," she said and smiled and walked back to the lobby, mentally noting the hotel's security-camera locations. The night before, she'd taken a roll of quarters to one of the few remaining pay phones near her apartment and called Hiltons in Cleveland, Denver, and Birmingham, Alabama. Under the guise of investigating a case, she spoke with the security manager of each hotel and got the corporate SOP for facilities, key access, and video recording and retention. There was significant camera surveillance, but there were also predictable gaps. All the elevators and each public entry and exit door would be covered. Most halls had one camera at the elevator bank on each floor but not at the stairwells. The lobby's cameras captured most of the bar and restaurant. Between the doors to the Decision Tree event ballroom and the first-floor public restrooms that faced them, there was a gap in video surveillance. A small loading dock at the rear of the hotel opened onto an alley. It could be accessed from the ballroom, and it was the only exit you could use without being filmed. Catherine guessed that Graves's security detail would take that exit in the event of an emergency. She turned her options over in her mind, visualizing a hundred different outcomes, searching for one in which she might get away with it. But she had a feeling in the pit of her stomach, deep down where the lies people tell themselves can't reach, that she would not.

She took the escalator up two levels until she found the rooftop bar. A short line of people waited to get in. Most were elegantly dressed couples about her age. Two security guards stood checking names off a list, then opening the door to let them onto the open-air patio one couple at a time. She walked past them and looked through the windows as she did. The rooftop was already crowded. Most of the guests must have arrived by now. She looked down at her watch. Seven thirty. She looked for Graves but didn't see him.

She walked down the hall to the bank of elevators. She thought about taking the stairs but figured the top floor would be inaccessible from the stairwell. She took a deep breath and pressed the Up button. A few moments later, the bell dinged and the doors slid open. She stepped inside and turned back to the doors. A woman was already standing there. She had a young boy in her arms, maybe six years old. A small girl stood next to her and hid behind her skirt when Catherine looked back and smiled.

"What floor?" the woman asked.

"Excuse me?" Catherine said.

The woman smiled. "I can hit the button for you."

"Oh, right." Catherine laughed. "Executive level," she said.

The woman frowned. "Oh, you need your key card for that floor."

Catherine feigned exasperation and made a silly face at the woman's children. "Of course," she said. "I'd forget my head if it weren't sitting on my shoulders." She reached into her bag and pretended to search for a key card. She pulled out her badge with one hand and held it against her purse conspicuously while pretending to look for the key. It worked.

The woman said, "I'm so sorry. Let me get it, Officer," and pulled out her own card, flashed it over the reader, and pressed the button for the executive floor.

"You're so sweet," said Catherine. No one else got on while the elevator climbed to the top floor. The doors opened onto huge windows overlooking the waterfront. Across the river, two massive gray warships sat in dry dock at the General Dynamics shipyard. The white sails of a dozen small boats dotted the glassy surface before them, delicate as water striders as they skimmed across it at sunset. She stepped out of the elevator and looked out the windows. The woman and her two children walked by behind her. "Thanks again," said Catherine.

"Have a good night," the woman said.

Catherine turned and watched them go down the hall and around a corner toward the rooms. She let them get ahead of her and began to follow them. When she rounded the corner, the family was gone. Two men from Decision Tree's security team stood on either side of the hallway. She could see three doors beyond the men but couldn't tell which led to the presidential suite.

"Can we help you find something, ma'am? This is a private floor."

Catherine froze for a moment, then felt the cold metal of the badge still in her hand. Her mind rolled through plausible reasons to be up there. She showed them the badge. "I was wondering if you've seen someone," she said. She gave Lamar's description on the off chance she'd catch a flash of recognition on either man's face, but there was none.

"Sorry," one of the men said. "Everyone on this floor is accounted for. No one fitting that description."

Catherine lowered her badge and said, "Maybe I have the wrong floor." She turned around and walked back to the elevators.

When she got back down to the main floor, she went to the hotel bar and sat on a stool. The mirror behind the bar gave her a good view of the lobby. Graves would have to go past her to get to the ballroom. After that, she'd only have to wait.

A young bartender came over and asked if he could get her anything. "Glass of white," she said.

"Do you want something dry or—" he began.

She cut him off. "Just your house chardonnay."

The Mets and Braves played under the lights at Turner Field on the flat-screen above the bar. Cat watched David Wright foul off pitches for what seemed like an hour before he finally hit a weak fly ball to short left field. She half turned on the barstool to survey the lounge. A few couples having drinks, a few solo business travelers. She thought she spotted a couple of Graves's security guys trying to blend in with the crowd, but if they were, they were good enough that she couldn't be sure. They wouldn't matter, though. Nothing was going to change her mind now. Graves would have to piss eventually, and she was willing to bet he'd be too proud to have an escort while he did. If she could get to the loading dock without being filmed, she'd only have to worry about eyewitnesses. And if there was one thing every cop knew, it was that eyewitnesses weren't worth a damn. She'd obviously be on camera all over the hotel, but she'd made no secret she was investigating Decision Tree. She had called Graves out by name to Demetrius, head of the Violent Crimes section of the commonwealth's attorney office. What counted, though, was that from start to finish, the whole thing would be in a digital black hole from which no useful information would escape.

"Got no pop in his bat this year," she heard someone say. She looked to her left and saw a man about her age, slightly overweight, wearing khaki slacks and a gold-buttoned blazer. He was balding and wore what was left of his hair in a last-ditch attempt at a comb-over. He got up from his stool, moved down the bar, and stood by Catherine but kept an empty seat between them. "You mind?" he asked.

She shrugged. "Free country, ain't it?" she said.

"Fair enough," he said and sat down.

"Lots of folks would take .320," she said.

"You're not a Mets fan, are you?" he asked.

"Would you leave me alone if I was?"

"Ouch," he said.

"I pull for the kid."

"Local boy makes good," the man said. "Bob Haskins," he added and put his hand out.

"Zelda Fitzgerald," she said.

"You're not gonna make it easy for me, are you?"

"Bob," she said, "I'm just sitting here drinking wine."

"Well, can I buy you another?" he asked.

She looked over at him. "You're a quick study, Bob Haskins."

Haskins waved to the bartender and ordered another glass

of wine for her and another Jack and ginger for himself. "What do you do for a living, Zelda?" he asked.

"I'm a police detective."

"No shit?"

She reached in her purse and pulled out her badge.

"Damn," he said, laughing. "I thought you were kidding." He looked around the room. "Anyone here committing crimes?"

She surveyed the patrons scattered along the bar. Out over the lounge area behind them. "I haven't decided yet," she said.

"Any likely suspects?" he asked.

She looked over at him. "Might be me, Bob. Like I said, haven't decided yet."

"I read an article somewhere," he began, "said there's so many laws on the books, most people can't go a day without breaking at least one. Don't even know they're doing it. Don't know what's legal and what's not."

"Could be," she said. "Ones I work are generally pretty cut-and-dried."

"*Salus populi suprema lex esto,*" Haskins said.

"What's that mean?" she asked.

"'Let the good of the people be the highest law.' High-school Latin. Stuck in my head all these years for some reason."

"From your lips to God's ears, Bob," she said and raised her glass.

"Yeah," he said. "Hey."

"What?"

"Aren't you supposed to ask what I do for a living?"

Catherine swiveled her stool toward him, cocked an elbow up on the bar, and rested her head on her hand theatrically. "I'm ready, Bob. Impress me."

"Okay," he said. "Here goes. I work for a private equity firm."

"I guess those loafers are real gator, then?"

"Ha-ha. You are a riot, Zelda. But hey, keeps the kids out of public school."

"So what kind of stuff do you invest in?"

"Defense industry companies, mostly," he said.

"You're here for the shindig, then?"

He looked at his watch and leaned back on the barstool. "I normally wouldn't be this gauche about it, Zelda. But by tomorrow morning, a bunch of people's kids will never have to work again."

She stared at him until he became uncomfortable. He wasn't used to being made uncomfortable. "Who needs a job when you're buried in Arlington, right?" she said.

He turned away from her slightly and grumbled, "Jesus. I never met a peacenik cop before. You sound like my fucking priest." He took a long slug of his drink and waved to the bartender, then mimed signing his check in the air.

"I'm not a peacenik, Bob. I've carried a gun more than half my life. I just happen to give a shit what happens when people use them."

He signed the check and thanked the bartender. He leaned in toward Catherine to whisper something in her ear. He put one hand on the bar and the other on the back of her stool, nearly pinning her against the long lacquered bar top. "You know, Zelda, before we started talking, I was gonna offer you fifty bucks to go upstairs. But I didn't want to overpay."

As he loomed over her, she instinctively reached into her bag and wrapped her hand around her revolver's grip. She looked up at him and said, "Bob, I've got a .38 pointed at that little pecker of yours. I'd maybe start thinking about being nice if I were you."

He leaned away from her stool and gave her a long look, attempting intimidation, belittlement, and dismissal. Then he turned around and began walking to the lobby.

"Hey, Bob," she said. He looked back. "Tell your priest that whatever he's doing, it ain't working."

She watched him disappear down the hall toward the ballroom. Couples from the rooftop bar had begun to make their way down the escalator in small groups, headed in the same direction as Haskins. At eight thirty, she saw the two security guards from the executive floor standing next to each other on the escalator as it descended to the lobby. Graves stood behind them. It took a moment to register, but the young woman and her two children were beside him. *Goddamn it,* Cat thought. He smiled at the woman as they reached the main floor, and she smiled back at him admiringly. He rubbed her back where her expensive dress fell open, exposing her skin from the nape of her neck to the small of her back. The kids seemed to glide across the tile floor beside their parents, oblivious to the reason for the evening's celebration but reveling in its excitement nonetheless.

Catherine ran through the layout of the first floor in her mind. Exits relative to the ballroom. Restrooms. A pair of smaller meeting rooms farther down the hallway. She walked to the center of the lobby and casually examined the placement and alignment of security cameras one more time. The hotel had at least one employee watching them in real time. Might be a Decision Tree contractor in there too. There was no way to know.

She went back to the lounge and told the bartender she wanted to sit at one of the tables. He poured a glass of white for her and said, "Sorry about the asshole. On the house."

"Right?" she said. "Don't want anything to do with a man who can't respect .300." She grabbed the wineglass and glanced in the mirror. That's when she saw him—sitting in a far corner of the restaurant area, dressed in a blue button-down and khakis. A lanyard hung from his neck. In a hotel like this one, he was a needle in a stack of corporate-travel, business-casual needles. Catherine looked away, not wanting to risk meeting his eyes. She took the picture out of her blazer pocket. There was no doubt—Chief Warrant Officer Christopher Miller. He was too tan and not nearly doughy enough to pass for a salesman or middle management under anything more than cursory scrutiny. She was a professional noticer, and he was a man who had lived his life outside, not in cubicles and members-only airline lounges.

She walked to an armchair closer to the lobby that had a better view of the hall. She could see the door to the ballroom, the alcove where the men's and women's bathrooms were hidden, almost all the way to the exit at the far end that led out to the hotel loading dock. She turned slightly away from Miller but kept him in her peripheral vision. Why was he hiding? He was clearly trying to blend in, but she couldn't figure out why. It was a Decision Tree event, after all. She wondered if he might be looking for her, but she had no reason to think anyone knew what she looked like. He was a variable she could not control, and it made her nervous. Catherine's leg began to shake ever so slightly. She tapped her foot on the carpet to try to keep it under control. After a minute, she stilled it. The band was playing from the ballroom stage, loud but indistinct, behind the closed doors. Jangling guitars and shuffling drums. It sounded like a Tom Petty cover band.

She sat there for the better part of an hour. Night had fallen outside the hotel lobby's windows. A dozen times or more, she got halfway out of the chair to leave, but something pulled her back down into the seat to wait. She finished her glass of wine, and the door to the ballroom opened. Music cascaded into the hallway and throughout the first floor of the hotel. Chief Miller got up from his chair and casually walked toward the ballroom. She saw Graves step into the hall. One of the security men followed him, but Graves waved him off. The guard lingered, and Graves gestured for him to go back to the ballroom. The door shut behind the guard, and Graves stood alone in the hall. Cat watched him turn toward the bathroom and disappear into the alcove. She caught sight of Miller again. He was fading into the crowd headed toward the event. She saw his eyes flicker toward a security camera. Catherine was sure he was there for Graves too. She stood up and matched his movement, joining a group crossing the lobby.

She lost sight of Miller. Behind the ballroom's closed doors, the music pulsed. Drums broke open a simple, driving groove. Again the bright guitar, the bass thumping like a heartbeat. She felt it as much as heard it, a voice not singing but speaking to her from a place much more distant than the stage behind the closed ballroom doors. She hadn't seen Graves come out. Catherine stood in the middle of the hall between the ballroom and the bathrooms. She shut her eyes and took a deep breath. Now the voice started to sing, almost screaming, gathering strength to break into the chorus that the song built toward.

Cat quickly took the four steps to the men's-room door, paused to reach into her bag and work the pistol's action, the song nearly reaching a crescendo, then walked into the bathroom and closed the door behind her. The world went quiet for a second while she processed what was in front of her. The music was now only a hum she felt buzzing at the center of her being. Graves stood at the sink, looking at himself in the mirror. The water seemed to run out of the faucet with a deafening roar. He turned to face her. Chief Miller was between them. He spun around and Catherine registered his confusion. She thought Graves was angry but then realized he was looking at her with disgust. He was offended that he'd been interrupted, and he was confused to see a woman there, but he didn't feel threatened until he registered the pistol in her hand, the barrel and the long suppressor held against the side of her leg. His face contorted with rage. She raised the gun and fired.

The sound of the subsonic rounds was subdued but hardly quiet. She shot Graves three times before he fell. She continued firing as he writhed on the ground. Brass casings were ejected from the chamber as she squeezed the trigger; they bounced off the mirror and off the walls and spun across the marble tiles of the bathroom floor when they landed. Miller wheeled around. She saw the knife in his hand and was mesmerized for an instant by the rippled steel of the handmade blade. Her eyes met his, and she thought she had him on the back foot, but he lunged at her with the knife, knocked her over, and landed on top of her. The force of the impact sent the suppressed pistol clattering across the tiles. He was crushing her with his body. She tried to scream but didn't have the breath for it. Miller's eyes tracked the pistol. He stood up and took a step toward it. She gasped for air when he got to his feet—he'd knocked the wind out of her. Instinct guided her. Still lying on the floor, she reached into her bag and pulled her service revolver. Miller bent over to grab the suppressed pistol. Cat lifted her head, found enough air for one word, and called his name. He turned toward its sound reflexively, and for a fraction of a second, he started to smile. She squeezed the trigger. When the bullet struck his forehead, he dropped as if a rug had been pulled out from under him.

Catherine let her head fall back and stared at the tiled ceiling. She dropped her revolver from her left hand, and pain washed over her, radiating from her stomach and drowning her entire being in it. Ringing deafness accompanied the pain. She put her palm on her chest for a moment, and her hand came away covered in blood. Motion caught her eye, and she turned her head.

Graves tried to lift himself to his elbows, but he slipped back to the floor in the slickness of his own blood. She'd hit him in the head and more than once in his chest. She'd shot one of his fingers off when he flinched into a defensive posture as she'd begun to fire. A bullet fragment had struck him in the upper lip and given him a raggedy cleft palate. He choked on blood and splinters of his own teeth. His eyes flashed crazily around the room. Miller lay dead beside her, the suppressed pistol trapped beneath him.

How much time had passed since she'd entered the bathroom? Ten seconds? Maybe twenty? It might as well have been her whole life. She took out her phone and called a number. Arman picked up on the second ring.

"Hello? Catherine?" he said, but she could not hear him. She couldn't even lift the phone to her ear. Cat let the phone drop onto her stomach without ending the call. A door opened behind her.

When the Decision Tree security team entered the bathroom, Arman heard their voices, but he did not hear hers. He listened to the staticky chaos for a few seconds. Then the line went dead.

Later that night, two detectives from Violent Crimes arrived on the scene. The guests were sequestered in the ballroom. The detectives ducked under the police tape covering the open door to the men's room. "Jesus Christ," the first one said. "How're we supposed to work with all this blood everywhere? I gotta call my union rep."

"You're such a prick," said the second.

"Yeah. I know. How many shots fired?"

"A shitload. That's a number, right?"

The detectives got as close as they could without having to kneel in the pool of blood spread across the marble floor. The first took out a notepad and started jotting a few things down in pencil.

"What's the story?" the first detective asked. "Did Wheel have some connection to these guys?"

"That's why we get paid the big bucks. Gotta find out."

"So what's up with asshole number one?"

"Disgruntled employee, seems like."

"Why don't we ever get to deal with gruntled employees, is what I want to know. Fucking disgruntled people are always ruining my plans. You never hear a bad word said about the gruntled."

"I heard the dead guy in the suit was like twelve hours from becoming a billionaire."

"No shit?"

"No shit. Corporate takeover or something. Wall Street–type shit. Way over my head. That's what the party was for."

"You know what my father used to say about those types?"

"What's that?"

"'Somebody ought to tell these sons of bitches shrouds don't come with pockets.'"

THIRTY

The two-tone pickup drove west through the newly arrived winter. Breaks in the roadside woods revealed the James River headed in the other direction, toward the Chesapeake and the sea beyond. The river's surface west of the fall line was as placid as if it had been frozen solid. Rolling hills sloped down toward it. Deer browsed stubble in the harvested fields. Their necks rose, and they watched indifferently as a few cars curved along the back roads toward the mountains, Butch Ewell's old Ford among that small number.

Sally pulled the truck off at an intersection about an hour later and looked at her map. The day was fading to the west. Beyond the fields and over the treetops, the Blue Ridge's rounded peaks were backlit by the setting sun. She found the town of Tyro on her map and pulled the truck back onto the hardball. She almost missed it when she drove through. It wasn't really a town as much as what was left of one after Camille broke over it in 1969. Catherine could have told her that if she'd had the chance, but Sally had no reason to think about the town now except as a reference for the turn she'd need to make five miles farther down the road. She stopped the truck again at the entrance to a gravel drive and referred to the map one last time. There was nothing on it but a mark someone had made for her with a red pen. She got out of the truck, rubbed her hands together against the cold, and opened the cattle gate. She pulled the truck ten yards past the gate, got out again, and closed it behind her. Snow was falling now, the sky so heavy and white with it that it kept back the darkness. Sally put the truck in four-wheel high, turned the wipers on, and went about a mile through the woods down the gravel drive until it opened up onto winter pasture.

A plain white house stood on a slight rise above the fields. A creek divided the pasture and ran off into the trees and up the low mountainside that held the little farmstead in something like an embrace. Smoke swirled up from the chimney and disappeared into the snowfall. Sally parked the truck and got out. Before she went up to the house, she turned and watched three horses stamp and circle each other in a nearby field. One broke from the trio and ran off on its own. The other two followed it at a trot and watched as it bucked and snorted smoke and ran lively through the swirling flakes.

Sally turned back to the house. Catherine stood at the top of the porch steps looking down at her. "I wasn't sure you'd find it," she said.

"Seems like that's the idea, huh?"

"No," Catherine said, "not really. But I'd be lying if I said I didn't put it in the plus column when I was looking to buy the place."

Sally walked up the steps. Catherine gave her hand a gentle squeeze and said, "It's been a long time. Come on in the house, girl. It's cold."

They went inside. Catherine opened the woodstove latch, put in three pieces of split wood, and closed it up again. Sally took her coat off and hung it up on a hook near the door. The room was warm and sparsely furnished. A small sofa sat near the front door, and there was a big kitchen table that took up much of the rest of the room. Catherine walked past the table to the small kitchen and poured two mugs of tea. She came back to the table, pulled out a chair for Sally and one for herself, and set the mugs down. Sally sat, and Catherine smiled at her in a way that seemed to Sally to emphasize the sadness in her eyes.

"Well," said Cat. "Welcome to retired life."

"How are you?"

"I'm fine, Sal. It was time."

"No, I mean—"

"Oh, that," said Catherine, instinctively reaching toward her stomach. "It's long since healed up."

"I mean, it must have been terrifying."

"Believe it or not, it happened too fast to get scared. Didn't get scared until it was over. By that point, there was nothing left to be scared of."

Sally slid over the first two of a series of articles one of her colleagues had written about the case. Catherine skimmed the top article and set it to the side. The second was about Lamar's disappearance, and she lit a cigarette and started to read. She stopped not three graphs into the story, looked up at Sally, and said, "I guess you would have told me if they'd found him."

"I would have."

"How's it going out there?" Catherine asked, gesturing vaguely toward the world beyond the little farmhouse's walls.

Sally knew what she meant. She shrugged and said, "It never ends, does it?"

"I think it only ends when everything else does," Catherine said.

"Package deal, huh?" Sally said.

"Far as I can tell," Catherine said.

"Catherine," Sally started, "they shouldn't have made you retire. You were a hero. They should have...I don't know... you should have been given a choice."

Cat put her smoke out in the foil ashtray. "Once I lost the laptop, retirement was probably the best I could hope for. But I always had a choice. I knew what I was going there for that night. I knew it was wrong. I did it anyway. Maybe I'd have gotten away with it. Or maybe, if that son of a bitch Miller hadn't gotten there first, you'd be visiting me at the correctional facility in Fluvanna. So who knows about should haves? Anyway, boy I grew up with just got elected commonwealth's attorney down in Lovingston. Asked me to come on as an investigator. Might find I've got another case or two in me."

"Do you regret what you did?"

Catherine sat there thinking for a bit. "No. But that doesn't mean it was right."

"I don't care if you got lucky. You wouldn't deserve to go to prison either way," Sally said.

"Says you. That's not what the law says."

"He was a monster. They both were."

"I don't believe in monsters, Sally. And if I did, who's to say I'm not one too? Christ Almighty. His kids were there. His wife. World's going to hell in a handcart and that's how it begins. Folks start making exceptions for themselves — 'Rules for thee but not for me.' It never stops once you cross that line."

"You sound like my father."

"I know. I sound like mine too."

"I'm sorry, Catherine."

"For what?"

"Shit, I don't know," she said.

"Well, I forgive you," said Catherine.

"For what?" Sally asked, smiling.

"Shit, I don't know," she said and smiled back.

"I never did tell you I was glad you called. That day. The trooper. She told me," Sally said. "It meant a lot." She took out a red poker chip and handed it to Catherine. "Another month, I get a yellow one. So, you know. I guess I'm fixed." Sally could see Catherine was thinking about something. "What is it?" she asked.

"Oh, I don't know," Catherine said. She turned the red poker chip over in her hand. Let it roll between her fingertips like a set of worry beads. She looked down at it. "I like how they do those chips, though. Marking time like that. I could see how that could come in handy."

"It's something to aim for, anyway."

"Yeah. Something to aim for. No, I was just thinking about my father. A long time ago, he told me that he'd only ever truly known one person in this world." She lit another cigarette, inhaled, and let the smoke spill out of her mouth before going on. "We were out walking the crest of this mountain called the Priest, not far from here. Aiming to tree a bear. Clear out of the blue, he starts telling me this story from when he was in Korea. How one day he's just walking and comes over a hill and runs smack into this Chinese soldier. Said they just kind of took each other in for what seemed a good long while but couldn't have been more than a couple of seconds, really. And then he said that he was *this close* to not getting his rifle up before the fella got his up." Catherine pinched her fingers together to emphasize how thin the margins were between living and dying. "So then they roll around in the mud until my daddy, being the bigger man, got the best of him. Told me he looked that poor son of a bitch in his eyes as the feller was dying. He swore up and down there was not a secret in this world they could have kept from each other in that moment. Didn't say nothing more about it. We just kept walking down the ridgeline. I sometimes wonder if he was thinking out loud and just didn't realize it, the way we just went back to walking down that bear. I wanted to ask him about it many times after but never did. Occurs to me I'm about as old now as he was then. I didn't think I'd ever understand what he was trying to get at."

Sally looked at her across the table. "What about now?" she asked.

Catherine got up and fed the woodstove again, then took her mug and cigarette to the front of the house. She looked out the window. "Do I understand now, you mean?" said Catherine.

"Yeah."

Night had fallen while they'd been catching up. The unblemished snow lay white across the fields, the whole of the hollow lit by the moon with an otherworldly glow. "I guess I do," Catherine said finally. "I wish I didn't. But I do."

———

Not long after she'd gone to see Catherine, Sally parked her father's truck in the white shells of the lot behind the Sea Breeze Motel. She opened the truck's door, and the wind almost pushed it shut again before she managed to get out. She ducked down, pulled her coat tight around her neck, and jogged to the entrance. When she stepped into the lobby, she shook off the cold and looked around as if there might be visible evidence of what had happened the summer before, but there was none.

The carpets had been replaced. The walls were patched and repainted. The front desk was now composite stone and natural wood, an upgrade from the 1970s-vintage Corian and wood veneer it had been before.

A woman stood behind the desk. Sally read her name tag: LUCY. "Welcome to the Sea Breeze Motel," said Lucy. "Checking in?"

"No." Sally put her hand out and introduced herself. "I'm Sally Ewell. A friend of Arman's. Is he around?"

"He went down to the beach. Don't know why. Freezing cold out there. But he's got his routines. You can wait here if you want. He shouldn't be too long."

"He's down at the park? Ocean View?"

"When he's not here, he's there. I tell him he ought to get a job at the post office. At least they'll pay you to walk around in this mess."

Sally laughed. "Thanks. I'll head down there," she said. "By the way, it looks great in here."

"Thank you," said Lucy, smiling. "Me and him are gonna change every inch of this motel before we're through, except that stupid sign."

"The sign?" Sally asked.

"You'll see it," she said. "Let me know if it makes sense to you, because it don't make a damn bit of sense to me."

"I'll take a look," Sally said. She left the lobby and stepped out into the parking lot again. She looked up at the big letterboard sign below the motel's name. THE REWARD FOR LIVING A GOOD LIFE IS LIVING A GOOD LIFE, it read. *She's not wrong, exactly,* Sally thought. She crossed the street at a jog, and when she entered the park, the trees broke the cold wind a bit. She walked to the gazebo and looked up and down the beach. The waves were white and broke sideways along it. The water gray as stone below the storm-dark sky. She saw a figure standing by the water with his back to her. He had a parka on with the hood pulled up.

She left the gazebo, stepped into the sand, and made her way down to him. She stood beside him and put her hand on his back to let him know she was there. "Hey, Arman," she said.

He turned to look at her. "Hey, Sally. I didn't know you were coming down here."

"Who could pass up a walk on the beach on a day like this?"

"Yeah. Fair point."

They walked back up to the gazebo together and sat on one of the benches facing the ocean. "It looks great, Arman. Mr. Peters would be really proud."

"I hope he would be. It's the least I can do. I never... You know, I'm grateful to him, even though I never would have guessed my life would turn out this way. But I feel guilty too."

"Because it's not what you wanted."

"Right. I had a life already. I loved Naza and Haydar. I was happy. It wasn't perfect, but I was happy."

"And then," said Sally.

"And then."

"I know it's not the same."

"I know," he said. "But you understand."

"I do."

The roar of fighter jets in formation rose over the sound of the sea. Arman and Sally waited until the noise faded and the fighters disappeared somewhere over the country behind them.

"Lucy thinks you should change the sign," said Sally.

He laughed. "Yeah. She's mentioned it. It was the last thing he wanted it to say, though. I guess if he'd known what was coming, he would have wanted it to say something else."

"Maybe," Sally said. "Maybe not. I think it's growing on me." They sat there for a while, wondering at the pieces they'd been left to remake their lives with. "Someone from the paper wants to interview you."

"You didn't tell them I would talk to them, did you?"

"Of course not," Sally said. "It's up to you."

"What are they going to write about?"

"It's a series. I think they want it to be comprehensive."

"Why don't you write it?"

"I can't, Arman. At least not for the paper. I'm part of the story."

"Do you think it will change anything?"

"For who?"

"Anyone."

Sally thought about the question. And whether telling the story ought to be about changing anything or not. Maybe it ought to be about telling the truth as it happened to the best of their ability. Was that enough for it to count? She wasn't sure. "People should know about Lamar," she said. "People should know what was done to you." She reached into her coat pocket and brought out a photograph. She handed it to him. "Catherine asked me to give you this."

Arman stared at the picture of Chief Miller. There was a big black X across his face. He turned it over. Graves's name had been struck through. "I wanted them punished," Arman said. "I wanted them to suffer."

"I know. Me too."

"Lucy told me I'm not allowed to hate anyone."

Sally laughed. "That's a bold declaration."

Arman smiled ruefully. "When I found out about Mr. Peters's will, I asked her to help me. I wanted her to be my partner. She knows the motel business a lot better than I do. Probably better than Mr. Peters too. Do you know what she asked for?"

"What?"

"That. Not a dollar amount. Not a specific percentage split. She said, 'If we're gonna be partners, you're not allowed to hate anyone.' That was her condition."

"How's that work?" Sally asked. "It's not like you can control how you feel."

"That's what I said. And I meant it. But she said I was wrong. 'You can want justice, Arman,' she said. 'You can want them to answer for what they've done. But hating someone is like drinking poison and hoping the other person dies. It doesn't work. You can choose to drink it or not drink it. But I won't be around it.' So that was our deal."

"You're a better person than me," said Sally. "I'm not there yet."

"I'm not there either. But I told Lucy I would try."

"You know what, Arman?" Sally said. "Maybe trying is enough."

He looked at her. "Will you come to West Virginia with me in a few days?"

"What's in West Virginia?"

"An observatory. A dark sky," he said. "Cassiopeia A. I haven't seen it in a long time. It used to be a star."

"What is it now?"

"Now it's something new."

She took his hand in hers and leaned against him. "I'd love to go with you," she said.

It was late afternoon. Between the storm out at sea and the coming night, visibility had diminished to less than a nautical mile. The cold December air pushed Arman and Sally even closer together on the wooden gazebo bench. They put their arms around each other, nothing more. Snow began to fall over the white waves, and they listened to a klaxon's long blast as a ship cleared Willoughby Spit and headed out to sea.

Acknowledgments

I will be forever indebted to Peter Straus for his guidance and advocacy. I also want to express my sincere appreciation to Judith Clain, Michael Pietsch, and all the other wonderful people at Little, Brown for the opportunity to publish another book with such an extraordinarily talented and hardworking team. Thanks to Anna de la Rosa and Betsy Uhrig for their attention to detail throughout the editorial process. And to Lena Little and Danielle Finnegan for helping get this book into the hands of readers. Dr. Tracy Roe gave invaluable assistance in copyediting, not only with her grammar and usage expertise but also her willingness to share her extensive medical knowledge. Gregg Kulick created the striking cover art, and I feel fortunate that his work will be a reader's first impression of this book.

Dave McGuinnes drew on his extensive law enforcement experience to answer my questions about police and prosecutorial procedures and culture. Where this is accurately depicted in the book, he deserves much credit. Where it departs from accuracy, I deserve all of the blame.

Although it is indirectly related to the writing of this book, I want to take this opportunity to thank the ER doctors and nurses at Dell Seton Medical Center, the kind and patient staff

ACKNOWLEDGMENTS

at Austin Bone and Joint, and especially Joshua Fox, MD. Their expert care quite literally got me back on my feet.

Finally and always, while I know I can never adequately express my gratitude for the love and support of my parents, my wife, and my kids, I promise to keep trying.

Read an extract from Kevin Powers' award-winning debut

'A masterpiece . . . a classic'
The Times

'Remarkable . . . every line is a defiant assertion of the power
of beauty to revivify'
Hilary Mantel

'Harrowing, inexplicably beautiful, and utterly, urgently
necessary'
Ann Patchett

THE WAR TRIED to kill us in the spring. As grass greened the plains of Nineveh and the weather warmed, we patrolled the low-slung hills beyond the cities and towns. We moved over them and through the tall grass on faith, kneading paths into the windswept growth like pioneers. While we slept, the war rubbed its thousand ribs against the ground in prayer. When we pressed onward through exhaustion, its eyes were white and open in the dark. While we ate, the war fasted, fed by its own deprivation. It made love and gave birth and spread through fire.

Then, in summer, the war tried to kill us as the heat blanched all color from the plains. The sun pressed into our skin, and the war sent its citizens rustling into the shade of white buildings. It cast a white shade on everything, like a veil over our eyes. It tried to kill us every day, but it had not succeeded. Not that our safety was preordained. We were not destined to survive. The fact is, we were not destined at all. The war would take what it could get. It was patient. It didn't care about objectives, or boundaries, whether you were loved by many or not at all. While I slept that summer, the war came to me in my dreams and showed me its sole purpose: to go on, only to go on. And I knew the war would have its way.

The war had killed thousands by September. Their bodies lined the pocked avenues at irregular intervals. They were hidden in alleys, were found in bloating piles in the troughs of the hills outside the cities, the faces puffed and green, allergic now to life. The war had tried its best to kill us all: man, woman, child. But it had killed fewer than a thousand soldiers like me and Murph. Those numbers still meant something to us as what passed for fall began. Murph and I had agreed. We didn't want to be the thousandth killed. If we died later, then we died. But let that number be someone else's milestone.

We hardly noticed a change when September came. But I know now that everything that will ever matter in my life began then. Perhaps light came a little more slowly to the city of Al Tafar, falling the way it did beyond thin shapes of rooflines and angled promenades in the dark. It fell over buildings in the city, white and tan, made of clay bricks roofed with corrugated metal or concrete. The sky was vast and catacombed with clouds. A cool wind blew down from the distant hillsides we'd been patrolling all year. It passed over the minarets that rose above the citadel, flowed down through alleys with their flapping green awnings, out over the bare fields that ringed the city, and finally broke up against the scattered dwellings from which our rifles bristled. Our platoon moved around our rooftop position, gray streaks against the predawn light. It was still late summer then, a Sunday, I think. We waited.

For four days we had crawled along the rooftop grit. We slipped and slid on a carpeting of loose brass casings left over from the previous days' fighting. We curled ourselves into absurd shapes and huddled below the whitewashed walls of our position. We stayed awake on amphetamines and fear.

I pushed my chest off the rooftop and crested the low wall, trying to scan the few acres of the world for which we were responsible. The squat buildings beyond the field undulated through the tinny green of my scope. Bodies were scattered about from the past four days of fighting in the open space between our positions and the rest of Al Tafar. They lay in the dust, broken and shattered and bent, their white shifts gone dark with blood. A few smoldered among the junipers and spare tufts of grass, and there was a heady mix of carbon and bolt oil and their bodies burning in the newly crisp air of morning.

I turned around, ducked back below the wall and lit a cigarette, shielding the cherry in my curled palm. I pulled long drags off it and blew the smoke against the top of the roof, where it spread out, then rose and disappeared. The ash grew long and hung there and a very long time seemed to pass before it fell to the ground.

The rest of the platoon on the roof started to move and jostle with the flickering half-light of dawn. Sterling perched with his rifle over the wall, sleeping and starting throughout our waiting. He jerked his head back occasionally and swiveled to see if anyone had caught him. He showed me a broad disheveled grin in the receding dark, held up his trigger finger and daubed Tabasco sauce into his eyes to stay awake. He turned back toward our sector, and his muscles visibly bucked and tensed beneath his gear.

Murph's breath was a steady comfort to my right. I had grown accustomed to it, the way he'd punctuate its rhythm with a well-practiced spit into an acrid pool of dark liquid that always seemed to be growing between us. He smiled up at me. "Want a rub, Bart?" I nodded. He passed me a can of care-package Kodiak, and I jammed it into the cup of my bottom lip, snubbing out my cigarette. The wet tobacco bit and made my eyes water. I spat into the pool between us. I was awake. Out of the gray early morning the city became whole. White flags hung in a few scattered windows in the buildings beyond the bodies in the field. They formed an odd crochet where the window's dark recesses were framed by jagged glass. The windows themselves were set into whitewashed buildings that became ever brighter in the sun. A thin fog off the Tigris dissipated, revealing what hints of life remained, and in the soft breeze from the hills to the north the white rags of truce fluttered above those same green awnings.

Sterling tapped at the face of his watch. We knew the muezzin's song would soon warble its eerie fabric of minor notes out from the minarets, calling the faithful to prayer. It was a sign and we knew what it meant, that hours had passed, that we had drawn nearer to our purpose, which was as vague and foreign as the indistinguishable dawns and dusks with which it came.

"On your toes, guys!" the LT called in a forceful whisper.

Murph sat up and calmly worked a small dot of lubricant into the action of his rifle. He chambered a round and rested the barrel against the low wall. He stared off into the gray angles where the streets and alleys opened onto the field to our front. I could see into his blue eyes, the whites spider-webbed with red. They had fallen farther into his sockets during the past few months. There were times when I looked at him and could only see two small shadows, two empty holes. I let the bolt push a round into the chamber of my rifle and nodded at him. "Here we go again," I said. He smiled from the corner of his mouth. "Same old shit again," he answered.